MW00619621

Ron Meszaros

BOOKS BY RON MESZAROS

The Secret Life of David Goens

A Long Good Walk

Six One-Act Plays

Gathering Leaves

Dedicated to Ellen

Ron Meszaros

Published by
Serendipity Press
Fairhope, Alabama
Http://www.serendipitypress.org

This novel is a work of fiction. Names, characters, places, and incidents either are the product of the author's imagination or are used fictitiously. Any resemblance to actual persons, living or dead, events, or locales is entirely coincidental.

Copyright ©2023 Ron Meszaros

All rights reserved. No part of this book may be reproduced or transmitted in any form or by any means, electronic or mechanical, including photocopying, recording, or by any information storage and retrieval system without the written permission of the Author, except small portions for review purposes.

ISBN-978-1-7323-174-6-8

The cover design and format of this book are protected trade dresses and trademarks of Wotan International Media (251) 504-2633

Printed in the United States of America

Type face: Goudy Old Style

Cover design by Ellen Grigg

Gathering Leaves

A young woman's arduous
Civil War journey
to find her wounded husband

A NOVEL

Ron Meszaros

Ron Meszaros

September 1862

It was early. She had not slept well. Lying there under a summer quilt, she thought of all the things she had to do. The list was not long, but carried a weight on her mind—what she needed to do first, second, and then third. When she had ten tasks in her mind, she reviewed them for a second time, then once more. She changed the order once, but felt satisfied all this was necessary. There, in the still of the night, she realized there was no reason to wait any longer, as there would be no sleep. Caroline Emily Duncan pushed back the quilt and swung her legs out of the bed, her feet touching the rough-sawed oak boards that made up the small bedroom floor. The thirty-three-year-old woman lit the coal oil lamp near their bed, and found her yesterday's clothes on the ladder-back chair in front of the opened window. It was still dark, but slight gray moonlight illuminated the back of the trees on a ridge not far from the house. Caroline reached into a drawer and pulled out her husband's pocket watch and held it to the light; it read the time: 3:36. Moments later she took the lamp and walked into the kitchen and, standing by the dry sink, she looked into the small pantry that ran six feet deep and five feet wide. The floor to ceiling canning shelves held the glass Mason jars filled with green beans, peas, tomatoes, lima beans, pickled cucumbers, sausage, pears, peaches, cherries, and plums. She knew exactly how many were there, as she had counted them twice the night before. Three hundred and thirty-seven. Most all of them were double quart Mason jars. Some were plain glass jars that bore no name and varied in shape. Each one was carefully topped with canning wax, to seal air tight, and then a galvanized lid was screwed over a red rubber ring. It would take many trips, she thought, but all of this had to be hidden away. The Union Army, now rumored to be within a seven-day march, could possibly sweep through this area on their push toward Memphis. They would take it all.

Caroline moved quickly and filled the wheelbarrow outside the kitchen door with the preserved green beans—she counted twenty-four jars. Walking to the gray-boarded shed, she took a well-worn, long-handled shovel and returned to the loaded wheelbarrow, then pushed off deep into the dark woods to the west of the cabin. A five-minute walk through the pine trees, and along a deer path, caused her to wipe perspiration from her forehead and push back her light brown hair from her eyes. She wanted all the hiding places to be far from the cabin—scattered and away from the well-worn trail used for dragging pine logs out of the woods. Finding a spot twenty feet from the trail, she pushed back the pine needles and then she quickly plunged the shovel deep into the sand. This was good. Sand was easy to dig, and she found no roots to slow her effort. She thought to herself, "This task will take the entirety of the morning." She had planned a day earlier that it would require seven hours to transfer the double quart blue-glass jars from the cabin, plus a few extras in the shed behind the cabin. Caroline knew it would result in fourteen trips and each trip thirty minutes. Three hundred and thirty-seven double quarts once seemed like a lot of food, but that amount was necessary to feed her family of five. Next spring's garden seemed so far in the future—a full nine long months away. So much could happen between now and then. Much of it bad.

After digging for ten minutes, the sky was getting somewhat lighter as the moon moved overhead. At two feet down, Caroline decided this initial four-foot-by-three-foot hole would hold forty-eight of the jars, and that would be a good start to this early before sunrise work. She understood she would need seven holes of this size to hide most of her canning. The night before, she had lined up eight jars wide and six deep for a total of forty-eight jars on the kitchen floor and measured its size. She pulled on the rope she had tied to a tree and pulled herself up out of the hole. Carefully stacking the jars in a circle around the hole, she lowered herself back down to the bottom of the sand pit and proceeded stacking all twenty-four jars of the preserved green beans. "One more trip and this will contain forty-eight jars. One of seven will be done."

Yes, it seemed simple enough, although hiding food in a hole felt odd. But what was the alternative? She would not starve her three children this coming winter. Nor would she only live on what they could trap. The war her husband was fighting could soon jeopardize her family right here 300 miles from where he was located in Virginia. Yes, this was western Kentucky, but the Union Army was moving quickly to the west, hoping to capture the Mississippi River. This was the workable solution she had thought of during her restless night. After the second trip that morning, she filled the hole with a total of forty-eight jars as she had planned. Quickly gathering pine needle straw, she spread the straw around the jars and over the tops. She used wood cedar shingles to cover the jars and then a foot of sandy soil. Her hands, now covered in sand and sweat, firmly grabbed the handles of the empty wheelbarrow and, with quickened steps, she returned to the house. She paused in the kitchen and poured herself a glass of water. Caroline found a chair and exhaled. She listened for several minutes to the silence of the homestead house. The only noise came from the squeak of the chair she was sitting in. She said quietly to herself, "One of seven is finished, and the boys can cut more shingles after breakfast. The first hole took fifty-five minutes and so we should be finished before noon. With the boys help it should go faster. Isaac and I can dig the holes. Priscilla and Noah can bring out the canning." She stood and looked out the window at the small shack to the rear of the cabin. "I shall deal with the smoke house soon, possibly tomorrow, but I need to bake this afternoon. I need to make butter. I need to do the wash." Caroline stood, took a deep breath, and walked ten steps to the stairs that led up to the sleeping children. "Children, it's time to get up! Tomorrow is here. Priscilla, you feed the chickens, gather the eggs, and start the biscuits. Noah, we need five buckets of water for the house and ten for the animal water trough. Isaac, get the cows and goats in and start milking. I will be hiding more canned goods this morning, so let's not talk but let's get to work. Remember, every task we do is to get your father home sooner. Breakfast will be in one hour. I do not want to hear anyone chatting. I only want to hear footsteps. I will be back in thirty minutes."

Caroline returned to her jars and started loading the wheelbarrow. Again, she carefully loaded twenty-four blue-glass Mason jars. She wrapped her hands in two rags to cushion the handles and pushed again into the woods, but now in a different direction, this time to the east and one hundred feet away from the first hole. The jars rattled but to her that was a good sound. It represented the work it took tilling the earth, planting the seed, watering, weeding the rows, harvesting the vegetables, and the hours over a wood stove preparing them and finally canning them.

Caroline Emily Duncan, at first glance, was somewhat plain, and yet in many ways, a delicate prettiness birthed her aura. She possessed an easy warm smile and bright hazel eyes that caught the attention of most who met her. To Caroline, no task was a difficult chore, but a chance to prove oneself. She was thirty-three years old, and a mother of three who lived in a small homestead cabin in western Kentucky, thirty miles from the nearest town of Hopkinsville. Her husband, Charles, eleven months earlier had gone off to fight, wearing a gray uniform in the War of Independent States. He was a first lieutenant in the Kentucky Volunteers. Charles had gone to college for two years and taken a job as an engineer, but that summer of 1847 he fell in love with the daughter of his pastor. Caroline was nineteen and Charles was twenty-three. She wanted to raise a family far away from the city, so they purchased a 360-acre parcel 169 miles southwest of her hometown of Louisville. The plot they chose was covered with virgin timber. Oak, maple, walnut, cherry, hickory, chestnut, and sycamore stood side by side. Three hundred trees could be counted to an acre. His plan was to build a steam-driven sawmill near town. But like all endeavors of business, seed money would be required and that was money they did not have. So they started small. They owned no slaves, nor did anyone within fifty miles, but he thought the future for him and his family was in the timber that ran up and down the hills. Unfortunately, the future was unexpectedly darkened. Civil war had broken out and Charles Matthew Duncan was forced to take a side. The side Charles chose was based on the land they lived on. This was western Kentucky. Yes, it was a neutral border state, but Charles had always thought of everything south of the Ohio River as part of the South. Truly, no one wanted war with their cousins to the north, but there were ugly rumors of Union troops invading from the north and killing women and children, burning towns and homes, and even stealing food and the slaughter of farm animals to feed the blue-coated armies. The families that were victimized were left with no food for the coming winter. Even schools and churches were torched. Some animals, cows, horses, and mules were taken or even slaughtered and left to rot for fear the Confederate Army would procure them for food or to pull their wagons and cannons.

Eleven months earlier, all of this had been discussed in the Duncan home over the kitchen table before Charles had decided to join with his younger brother, Benjamin, in the gray-coated army of Kentucky Volunteers. To him, it was not about slavery, but about the sovereign right of Kentucky to choose its destiny. During those conversations, Caroline insisted their children, now aged 13, 11, and 9, hear all of this reasoning, and to understand where their father was going—how it was up to them to share the burden. That meant cutting and splitting the firewood, working long hours in the garden, milking the three cows, picking the peaches, plums, and cherries, carrying the water from the well, and finishing the construction of the new barn, now only half done. After their father left, there was just a single hour of schooling for the children, as work occupied most of their time. Caroline had stopped calling them chores, for chores were things you did for an hour or so a day. She told them this was now to be called "a full day's work." It was not easy, but for the family to survive it had to be done. "I still love you all, but now I must be more serious with you. I won't smile as much, for I have my work to do also. No one shall complain, for complaining is the work of the devil." From that point on, there was not a lot of laughter there in that small homestead house. The oldest boy, Isaac, would take the mule as his father had done and go deep into the woods to cut pine for the new larger barn, oak for next year's firewood, and locust for fence posts and rails. His younger brother, Noah, would trail behind, carrying the large, five-foot, double-handle cross-cut saw and the double-bladed ax. Caroline and Priscilla worked the garden, weeding and hoeing, and in July together they started canning early vegetables. A pig was butchered and hung away to cure in the small smoke house attached to the barn. In the evenings, they sat around the kitchen table and explained what they had done that day. Each child, Isaac, Noah, and Priscilla, would give thanks to God for the strength He had provided. Priscilla was always chosen to be the last to pray. She ended her prayers asking for thirty-three angels to protect her father. For thirty-three was her favorite number.

That September early morning, Caroline and the boys dug a second hole and then five more, scattered nine hundred feet from the cabin. All seven were filled with double quart blue-glass Mason jars following the plan she had prepared in her mind. All in all, 337 jars were buried. Cedar shingles and then pine straw covered the jars. A foot of red sand covered that. On top of the sand at all the seven hidden holes, Noah and Priscilla spread fresh pine straw and fallen pine branches. Trees nearest the holes were marked with three small marks. Isaac drew a map of the locations. On the shelf in the kitchen, fourteen jars of green bean and tomatoes and yellow peppers stood. If the blue-coated soldiers arrived, she would tell them the Confederates had taken all their food, leaving only what could be seen on the shelves in the pantry. She would also ask the Union soldiers for any hard tack and salted pork they could spare for her family. It was a plan she had thought of in her restless nights.

But three day later, all her plans changed. After riding to town on the mule to post letters and receive letters from their father, Isaac returned with three pieces of mail. One was an official letter from the Army of the Confederacy, and the other two were from his father last somewhere in Virginia. Caroline read Charles's letters first. The children gathered around the kitchen table to hear the news. Their father had been in three battles and was wounded slightly in the hand by a stray bullet and his hand was sore but healing. The second letter joked about how much weight he had lost, but that he had grown a beard, and his hair was long over his ears. He asked many questions about them, but revealed little about his situation.

Caroline put Charles's letters into her lap after reading them aloud and thought she should highlight the good news and ignore the bad. "Your father is in good spirits and I am sure he cannot but wait to return to us, to see all we have accomplished since he has left us." Caroline, looking into each child's eyes, smiled. "I am sure we wish for that day, which will surely come, that we see his big beard and long hair and his skinny, skinny body. We will all laugh and sing and then we will have the biggest supper we've ever had. Much like Christmas with pheasant and ten dishes all from our harvest bevy we have raised in the garden and you children have helped to preserve. We will celebrate Daddy's coming home for a whole week, a new pie every day with singing and dancing."

Caroline opened the third letter. She was certain it was yet another letter from the Confederacy, announcing Charles's pay had been delayed again, the money to come shortly. But that was not the case. The letter was from a Confederate Army surgeon, Captain Detwiller. Caroline read it silently as the children looked to her eyes for clues. She gasped at one point and raised her hand to her mouth. She quickly reread the letter to herself. Glancing at the children's faces, she slowly forced a smile. "Well, it seems our brave husband and father has ended up in a hospital for the second time. And this time it is a bit more serious than his finger. He has been wounded and it is a bullet wound in the shoulder, which is probably why he has not written to inform us. I assume he possibly cannot move his right arm to write, as it may well be in a sling. We do not know. But he has been wounded and is located at a hospital tent somewhere, could be in Kentucky or perhaps in Virginia. Maybe he will have a nurse write for him and we may get a letter in the next day—so Isaac will have to ride to town each and every day to see, won't we children?"

Noah was the first to speak, "I want to go with Isaac when he rides to town. Is that permissible, Mother?" Isaac spoke next. "No, it is not; you have to stay and help Mom. I can ride faster without you back there." There was more discussion, but in the end it was decided only Isaac would go. Priscilla, the youngest, never said a word; however, her tears were visible to everyone who sat in silence around the table.

Caroline broke the stillness and stood. "Well now, enough of that. We have a wounded father, and he would want us to carry on. I am going to write to Captain Detwiller, of the 1st

16

Kentucky Volunteers, to see if he could determine where your father is as I may want to travel to him—depending how badly wounded he is. I might have to stay a month or more until he is well.

But in a state of war things happen quickly. On the second day after the Confederate Army surgeon's letter arrived, another letter was waiting at the post office, written by Missus Ruth Abernathy, a nurse. It stated Charles had been hit with not one bullet but two—one in the shoulder and a second in the calf of his left leg. The bullet had passed cleanly through his leg and Nurse Abernathy stated it was an "easy wound and no amputation was necessary, but an 'infection' had set in on the shoulder wound, and sulfa medicines had been applied." She stated Charles had experienced "strong fevers" and was evacuated to a compound field hospital in Northern Kentucky. "Surgeons are attending him, but our surgeons are in short supply, as most travel with the army to address immediate wounds inflicted on the battlefield." She further stated there was fear that the Union Army would soon occupy the area and the wounded would be captured and sent to a prisoner of war camp in Ohio. Nurse Abernathy said one nurse was attending twenty-six wounded men, and six ladies from a local church had been helping around the clock. She stated she would write in a few days or if something new had developed. She said the women who were helping were members of the local Baptist church, but as a CSA Army nurse in service to the Confederacy, she was not permitted to reveal their exact location. The letter was postmarked Shelbyville, Kentucky.

17

As might be expected, the new letter sent a chill through Caroline. Her hand, grasping the letter, started to shake, but she attempted to hide it from the children, placing the letter in her lap and quietly folding it closed. While the two youngest children did not notice, Isaac did, and placed his hand on his mother's shoulder. Caroline's hand, still in her lap, started to spin her wedding band in circles on her finger. She thought to herself that this is not a simple flesh wound, but this could be an unstoppable infection, deep sickness, and possibly even death. She thought of what she could do. Shelbyville was east of Louisville. It was 190 miles away from her. Recently, stage service to Bowling Green had stopped due to outlaws, deserters, destroyed bridges, and the war. Train service from Bowling Green to Louisville was out of the question, as six of the nine trestles had been burned weeks ago. Her plan previously was to hide everything from the Union Army should they come this way, and to travel deep into her woods with the children should she hear the sound of marching feet or the thunder of horse hooves. But now, today, circumstances suddenly changed and she could think of but one thing. She must travel to her wounded husband. Maybe his life depended on one application of a sulfur drug, one cup of water, one cold compress on his head, or a fresh bandage. And maybe just her hand on his in prayer.

The following morning, Caroline traveled by foot to the Millars, who lived a mile and a half away. She heard more ominous news from them. The Millars had started to hide their preserved goods upon hearing rumors the Union Army was camped six days away. The latest news was startling. The blue-coated army had grown in size and was moving west toward Hopkinsville, a town east of them by thirty miles. Mister Millar, who was not seated with them at the table, but sat in a chair by the front window looking out onto his front yard, stated vehemently he was going to stay and try to protect the farm. He said that he would hide his four cows and pigs deep in the woods near a natural cave deep in a ravine. He noted his wife had moved all her preserved goods except for a few weeks' supply also to the cave. Missus Millar revealed that she had filled three wooden crates with their preserved smoked meats and was preparing to lower them into a pond three hundred yards away. Her husband would, upon hearing the army approach, toss the crates into the pond, and then stir the waters till the silt covered the crates hiding them from view. He would leave one cow and one sow pig near the house as a sacrifice. Mister Millar said other homesteaders were taking their farm animals and letting them loose in the woods, as they might stand a better chance if the Union Army came searching for food. "Caroline, let them have the chickens and your three goats, and leave some preserved foods on your shelves. Maybe that would be enough for them. But if you go and hide in the woods, prepare to find nothing when you come back. I hate to say it, but they have burned houses and barns in Ottsville according to my brother who lives there."

Caroline explained one plan was to hitch the mule to the wagon and she and the children travel to her husband. The second plan was more complicated.

Before Caroline could tell of her new plan, Missus Millar was shaking her head back and forth. "No. No, Caroline. It is dangerous for you and your children to be traveling alone." Mister Millar agreed and said he had heard of gangs of criminals seen traveling about robbing and pillaging as they traveled. Further, he stated a bank had been robbed in Maplesville and several women had been kidnapped and possibly harmed by these outlaws. One gang had been identified as the Willems Gang. A farmer in Pricket Springs had been shot to death while defending his home, and a woman had been taken for ransom. Finally, Caroline interrupted and said she had a new and complicated plan. One that she was now sure of. It was her final decision. That she would travel alone to where her husband was, and she would leave the children at the homestead or in the woods to care for themselves.

Mister Millar stood from his chair and interrupted the conversation. "I think you traveling by yourself is noble but quite the risky plan. As you know, the Overland coach to Bowling Green has stopped, so you would have to walk to get there. But the trains have stopped! Caroline, if there are no trains running to Louisville, that leaves you to ride your mule all the way. But either army, North or South will appropriate your mule. So that leaves you to walk all the way. Shelbyville is close to 200 miles away. A man could walk it in nine days in good weather, but if it rains it'll be slow going. Why don't you just wait and see what happens? I'm sure the army doctors..." Missus Millar interrupted her husband by speaking directly to him, "But, Thomis, it's her husband. She can help. I'd do it for you, Thomis. I would. I would come to help you, but Caroline knows herself, she knows she has the stamina and courage to do it." Missus Millar turned to Caroline and rested her hand on her shoulder. "If you made up your mind to do this, then remember what I am about to say. Dear, it's going to be a long journey. Longer than you think. Because of the war, there is no law around. You will be in severe danger most of the time. You'll need good shoes. You can't carry much, as it will slow you down. You will have to find food along the way. You may have to borrow. You may have to, and I hate to say it, Caroline, you may have to steal. Look for homesteads like ours along the way. Homesteads and not shacks. But when you find them, do not rush in—no. You watch to see if there is a woman around. If you only see men, you stay away. But above all, you take care of yourself, as it will require all your strength. God may help you, but you have to help yourself. That said, if you are determined to go to your husband, then let nothing on this earth stop you. You go and you go hard."

Mister Millar took a deep breath and pushed it out slowly. "Looks like it's two to one and so I surrender. So, let me say my last piece. Do not take the well-traveled roads. No, you stick with the roads homesteaders use. The wagon roads. So, you start in Hopkinsville, but there you turn north to Crofton and Morton's Gap. That's a day and half walk, but then on the second day you turn east and to Echols and Nealus. It's a long stretch to Elizabethtown, and that should take six days. Try to walk around Elizabethtown, as there are many men there. And if they see you alone, one might trail you a mile behind until there is no one around. Take the Lebanon Junction to Shepardsville and that should be about seven days; the last two days will be from there to Shelbyville. Nine days total. That is if you walk twelve hours a day. If you walk fourteen hours a day, you will make it one day less. There are some mountains too, and they will slow you down. Then there is the weather. October is upon us, so you will get fall rains."

Caroline smiled slightly. "I hope to catch a ride now and again on a wagon, and that would reduce some days maybe down to eight. But since the war started, there are not a lot of wagons. People are staying close to home. But, Mister Millar, I am a fast walker. I might be able to make it without a ride in nine days. Nine days is my target."

Mister Millar stood; walking to the screen door, he looked onto the yard, slowly speaking over his shoulder. "Then you will be walking fourteen hours a day. A strong man could do that, but you are small boned and take women steps. I would say ten, maybe even eleven days at best."

"I assure you, Mister Millar, I have stamina, and I have worked side by side with my husband when we cleared this land. I will do this in nine days."

Caroline looked to Missus Millar's eyes and took her hand. "No matter how long it takes, I will do this. You see, I am not worried about myself, but you are correct, Missus Millar, I worry about my husband. I could be there nursing him round the clock, night or day. I could wipe his forehead with cooling cloths. Help him move. Watch for infection. Remove bandages and look for gangrene. Apply poultices. Wrap new bandages. Give him cool water. Then I could bring him home. I will pay for a wagon. But I also worry about leaving the children behind."

"The children, yes, your children." Mister Millar turned to the kitchen table. "I could stop over now and then to see how they are doing, but if me and Missus Millar were forced to flee ourselves—if we had to leave here, flee here in the middle of the night because of gun fire, then we could not look in. The three of 'em would have to fend for themselves. The boys could do it, but the little girl, Priscilla..."

Caroline shook her head. "I realize that might happen, and Isaac is thirteen and he knows the woods well. He knows where to hide, and how to locate food. For the three of them, it is a danger far off in the future, and the future is full of maybes, but to my husband the danger is at hand—right now and imminent. I have weighed the two and I feel an unrelenting pull toward my husband. It is within my power."

Caroline could see Missus Millar's face had changed, and deep furrows appeared. It was more than a worried look. There was sadness there.

Missus Millar took hold of Caroline's hand. "It is with patience, fortitude, and sagacity by which evils are overcome. If you have found peace in your heart, Caroline, then you go. But you are like the daughter I never had. So I am shaking inside at the thought of you traveling alone. I know this. God will protect you, and I will pray for you every day. But Caroline—Caroline Emily Duncan, you listen closely now, this is the wisdom of a mother to a daughter. Caroline, you carry the sharpest knife you own. And you keep it hidden in your clothes." Caroline said she had planned to take a kitchen knife and nodded and started to stand when Missus Millar gently put her hand on Caroline's shoulder, stopping her. "I have more to say and some of this will change your plans, for I believe it will be wise to travel as much as you can at night as not to be seen. For at night there is darkness everywhere to hide. You stay on the roads, but if you hear many horses coming, you will have time to run deep into the tall grasses. Always lay flat, cover your face, and you will blend into the darkness."

Mister Millar cleared his throat. "But daylight can be equally dangerous. Maybe more so. If you travel by night you'll have to sleep during the day and therefore visible to anyone who walks near. Caroline, you'll need to sleep far into the woods. Put out your bedroll first, then you set out gathering leaves to cover yourself. The more leaves you gather, the more invisible you will be. Pile 'em half a foot high if you can. And if you hear men, you stay still. Do not get up and run. If they can't see you, they can't hurt you. This alone could save your life.

Missus Millar sat back in her chair and spoke softly. "And if you encounter a single man or even two traveling at night or day, they can be the most dangerous. Be friendly, but do not stop to talk. You walk on and if he stops you, then you can soon tell what he is intent on doing. If he comes intimately close to you, if he touches you, then he is on his way to becoming a rapist. Now listen closely as you have never heard me before. Caroline, as he grabs at you, you say 'no' and push

24

back, and if he continues then you know he will not be stopped. Again say, 'please no!' If he continues and grabs you, then you should act as if you are giving in to his desires. Yes, you surrender. First he will push you down on the ground, and you lay there, do not look for help as there is none to come. You lay there quiet, but all the time thinking about what you are about to do. Watch his eyes closely and as he is about to get on top of you, there will come that moment the rapist reaches down and pulls up your clothes. As he unbuttons himself, that is when—hear me now—that is when you pull the knife and stab instantly."

Caroline interrupted. "Missus Millar, I think I can protect myself." Missus Millar shook her head. "There is only one way to protect yourself. You attack! Because, Caroline, there is no simple pushing back against rape. The first place to stab is his neck. And you stab under his ear and pull it toward you. After your first strike, you twist and bend your shoulders to your right and duck your head under his left arm so he can't hit you. And you stab the man in his back at least five times in quick succession and keep stabbing as long as you can. Nine, ten, eleven times. Now he will try to strike you to stop the stabbing, but your hand, holding the knife, is well behind him. He may roll off of you, away from the stabbing, but he is in pain, bleeding, and fatally wounded. At that point, you get to your feet. And you run as fast as you can." Missus Millar looked to her husband and back to Caroline. "He is a wounded animal as he has allowed Satan into his mind. It will take at least one minute before the man loses strength and falls to the ground." Missus Millar sat back in her chair shaking her head left and right. "Do not think you are killing a man. Think you are killing something evil. For he comes to destroy your very womanhood. And if he has his way, he will."

Caroline sat with opened mouth, amazed that her church going Christian neighbor had just given advice on how to kill a man. "How do you know all about this and how to fight back? How to kill a man?" Missus Millar looked at her husband for a long time, and then back to Caroline. "I have not spoken about this to anyone." She turned to her husband who sat transfixed on his wife. "Mister Millar, Thomis, I bear shame, pure and ugly shame within my soul as I have not told you. It is a shame I carry daily. It was—Jesus, help me with this—it was when I was, when I was fifteen. I was walking home early evening and a man came from behind and pulled me into the woods. I could not stop him. I tried, but it was for naught." Mister Millar, who had been looking at the floor, looked up quickly at Missus Millar. "For thirty-three years, I have carried that shame. It haunts me. I feel not worthy of Mister Millar. But I have kept that secret long enough and I am telling it now for one reason only. I do not want it to happen to you. And so for these thirty-three years, I have thought hard and long how I would do it if it happened ever again. I have thought about the knife and how I would take action. At unexpected times I cried in my shame. When it happened to me I did not tell anyone but my mother, and she said to tell no one. Not even my father. When I met Thomis, Mister Millar, I thought he would not want me as a wife if he knew." Missus Millar turned to her husband. "I am a liar, Thomis; I have been with another man before I met you.

Once. A rape. I was spoiled goods. And still am to this day, to this very minute. I am not worthy of you."

Caroline reached out. "Missus Millar, you did nothing wrong. How can you blame yourself?"

Missus Millar's demeanor suddenly changed. There was anger there. A wound that would not heal had been revealed. "I will no more speak about it, tonight nor ever again. I feel like Jesus has turned his back on me. I felt unclean and not worthy of any man's love! I only now speak of it after thirty-three years so you will not have this visited upon you. No one should bear this all their days, but I have. I am unclean." Missus Millar stood; her face grew red. She quickly picked up a coffee cup, paused for a moment, and smashed it hard on the floor into many pieces. "That is me there, Thomis. I am broken. I cannot be put back together again as I once was. Look at the shards. That is how I saw my life until I met you." Tears started to fall. "Now I am going to my room. Thomis, if you come to sleep beside me, I will hold you tight; I will welcome your love. And if you don't join me, I will understand." Missus Millar turned. "Goodnight, Caroline. I hope you have listened to what I said; it has cost me greatly with Mister Millar." Missus Millar stood and hugged Caroline. After a moment she turned and walked to her room with soft footsteps. Mister Millar did not move, but only sat looking to the floor and then to the broken pieces that lay scattered. He closed his eyes.

Walking back to the cabin along the creek, Caroline fought tears, still amazed at what Missus Millar had said. She had

known Missus Millar for thirteen years and there had never
been a hint of tragedy about this woman. Yet there it was. The
shame of the rape. Caroline thought of Missus Millar's advice.
Traveling at night. How to hide. How to kill. But her thoughts
slowly turned to her wounded husband and those things she
needed if she were traveling to Charles. She tried not to think
about a knife, but Missus Millar's advice stood center. She
also remembered what Mister Millar said about the farm
animals hiding safe in the woods, which would also be true
for the children. After all, Isaac was thirteen and he could take
care of the other two, especially Priscilla who, while only nine,
had become quite self sufficient since her father had gone
away. The children knew where the food was hidden, where
they could hide the cows, the pigs, the chickens. The woods
behind their house ran for six miles to a river which bore no
name. This was virgin forest known only to the Indians and
trappers. The boys had walked deer trails to the river many
times to swim and catch fish. Between the river and the
homestead, the woods were full of wild turkeys, grouse,
pheasants, rabbits, and squirrels. That afternoon she felt
confident the children, and especially Isaac, knew the 360-
acre homestead and their woods as well as her husband did.
Caroline further reasoned the Northern Army, if it came this
way searching for food, would be here only a day at the most.
But more importantly, they would not go deep into these
woods for they feared what could be hiding there. A
dangerous gray-coated army prepared for an ambush.

By the time she got back to the cabin, the plan had become
fixed in her mind. It would be alright to leave the children to

themselves. But she worried most for Priscilla, who many times crawled into Caroline's bed when frightened by the night's wildlife sounds. And tomorrow night, the three children could all sleep together in the big downstairs bed—it would be comforting and especially for Priscilla.

That afternoon Caroline informed the children of the upcoming plans. She explained that they were safe here on the homestead and that their father was in danger up there. "Which would you choose for me to care for? Your father or you three? I will abide by your decision. Do you want your father to come home, or do you want me to stay here and take care of you?" Surprisingly, Noah spoke first, "Go get Daddy." Isaac nodded. "Yes." Priscilla started to cry but wiped her nose with her hand. "I want both, please, Mommy." Caroline took her hand. "You can only have one. Which is it? I will stay here or I will return with your father." Priscilla thought for a moment. "Get Daddy."

That afternoon, Caroline, with Priscilla standing by her side, counted twenty-one double quart blue-glass Mason jars with green beans, tomatoes, and plums on the kitchen shelves, enough to feed the children for three weeks. Further, most of the smoked bacon and hams were wrapped tightly in canvas bags, then taken to the rock pile near the small barn and spread on the boards. Rocks were stacked on the meats until the rocks were three feet high and five feet wide. Two hams and a slab of bacon remained in the smoke house. Caroline told the children if the Northern Army comes though and leaves, the children should not retrieve anything, as the army could return days or weeks later for a second search. "Let them find only a deserted homestead."

Caroline likewise gathered all her husband's personal letters and the few letters from the Confederate Army and burned those together. She told the children that if Yankees discovered them to smile and say, "I am glad you are here to protect us." But under no circumstance were they to mention their father wore a gray uniform. She told Priscilla to pretend she was a mouse and could not speak. "Just point to your mouth and shake your head 'no.'" At once, Priscilla began practicing.

That evening's meal was beyond somber. No one said much. Caroline recited the 23rd Psalm aloud three times so the children would hear it. She would say, "We, all of us, are going to walk through the valley of the shadow of death but we are to fear no evil, for Jesus is with us. You, me, and most of all Daddy. Now, I will be away for maybe three to four weeks. Will you take care of each other until I return with your father?"

After sundown the children went to their space in the loft. Caroline climbed the steep, narrow stairway after them and watched them dress for the night in total silence. She said little to them, as there was little left to say. "I love you and I will be back with your father. That is my promise." Caroline turned and climbed down the stairs and went to her bedroom. She wanted to sleep for an hour, but she only lay there thinking of what she was about to do. After a few minutes, she rose from her bed and dressed in a dark brown dress with a dark brown jacket and took a canvas haversack from the shelf. She filled it with a day's worth of cornbread, sausage, a few carrots, and a single apple. She took a gray wool blanket and rolled it. Tying the ends together with two leather straps, she slung it over her left shoulder. She quietly walked toward the homestead's door, and then she stopped for a moment and walked back to the kitchen counter and pulled out a single drawer. There, she spotted the sharpest knife she had. It had a bone handle and was ten inches long. Caroline wrapped it in a small piece of dish cloth and put it in her waist band then walked out the door. It was dark and there was a chill in the night air.

It doesn't take long after setting off on a long unexpected journey to realize the road ahead is unending, and offers no clue as to what lies ahead hidden. Further, these journeys possess unimaginable challenges that may drain the spirit. Caroline walked north with the moon over her left shoulder illuminating for the most part the grassy wagon and horse trail that connected this small community of young homesteaders. When she had traveled to the main dirt road three miles from her home, she felt the task somewhat easier than she feared. Occasionally as she walked by a homestead, a dog would growl and bark, but would retreat into its silence and to its outpost, only to let out a single acknowledging bark to signal it had done its duty. But after leaving the little settlement, which now bore the name Green Mill Crossing, a vast expanse of fifteen miles stretched to the east and the next settlement. During this walk, there were no fences, no houses, no barns, and no cows grazing. This was virgin untouched woods. The road was an old Indian trail that snaked into woods so thick sunlight rarely touched the road. When a welcomed clearing came, a vast meadow would greet the traveler with creeks and streams and ponds filled with wildlife. Occasionally, young saplings attempted to crowd near the open road, but thick briars kept the trees from crossing—holding that line with angry spikes that would tear your flesh if you tried to enter the woods or trap you if you tried to leave. This was the rule of western Kentucky. Dense and dark with sounds that, while familiar at home, were somewhat upsetting out here in the cool midnight air. At one point, after three hours of walking and after fording a creek, she rounded a bend and smelled a campfire. She quieted her walk and could smell 200 yards up a hill in a clearing, a campfire still burning. She saw a shadow of a man standing by the campfire. Caroline heard the voice of a man and perhaps the voice of a woman. It appeared to be an intimate moment but she saw nothing. She noticed ten horses all gathered together and tied to a long rope stretched between two pine trees. Were there other men up there sleeping? Was the man by the fire a guard? What of the woman? Who was she? Was she the wife of one of the men? Why were they out here hiding? Were they Northern Army scouts? Or were they from the South? Were they trappers looking for new territory? Or were they the famous Willems Gang? Did they have a captured hostage woman with them? "Yea, though I walk through the valley of shadow and death, I will fear no evil." Caroline walked on, tilting her head low and walking slowly as to not make a sound. She had traveled for a hundred yards when suddenly a dog from up near the campfire barked. It echoed in the trees and soon sounded like it was running toward her. The dog ran out of the woods and through the tall grass, on a direct route to her. She broke into a run. She was sprinting, but soon realized she could not outrun the dog quickly gaining on her. The animal, now just a shiny black-coated form, was barking non-stop with its mouth turned up baring its white teeth, so she stopped and turned facing the approaching dog. Desperately looking around, she spotted three pieces of sandstone and pulled up the largest chunk, then, raising the stone over her head, she turned back, waiting for the dog. At six feet away, the growling dog started its leap to her thigh, its mouth wide open and its head turned. She stepped sideways and swung the stone hard and caught the dog square on the side of its head. The black animal let out a partial yelp, but fell unconscious to the center of the road. Silence returned. Caroline was breathing heavily. Was the dog knocked out or was it dead? She listened to the men and heard a man's agitated voice. Would this dog awaken and continue its attack? What was she to do? She looked up the hill to the man by the campfire He was moving out of the tree line and in her direction. The dog stirred and tried to find its feet; blood ran from its ear. The dog looked at Caroline and started to growl. It took a halting forward step but its front legs were wobbly and the black animal was fighting for balance. The dog growled and bared his teeth again. Caroline raised the rock and swung hard with both hands against its skull. She heard a crack of bone as the dog fell instantly to the road. Again silence returned except for the sound of a man rushing out of the tree line and into the grass, his footsteps quick and forceful. Caroline hurriedly grabbed the rear paws of this black dog and pulled its sixty pounds hard into the deep grasses alongside the road. Quickly walking into the dark shadows, she ducked low to the ground in the tall grass, turned her face away, and listened to what was behind her. The man stopped thirty feet from her in the middle of the road and with a gruff voice called out, "Blackard, where are you? Blackard?" The man turned his back and hollered in the opposite direction. "Blackard, come." Caroline waited for his footsteps, but hearing him walk back along the road, she rose and walked away slowly and quietly. The man continued to call out for the dog, still lifeless in the deep in the weeds. "Blackard!" A woman's serious voice could be heard up near the campfire. A moment later, Caroline heard the woman's muffled cry. Caroline hesitated then walked on. It was a mystery and she was powerless.

For the next fifteen minutes, she walked with the bloodied sandstone in her right hand. Realizing there were many rocks along the road, she tossed it aside. The rock had become a new tool—an implement that had protected her as it silenced the attacking dog, maybe killed it. But what was she to do? She hoped in the next nine days she would not have to make another decision like this one. A quick one like she had never made before. Caroline was surprised at herself.

In the night air, as she moved far away from the attack, she welcomed the silence around her. Except for the sound of her shoes on this packed dirt road, there was nothing more out here in the darkness. This wagon trail turned left then right, up and down through these hills. But there was something strange. There was a night noise that she had never heard during the day. The sound was the faintest breeze—less than a whisper through the tall, moving grasses and it rippled the tree leaves that fluttered on the lowest branches. It was not wind, nor a breeze; it was the sound of night moving from one hill to another.

Out here in these uncharted hills were families of trees that had grown up together. They could hide you if necessary or hide bad things from you. They took no sides in this dispute. Yes, there were bear here, there were known cougars, there were even sightings of wolf packs. But she encountered none of that this long first night. After a time she noticed the wind would stir tree leaves behind her and then a moment later, trees from in front of her would answer back. It was like they were calling to each other—maybe relatives from the same mother tree, birthed by whirly spinning seeds from an ancient oak spread by winds hundreds of years earlier. Once after cutting a giant oak, her husband counted 367 rings. She dated the tree's start to 1494. Yes, during this first night's walk there was a comfort in the age of the trees. Comfort also in the shadows the huge trees provided in this moonlight. She thought often of Missus Millar's advice to travel in darkness and how this experience, this understanding, would have never occurred to her on her own. As long as the moon was visible, this was an excellent idea. But if the moon went behind clouds, things grew incredibly dark. The road would play tricks on her and disappear from her footing. Caroline reasoned if she could not see, then no one could see her. At one point, the road turned north, and she rounded a corner then climbed a small hill. She stopped for a moment and experienced for the first time that night the sound of crickets and frogs in concert with untold thousands of fireflies, all floating like a sparkling river dancing within the borders of the valley, setting the road alight. Because of this, Caroline could see the snaking valley several miles ahead. Only a few fireflies stayed in the woods, as most had come out into the opening and flew above the warm road. Maybe it was a mating ritual, or maybe it was a signal. As she walked, she turned and looked behind her to see the fireflies. They moved in randomness, like stars speaking to one another in the night sky. They seemed to ignore her presence completely—occasionally one, followed by two, three, or even a dozen would land on her and move up her arm, across her breast, blinking their magical effervescent light. Several landed on her dress above the knees. Yes, she thought, this is a sign. A sign from God? A sign from her husband? Whatever it was, it was a welcomed sign. She thought, "I am not alone. I am being guided."

At hour seven in this journey, and about four in the morning, it started to thunder. It was off in the distance, but ahead of her. Caroline walked on. There was no preparation made for this occurrence, just to keep moving. As the lone heavy drops started to strike her face, she looked for a tree to shield her until it passed. Nearly one hundred feet ahead, she spotted a hickory tree that overhung the road. She quickened her steps and at times started to run. As she approached the tree, but still fifty feet away, a brilliant flash filled the sky several miles to the east. A second later, the sound rolled across the landscape, down the valley, and collided with the still air in front of her. The earth's stillness under her feet shuddered and momentarily surrendered its domination of the landscape to the rumble. A full moment later, there was a pure intense light. An explosion of red-white brilliance, so powerful it sucked the night's quiet air from her lungs. There were no mountains, no trees, no valley, just piercing light and heat. In the space of a blink, Caroline felt she was forcibly hurled upwards with great speed, and maybe above the clouds and far above everything she was familiar with. The earth appeared purple beneath her, and at a great distance, but now, as if the brilliant, angry force had changed its mind, the earth began racing toward her. She was being hurled down through the clouds and toward the earth. Caroline realized the force could tear you up or toss you down. In the next moment she collided with the ground hard. The impact was like nothing she had ever felt before. It snapped her head backward. Her arms and legs were powerless. Caroline lost consciousness for a moment, landing twenty-five feet off the road. Her blanket roll cushioned the fall somewhat. For a moment she was disoriented. She wondered where she was, and what happened to her. Looking to her shoes, she only saw her stocking feet sticking out from her dress, now muddy from the rain. What was going on? Where were the children? Where was the cabin? Did Charles see that? Caroline cried out, "Charles, help me! Charles, help!" She tried to raise her head up to see where Charles was. Was he coming? Caroline laid her head back down and gazed upward. Why was it so dark? Where was Charles? Rain splattered her face. She knew she was somewhere unfamiliar, yet strange. Priscilla was smiling while quickly running up the hill. She had picked some blackberries and had them in a tin bucket. Priscilla was very proud of her pickings and said she wanted to bake a pie. The dog followed and was running in circles, then ran off to chase a rooster. Caroline saw herself standing in the kitchen; her husband, Charles, was seated at the table. A plate of biscuits was in her hand, and she was moving toward the table. The ringing in her ears slowly drifted away and she opened her eyes—again looking at her feet. "Where am I? What is happening? Is this a dream? How did I get here?" Attempting to rise up, she fell back and slowly fell into a deep sleep. "Everything will be alright; I just need a few moments to myself." Thirty minutes went by before she woke again. She sat up. "Yes, there was rain and a thunder strike. Was I struck by lightning? I must have been. Yes, that is what happened. I was struck, and have been knocked out. But for how long? An hour? Two? Maybe more." She gathered herself up and slowly stood. She picked up her bag. Caroline walked out of the weeds and down to the road. She found her shoes in the middle of the road, then sat in the grass and put them on. She started walking again. Another lightning strike echoed off the hills ahead and bounced behind her. The light rain continued. After a moment she thought, "Maybe eating something will help." Taking out a piece of cornbread and an apple, she said to herself, "This should help. I know who I am and what I am doing. I am walking to find my husband. Yes, that is what I am doing." The rain slackened slightly and she could hear the thunder way off in the distance. As she walked she started to quietly hum a church song. God was with her she thought. Maybe this was the worst part of her journey, and getting struck by lightning would be the sacrifice she had to pay. "Yes," she thought, "this is but an inkling of what my husband had probably gone through, and now, maybe I understand better than most what war was like." Her hair danced around her face and at times stood straight out and made a crinkling noise as she walked. There was a burnt smell on her clothing. "Maybe there is a campfire nearby, and then, too, it could be from the lightening. Maybe this is what a battlefield smells like from the cannon shot and the musket rifles." Was this God telling her to be prepared for the worst? Not knowing what the answer was, she prayed as she walked, "Father God, thank you for bringing me this far, thank you for letting me know what lies ahead. For now I am prepared for whatever may come. For if this is but a shadow of the valley of death, I see now you are preparing me to accomplish this. If this takes the hand of death away from my husband, let it be so. I am ready, Lord, for you have sent me. You have walked beside me. I am your daughter. Amen."

On a level dry road, the average person can walk two to three miles an hour. On a muddy, rolling terrain, the speed may be as slow as a mile an hour. Caroline was aware it was muddy from the rain, and the terrain in Kentucky hill country was challenging to both man and beast. Many of these roads follow the rivers, age-old Indian trails, or follow deer trails. Further, when Caroline observed the stars she could tell the North Star would move to her left then to the right. She thought to herself, this meant that she was not walking in a straight line, and the time it would take to reach her husband, located somewhere near Shelbyville, would be possibly more than she had planned. What she knew for sure was this dirt road would take her to Echol, which lay twenty-one miles to the northeast. Then at Farmersville she could take the Elizabethtown Road for nearly eighty miles. She had been told by Mister Millar that Shelbyville lay seventy miles due northeast of there. That would be a total of 193 miles. If she walked twelve hours a day at a pace of two miles an hour, she needed eight long days to reach there. However, if it rained and traveling was slow going, or if she got sick—if she had to hide in the woods for any length of time, or if she injured herself, even getting blisters on her feet, things could go markedly wrong. At one and a half miles an hour or eighteen miles a day she could walk it in eleven days. Which is what Mister Millar said it would take to get there—if you were a woman. She realized her brogue shoes were old, and in her haste she had only brought along one pair of socks. If they got wet, blisters would follow. Caroline knew those eight days could turn into eleven days or maybe more. "But I have no other choice. All I can hope for is one good day tomorrow—followed by nine others."

The moon was no longer lighting the sky, but a gray glow from the east was starting to illuminate the road ahead. She had been walking what she thought was nine hours and being there was no evidence of danger ahead, she decided to walk on in broad daylight for a few more hours. She stopped briefly to eat some dewberries growing by the side of the road. She had a piece of cornbread and after finishing that, she stopped by a creek and knelt on her knees. She cupped her hands and gathered some cool water. She brought it up to her lips. As she was drinking, she heard footsteps behind her.

"Don't ya think a person should ask the owner of that water if it is okay to take some?" A tall yet heavy set man with an oil-stained hat walked up behind her and stopped about fifteen feet away. Caroline turned and observed a dark figure who wore a pair of well-worn gray pants and a black jacket filled with holes worn through at the elbows and which bore only one button to hold it closed. His leather shoes were not a matched pair. One was a brown boot with a brass buckle on the side and the other was a black riding boot whose stitching had been ripped apart. He glanced over his shoulder to the left then to the right and returned his eyes upon her. He measured her from top to bottom, and quickly drew a picture in his mind that she was alone and walking. Caroline instinctively turned to his direction, and her hand went to the knife handle she had hidden in her waist band. The man took three steps toward her then took off his hat, holding it in his hand. Caroline rose and stood facing the man. "I will start. My name is Jacob and this here is my land ya be standin' on. Two miles that away and four miles that away. May I ask what be yourn intention?"

Caroline took a step back and dropped the sack beside her. "Sir, I have no intention except to walk toward Farmersville today." The man grinned for a moment, laughed, and then spit tobacco to the ground. "Ya won't maketh no Farmersville today. Ya might maketh walking sometime in the morrow. Hell! I walked it oncet and it tooks me thirteen hours straight with two stops. Sunup to sundown. Plus ya will find two rivers to cross and both of 'em is up this time of the year. Ya looketh a little lady-like and may not have the stamina I possess. Ya appear like ya need a rest. Watching ya, which I have been doin' for the last ten minutes as ya walked up, I observe your weakness." The man shifted his stance and pointed to the right and up a hill. "Now that away, I possess a shack 'bout a few minutes walk from here if ya would like to rest there, maybe layeth down and sleep for a spell. I would be glad to show ya the way, and I would even sit out on the porch and keep ya in my safety. There's also a stream up there feedin' this 'un and a small waterfall. Ya could take a bath and refresh yourn being. There is no one there to bother a person of your quality. As I said, I do not see a lot of ladies, like yourself— pretty like—walking these here roads. And since this here is my God given land, I feel an obligation to watch over 'em and give 'em a place to rest. I could fix us breakfast afterwards. A man gets lonely out here by hisself. You would be pleasant to talk to."

Caroline said nothing, but reached down and picked up her haversack, then turned to step around the man, but the man turned also, cutting her off. "My wife died three years ago, and so no one has been in my shed since I buried her. I see your dress is muddy from the rain, and luck is on your side, as I still have some of her clothes and ya are about the same size and so ya could change right there after your bath. But this here land is all mine. That over there on the other side is free of ownership. There is no one else out here but me and yourself."

Caroline smiled and then raised her hand, pointing ahead. "Sir, take no offense, but I cannot slow for a moment. I am on my way to Farmersville to meet my three brothers and to return by here in the next days. All three are very strong hunters like you and would enjoy your company." Caroline took another step, but the man took a sideways step and blocked her. She kept her hand on the handle of the knife still hidden in the fold of her skirt.

"I do not take it as offense, but when a man offers hospitality and a place and time to rest to a stranger walking these roads, he does feel a lowering down and sinking of emotions when that offer is declined. So if ya excuse me, I will mention again my place for ya to wash up; as I have said, I have fresh clothes for ya, pretty things too. I see yourn clothes do appear ragged. Please do not resist my hospitality. For ya will walk far to find another as kind as I am. I do insist."

Caroline took a third step to the side and the man did the same. "Again, thank you. But I am late for this meeting with my brothers." The man rubbed his two great hands together and fell silent for a moment. Looking over his shoulder and in all directions, he placed his hat back on top of his head. "Ya know they tell me, and it is common knowledge, some women like a strong man to tell 'em what to do. Some women will pretend they don't want to enter into it, so therefore they can claim it is not their doing, but they were forced. Could you be one of them?"

"Sir, I am not one of those women, as I am a Godly woman and I am married with three children. I do not seek out your company. I too am strong willed and a fighter. You will not insist on me."

43

"Why? I am stronger than ya. I have always taken what I want. I want to see ya bathe, be in my cabin, and be in my wife's clothes."

Caroline fixed her jaw tightly. "Kind sir, I seek nothing from you, and I am sorry for the handful of water I took. I meant no harm."

The gruff man looked over his right shoulder again. "If I were to knock ya out and have my way with ya right here, will that be a harm? Ya will not know what has happened to ya. Ya will be the same as asleep. You would be innocent to any event that happened. But if ya come to my shed, ya might find enjoyment in it. And I would enjoy that better too. A man and a woman were meant to do it. Meant to have relations. The good book says so. That is what I am offering."

"Sir, if you fear God, you should fear any actions you would take upon me. God could strike you dead if He chose to do so, and I have seen it with a sinning man only six months ago. God has given me traveling protections, and you would be wise to observe them. I cannot be responsible for your life should you attempt anything untoward to me."

There was only silence between the two of them standing near the dirt road ten feet away from each other. The tattered man took off his hat again and brushed back his coal black hair. He turned and looked over one shoulder a third time. He then quickly turned in a complete circle. "Damn my luck. I saw ya walkin' and thought my luck had changed. All I wanted was ten minutes with ya in my shack. But now I am willin' to pay. I wasn't afore, but now I am. I will offer ya a week's wages. I have five dollars. That's a lot of money. I will give ya five dollars for ten minutes. And if ya don't take it, I will take ya as I want, and where I want. And many times."

"Alright then," Caroline replied, "I only want to know where you want buried. For as you touch me, before you start your fornication, God will strike you dead, and I will have your five dollars. I will burn down your shack, with you in it, and be on my way. Let us go now to your shack and start." Caroline looked to the sky. "Jesus, I have given him fair warning."

"Not so fast. Why are ya so damn sure this'll happen?"

"It has happened twice in my life, and once two weeks ago. There was no lighting, no thunder. The man, this rapist, fell dead to the floor only minutes after abducting me. And there was a sulfur smell about him as he lay on the floor. Yellow foam came out of his mouth, and I could smell the putrid odor of fire and brimstone. From a burning hell. God killed him and he went straight to Satan. Now let's get up to your shack and get this over, for I am tired as I have more to walk this day."

The tall man kicked the ground and dragged his foot in a straight line across the grass. He looked at her and spit on the ground. "Wait a minute! Let me think. Damn! Ya know, if ya would have runned, I would have runned after ya and knocked ya down. But you stand there looking at me, eye to eye. That scares me. So damn you! This is my land. Get off of it! Get off of it now! And do not come back this way with yourn brothers, for I am liable to shoot one or all three. Go ahead, get the hell out of here."

Caroline looked the man straight in his eyes. "Even though you are a sinful man, God has a plan for you if you change your ways. Repent. And seek Him."

"It's too late for me. I know I am bound for hell. I just do not seek to go now. I said it oncet and I will say it again, get the hell off my land. Now! Damn it!" The angry man turned and quickly walked up a slight hill, through the tall grass, and back into the woods. He shouted out one last time. "Get the hell out of here." He disappeared in moments mumbling to himself. Caroline stood there and watched. Indeed, God had walked with her through this valley's shadow of death. She did not fear any evil. She feared something worse.

Nearing ten that morning, Caroline felt exhausted. She knew she had walked for twelve hours and desired only to sleep. She walked on for the next mile until she spied what appeared to be a hidden collection of elderberry bushes fifty feet off the road, and up a slight hill on her right. It would be impossible to see her sleeping there as it was shaded heavily—further the elderberry shrub branches came low to the ground and would provide a wall of green leaves to screen the sun.

As she left the road and walked up the hill, she heard the sound of horse hoof beats, and ducked low to watch two wagons come over a small rise, heading west. She observed a lone woman with a small girl child sitting next to her. Caroline stood then waved but the woman did not see

Caroline; instead, she stared straight ahead. A milking cow and two goats were leashed to the slow-moving wagon that carried several wood and wire crates—one with chickens and one with ducks. The second wagon was pulled by a pair of large black mules covered with sweat, and carried three elderly women who looked to be sisters. Someone had painted crude red crosses on the canvas sides. All three women wore white dresses with white bonnets. She again waved, but the women did not notice her standing uphill near the tree line. Caroline realized it was easy to blend into the trees and not be seen even in the daylight. But this sighting was a good thing, as her experience this first night had been all bad. And each of the three occurrences could have been fatal. But the sighting of the two wagons meant there could be good people traveling these roads in the next nine days. She hoped this was a fortuitous sign.

The elderberry bushes did provide shade for her, and the grasses mixed with ferns beneath the canopy looked to be welcoming. She ate several handfuls of berries and ate the last piece of cornbread. Walking to a nearby beech tree, she set about cutting the low hanging branches. She unslung the rolled blanket bedroll and then covered herself with the gathered beech leaves. Now nearly invisible, Caroline collapsed exhausted inside the blanket and laid there for a moment. The wool blanket felt scratchy on her, but it felt like home. She closed her eyes.

Charles helped her off the wagon and they both stood there looking at the circle of grass all knocked down. "Look here, Caroline, even the deer like this place. We can build our

47

cabin right here. The deer won't like it, but you and I will. Here, turn around as this will be the view from the front porch. And when the first born comes along, you can sit here and nurse him or her and watch the black birds land on the fence posts that surround the corral which I will soon build to hold our horse. The sun will set over those hills."

Caroline smiled. "How do you know I am not already pregnant? Maybe I have not told you something of importance. For I know in my heart when I sit on that porch I will be nursing a son."

A small smile crept across Charles's face. "How do you know? Why are you so sure it will be a boy?"

"This morning while you were shaving, I floated a blade of green grass in my morning's pee and it pointed toward you and not me. That is how I know it will be a boy."

"But how do you know you are pregnant?"

"God told me in a dream. He said we will have a wonderful life right here. He said we would have two boys and a girl. And the first would arrive before Christmas."

Charles took her hand. "Did he tell you how much I love you?"

"Oh, no. You first told me that in a church pew in the back of my father's church. Then you kissed me. You were not a good kisser then, but you are improving. And I will teach you the art of a tender kiss."

Charles released her hand. "Improving? There is no time for kissing lessons then. I must pitch our tent and gather wood for our fire. Perhaps you can go down to the stream and bring back some water, while I unload the wagon."

"There will be no water and no unloading of the wagon and no dinner. I will stand out here all night by myself until I get the first tender kiss on our first homestead."

"I think you are bluffing."

"Mister Charles Matthew Duncan, soon you will see, while I am very good at bluffing, there are times I do not bluff at all. This could be one of those times."

"Okay, but you never told me nor showed any signs before I married you how strong willed you were. Some would say stubborn."

"What you see before you is not as it appears. You think I am weak. I assure you, Mister Duncan, I am not. Now, kiss me or suffer sleeping by yourself with me out here standing in the dark waiting for you. And I will do that. That is my deal."

Caroline woke suddenly when she heard the sound of grass stirring on the ground near her. A mother deer and a yearling doe stood eating elderberries. The sun was low on the horizon but, turning to her left, she could make out five other deer standing in a row of shadowy trees sixty-five feet away. Caroline realized she was thirsty and she slowly stood and gathered her bag. Rolling her blanket into a bedroll, she hung it over her shoulder and head. She saw the knife and placed in back inside her waist band. She quietly pulled a handful of elderberries as she cautiously walked down the rise to the dirt road. It seemed to her it was about eight in the evening. An owl flew out of the trees behind her and circled silently overhead as she started walking again. Caroline watched the owl, as this was something familiar and normal at their homestead. She felt strong. She felt good.

Five miles into this second night's walk, she heard the sound of water rushing over some rocks and so, she turned to her right and walked down a small embankment to a wide stream. The soil beneath her feet felt soft and rich. It was the type of soil that comes from years of spring rains and flooding which washes the rich top soil out of the woods and fills the valleys. As she drank, she spotted a round patch of watercress. She stepped forward and started pulling the watercress and eating it. It was cool from the spring water and yet had a fresh spiciness to it. She reached into her bag for a piece of cornbread but found only crumbs. This would be her meal for tonight. She took off her shoes and rolled her dress then waded deeper into the water. She pulled up several handfuls of the watercress and placed it into her bag. This might be the only food she would find for the next period of time. She spied several crayfish along the embankment, but having no way to cook them, she only thought of how good they would taste if she made a fire. She turned and walked out of the water, put on her shoes, and walked back up to the wagon tracked road. There was no time to waste and make a fire for a meal. Thirty minutes was a mile traveled and not something she could waste on herself. Her husband lay badly wounded in a hospital bed 190 miles away, battling for his life. There was no other choice but this.

Moonlight, like sunlight with its shadows, can deceive the eye. At times, as Caroline walked, she caught a moon shadow in mischief. Irregular shapes and distinct forms seemed to move, and then join into larger threatening shadows. During the day, she could see clearly and know that nothing was hiding behind a tree or bush. But in this early night's light, there were moving shadows everywhere, and any shape could be hiding something. It could be a bear, a wolf, or even a man hiding—maybe several men hiding. She thought of the advice Missus Millar had given about encountering a man, but what of a bear? Worse yet, how could she fight off a wolf? Where would she stab it? How much time would she have to prepare, and what if there were two or three wolves? She knew she would have to be quick. Not only quick, she thought, she had to dodge and sidestep. The more she thought about it, the more she knew she was poorly prepared for such an attack. Caroline spoke aloud to herself, as if this would help contain her fears. "Caroline, you may be entirely insufficient to sustain this endeavor. This is not an easy task before you, and you cannot always depend on God. You will have to help yourself. You have a plan, but this was a beginner's plan. You need more than that. You need an evolving plan. So what are you afraid of? Bears and wolves come to mind. So take out your knife. How do you hold it? If I hold it down low like this, then swing up, it is not wise, as a bear's paw swinging down onto me could stop my arm, or cause the knife to be knocked from my hand. But since he would be running at me, then I need to keep my knife held high and over my head, like this. Then I must swing down and hard like this. And I must stand my ground until he is upon me. I must not run, I must stand my ground. When he is but within five feet of me, his paw will reach out to knock me down, but I must twist left and step back quickly to the right. And I must swing down hard with the knife as he passes. I should aim for that part under his head, like a neck. Yes, where his head joins his body. But one knife strike will not be enough. He will turn and charge again. Then I must repeat my same moves. Wait until he is within five feet, turn left and then step back to the right, and swing down the knife again. This fight will go on for some time. Watch him closely, as he might change his tactics. He might stand and try to fight me on his back legs. He will try to frighten me. I must step backwards and make him come down on four legs. Every time he stands, I must move backwards. I cannot attempt to fight him, because he has the advantage on his back legs. Keep him down and moving, let the wound do its course, let the blood flow and it will weaken him. Also, when I see him coming, I must drop my bag and bedroll, as it will slow me. Now, I must stop here and practice." Caroline stopped in the middle of the road. She took a deep breath. "Quick, get rid of the roll. Drop the bag. Take the knife. Raise it over my head. Wait until he is ten feet from me. Twist to the left. Step back as he passes, and plunge the knife down. Again, do it again." Right there and then in the middle of the road in the night's darkness, Caroline practiced her bear attack defense a second time. Caroline picked up the bedroll and the bag; she placed the knife back into her belt. "Quicker this time. Get rid of the bedroll, now the bag, pull the knife, raise it, twist to the left, step back as he passes in front of me, and plunge it down. Now turn, because he will come again. Raise the knife, swing to the left, and swing down hard the knife. Harder, you are not cutting a chicken's head, you are killing a bear. It has to be hard to cut through the fur. Maybe I should use both hands on the knife. Yes, Caroline, be mad at that bear, for he wants to keep you from your husband. He is evil. I must show great strength. I must be angry. And I need to scream at each plunge of the knife. I must show the bear that I am stronger than he." Caroline picked up her bag and haversack. "If I only had my husband's gun, I would not be so frightened. But I have what has been given to me. It is a knife that I once peeled potatoes with. It is all I have. And what I have can be enough."

Caroline picked up her bedroll and bag, and then placed the knife back into the fold of her waist band. "Jesus, thank you for that lesson. David killed Goliath and I am prepared to kill a bear, or if it happens, a wolf. Maybe later you can show me how to kill a wolf. I fear there might be two or three and so I will need new instructions. Put them into my mind like you did for the bear, for I could not have thought of that on my own." As Caroline walked on, she had no thoughts of how to deal with several wolves. She thought she could deal with one. But what of two or three or a pack? How would anyone fight a pack of wolves? For the rest of that night, she thought, but no answer came. At about three in the morning, she caught the smell of something burning. Then she changed her mind. It was not a recent burning, but that of old ashes now wet. This smell of a fire filled the air, and yet she could see no smoke in the moonlight. As she walked on, the smell grew stronger. Wherever it was, it was once a big fire. She knew there was a small settlement on this road, and thought the settlement was still ahead in the distance. She walked for the next six miles as the smell grew stronger. Additionally, there was the smell of something dead—something that had been dead for three or four days. It was large. It reminded her of the time she and Charles encountered two dead deer, antlers locked and deep in the woods. It was a stench that filled the back of one's throat causing the muscles to tighten in a gagging reflex. Yes, she thought, something is dead and decomposing. The next mile proved to be even worse and she pulled a scarf across her nose. Her throat tightened more to ward off the intense choking reflex. She could almost feel the rotting flesh in the air, like a humid blast of festering decay. There was silence everywhere except for the ever increasing buzzing noise. Thousands of large, black flies were swarming directly ahead and she turned to the left of the road. As the flies increased, she left the road and walked high up through the tall grass fifty feet from the road and to the tree line of young maples, which she thought would offer respite from the flies and putrid smell. But it was to no avail and the grasses only slowed her steps. She tried to hurry and hold her breath, but the weeds were so thick it only pulled at her feet and proved difficult. She gagged once and placed her hand over her mouth. Then she saw it. There in the middle of the road was a dead horse. Its brown coat no longer held a sheen but was dull and lifeless. Bloated, it appeared to have been dead for a week. She tried not to look at it, but there was more than a dead horse before her. In its opened mouth, was a nickel plated bridle with reins lying on the ground. On its back was a military saddle; brown blood clung to the black leather. As it rotted and distended for those days, the underbelly strap had grown tighter and tighter until it had cut into the horse's belly. Its once dark brown coat had split from the heat, and pink-red flesh was visible clinging to its white ribs. Carnivorous animals had come and eaten on it. Flies and a sea of maggots moved in waves in the moonlight. Caroline averted her eyes and ran through the small trees and down onto the road and continued to run from the gagging smell. It took thirty minutes to distance herself from the dead animal, but still in her nose she could sense it. Finding a small stream of water, she stopped and washed her face, splashing water up into her nose, hoping to erase the putridness of it all. It was of scarce help.

As she walked, she wondered whether it was a Confederate horse, or a Yankee horse. There was no way of knowing, but she thought it had to be one or the other, which meant the Yankees were there recently, but where had they gone? Mister Millar said he had heard they were several days away, and maybe he was correct. But what happened to the horse? Was it shot? Did the Yankees shoot a Confederate horse? Did the Confederates shoot a Yankee horse? But there was more. What was the fire smell? Where did that come from? She stopped and again smelled the air. It was still there, and, yes, even stronger. The road dipped down to a stream and she walked through it and then up a rise and now could see something hidden in the shadows. It was nearing five in the morning and the sun had yet to show itself to the east, but the coal black sky had turned light gray, the color of rain clouds, yet there was no rain. Early morning birds had not started to leave their branches, but were calling greetings to each other from the trees that held this road in place. While these sounds seemed so normal, the birds were ignoring the devastating sight that revealed itself in the morning light. Before her, hidden in the darkness, appeared a small settlement of sixteen houses and a single school building. All burned to the ground.

The birds sounded so normal, so regular this morning, as if they were oblivious to what had happened here or maybe in spite of it, as something man did to his fellow man now and then but never to them. All the buildings, every last one she could see, had been burned and turned into ashes. There was still smoke rising out of several, and small flames emanated from one small barn. Several years ago, she had passed through this settlement on her way to visit her mother and father in Louisville. But at that time she was in a wagon while Charles held the reins and the children rode in the back on straw mattresses. Caroline raised her hand up to her mouth, aghast at seeing the absolute destruction of this little settlement. It had been a handful of innocent buildings and a small school by the side of the road. There was evidence in the distance of three houses clustered together near a small creek 800 feet to the east. Walking closer, Caroline saw those three houses near the creek had not been burned completely, while the others were totally destroyed. A clapboard wall on one house still stood, charred black except for a small amount of whitewash that survived under its burned out windows, as if the owner tried to extinguish the fire but could save just a single wall. Caroline thought, days earlier people like her lived here. Mothers preparing dinners. Children playing. Fathers building rooms to their homes, ready for a newborn. But today merely an echo remained. Caroline walked toward the houses. And while she guessed the time was about five in the morning, she called out, "Hello, is anyone here?" She turned in the other direction. "Hello. Hello. My name is Caroline, is anyone here?" In the distance she heard a dog barking, but it did not come near. She moved to the nearest house. The stone chimney stood there, unmoved, rising two stories high and marking the spot like a cemetery stone—waiting patiently hoping the owner would return and build a house surrounding its charred stones. Caroline stepped over a small fence that had been knocked down into the yard. In the ashes near the kitchen, she spotted some broken dishes and several pots and pans. She noticed a piece of the kitchen roof had fallen and its slate shingles had smothered the fire. Parts of the kitchen dry sink were still visible. A chair and a table were thrown into the side yard. Maybe the owner attempted to save something, anything, from the fire. As she turned, she noticed all around the houses the burnt grasses stood as silent witnesses to the ferocity of the flames, forming perfect brown circles, each one surrounded by green yards where children once could be found. But standing at this one house, Caroline's eye caught sight of a glass jar, broken with its contents spilled. Picking up a stick, she pushed back a piece of the slate roof, and spotted more broken glass and there among them were several unbroken and full jars. "Peaches! I see peaches." Caroline reached down and pulled up a quart jar of peaches. She looked around again. "Hello, my name is Caroline. I want to talk to you. I am going to eat some of your food. Is that okay? I am from west of here. I am walking to find my husband. If no one answers then I will eat some of these peaches." There was no sound. No one answered, and so Caroline sat down in the green grass, gazing at the burned house before her, and opened the jar of peaches. Cutting the wax with her knife, she licked the bottom of the wax sealer and then she drank the peach syrup; reaching in, she pulled out a single peach and ate it. "You did an excellent job with these peaches, for they taste wonderful." It took Caroline ten minutes, but she took her time eating the whole quart jar of peaches. It was the first full meal she had that night.

The sun was starting to rise above the valley to the east, and for some reason, she felt at home here in this burned down settlement. Maybe it was the idea that families had lived here recently and that a mother, maybe her age, had canned these peaches a month earlier. But that feeling lasted merely a moment as Caroline felt a sense of dread as the sun rose and she saw a clearer picture before her—a picture of the emotional turmoil the families endured. These were families who stood frozen in their yards as their homes were set aflame by men who smashed coal oil lamps to the floor and tossed a single match. What took a year to joyfully build was destroyed in a moment of hateful anger. At a home 200 feet away, a clothesline still held laundry hung out to dry on the morning of the great fires. A young girl's bright blue dress danced rhythmically in the morning breeze, never to be worn again— yet waiting for the girl to dance with it once more. This missing family caused Caroline to see the possible future of her own family only two days and fifty miles behind her. Total war was not something she expected to see on these back roads inhabited only by a small settlement of homesteaders like hers raising families. As she gazed upon the fluttering blue dress, she started to tremble. Emotions rose. She could not contain it. Slowly, tears filled her eyes and ran down her cheek for the family she would never meet and the one she had left behind. Her own. She said one word aloud. "Priscilla." She pictured a young girl in that blue dress happily dancing in the yard and she pictured her daughter standing by their burned homestead crying out for her mother. She whispered the name again as if her daughter was standing there. "Priscilla." She wiped a single tear off her cheek. There was a long silence. "Priscilla, you listen to me. You hide deep in the woods. You hide well. I promise I will come home with your father, but you must be strong. I will return with your father, but it will take time. Now don't bother me again as I do this, for it surely will weaken me and I might falter. Now go and hide in the woods with your brothers. And if they burn our home, worry not, we will rebuild it. You, me, the boys, and Daddy."

Caroline fell over onto the grass and closed her eyes, but the images of what might it have been like to be here with one's family days earlier haunted her. She saw the confusion and the fires, the emotions. This little town could be the homesteads around her home. This home could be her home. These jars of peaches could be her jars. And while she did not know these people, they were indeed related—fellow homesteaders. She thought to herself, "This is but the second day and what will I encounter in the next nine days? Will it be more like this? Will I see dead people, women and children killed near their homes?" Caroline had not imagined the enormity of it all, but this little village made it clear what lay ahead in the future. "Please, sweet Jesus, take this cup away. Please, please take this cup away. I do not want it. I do not want any part of it." After a few moments Caroline, with tears on her cheeks, grew silent and fell asleep. There, in front of a burned-out house in what was once a fenced yard, with smoke still rising from several homes nearby, with two quart jars of peaches now gathered around her, Caroline Emily Duncan slept for what seemed to her was just a moment, but in reality was six hours.

"What 'cha doin', lady? You sleeping or are you a ghost?" Caroline stirred at the sound of a voice. Her hand went to her waistband and the knife.

"I've seen 'em before. Ghosts. Lots of 'em. Right here, the day after the Yankees came."

Caroline opened her eyes to see a young boy standing over her. The young child looked to be about the same age as Isaac, fourteen at most, and was dressed in an over-sized wool suit and wore black shoes two sizes too big. "My name is Esau, and I used to live in that there house down by the creek. It's gone now. Over there." The young boy pointed to a pile of lumber, burned, and a stone chimney still standing. Caroline looked in that direction and then back to the boy. He carried no musket in his hands, but had a shovel in his right hand. He wore a brown rough-cut leather belt around his waist, and a

60

blue steel revolver stuck out beneath it. "Burnt. It was fast. When they came, I was down by the creek with my sister. I was fishin' and she was collectin' dandelion greens. Mister Stimonds and his sons were far away, near the road. When the Yankees came ridin' down the road yonder, you could hear 'em. There was only about five of 'em. With big black horses. We didn't know no how that there were about sixty a half mile back. The first Yankees were scouts. Mister Stimonds lost his oldest boy Neval, only a month ago. So he was still mad. The Yankees started shooting at the stars and bars flag we had flyin' by the school."

Caroline looked again at the boy and noticed in the grass at his feet, barely visible, was a long rifle musket. Part of the wooden stock had been burned black. When he turned to point, she saw the belt around his waist held two bone-handled knives behind him. Dirt from ashes covered his hands as if he had been digging in the rubble.

"Mister Stimonds went into his house and got his shot gun. He ran out screaming. His sons were right behind him with their guns. That's when all the shooting started. So the Yankees jumped off their horses and started shooting back. I grabbed my sister, Lucy, and we hid by the bank over there. There were lots of shots fired. Mister Stimonds second oldest son, Fredrick, was first hit, and then the younger son, Tyler, was hit. Some other men of the town, the Bennetts, the Hindmenths, the Felkners, even old Mister Wiley grabbed their guns and started shooting. There was blue smoke everywhere. My dad ran out of the house with his musket rifle—a brand new one, not this one here, this one belongs to

61

Mister and Missus Carlton and he was shot over by Missus Sumner's house. By then, the rest of the Yankees got here. But we shot and killed all five of 'em. That is at the beginning. Before the big Yankees got here."

Caroline stood up and looked in all directions. "When did this happen?"

"Oh, about five days ago. I been up in the woods sleepin' in case they came back."

"What happened to your family, your mom, your sister?"

"I was supposed to go with 'em. Mama took the wagon and Lucy and Grandma. All of 'em and ole Missus Sumner are headed off to Aunt Edna's house. It's way out in Narvon's Creek."

"Why didn't you go with them?"

"I told them go on and I'd catch up. I had to bury Daddy first and then Mister Stimonds and Frederick and Tyler. Everybody else buried everybody else. Most are buried over where the church used to be. You can see the crosses I put up."

"I repeat my question, why are you still here?"

"Because of the ghosts. I've seen 'em. I stayed the first day up in the woods, but at night I heard 'em singing. So I came out to the edge of the woods and watched them walk around. I saw my dad, and they just walk from house to house. Singing.

They don't see me. The reason I know they are ghosts is they're all, everyone, dressed in white. I hollered to Pa, but he don't look my way. He is just singing. Like all the rest. I never heard this song before but it is beautiful."

Caroline looked at the boy with concern. "Why did the Yankees burn the houses?"

"Well, like I said, we had the stars and bars flag flying down by the school. I guess that made 'em real mad. In the end, I think we kilt about nine Yankees. Course they kilt sixteen of ours. Well, most of the men, and then they went around and burned everything. I come down each day to get some peaches just like you." I ain't going to Narvon's Creek or even Paducah. I am staying here. This is my home, and so I am going to build a shack right here. The creeks got fish and I took our cow up into the woods." The young boy took a step back and smiled to show himself. "I got this suit from the Pattersons. That house didn't burn all the way down. He was three years older than me, but he's dead too, so I got most of his clothes; it's all up in the woods. I got a tent. I got guns. I got ammunition. If I see a Yankee by himself, I'll put him in my sights. Bang, he's dead. But what is your name?"

"I am Caroline and I am on my way to Shelbyville to see my husband. I am from west of here about fifty miles. I've been walking for two days now."

The young boy looked to his west. "I ain't never been west of here. But Shelbyville is more than a nine-day walk from here. Down this road. That's where the Yankees probably come from. But you can have all the peaches you want. Missus Patterson had nine peach trees in the backyard and she shared. We had peach jam, peach cobbler, peach turnovers, peach relish, peach upside down cake. We had forty chickens and ducks, so she got all the eggs she wanted."

"That's very kind of you. I will take some preserved peaches." The boy pointed to a pile of burned lumber sixty feet away. "There's green beans and lima beans and peas all under that. Most of it didn't break. It's still good. I figure with just me, I could live here for three years and worry not about food. Mom could come back by then and we can rebuild the house. That way we would be near my pa."

"You say Shelbyville is a nine-day walk from here? I thought it was about seven days away."

"No, ma'am, you would have to walk real fast to make it. There's the Shivers River, and I heard it's up real nasty like, so you may have to detour upstream to Nelsville. They got a strong new bridge there. But that is eleven miles up and then eleven miles back to the road. That's probably how Yankees come 'cause no one is gonna cross the river on this road. We used to have a rope and horse ferry, but that washed away last spring and ain't nobody yet built a new one. But if you try to swim that river, you'll drown surely, there is not a doubt in my mind. Last spring, I seen a whole house float down that river."

"I am a good swimmer, Esau. I have swum in the mighty Ohio River from Kentucky across to Indiana. If I find a rope and tie it to myself, I could—if I had trouble—pull myself back."

"No. You shan't survive. Last spring bodies floated down that there river. Me and my pa stood there in April after the big rain. We watched it all. I saw horses and cows and pigs. All dead. And I saw a man, face down and blown up like a rubber balloon, float by. The waters had ripped off all his pants and shirt so he was buck naked." The young boy removed his hat, scratched his head, and then put it back on. "My ma said God is mad that his fellow creatures are having war with each other. I think God is still mad, 'cause he is sending all this rain causing all this here flooding."

Caroline looked to the east and toward the river. She shielded her eyes from the noon sun. "Alright then, I will have to fend for myself. I do not want to go eleven miles up and eleven miles back. If I swim with the river and not try to fight it, if I swim and let it take me downstream, then I should survive. Thank you, Esau, you have been most helpful."

Again, Esau took his hat off his head and held it in front with both hands. "Then I want to pray for you. You could be dead this time tomorrow. Can I?"

"Yes, go ahead."

"Dear, Jesus, this is Esau talkin'. I know you have some. So send some extra angels to help Caroline. She is stubborn beyond my belief, and she is fixed to swim the Shivers River.

I think enough people have gone and died here, don't you? I bet you do, so you don't need another one. So I just wanted to let you know what's happenin' today. Amen."

Caroline gathered her things off the ground, including two double quart jars of peaches. When she turned to say goodbye to Esau, she saw he was already walking toward the church with its new white crosses. Over one shoulder was a shovel and over the other was his musket. Two knives hidden under his belt in the back caught the noon sun and reflected toward Caroline. She turned and walked back to the road, giving one last glance at this little settlement. It was dead, but the Shivers River was very much alive.

As she walked past the homes, she looked for things she might need in the future, but specifically she looked for some rope. At the edge of town, near the last burned out house, she found a clothes line with men's clothing hanging on it. She saw several pair of men's trousers and five men's shirts all small in size. Caroline stopped and pulled down the clothing and piled it on the ground. She untied the rope at one end and then the other. There were six lines of cotton rope hanging there and she took all six. She looked around to see if the boy was looking her way and she saw that he had disappeared. Caroline took off her bedroll and then her dirtied and tattered dress. She bent down and lifted the dark brown trousers. She stuck one foot through the pant leg and then the other. She buttoned up the pants. She thought she would need a belt or a piece of rope. She lifted up a man's white dress shirt and slipped her arm into the right sleeve then the other arm into the left sleeve. She had never worn men's clothing before, as it was strictly forbidden in the Bible for a woman to do so. But this was a different time now. She lifted a second man's white shirt from the pile and ripped off a sleeve. She rolled it and pulled it through the belt loops and tied it in a knot, creating a makeshift belt. The pants seemed roomy, and fit around her hips. Caroline slipped her kitchen knife under the waist band. She pulled her shirt tails out, covering the belt and the knife. Looking down into the pile, she spotted a man's black woolen vest; picking it up she slipped it on.

To anyone who would pass by her, and especially at night, she appeared at a distance to be a young man. And she thought if she wore a hat with her hair hidden underneath, the disguise could be sufficient to fool many. Looking down again at the pile of clothing, she spied the second pair of men's wool trousers. She pulled them up to herself and pulled out the knife. About twenty inches up from the bottom of the pant leg, she made a cut all the way across. She pulled the pant leg over her head as you would a cap. She pushed her hair up under the gray wool cap and allowed the top to flop over to one side. Now she had a man's looking cap that hid her hair and made her disguise complete. As she walked from the town, she looked back one last time. She saw the flagpole that once flew a confederate flag. It was bare.

She could hear the river long before she got there. It was a roar like she had heard during big bonfires when she and Charles cleared the homestead of hundreds of trees, and flames from the slash reached 300 feet, roaring into the air. Standing in the sun she cupped her ear to hear the river. Just the noise alone was enough to tell anyone this runaway creature was a force that ruled this valley. She was still a mile away and it drowned out all other noises. Deep and steady. Powerful. Dangerous to anyone who ventured close. This roar shook the leaves on trees that lined its banks, echoed against the mountains, and, finding nowhere else to go, this thunderous cacophony of noise climbed through the clouds proclaiming to the sky its power.

Upon approaching the river, she felt the ground tremble. She went up a short hill and then from that distance she looked down at this creature of immense power. She stood there and watched the other side for any sign of life. There was none. Everything was still except for this mighty river's domination. No, there was no one over there that could help her if she got into trouble. Just an empty and unused road. Caroline sat and watched the river, judging where its hidden forces were hiding. How it moved. What were its dangerous places out there she should avoid—like swirling waters that pulled you down into its depths. As she sat, she ate half a jar of peaches while watching for any sign of the river's weakness. To her, the distance across seemed 170 feet. Occasionally, a tree torn from the earth would race by, turning and tumbling, surrendering itself to overwhelming authority. Caroline walked down the hill and into the shallow valley carved millions of years ago by the forefathers of this river—for this river's will had always been here. She took out her six ropes and tied the ends together in square knots. She realized she did not have enough rope to stretch to the other side but there was enough if she ran into trouble, she could pull herself back. She unrolled her blanket on the ground and placed her shoes in the middle along with her new cut off pant leg hat, trousers, vest, and shirt. Lastly, she poured out the remaining peaches onto the ground and secured the galvanized tops with their red rubber seals. Caroline placed those two empty double quart jars next to her shoes. Carefully rolling up the blanket, she tied the ends together. She slipped the bedroll blanket over her head and under both arms. "The air trapped in the jars should give me an element of buoyancy. Not a lot, but some, maybe enough to help." She looked for a tree nearest the riverbank and remeasured the distance across. Caroline decided for the second time it indeed was 170 feet to the other side, but she realized the current would pull her fast downstream. So, if she could keep her head above water, and if she made it to the middle of the river, Caroline felt she could make it the rest of the way. In the middle of the river, she would untie the rope and swim safely to the other side. The question she had was a new one to her. Would the trailing rope be a pull on her? Would it drag her under, and could she untie it fast enough to free herself? She tied the rope, not about her waist, but under her arms chest high. She looked at the knot she had tied and questioned whether, underwater and blind, could she untie it in time to surface. She thought about the time her husband had taught her a quick release knot. It took but a single quick pull, and it fell apart. She untied her previous square knot and started again. "Yes, this goes over here and then under here and this part pulls into a loop. It is that single end I pull to release, and not the loop, which will only tighten the rope and surely then I would drown."

Caroline walked upstream twenty feet to a small hickory tree five feet from the riverbank. She tied the rope to the tree. She pulled hard to see if it would hold. It did. "So, if I jump in here I would be swept down the river and surrender, letting the river carry me. I would not resist but only guide myself to a spot about 200 yards downstream." She said a quiet prayer and said out loud, "Do not panic. Let the river take me for a ride and when it is finished showing me it is the boss-man, it will tire of me and spit me out on the other side. I have done this before in the mighty Ohio River, and this one is smaller. I know its tricks. It will try to scare me. I will not be frightened."

With that, Caroline took several deep breaths and turned and ran full speed into the river with the seventy-foot rope trailing behind. The cold water splashed in her face and up her nose into the back of her throat. She coughed once and spat out the water. She lifted her head and spied the point she wanted to target. She kicked hard and stayed above the water, but without warning a second wave swept over her and filled her nose with water, which she coughed up and spat out. She swam hard, not against the current but hard into its midst. Thirty feet out, she turned and looked back at where she had entered the river. It was quickly moving away from her. But there was a more immediate problem. It was a problem she had not thought of. She realized the trailing rope was being pulled hard downstream by the river, and thus dragging her back toward the side she had left. She thought of her planning, and how this was to be a safe line, but in fact it was of no use. It was the opposite. The rope pulled hard against her, and she was making no headway. She thought of her father who had once said, "Only a fool ignores what he sees." Caroline decided to pull the end on the rope and push on without the safety it could afford. In one quick pull, she felt the rope slip away and race downstream dancing on the surface of the waves and toward the west bank. It was worse than no use. It could kill. She turned to her right to see her target point rush by, and she was only forty feet out. The current was tiring her as she kicked and pulled at the river with one arm then the other. She gasped for air at times as water splashed into her nose and mouth. She was making progress, but keeping her head above water was extremely tiring, as the water tried to pull her down. She glanced at the other side and decided she was now only a quarter ways cross the river. She was using much of her strength and was tiring quickly. Another wave came and splashed over her head then pulled her down deep into the swirling water. She fought and kicked hard to get back to the surface. The water turned her upside down. She started tumbling out of control underwater, rolling over and over. Her shoulder bumped hard into something, but she had no idea what it was. She pushed her arms out from herself and stretched her feet far apart and this was enough to slow the spinning, but Caroline was unaware which way was up and which way was down. She opened her eyes but everything was greenish black. Her body wanted to exhale, so to take in fresh air and her lungs started to quiver, but she fought hard against that reflex. "Caroline, do not panic, but which way is up?" She stopped tumbling and thought, "Don't panic. I think it is okay to grab my knees and roll into a ball and I may pop to the surface. Be like an apple in a water barrel. Be an apple. Just relax and be a bobbing apple in a water barrel." Seconds later Caroline's back side broke to the surface. She felt it, and quickly raised her head above water to take the first rushed breath she had in the last two minutes. She quickly looked around to see how far she had come. She was now 500 feet downstream, but she was only sixty feet from the east bank of the river. The river was not satisfied and tried to pull her under again. Caroline fought back, kicking quick and hard. More water splashed into her nose and she coughed it out. She pulled hard with her arms against the current trying to move to the other side. But she could tell her strength was ebbing. Her arms felt heavy, her legs were growing numb. She turned upriver to a noise and saw an oak tree ninety feet long racing down the river. She screamed at herself, "Caroline, you can do it." She mustered more strength and kicked hard to barely keep her head above the water. She saw the tree with all its leaves still intact being swept faster than she was swimming. It was sixty feet upstream and she could hear the noise it made churning in the water. From its speed, she thought it would pass by incredibly fast and it would be like jumping bareback onto a running horse. She had done that many times before as a young girl in Louisville. As the huge tree went by ten feet away, she kicked hard and reached out, grabbing a single branch on the main trunk with both hands. It was traveling even faster than she thought, and so it jerked hard on her arms. Her left side ribs slammed against the twenty-inch diameter trunk, knocking the air out of her lungs. For a moment, things went black. Instinctively, she grabbed hard with cold fingers against the branch. But her arms were so

weak and numb they could barely hold on. She did not like
the great tree's speed, but her head was staying above water.
"Rest, Caroline. Rest. Gather your strength. Be patient. God
has sent an ark for me. Wait for a moment and there will be
a time when the river turns sharply to its left and we will come
close to the right bank." What she thought was correct.
Within three minutes the river turned left and with one hard
push she was alone again without the aid of the tree,
swimming hard for the bank. Water splashed over her head
and the river tried to pull her down, but the river was using
all its energy on the tree and the Shivers River let her go. She
realized what the boy said was true, "The river has its own
mind, and it travels on, hoping to snag another victim. Horse,
cow, pig, or man. To the river, it does not matter. It only
wants to show its authority."

Caroline's feet hit something firm. She thought it was
probably a large river rock, and it meant maybe there would
be others. She was barely keeping her head above water.
Moments later, her feet touched another rock and she pushed
herself up and forward toward the bank. She moved her feet
quickly as if she were running, hoping to land on another
rock; this time there were several and she pushed hard against
the river's rocky bottom and pulled with her arms. Now she
was fifteen feet from the river's east bank, and she understood
the river was using its mightiest forces in the center of the
river, and the pull along the bank was less. But still the Shivers
River pulled her downstream. With each step on the river
bottom, more of her body was emerging from the water, so
the river had given up and moved on. With six hard-fought

steps, more of her body came out of the water, and she was finally up to her waist. She pushed hard with her feet on the rocks and pulled the water with her hands, and then with one last push she threw herself to the bank. She was now over 1,300 feet downstream, but the important fact was she was on the other side—the east side. The side that was closer to Shelbyville, and closer to her husband. Caroline collapsed to the ground and lay exhausted. Breathing deeply while on her back, she closed her eyes as the dapple sun danced on her face. The river continued to roar, but it roared for a new unsuspecting victim, not her.

After fifteen minutes lying on her back, she sat up and pulled off the bedroll then unrolled the wet blanket, taking out her pants, vest, shirt, hat, and shoes. She slowly started dressing while still seated on the ground. It took all her energy but with only her underwear on, she felt vulnerable. She pulled on her wet shoes and hat. Caroline looked down at the two empty double quart jars that sat at her feet. These jars held air and the air gave the blanket-roll needed buoyancy; it may not have been much, but it could have been enough to keep her afloat and alive. Yes, they were just two double-quart Mason jars, and they looked like those she buried at home, but emptied, these looked sad to her. "How little I have. How much I have left behind." At that moment, a chill ran up her spine as this new and different thought rushed into her mind. "I have been stripped of everything valuable. This is all I possess in this world. A stranger's clothes and stranger's Mason jars. There is nothing of me left. This is all I possess."

Despite all that river noise, there was stillness in the air above her head—stillness in the trees that looked down to the river's anger and stood watching. It was an acceptance of the river's given authority. This stand of age-old hickory trees bent to the river's anger, saying, "You can travel where you desire while we stand immovable. You can rip out centuries-old trees from your banks and carry them away. Yes, mighty Shivers River, we will wait until you have spent your anger and you are at peace with us again. Then our roots will drink from your waters, and you can do little about it."

As pieces of lumber from houses, barns, and buildings swept by in front of her, she could not remove her children from what she was watching. They were children that belonged to these homesteaders upriver that caused her stomach to tighten. These children alone were unprotected. She turned her face from the river, not wanting to see a child face down floating by, and so she remembered the last thing she and her children had done together. She remembered how they, as a family, buried the double quart jars. An image grew in her mind. The 337 jars now in seven holes she and the children had covered with pine straw and sand. Seated on the ground, Caroline looked again at the two familiar blue-glass Mason jars at her feet. They represented a faraway home. Still exhausted, still chilled from the cold waters, her spirit continued to lessen. Too weak to even stand, she sat there. She placed her hands on the pulsing pain that emanated from her ribs. The doubt increased in her mind and she found little strength to fight it. "This is but day two. I have been tested. I have won little, but I have lost a lot. I have little strength left for this day." She closed her eyes to rest and within a minute an image of her wounded husband holding out his hand came to her, and so, still with eyes closed, she said quietly to all the Carolines who had come before her, the six-year-old Caroline, the thirteen-year-old Caroline, and the seventeen-year-old Caroline, "Yes, I have done hard things before. I will do them again. No. I will not dwell on this! My children are safe. It is my husband that is not." Resolve and clarity redoubled itself. "This river has proven something to me. I can do this. I will do this. Did I make the right decision in leaving the children? Yes! But that doubt will chase me every day that I walk. Maybe my husband is dead and all of this it is for naught. And when I return to the homestead the children are gone...dead? Maybe not by Yankee gunfire, but by wolves, bears, cougars, or gangs of criminals. If that be what happens, then that is what the Lord desires. Lord, keep telling me that I am right in doing this, for I can become weak." There was no answer from the woods around her, from the clouds above her, or the earth below her, but slowly in a new breeze she heard a voice at a great distance whispering something. Whose voice was it? What were those words? It was a young girl's voice. Was it her own voice? "Yea, though I walk. Yea, though I walk. I walk through the valley..." That wonderful idea came rushing in like a warm gentle wind. Her fear started to dissipate and turned to hope at the thought. "I am to walk. I am to walk. Yea, though I walk." Caroline wiped away a tear. "Yes. You carried me across the river. How unthankful I am! You were with me every moment I was out there. You sent that tree. You placed a rock beneath my feet. Forgive me, Lord, for doubting you. You will be with me every step I walk. Now, please speed my stride to my husband." Caroline stood. Still cold, still exhausted, but she knew she had to travel on. She turned her back to the river and made her first step. Her ribs ached, but she was alive. She was walking again.

The first miles were slow and tiring. Her legs had surrendered most of their strength in the river. Her arms ached as they hung by her side. With each breath, the pain of the battered ribs stopped her from fully inhaling. Her wet clothes weighed heavy and the bedroll was still soaked and pulled her down. So, Caroline slowed her pace; it was all she could do to continue. She encountered no one on the road, but only saw evidence of a deserted shack with its roof open and door collapsed on the front porch. A small tree grew inside the shack, poking its branches up through the roof, attempting to erase any evidence that man had once been here feebly attempting to conquer the woods. She stopped twice to drink from a stream and eat some watercress that she discovered growing there. Then she rubbed comfrey on her ribs and filled her still wet shoes with its healing balm. Around four in the afternoon, she smelled the fragrance of food cooking. She walked on another thirty minutes until she spied a homestead. White smoke rose from the chimney. Caroline left the road and walked a while in the tree line, up off the road as not to be seen. She watched the home for a long while and saw no one outside. She spied laundry hanging from the clothesline near the side of the house. She counted eleven chickens near a shed. Then a woman came out of the home with a cane basket under her arm and took down some laundry. Caroline saw no one else. She rested, sitting in the woods, and watched for the next fifteen minutes. Still there were no men around. At times she could identify the smell. It was burning cornbread. Caroline stood and walked out of the woods down the hill to the home. Walking across the road she shouted out, "Hello! Hello. My name is Caroline Emily Duncan. I am traveling to Shelbyville and I am by myself."

A woman came to the front door and looked out, and then she came out onto the porch. "Stand there still and let me see you over." Caroline noticed the woman held a revolver in her hand. The woman was about fifty-five and wore a large apron over a tattered dress. She was barefoot.

"I will do as you say. I am from Hopkinsville and I am on my way to Shelbyville where my husband lies wounded. If you could but spare me a piece of cornbread, I would do some chores for it."

The woman on the porch shielded her eyes from the sun with her left hand but kept her right hand by her side with the revolver. "I can take care of myself. I need no one to do chores, but my husband died three days ago and he is in the house resting on his death bed. I do not possess the strength to move him, but if you deign to help me carry him from here, for I have already dug a burial hole, then if you would lend your hands, you can have what I myself am eating. It will be a poor man's dinner."

Caroline took a few steps forward. "I will do that. I will help. Let me put my roll and bag down here and let me come inside."

The woman, who identified herself as Missus Billows, said her husband died from smallpox, but she had shown no signs of it herself. Caroline entered the house, and the stench was overwhelming. She held her nose with one hand, but could feel the odor on her face. Missus Billows pulled a damp handkerchief wrapped around sprigs of mint from her apron, and held it over her nose, then led the way into the room. Standing at the foot of the bed, Caroline could see several blankets and a quilt over the top of a hump in the center of the bed. No part of the man was visible. Without a word and wanting to work quickly, Caroline walked to the top of the bed and took hold of the sheets. Missus Billows reacted and took hold at the foot of the bed. Together, the two women pulled and lifted the body, with the sheets, blankets, pillow, and quilt. The man must have weighed well over 200 pounds, and so the lowest part of him hit the floor as they pulled him out of the stained bed. Both women paused for a moment and took new grips on the sheet, then carried the man through the kitchen and out the back screen door, down the three steps, and into the fresh air. At that point, both women dropped the body to the grass and quickly walked away to gasp fresh air. With a nod of her head, Missus Billows pointed to a spot about a hundred feet to the rear of the house, and to a pile of fresh-dug earth. Caroline took the lead, grabbed the sheet again, and walked there backwards, looking over her shoulder as she walked. The two women stopped at one point, rested, and then resumed their walk with unsteady steps. "I appreciate this, I really do. Mister Billows was too heavy for me." They stopped at the side of the hole. "Let's just roll him in. He won't know if he is face down or face up. God don't care." Missus Billows tried to push him in tenderly with her bare foot, but when that attempt failed, Caroline pushed hard on the object with her shoe, and the man rolled in. There was no way of telling whether he was face up or face down. It was merely a hump of blankets, quilts, pillows, sheets, and a husband.

Missus Billows took the long-handled shovel standing at the head of the grave, and started shoveling dirt on top of Mister Billows, now possibly face down and five feet deep in this dirt pit. After ten minutes, she handed the shovel to Caroline. No words were spoken, but none had to be. Caroline finished the rest of the dirt. Both stood there looking at the grave. Missus Billows spoke first. "God, you gave him to me and now you took him away. I hope you know what you are doing. I think you don't. Amen."

The two women stopped by the cast iron siphon water pump and washed their hands repeatedly. A bar of recently made tan soap, irregular in its shape, was passed back and forth several times. A worn out, yellowed towel hung on a rail-post next to the well. The woman took off her apron and tossed it to the ground. "No matter how much I wash, I do not think I will get the smell out of my nose or out of this house. I have burnt cornbread, I have burnt bacon, I have burnt ramps, all on purpose to get rid of the smell, but it did little. I have burnt horse hair rope to no avail. With all the windows open, it will take a week I fear." Missus Billows picked up the apron and threw it into a wash tub near the well pump and started walking toward the back door. "We shall eat out front, as I have been eating out there far from the bedroom as possible.

80

I could not sleep in the house and have been sleeping out in the barn. I consider myself a fair smart woman, but I did not know what to do about Mister Billows. Thank God, Missus Duncan, you came along. No longer could I keep the flies from the house."

The two women ate a meal of cornbread and lima butter beans, including a bowl piled high with sliced tomatoes. Each shared a single thin slice of smoked pork. "I would cook a chicken, but I am down to eleven and I will need to live on their eggs for a while. That damn gang came and took the cow and three goats. I have no milk for biscuits and no milk for butter. Mister Billows hid the pig and the mule weeks ago up in the woods. I will leave them up there, but I fear a bear or a wolf will find them."

The food tasted very good and familiar to Caroline. She had not eaten anything except a quart of peaches that morning in the burned town, but all of that had been expended crossing the river. "What men are those which you speak? The gang?"

Missus Billows shifted herself in her seat. "The Willems Gang. There were twelve of 'em and I heard them talkin'. Couldn't make out much what was said. But everybody says Sercint Willems is the leader's name and he looked to be the tall skinny one with the short black beard. I saw him. I hid out in the barn. There was no time to get further away." Missus Billows put down her blue enameled tin plate on the small table and took another helping of butter beans from the pot resting on the planked front porch between the two of them. "Of course, Mister Billows was direly sick, covered with pox sores and fevered for a week. Breathing shallow like. I had not choice. I left him there and rushed out back when I heard all 'em horses and all these cows mooin' like they were in pain. I couldn't have done nothin'. So I covered myself with hay. They killed half the chickens and cooked 'em over a fire they started out by the barn. Then they took my cow and goats with 'em. They had 'em all tied up with ropes. One long line of cows. Goats tied to the last cow." Caroline interrupted, "Did they harm Mister Billows?" The older lady put down her plate again. "Well, no. Mister Billows was no threat. He had not spoke much in the last six days because of fever—his tongue swollen nearly big as my fist. I suppose the Willems Gang recognized the smallpox, because they ran out of the house fast, and ne'er went back in. They did not even search it and there was eleven dollars in the coffee tin atop the shelf of the pantry. Only 'bout two hours did they spend here afore they took the animals and added them to the herd they had. About thirty by my count." Missus Billows picked up her plate and started eating again. Caroline put her plate down and looked out to the road. "What are they doing with the cows?" Missus Billows tilted her plate so the butter bean juice would run to the corn bread. "I hear, and they'll be all truth in it, they sell 'em for a high price. A twenty-dollar gold piece is the going price. The homesteaders who lost their cows to the Yankee Army east of Elizabethtown are buyin' 'em back. Because that's what I hear they do. But if you got money hidden away, they will take it. And this is the saddest part, they will kidnap and ransom—especially young girls and wives."

Caroline waited for anything more to be revealed about the Willems gang, but Missus Billows said nothing more. Instead, Missus Billows looked at Caroline with a nod of sadness, then resoluteness, finally of concern. "Tell me something about you, dear. Why? Why are you traveling out here by yourself?" Caroline took a moment and explained, for safety sake being a young woman traveling alone, she had chosen to mostly travel by night to reach Shelbyville and her injured husband. Caroline then interjected, "Would I might, would it be agreeable to sleep the afternoon out in your barn?" Missus Billows nodded and said there were already blankets on a pile of hay in the grain room. Caroline looked over the well-cared-for homestead, mentioning the straight green rows of pole beans that ran one hundred feet. "I have never seen a fuller, more ambitious garden, but what are you going to do now, with your husband dead? And better to the point, what future do you see for a single woman out here now?"

"I am fifty-five and have some years left in me. I have put a man's work into this homestead. Eleven years here. I am not forfeiting it to fear. In the spring, I will buy another calf, and I have my pig to get me though the winter. I need to burn that mattress and construct a new one tomorrow, but the house for a week will smell." Missus Billows waved away the flies that circled near the two of them, and then reached over and fanned them off Caroline's face. "This afternoon while you sleep, I can bake another batch of water biscuits, and half you can take." Missus Billows stood and reached out and touched Caroline's shoulder. "Missus Duncan, how do you know your husband is still alive? Many men folk who get shot goes to gangrene or worse. Some get pneumonia and in a week they've crossed over. No. There won't be many men whole for me to hire when this war is no more. Many will be without arms or legs and what use would they be to me here?"

Caroline reached over and touched the woman's hand with both of hers. "Missus Billows, I have seen a one-armed man work as hard as a two-armed man, and glad was he to have a job. That man would not be outworked by anyone with two arms. You find one of those, and you will be content with his work. There will be many when this war is over."

That afternoon, Caroline slept in the barn on top of a hay mound. She did not want to sleep the night as she wanted to get back into her routine of walking in darkness, which so far had proven itself. At about eight, Missus Billows came into the barn. She carried a cup of black coffee in a tin cup. "It's almost eight and you said you wanted up. I have made a batch of water biscuits and you are welcome to half. While you slept, I pulled the tick mattress out of the house and burned it on top the grave. All of him lies forever there now. Few have traveled the road since you arrived, and I think it shall stay that way as long as the two armies skirmish in these hills. People are dire afraid, and who would blame 'em? I will feel isolated, so I do so hate to see you go. You have done me a great service, Missus Duncan—something I could not do by myself."

Caroline got up from the hay and put on her pants and shoes and shirt. "Thank you for your attention. Thank you for the barn and a good sleep. And thank you for the biscuits. I need to be on my way. This is only day three for me, and I have now been told it is a long ten-day walk. I have seven to go."

Missus Billows reached forward with a tied handkerchief. "I have suspicion you have no money and so I will loan you some. This is a dollar in gold coin. When you get to Elizabethtown, you find a proper hotel to sleep in, and you have a proper meal, with meat. You will need that for the task you have chosen. Should you come back this away with Mister Duncan, you can stay as long as you wish. Maybe this damn war be over by then. That is my mind. That's all I have to say."

It was half past eight in the evening when Caroline started out. The sky had a red glow about it, and the road stayed rolling to level for the first ten miles. Sometime after midnight, she came to a deserted homestead. No dog barked at her. Three broken chairs lay upside down in the front yard along with scattered items of clothing. She avoided calling attention to herself and quietly walked near, keeping her eyes on the house and barn. In the full moon, she noticed the windows were open and the curtains flapped casually in the breeze. There was no light from inside, and so she wondered whether someone was dead inside the house. She smelled the air, sensing nothing out of the ordinary. A little past the house, she noticed a long and narrow vegetable garden that ran from the back of the house forward and toward the road. She barely could discern tall tomato stakes and thought there might be tomatoes still hanging. She crouched low and quietly stepped off the road and to the garden. Caroline pulled two tomatoes from the closest stake. Back on the road, she started eating one with a lone water biscuit from Missus Billows.

All through the night, fireflies fluttered in randomness, much like stars twinkling and reflecting in a pond of water. Caroline delighted in the fireflies, which kept her company and lit the road. These little glowing insects had become her friends, possessing no fear of her. They flew inches away from her face, giving her a peace and comfort, a reminder of home. There were long stretches of nothing but maple on both sides of the wagon trail, running for miles as if the maple trees found favor with the land and reproduced uninterrupted for 500 years. Once she descended from a hill, she found the low-land meadows, where two streams bubbled and wandered across the road. In the deep tender grasses 300 feet from her, between the two streams, she spied a large nearly uncountable herd of white-tail deer sleeping in the meadow. The largest deer, with antlers four feet wide, slowly stood and turned its huge head toward her but made no movement other than its tail, which the stag flicked back and forth rapidly—the only outward sign the deer was not happy to see an intruder. Its ears followed Caroline's steps, as the male deer remained fixed on this lone traveler. Obviously, deer had seen people before, but rarely at night, rarely by themselves, and rarely walking quietly away.

As she approached the first stream, she noticed earlier homesteaders had placed a walkway across the stream with spaced flagstones, so it was easy to cross over dry. But thirty minutes later at a wider and deeper stream, she stopped and removed her shoes and walked through the cool water which came up to her knees. Caroline had discarded her socks at Missus Billows, as she had worn through them in the heel, and now relied on the comfrey leaves to protect her feet. At nearing two in the morning, a solitary great horned owl flew low over her like a ghost, and she felt a pulse of air as it passed ten feet over her head. She glanced up in the moonlight to catch its familiar silhouette as it slipped away. Moments of silence passed, then the great bird returned a second time but it came from a different direction, sweeping low over her head to inspect this night's visitor to its realm. Within the next minute she heard a rabbit squeal. The owl, still silent, flew away with the prey crying out, as if that would do some good. Maybe its cry was a protest or maybe a warning to other rabbits. Caroline could hear the creature's last whimper a moment later and far to the west. Then only silence.

After mile twenty-three that night and nearing five in the morning, as she rounded a turn in the road she came upon a wrecked wagon. Its front wheels had been broken. The metal ring on one of the wheels had fallen off the wheel, and several wooden spokes were cracked and two were missing. The wagon itself had been over-turned on its right side as it traveled west. Caroline stopped and allowed a picture to form of what could have happened. She looked in a full circle to see if there were people around and, seeing none, she stepped forward slowly and approached the wreck. Toward the rear of the wagon, three suitcases lay scattered along with seven overturned wooden crates. All had been opened and their contents strewed on the road as if being searched for something of value. Tossed in the dust were several female dresses, children's clothing, and a man's work shirts. Near the boxes, she found broken dishes—bowls, and plates—all once cushioned in yellow straw, but now mostly shards. She returned to the front of the wagon and came face to face with the wagon's seat now positioned vertically. There on the seat, she recognized blood. On the floor of the wagon under the seat, there was even more blood. Both were no longer red but now dark brown stains. Seeing that, Caroline decided to move quickly away as maybe this was a sign the Willems Gang was nearby. She looked over her shoulder at the wreck one more time and observed the mystery, its gray silhouette quickly enveloped under the dark sky, only the wheel's steel rim reflected the moonlight. She had traveled nearly a hundred feet when she heard a pronounced rhythmic resonance behind her. It was the sound of someone following. Caroline stopped and looked back toward the wreck and saw only shadows on the road. She listened for footsteps. They were about a hundred yards back, but after a moment they too stopped. Was it a man? A wolf? A bear? Quickly walking away, she heard the footsteps again. Caroline instinctively stepped off the road and rushed up the hill to the right of her. She ducked low into the tall grass. There was still a partial moon above to give her position away and so she laid flat in the grass, her left arm tucked to her side, ready to spring if necessary. Caroline's other hand went to the knife in her waistband. She listened but there was only silence. She thought if it was a man, she should not show the knife as Missus Millar said, instead to pull it as a surprise and attack. "Caroline, pull it only when he is attempting to lay top of you, then without hesitation stab repeatedly." Yes, she was on her mission to save a human being, and yet to accomplish it, a trade may be necessary. A life for a life. Further, that person would be someone she did not know—a stranger. She raised her head slightly and listened.

Silence surrounded the air, and she searched in the silence for any sound. Five minutes passed. "Well, time is wasting, Caroline." She stood and waited for a moment; she heard nothing. Maybe it was a rabbit. A raccoon. Maybe it was wind in the weeds and trees. Cautiously, she walked back down the hill and through the tall grass to the road. To her surprise, standing there silently, frozen in her direction in the darkness, stood a very large black and brown dog. Caroline stopped still and watched the dog's eyes, they appeared to be relaxed. There was not sound from the dog. After a moment, she took a step to the right. The dog's head turned and followed Caroline, who waited for a reaction. Would the dog growl and bare its teeth? Still there was little to reveal what the dog was thinking. Caroline took a second step. The dog again turned its head but made not a sound. Judging by its size, this dog looked to be eighty pounds, and probably not afraid of anything even twice its size. Caroline slowly circled behind the dog, her hand on the knife, and noticed the dog's tail wanted to wag. But the dog fought against it. And so, Caroline quietly spoke, "Are you a good dog or a bad dog? I need to know this." Caroline waited for an answer, but none came. "I am a good person. So are you a good dog?" There again was no answer from the dog, who now only stared straight ahead. "Or do you bite? Do you bark a lot? I have little to no use of a dog that barks." The dog blinked his eyes and then turned his head toward Caroline, trying to understand what this woman was saying. "You appear to be like my mule, as he does not make much noise. I bet you came with those people who were on that wagon. Were you among them, and if you were, then what happened?" The dog, now tiring of this, sat down. "I see you don't want to talk about it. Well, it is nice meeting you, but you stay here, as your people might come back and they would look for you. Goodbye, big dog." As Caroline started to walk away, the dog stood and watched for a moment then he turned and walked back toward the wagon. Caroline walked on, occasionally looking over her shoulder. She could see the dog approach the overturned wagon and appeared looking for something. Then digging with his nose in the clothing, the curly haired animal found something and came trotting back with it in his mouth. When the dog caught up to Caroline, she could see it was a pink sweater of a small child. Still the dog did not make a sound, but trotted ahead of Caroline as if it were in charge and leading the way.

With Caroline following thirty feet behind, this dog continued silently for the next two miles and at that point the dog slowed and started walking beside Caroline. "Decided to join me, dog? Well, I would welcome you, but I cannot see how you would be any help for me. I have little food, and I cannot be slowed by you running off to chase a rabbit or squirrel. But if you remain silent and stay close without giving me away, you are free to travel with me. I am on my way to Shelbyville to see my husband. He is a first lieutenant in the Army of the South, and he has been wounded. I hope to reach him in seven days from now, maybe eight." Caroline stopped for a moment and readjusted her bedroll over her shoulder, then continued on. "Oh, yes, my name is Caroline and I am from Hopkinsville, which is three days back that way." Caroline pointed over her shoulder, and past the wagon toward the west. "I have three children and they would love to have you as their dog, but that is a sure impossibility as they are now miles back, and I am not heading that way."

Caroline rubbed her left shoulder and then stopped again and moved her rucksack to the right shoulder. The dog dropped the pink sweater to the dirt road and sat down. "Here, if you give me that little sweater, I will put it in my bag and carry it for you." Caroline reached down to take the pink sweater, but the dog quickly picked it back up. "Have it your way. You found it and not me. But I have a question since you were probably there. Did this sweater belong to the little girl that was on the wagon?" The dog only stared down the road to the east. Caroline looked in that direction. "And how long ago did that happen? And where are her mother and father?" The dog curled his eyebrows trying to figure out what the woman who was dressed like a man was saying. Caroline started walking again, and the dog stood and followed three feet back and to the right. Caroline glanced over her right shoulder. "I know you saw it all and would tell me if you could. It looks to me the wagon was pointed west, and we are walking east. So where did you come from?" Caroline realized all these questions might be confusing the dog, and so she tried another approach to sooth the dog who may have witnessed a tragedy. "But you are a good dog. Good dog. And a handsome dog. Good boy." The dog did recognize "good boy" and he liked what he was hearing. So he relaxed his face muscles and he trotted ahead of Caroline. To her, it felt good to think aloud and to question aloud. It made her feel like she was not alone on this darkened road. She waited for answers but knew the dog could not answer. So, she started the questions again but quietly, as if she were asking them to herself. "There was dried blood on the seat, so that was either a man's blood or a woman's blood, and which way did they go after the accident? East or west? Or does that matter?" The dog again listened to these endless questions, tilting his head, trying to understand why this woman was talking so much and who was she talking to. It wasn't him, as she was not looking at him. But by the tone in Caroline's voice, the dog came to a simple but correct conclusion. He felt he had found a friend. And this new friend was walking in a direction familiar to him, and so the black and brown dog did not turn his head toward Caroline as if listening. He ignored her and only smelled the air ahead searching for his family. Caroline again said, "Good dog." But the black and brown dog had grown tired of this game. A smile came across Caroline's face, followed by a new thought. She realized the value of having a traveling companion was that it helped pass the time and took her mind off the pain in her ribs. "Hey, dog, if you want to be my silent friend, then I will talk and tell you of my thinking." Caroline started walking again, as the joy of companionship was lifting her spirits after the Shivers River's dark experience. Having a conversation felt good to Caroline, as it seemed normal and uplifting, as when she talked to her mule back at the homestead. All her children, and especially Priscilla, did the same with the goats and the pig. No one talked to the chickens, as it was felt they had little to no brains. A second smile appeared on her face. "This is not a requirement for my companionship, but I do appreciate your company. I only hope you bark loudly if you see or smell something dangerous. It's okay to alert me. You do look like a well cared for dog and that must mean the people you were with are nice people—I hope nothing untoward has happened to them. One last thing you should know, dog, I intend to push on deep this morning, as I have lost time. But we will rest for the night before noon. You can join me if you so choose."

For the next mile, neither Caroline nor the dog interacted, as she had said all that she wanted to say. The black and brown dog understood little but that he had found a new friend, and so at times would slow and wait for Caroline to catch up. Caroline suspected the dog knew where the people from the wagon had gone, and was walking in that direction, but she wondered why they had left their dog, or possibly did the dog stay on its own? There was a mystery there and yet so far there was no clear answer. If the dog could talk, it would reveal that a young fifteen-year-old girl was shot there during a robbery, and her parents had buried her a hundred feet uphill from the wreck. Three rocks stood on top of one another to mark the place where a girl named Samantha rested. While the dog laid by the grave site, he watched the man and wife take their second daughter and young boy and start walking away from the tragedy and back home. The dog stayed for the next three days to guard the grave, and to mourn the death of his closest friend.

Nearing nine o'clock in the morning, with a new sun to light the dirt road and sycamore tree covered hills on both sides, Caroline spotted a white painted homestead 600 feet from the road and nestled up near the tree line. An unpainted barn stood halfway to the road. Caroline stopped as she approached the horse path that ran up to the homestead. The house was still, and three mules stood up and walked to the split rail fence that ran near the road. The mules in unison hung their heads over the fence and gave their full attention as Caroline and the dog stopped at the road's edge. Shielding her eyes from the rising sun in the east, she focused on the house, still in the shadow of the trees. "Is it safe, dog? Do you see something I do not see? The dog dropped the pink sweater he had been carrying in his mouth. The dog smelled the air. The dog then picked up the sweater, turned, and walked on. Caroline was not sure about the house, and decided it was no use to her as she had food, and there was still a half hour she could walk before the full sun had warmed the night's air and chased the morning dew from the grass. Caroline turned from the home and followed the dog. Unknown to her, a lone raven-haired, fifty-year-old woman named Ida sat on the front porch in the shadows, dressed in black with a black shawl over her shoulders, a fully loaded Colt 31 revolver resting in her lap. Her eyes followed Caroline and the dog. She said nothing, for there was nothing to say that would bring back her husband and son now resting side by side in a wide shallow grave, dug three days earlier east of the house.

In the next mile, Caroline and the dog crossed three streams and each time, Caroline sat down, taking off her shoes, rolling up her pants legs. The dog crossed before her, and once on the other side turned and waited for Caroline. Each time, the dog sat and wondered why Caroline had to remove her shoes, cross the water, and then put them back on. Nearing ten that morning, as the birds were in their second chorus of singing, and early morning dragon flies flirted in the air catching the light with their translucent wings, Caroline heard horse hooves on the road ahead coming from the east. She quickly turned and rapidly climbed the hill to the left, then to the tree line. She went in deep until she found a stand of cypress trees that would shield her from sight. The dog, sensing something ominous, followed closely behind, but part way up the hill, and fifty feet from the tree line, the dog stopped and lay down in the tall grass sixty feet from Caroline. As the noise of the horses on the road grew louder, she stepped deeper into the shadows and behind a large pine tree; Caroline tossed off her bedroll then ducked down, barely able to see the road. Within minutes, eleven horses and nine riders appeared. The horses were not running in a gallop but were trotting in quick steps. None of the men were speaking to each other, but rode in a spread out, long, staggered line, each rider looking both left and right as they rode. The last rider held the reins of three unsaddled horses. Caroline rose up slightly to see that none were in uniform, but all carried musket rifles slung over their shoulders. All eight carried revolvers tucked into their leather belts or in holsters. Around their waists were black pouches containing cartridges for their revolvers. Two of the men wore Confederate uniform caps. They rode uneasy, glancing occasionally to each other and behind them. As they approached where Caroline and the dog were hiding, the dog suddenly stood and started to growl. It was low and contentious. This was the first sound the dog had made in hours and surprised Caroline. She wanted to shish the dog, but the riders were too close. One of the riders, a young man, riding next to the last one in the line, wearing a torn blue army jacket and a bandage on his right hand, pulled up the reins and his horse stopped. "Sercint! There's that damn dog again. I'm getting it this time." The young rider jumped off his horse and pulled his revolver from his belt. "That's right, you damn dog, you stand there and mock me." The rider took several steps off the road, came up into the grass, then he stopped and checked the Colt 36 revolver. The dog moved slowly to the left and away from the gun yet continued his growling. The young man, sensing a sure hit, pushed back his hat, lifted his revolver with his bandaged hand, slowly aimed, and fired a shot toward the dog. "Bang." The dog, seeing the revolver sights following him, jumped to the right and the shot fell to the left and dirt exploded into the air. The lead rider, Sercint Willems, turned and shouted, "Creech! What in the hell are you doing? Don't waste shots on a damn dog, you stupid son of a bitch." The young rider, Ryland Creech, took a second aim on the dog, which was standing in a challenging posture and staring at the rider. As the man lowered the gun sight across the chest of the dog, the black and brown animal jumped again at the last instant as the rider fired a second time. "Bang." The red hot bullet sailed high past the dog deep into the woods. The young rider started running after the dog, which, seeing this man run toward him, turned and ran into the woods fifty feet from Caroline. The bearded leader of this gang, dressed in a black coat covered in road dust and with brass buttons on the sleeves, again shouted. "I said, Creech, what the hell you doing? Leave the damn dog alone. All this stupid shooting is going to alert someone and we don't need that crap. Get back on your damn horse." The young man stopped and turned to the lead rider. "That damn dog bit me when we took that wagon. I lost two fingers, and I will shoot..." The lead rider drew his gun. "If you don't get back on your horse, I will shoot your sorry ass and leave your body to rot right there. You are the most ignorant man in five counties. Now get on your horse and shut the hell up." The young man holstered his pistol. Then he turned to where the dog ran into the woods. "This is not over, you shit ass dog. I will find you and cut you real bad; I will cut your damn head off and put it on a fence post." The young rider arrived at his horse and got on, spitting once in the direction of the dog. Caroline peeked her head out from behind the giant pine, her left cheek tight against the rough bark, and watched the nine men as they rode away. She tried to study each one, and especially the leader. Could this be the famous Willems Gang? She realized they had mentioned a wagon. So these nine men were responsible for the overturned wagon. And she had heard two names. Creech and Sercint. She also heard, in defending the people in the wagon, this black and brown dog had bitten one of them. A man named Creech. But where were the people of the wagon? Whose blood was on the seat? And what was the story that lay hidden in the dust and debris on the road?

Caroline waited for ten minutes in case the riders came back, then walked out of the tree line. The dog came trotting out of the weeds with the child's sweater in its mouth. The dog rushed past Caroline for about fifty feet and stopped and turned to Caroline. It barked once. Caroline started walking toward the dog. "I thought you were smart. But you growled. You should have not done that. You almost gave away where I was hiding. And you almost got yourself killed. Nothing good has come from this. Except now I know you were there when that wagon overturned and you bit one of the bad men. A man called Creech. But there was another named Sercint." Caroline adjusted her bedroll over her shoulder. "Wait, there is one more thing. If I run, you run. If I fight, you fight. But for the most times we need to be like phantoms. Unseen and unheard." Caroline pulled her hat down tight over her head. "I see now that we must survive each and every day. For each day arrives with its own unsuspected dangers. This was a true danger we have escaped. But barely. Now, you and I have not eaten much all night and I am going to have the last biscuit and the last tomato. Would you like to share a biscuit?" The dog walked on as if he had heard or understood none of this conversation. Obviously, he too was on a mission.

An hour later, with her legs tiring and her bruised ribs throbbing with each breath, Caroline held up her opened hand and measured the sun's distance from the horizon. The sun was up a forearm, or about eleven in the morning. Caroline had been thirsty for the last hour, and was hoping to soon find a stream. After twenty minutes, she spied a small creek and went down through the green grass and wild lilies to the edge of the water. Watching some minnows swimming in small schools, she took off her shoes and waded out into the center of the stream. She cupped her hands and drank several hands full of water. After washing her face, she opened her shirt and splashed water under her arms. The dog had noticed Caroline's excursion and trotted into the water fifty feet upstream of Caroline and lapped at the water freely. The dog, spotting movement near him, chased a school of minnows and catching none, he lapped at the water again. "If you are hungry, dog, I have a single bite of biscuit for you." The dog ignored Caroline and, spying several large frogs sitting on the bank asleep, the dog charged and caught one with his paw. The dog looked at Caroline, and then ate the frog. Moments later, the dog spotted another group of frogs and charged at those, repeating the action, catching two frogs. This time the dog ate the larger one, and the second escaped into the grass. The dog gave pursuit, but it disappeared into the tall weeds. Caroline watched as the dog jumped into the air several times and dove face first, pushing his head deep into the grass. Caroline was amazed at the speed of the expert hunter, as his head came up shaking violently left and right, and he turned and returned with a limp, small, black snake. The dog walked over and dropped the dead snake in front of Caroline. "A black racer? You are quick. But I am not hungry enough to eat that. You caught it and you eat it." Sitting down in the grass, Caroline put on her shoes. She watched the dog put one foot on the snake and bite off its head. This was repeated until the snake was finished. The dog waded back into the stream and lapped the cool water for a moment, then left and walked back to road, picking up the sweater in the grass. Glancing at Caroline as he walked on, he let out a small quiet bark and started trotting east again. It did not take long but within ten minutes, the dog had to stop and wait for Caroline, who was struggling to keep up to the dog's pace. "I wish you would slow down, but you are in a hurry to get somewhere unknown to me. You have four feet and I have but two and both have blisters. I hope you wait for me, as you are good company."

For the next half hour, Caroline walked slowly behind the dog and nothing more was said. As they approached a sign near a fork in the road, the dog stopped and sat in the middle of the road waiting for Caroline to arrive. The sign-post had two signs. One pointed north to the left and the other east to the right. The one pointing north read, "Louisville." The other sign read, "Leitchfield." By the height of the sun, Caroline figured it was about noon. It had been a long night and she was truly exhausted. Caroline left the road and walked up a small hill into the tree line. She called to the dog and the dog stood and followed. Thirty feet into the woods, she found a grove of young hickory trees. Gathering leaves from under the trees, she piled them six inches high and unrolled her bed roll then took off her shoes. Remembering the eight men and realizing she might have to move fast, she put her shoes back on, but left them unlaced. The dog came walking though the tall grass and into the grove. Seeing Caroline sitting on the bedroll, the dog lay down ten feet from Caroline facing downhill toward the road. He dropped the pink sweater and rested his paws on top of it. As Caroline lay there, she closed her eyes and did the math in her head. Fifteen hours at two miles an hour. She decided she had traveled thirty miles that day. With that satisfaction in mind, she slid inside the folded wool blanket sideways, gathered the hickory leaves on top of the blanket, smiled, and fell asleep.

A cold nose awakened Caroline. The dog stood over her. It made a low growl and turned toward the road. Caroline sat up instantly and looked. She saw nothing. "What is it, boy? What is coming?" The dog did not turn but kept his head facing the road. Caroline looked at the shadows on the ground. It appeared to her to be about five o'clock in the afternoon. The air felt dry. Getting to her feet, she rolled her blanket and tied the ends, slinging it over her right shoulder. She positioned her bag over her left shoulder and pulled on her hat. "What is it? Who's coming?" Things in the woods grew silent and the birds stopped their singing. In the next moment, Caroline heard the noise of horse hooves. It sounded like the roar of the Shivers River. In that moment, this cacophony of noise grew louder and appeared to be coming from all directions. But, after cupping her hands around her ears and turning her head in all directions, she realized it was coming from the east and heading west. In the snap of a finger, the Army of the North roared into view. Caroline ducked low and started counting the soldiers, who rode by five abreast. She counted twenty-five, thirty-five, forty-five, fifty-five, sixty-five. Seventy horsemen all dressed in blue, led by men with gold braids on their hats and gold medallions on their shoulders. One rider carried a red, white, and blue stars and stripes flag. A second rider beside him carried a white, red, and black battle flag with crossed swords and the words "Ohio 1." They were followed closely by eight wagons. Each wagon carried what appeared to be twelve men, all seated with their backs to the side of the wagon—their rifles with bayonets in place pointed skyward and the wooden rifle butts tucked tight between their black boots. Teams of four dark brown horses, splattered with mud, pulled each of those wagons. One hundred feet behind that, came twelve wagons loaded with seven men to each wagon, plus a driver and assistant. The assistant on the left rested a musket rifle across his lap. Caroline could see each wagon carried six wooden powder kegs all crudely chalk marked with a skull and cross bones on the sides and an equal number of unmarked large wooden boxes. Then to her surprise, she saw something she had never seen in her life. Six pure black horses pulled a shimmering, highly polished Napoleon brass cannon eight feet in length, attached with forged iron straps to a wood cradle bolted on two enormous wheels. Connected to the cannon, like a leg is connected to the torso, was a smaller caisson wagon, yanked down the road riding on two smaller wheels and loaded with cannon ball and even more gun powder. But it wasn't just one cannon, there were ten cannons in total. Ten teams of six pure black horses, ten long brass cannons, and ten caissons. Sixty black horses, and drivers whipping the reins over each team of six. The wheels of these caissons were covered with mud, but toward the hub she could see a shiny gold stripe down each olive green spoke. Finally, Caroline could see the enormity of what war was about. This was a killing machine. Meant to kill as many men as possible in the smallest amount of time necessary, then to move quickly somewhere else and repeat the killing. Caroline listened as they passed, but there was no sound from the men—no talking, no laughing, no singing; it was as if they were numb from what they had come from, or numb from fear as they headed off toward an unknown battle field. The only sound was the wheels on the dirt road, the hooves of the horses, and a rush of wind as they sped by. This was a frightening sight for Caroline, as she realized the enormity of the awesome Northern Army, which her husband was fighting. Beside the power and speed it exhibited, Caroline was struck by the fact that everything was painted an olive green color. Every wagon, every caisson, every box, every keg of gun powder had a dead seriousness about itself. Like a complicated and nefarious machine, hammer-forged in a smoke-filled factory, then plunged into huge vats of thick olive-colored paint, this machination was now finalized and readied for God-fearing men to accomplish one single task. To kill other men.

Caroline, still hidden and crouching low, watched as they disappeared to the west, down the same road she had walked only hours earlier. The dog stood and watched the dust drift southward across a meadow. He turned and looked at Caroline, and then trotted down to the road. Standing up, Caroline felt dizzy for an instant, her stomach starting convulsing, and so she steadied herself. "I cannot get sick. I cannot. That would be the worst thing to happen." Black and white spots appeared circling around her, and she was losing her balance. Not wanting to faint, Caroline quickly turned and walked about ten steps out into the tall grass. She desired to get down to the road and to a stream of water, but her feet only took halting steps. She stood there looking down toward the dog, but the dog was gone. "Where am I and what is going on?" She took a single step backwards, and then Caroline collapsed into the grass.

"Well, you have been out about twenty-four hours now, and how do you feel?" Missus Hollette Bellforest, the midwife, looked down at Caroline as she lay in bed. Caroline exhaled. "I feel okay. A little lightheaded. How's the...how's the baby?" The midwife glanced over to a handmade pine cradle. "The baby is doing fine. You said you wanted a girl, and Missus Duncan, well, you got your wish. She's a she, okay. But she's a hungry one. I gave her my breast three times today, and I think it may be time for you to meet your daughter. Would you feel up to that?" Missus Bellforest turned and walked to the cradle and picked up the baby, now only hours old, and brought the tightly wrapped infant to Caroline, placing her on her stomach. "Give her your breast; she will soon prefer yours to mine." Caroline pulled down the top of her gown and the baby started feeding instantly. "I still feel dizzy though." The midwife took out a handkerchief, dipped it in cool water, and wiped Caroline's brow. "Well, it was not an easy delivery—about three hours, and you lost a lot of blood. Sometimes it takes a good while to stop. Mister Duncan and me debated going out to Greenton to get the doctor there, but I told him I been down this road afore and you're good stock. I knew that with your first and second one, and so I said all she needs is a whole days sleep. And look at you now. I was right."

Caroline glanced out the window. "Where's my husband?" The midwife laughed. "Coincidences are a plenty. The Millars' cow was full of problems delivering a calf and Missus

Millar came running about three hours ago to get him to help Mister Millar. Your boys went along to watch. I told them to go, that everything was going as expected and you'd come around shortly." The midwife stood then pushed her chair backwards across the oak floor. "I suppose you're hungry and that is a good sign, for I made a nice chicken broth to bring your spirits back. Oh, by the way, what you're going to name that precious little girl?"

Caroline smiled. "This is Priscilla."

Caroline suddenly awoke. She lay there looking into the pink clouds, then she sat up and, while still somewhat dizzy, she felt well enough to stand. The dog returned without noise, and then lay fifty feet south of her in the tall grass. When Caroline stood, the dog stirred and twisted his head toward her. Its gaze had been fixed on the road, both east and west. The dog stood and let out a small bark, as if to say, "I am ready if you are ready." Caroline slowly gathered her bedroll and bag and made her way out of the grass and down to the road. Judging by the shadow she cast, it looked to be about eight in the evening. She reached into her bag for another biscuit, but remembered she had eaten the last one earlier. Glad that the dizziness had left her, she knew she needed to drink some water, as possibly lack of water caused her to be faint. Ten minutes into this walk, she was happy to hear running water and came to the first creek she had seen since the late morning. Stopping as the stream crossed the road, she turned and walked upstream about fifty feet, then sat on the grassy bank, taking off her shoes. Wading out into the very cold stream, she realized this water was coming from an artesian spring far up into the rocky hills on the right. She crouched herself down and dipped her hands to drink. Feeling vulnerable out in the open, she looked back at the road and, sensing no one, she drank a second time. This cold water was full of bubbles, so it tasted unusually refreshing. The dog watched as Caroline splashed water in her face. He barked once and ran past her upstream a hundred feet. Finding a group of crawfish, the dog started feasting on the catch. Caroline could hear the crunch of the shells as the dog repeatedly ran upstream finding more and more to eat. At one point he stopped and, spying a rabbit, he took off after it but returned when the rabbit found a hutch in which to hide. Caroline, likewise, caught a crawfish and took out her knife. She cut open the belly and pulled out the meat. She had never eaten a raw crawfish before but she knew she needed to eat something for strength.

She was surprised at her first bite, as the raw crawfish meat was cold and earthy tasting. She found some watercress and bit into that too. Together, they had an acceptable taste. Quickly locating a second crawfish, she sliced open its belly and pulled out a thumb-sized piece of meat. Again, it was cold from the spring and very tender. Caroline continued finding crawfish and eating until she consumed nine of them. With each one, a handful of peppery watercress followed and seemed to make them palatable—maybe it was the spiciness or maybe it tasted familiar. Hundreds of times at the homestead, she had eaten crawfish, but always cooked, and usually with tomatoes, onions, okra, wild rice, and cut corn. Yes, this taste was familiar, and not as gamey as she would have expected.

She watched the dog as he continued to eat, and she said, "Aren't we a pair, dog? I am no different from you; we both possess peculiar natural hunting skills. There comes to mind one particular difference. You prefer to eat your food raw with a gamey quality about it, while I will attempt to disguise mine. But I will eat dirt before I will eat snake."

At nine that evening, as the clouds in front of her turned a peach color and the sun was warming her back, she knew she needed to walk on through the coming night. She realized this was only day four of this nine-day walk. At times, she imagined that maybe by the time she got to Shelbyville, her husband would have died, or that he had gotten well enough to be put back into action. Then too, he could have been captured and was—this very day—moving further away from her on the way to a prisoner of war camp in Ohio, Pennsylvania, or Maryland. This was not a new thought, as she had already wrestled with all of those possibilities for a whole day before leaving on this long undertaking. Nonetheless, her final and deciding thought had been, "I will not go through the rest of my life thinking I could have done something to save my husband if only I had gone to him. It would be a dark, unrelenting, remorseful life—worse than would be bearable for me. And for my children, they would think less of me for all my days. No, this is the right decision."

Five miles later, Caroline passed what appeared to be a deserted homestead. In the moonlight, she could see a whitewashed, two-story house high up a knoll and near a tree line. The barn looked to be only partially finished, with only a roof in place and no sidings. She could see the house had been ransacked. Items of furniture had been tossed out through windows; the front door had been pulled off its hinges and lay flat on the porch. The fence line had been pulled over, releasing the animals. In the front yard, only twenty feet from the front door, there appeared to be a man's body lying face down. A dozen crows circled overhead and a lone buzzard stood beside the man pecking at the man's face. She thought, "I can do faint good to go to him. And if his people are hiding, they are better off staying hid. Whatever or whoever killed him may return." Caroline walked on quietly and was careful not to make any noise. As she walked, she heard the cry of crows as more coal-black scavengers were arriving from the east. Soon the buzzard would have his fill and depart. The crows waited patiently.

About midnight, she came upon a second homestead and this one was not deserted as the last, but had a single sign of life. From a thousand feet away, she could see a coal oil lamp burning on the front porch. Moments later, she saw a dull orange light from a side window near the rear of the house. This, she thought, would be the kitchen. She stopped, watching for movement inside, and saw a shadow move by the window. It returned a moment later with what appeared to be a match flaring alive to light a pipe. She listened and heard a woman's voice. Caroline thought it would be safe to stop there but there was nothing she needed. She had eaten and was intent on walking all night until sunup when she would sleep the day. It felt good to see something so normal as a homestead and people who appeared unaffected by the war. Suddenly a dog, not visible until now, stirred on the porch. It barked loudly at the sound of her footsteps and also the sound of the four-legged black and brown dog, which accompanied her on the road. The unseen dog continued to bark. The man seen in the window walked past the light and moments later came out onto the porch. He looked to be carrying a long musket. "Who's there? Anybody out there?" Caroline did not answer but froze. "I said is anybody out there? There are six of us and we are heavily armed." Caroline watched the silhouette of a man, who looked left and right. He strode back and forth on the front porch looking in all directions. She realized the moon was waning and too dark for him to see her. Slowly, she started walking away as the dog on the porch moved to the front yard continuing its barking. The man shouted out again. "You would be wise to know, but I got my four boys circling around right now, so you better be on your way. They will shoot to kill and they are damn good shots. Bull's-eyes! You hear me? Get on going." Caroline caught up to her dog and was glad he had not returned any barks back to the unseen barking dog in the front yard. Caroline walked on for the next ten minutes, and could hear the homestead dog continuing to bark in her direction. She also heard the echoing of a man's voice shouting out into the darkness, then the sound of two young boys answering back to the man with the gun. After the next big rise, she heard nothing behind her.

The rest of the night, she encountered few signs of human life. These woods were once virgin forests that ran a hundred miles in all directions. For a time, they belonged to the Indian tribes who passed this way once a year following game. Then came the French invaders, who would build shacks and trap beaver, fox, and bear. Living off the land for a season, the trappers usually moved on—like the Indian tribes—always heading west and north. Many early settlers would claim with pride a single squirrel might cross from Virginia into Kentucky and travel all the way to the Missouri Territory on the tops of trees—all 480 miles—never touching the ground. But there were other things besides squirrels in this forest that kept Caroline company. There were sudden noises in the lowland grasses and high above the tree line that caused her to freeze for a moment. Hearing nothing approaching her, she walked on, occasionally stopping to listen for a second time. She also took comfort in the dog, which walked fifty feet in front of her, who at times would stop and smell the air, turn and look to Caroline, then walk on. Once, she heard a wolf, far off to the north, howling in the still night air. After a moment, she heard another wolf, possibly five miles away to the south, howl in return. She thought how she could possibly fight two wolves at once. But she had no plan.

At six in the morning, as the sun started to crack the blackness, she approached a small scattered settlement of twenty-three whitewashed clapboard houses. The little settlement formed itself above two small valleys. Three gently sloping hills held two streams in place, which flowed into a single stream forming a 'Y'. The newborn larger single creek, taking fresh energy, flowed downstream, disappearing into the ravines and hills. There were no streets connecting the homes, but only foot paths and a few wagon trails. The houses were scattered in a random pattern, but all were facing downhill toward the streams. Taking prominence in this settlement was a freshly constructed and still unpainted schoolhouse, which, like in many such settlements, became the church on Sundays. The tall steeple with a green copper lightning rod held an oversized bell useful for both purposes. A single lone store stood in the center of this little settlement. It bore a gold sign that hung over the door. It read in freshly painted black letters, "C.C. Bennett General Store." Twelve wooden chairs, all with twisted wires cross pulling tight the legs, stood six to a side. A wide space to enter and exit held center to the front door. A man whittling on a black walnut sapling sat on the right-side chair closest to the door. A pile of skinned bark shavings sat on the top of his boots and also in his lap. The man, seeing Caroline walking down the middle of the road, started to wave and she returned the gesture. "Where you all coming from? You by yourself? My name is Edward and this little town is called Moorehouse Bottom. Where did you say you are coming from, young man?" Caroline stopped for a moment and, seeing the empty chairs, walked over, climbed the three steps to the landing, and sat on a chair about six feet away. The dog walked to the porch but did not climb the steps, sitting down near a water trough. Caroline removed her bedroll and thought for a moment. "Should I tell the truth or hide in a story that gives me protection?" She removed her hat and her hair fell over her shoulders. "My name...my name is Amanda and I am walking to visit relatives in Elizabethtown. I am a school teacher. My husband...my husband is a pastor."

The man, wearing bib overalls and a faded red flannel shirt, stopped whittling and turned to her. "When I first spied you,

I thought you was a very young man. Now I see you ain't. How come you dressed in a man's clothing?" Caroline was ready with a conjured answer. "All my clothing was burned in a fire, and so I am wearing this until I get to my relatives in Elizabethtown."

"Well, we all do what we have to do to stay the course. My name is Edward Dawes Higgens. I am originally from Ohio but right now, right here in Moorehouse Bottom, well this is my home. This store will be open in another hour. Mister C.C. Bennett is prompt. You might find some clothing here if you want."

"No, that is okay, Mister Higgens, I do find it easier to walk in men's clothing. I have been walking all night. Is there a place out of the way I could sleep for the day?"

The man pointed down the street. "Third house down that away is the widow Hudson's place. You stop in there, and she will let you sleep in a spare bedroom. She won't let that dog in the house, though. Last year, Mister Hudson cut deep into his own leg right above the knee up the woods with his own ax, and bled to death before anyone knew of it. They found him 160 feet from his bloodied ax. Some say five minutes is how long it took him to bleed to death. I knew the man. Elgood Hudson. Honest, hardworking man. Maybe he worked too hard for his own good. Anyhow, the widow Hudson started taking in boarders after that, so she will charge you for the room. I hear she gets twenty-five cents a night. Another ten cents gets you a biscuit gravy breakfast, though."

"That sounds reasonable. But I have little money to my name, so I will just sleep over by the school in the grass."

"That won't do. No. Now, my house is the seventh one down there. I have a barn to sleep out back. Or better yet, you stop in and tell my wife your story. I have a back porch, and we sleep out there when it gets real hot. There's two small beds there. Tell my wife your story. Tell her to show you the back porch. Her name is Saorise Presence Higgens. Tell her you saw me. She's a good Christian woman, so she will take you in. There should be some leftover biscuits and gravy. Get some of that before you bed down." The man brushed some whittlings off his lap. "We have supper about five, so I will wake you for that, and then you can be on your way."

Caroline stood to thank the man. "You are very kind, Mister Higgens. I will take you up on your offer, but as I said I have nothing to offer in return except chores."

"Amanda, you look like an honest Christian woman traveling far from home, and my daughter would be about your age. And it is during these terrible and wretched times we people must come to the aid of each other. Not expecting nothing in return except for a simple thank you. My daughter, were she still alive, would want that, and that is what I would want for her. Today, you are my daughter."

"Thank you, sir."

"Seventh house on the left. Tell Missus Higgens to make you comfortable."

Caroline stood and took a step forward and extended her hand in a handshake. The man stood and took off his hat. He reached down and kissed her on her cheek. Kicking his whittling shavings off the porch with his right shoe, he turned and walked down the stairs, humming a song.

It was as Mister Higgens said. Caroline met his wife, Saorise, and told her story, except she told none of the truth, but she had decided to stick with her fictional story. Knowing that parts of Kentucky were sympathetic to the Northern Army, but not knowing whose side strangers were on, she thought it would be best not to mention her husband wore a gray uniform and lay wounded in Shelbyville. It would be best to be Amanda and on the way to Elizabethtown to see her mother, hospitalized with a badly broken right leg in which gangrene had started. She thought that would create sympathy and give enough details as to be believable.

Missus Higgens took her hand and said she would pray for Amanda's mother. Hearing that made Caroline feel bad about lying, but it served a purpose now, and maybe would serve a purpose in the future. Missus Higgens walked Caroline through the house to the back porch. "You are taking a dangerous chance in walking to Elizabethtown. I understand why at night, but in the last day I have seen on this very road, right in front of my house, I have seen in broad daylight a band of twenty Negro men on horseback, all armed with rifled muskets. I have seen the Northern Army, thousands of them, with horses and cannons, and all sorts of wagons loaded with gun powder and cannon shot. I have seen Confederates, ragged and torn, yet angry for a scrap. I have heard tell, but not seen, a band of men called the Willems Gang, full of deserters and escaped prisoners, who are out stealing and robbing. They have taken a woman in Tylerville and have ransomed her back to her family. But some of the women, especially the younger ones, have been violated. Violated is the respectable word I can use. And I have heard only last week three men have been shot to death down in Bee Spring trying to protect their families. You will be easy prey for them."

Caroline shifted her stance. "I know of the dangers out there, and I assure you, Missus Higgens, that God will provide a safe way for me to travel. I have traveled now many days and have but seven to go. But I must sleep now, as I have walked all night and I am very tired. If you have something for me to eat, I shall appreciate it and will do chores when I wake, but as for now, let me sleep." Caroline nodded toward the dog that sat listening to the conversation. "Do not mind my dog as he will scare up a rabbit or squirrel in the woods out back, but please put out some water for him. I hope to wake about sundown and be on my way. I would also like to buy two penny's worth of goose fat to salve my feet, for I find the right shoe is unforgiving. A blister has manifested itself. And it is painful to walk at times."

After eating several biscuits with pork sausage gravy, Caroline fell into a deep sleep there on the back porch. She woke once and found the outhouse to the rear of the house, and then returned to her sleep. The dog went into the woods only once, found several young, slow-moving squirrels and had his dinner there. He returned to the back porch and slept by the step throughout the day. Caroline stirred a second time and went to the well and took some water and returned to her bed. She quickly fell into a deep sleep again.

It was late morning. The sun had broken through the clouds after a night of light rain. Sitting on the front porch with her husband sitting beside her, Caroline looked out over the pond. A peck basket of fresh picked Winesap apples sat on the floor near her and in her lap rested a bowl and a paring knife. It was after breakfast, and the pasture in front of their cabin was beginning to come alive with hundreds of dragon flies, small yellow butterflies, and bees of all manner. She looked at three quart jars, each one bursting with red clover blossoms, honeysuckle, and Carolina jasmine picked near the creek earlier that morning, now resting on a small table in front of her.

"Tomorrow is our anniversary. Not today, Charles. But I assume you picked these three bouquets this morning because you are preparing for tomorrow. What surprises will you have for me then? And I, likewise for you. Yes, dear husband, a wife remembers these things too. Three years ago tomorrow I said 'I do,' and I can still see your smiling face when I quietly spoke those two words as if, perchance, you thought I might not speak those two words at all. 'I do take him.' Would you like to say something sweet to me, this morning?" Caroline turned away with her paring knife, and started to peel an apple.

Caroline glanced over to her husband, who was repairing a leather bridle for the mule. He smiled. "You were the prettiest young woman in all of Louisville. Maybe yet that is wrong.

The prettiest young bride in all of Kentucky. I knew you were the prettiest, but that day you were so serious, I was afraid, until the last minute, that you might change your mind, because you looked mighty hesitant when you walked down the aisle. There was scarce a smile on your face."

"Truth be told, I was nineteen. The thought that in several hours I would be alone with a full-grown man, and he would expect me to disrobe in front of him then get into bed and be intimate. Well, you may have been handsome, and we may have held hands and kissed, but for you to see me naked was overwhelming. I thought I surely am not enough. The women in our church possessed these full-size bosoms, and what if mine were too small? And what if you looked upon me and saw a teenage girl of nineteen, with these small bosoms and a flat back end, not like many grown women in town? So I kept thinking, maybe I should go not into our new home until it is securely dark, and then undress in the blackness—maybe with just one lamp a distance in the kitchen. But to my concern, you pulled me away hours before sunset and so my plan was challenged. I quickly devised another, which was that you would not be allowed to come into the bedroom until I was in bed with sheets and covers, but you carried me across the threshold and right into the bedroom and undressed me, button after button. Which I quickly rebuttoned as fast as I could, and you thought it was a game but it was not. Then when you finally won the game and I stood there all unbuttoned. It was then, and only then, I could see in your eyes for the first time that I was good enough. That I measured to others."

"You will always be enough. Thank God, you still do not know how beautiful you are. Sitting there in that wore out apron, hair in your eyes, slicing apples for an apple pie. Sitting there, still perfect and still barefoot."

"That's because I have these small tender feet and no shoe fits me proper. But if you like me the way you see me, then surely God has put a crystal in your eye." Caroline put down the knife, pushed her hair out of her eyes and turned to Charles. "I was saving this for tomorrow, but now that our firstborn is approaching two and Isaac has left his small cradle, might tonight we try—might we try for a second? I believe I am ready."

In her sleep, Caroline reached down and rubbed her bare feet. She was not aware, but smiled in her sleep and pulled the pillow to her bosom and held it tight. Caroline rolled over, opening her eyes and gazing out onto the back yard. The clouds had turned sunset pink and it was time to move on. She looked down at the dog resting at the foot of the porch. "It's another day and I am so glad you are still here. Today will be my fifth, and a day closer. We have but six more days and I shall not waste a minute more."

Missus Higgens came out onto the back porch as Caroline was dressing. "I never saw a woman dress in man's clothes, yet the Bible talks about it. I suppose walking all the way to Elizabethtown, it might be an advantage. Anyhow, we had chicken for dinner with corn on the cob, and I have wrapped part of the leftovers in this paper. There is some goose grease for your shoes too. I am sure about midnight tonight you will be twelve miles down the road, and pretty hungry. Do take care of yourself, as you know there are plenty of dangers out there, and dressing like a man will help." Missus Higgens pulled her hair out of her eyes and tucked it behind her ears. "Three days ago a family of four came walking, heading east back home. Robbed and their horses stolen. Their wagon wrecked. The woman, about your age, had a baby boy and a six-year-old daughter with her. Quiet folk. Mennonites. Neither she nor her husband wanted to talk about it, only get home, merely had just the clothes on their backs. That poor woman, bless her, looked a lot like my daughter. She's passed now." Caroline saw Missus Higgens was starting to tear up and Caroline took her hand. The gray-haired woman put her hand on top of Caroline's. "This damnable war has turned men's hearts evil. I hope God strikes dead these men who call our young boys to kill each other. Maybe he will."

Caroline interrupted her, thanking her for the food and offered now to do chores, but Missus Higgens declined—wanting nothing in return. Missus Higgens said if Caroline came back this way, she was welcomed to sleep on the back porch again, and maybe she could sit down to a proper meal around the kitchen table. When Caroline made the first step off the back porch, the dog stood and stretched his front legs and arched his back, then moved to Caroline's side. Caroline waved goodbye to Missus Higgens, and looked the dog in the eye as if to say, "It's you and me together again." The dog acknowledged with a low quiet bark, then ran ahead leading the way.

The first nine miles that night were uneventful. The moon was fuller and so she felt confident about her safety this new night. A light breeze from the west blew at her back and helped her along. She was on dry ground and her blisters had not been a problem so far with the new goose grease lubricating the shoe. Her ribs only ached when she encountered steep hills and her breathing had labored with each step. Caroline sensed her pace was swift and knew she was making good ground as she encountered eleven scattered homesteads, all without light and all silent. Only the farm animals were aware she was passing by, although at one homestead a dog barked out into the darkness, and the black and brown dog barked quickly back as if to say, "Quiet! I am much larger than you and have authority to pass." The dog made no second bark, understanding the pecking order of things.

At about one in the morning, she encountered a high-pitched chorus of tree frogs in concert that seemed to come from ten thousand little green amphibians trying to outshine one another. It made no sense to her that they would be in this one particular woods, but she decided there must be a swamp nearby, unseen from her vantage point. The dog ran into the trees but returned a few minutes later with nothing to show for his efforts. The road climbed and then rounded the top to reveal a new vista—a canopy of trees that ran forever and hid what lay below. There at the top of this large hill, standing by the road, were five rocks stacked on top of each other. A dried collection of flowers rested on the top rock. Had someone died here? Was this some sort of memorial to some event? Caroline could only guess. She picked several wild flowers and some red clover blossoms growing nearby and placed them with the others. From that point on, the road descended quickly down, and at one point dropped deep into a grassy valley that became narrower as she walked. Under this moonlight she could observe this valley gave way to a ravine, and as she descended slowly lower, the walls on both sides closed toward the path and both sides became walls of granite stone that rose nearly ninety feet high on both sides. While it was tapered, it remained wide enough for a single wagon or even a stage to pass—the ruts of the wagon wheels were clearly visible in this darkness on the crumbled stone road. Artesian spring water ran down the fern-covered south wall and collected into a stream held in place by gray-black crumbled rocks, once part of the wall. This ravine continued unchanged for well over a mile. There was a peacefulness that enveloped itself here. Maybe it was the stars above or the moonlight reflecting on the mist collecting on the ferns, but Caroline felt the outside world was hundreds of miles away. Rain, sleet, snow, or storms would be held at its boundary, unable to invade this secret sanctuary. At one point, half way through, she stopped and cupped her hands at one small dripping waterfall and drank for a moment. The water was ice cold and tasted of limestone. The dog likewise stopped, and seeing Caroline drinking, walked under the waterfall and disappeared into a small crevice, not large enough to be called a cave, but large enough for him to disappear into the darkness and reemerge eating something that could have been a frog or salamander. Maybe a water snake.

But as unprepared as she was for the ravine's appearance, so was she unprepared for its departure. Caroline saw light ahead and sensing warm dryness in the air, she walked out and looked down into the open valley. The ravine's stream met a second larger stream and they joined forces, pushing the road one way and randomly pulling it the other. The stream could never be tamed by the land, because it was birthed from mother earth thousands of feet deep, where all streams are born. Indians believed that moving water held dominion over the motionless land. The land, in turn, exerted dominion of all trees that sank their roots into its soil. The great trees, in turn, possessed dominion of all who roamed under its green protective mantle. And lastly, man stood empty handed, with only dominion of himself.

Three hours later, after travelling this cooling valley, Caroline and her new-found black and brown friend came to three streams all from different valleys and flowing toward each other, pulled by gravity down into a new valley. All three originated from the same aquifer six miles deep yet sprang to the surface from separate artesian springs miles apart. Once one, then three, now one again.

Caroline stopped and she and the dog both drank from the new stream. The cool mountain water was the first they had encountered in the last nine miles. She sat on the moist soil and took off her right shoe and rubbed her foot. The goose fat had softened the leather, and her blister was not as painful. She pulled the leaves of a plantain herb growing there intermixed with the stinging nettle and milkweed on the side of the stream. Placing several leaves in the back of her shoe, she decided this was a good idea for the other foot and so, she removed her left shoe and did the same. She slowly slipped her feet back into the leather shoes, making sure the plantain stayed in place. Standing, she walked in a circle for a moment, and decided the plantain acting with the goose grease was soothing. Picking up her bedroll, she slipped it over her head and, with the haversack on her shoulder, she continued on. As they traveled, the moon shadows ran ahead of her, then at times, when the road turned, the shadows moved to the right and followed her step by step. At one time, the shadows disappeared as darkness briefly fell from the cloud cloaked sky. The road turned and climbed sharply to the right and a half mile later it switched direction, turning to the left. This went on for more than an hour. Left then right. North then south. It was the steepest terrain she had encountered and it drained her of her strength. Her calves ached and thigh muscles burned. She stopped once and sat alongside of the road, then removed her shoe, adjusting the plantain leaves for a second time. At about five in the morning, she stopped and took out the chicken leg and the cob of corn that Missus Higgens had given her. The dog, having been silent until this point, barked once and ran down the road looking back. But Caroline did not stir until she had finished her meal. There was no stream nearby, and she wished she had something in which to carry water, but she knew at the bottom of the mountain there would be a stream. She eventually reached the top of the small mountain, and looking down she could see a stream of water which caught the moon light. Bright white reflections sparkled, dancing in the pitch black darkness like little fireflies moving to an unseen and secret place.

Caroline thought if she were bird, she could have flown over the torturous mountain in moments instead of the last hour which had taken its toll on her stamina. Coming down the mountain proved much easier as the dog ran ahead of each switch back, stopping at every turn and ensuring eye contact with his new woman friend. But at one point, the dog ran into the weeds and disappeared. Caroline called out once, but the dog made not a sound. At the fifth switch back, the dog reappeared down the hill from Caroline and sat in the road until Caroline approached. Caroline thought the dog had probably gone after something to eat. But the thought occurred again that the dog never once begged for food, but always fended for himself. Nearing the bottom of the mountain, a stream ran over a rocky ledge three feet high and fell into a stream bed. She walked to the waterfall, took off her hat and plunged her head under it. This felt good. The walk up the mountain and even down had caused her to heat up. Her perspiration had matted her hair. She took off her shirt and splashed the cool water over her arms and down her front and back. She sensed the salt being washed away. She thought it might be close to sunup and maybe this could be a good spot to sleep. Indeed, the mountain had taken several hours to climb and descend. Glancing up into the stars, she spotted the North Star and located Venus. She assumed it was about five in the morning. Caroline wanted to think out loud, and so she turned to the dog. "Hey, dog. If we left the Higgens at six last night and if I am right, it is about five, dawn. It means we have been walking eleven hours. Times about two miles an hour, because of these hills and this mountain, so we may have traveled twenty plus two, so let us say twenty-two

124

miles. I could go on for another hour, but this place with the waterfall is so peaceful and perfect a place to hide, let us call it day four and let's get sleeping." The dog did not know what Caroline was saying, but when she walked to a high grassy knoll and took out her bedroll and lay down, taking off her shoes, the dog knew what she had said.

Caroline had consumed a lot of water at the waterfall, and so midway that morning, she arose from her sleep and went into the weeds twenty feet away to relieve herself then returned to her bed. It looked like it might rain that morning, but Caroline could not be disturbed by the weather, for no matter what it was, she was going to walk. Watching carefully the large black clouds, she listened for thunder but, hearing none, she went back to sleep. Somewhat later, a solitary bee landed on her face and inspected around her mouth. She pulled out her shirt and draped it across her face, with only her nose sticking out. At around noon, she woke to the sounds of horse hooves coming from the east and heading up the mountain. She did not stir, but took comfort in the fact she was 200 feet from the road, and hidden on a grassy knoll under a stand of young dogwood trees.´ After the unseen riders and horses passed, she stood and walked to the waterfall and drank again. Returning to her bed, she glanced at the dog and realized the dog was always staring at her as if he knew when she was about to look at him. She turned away, but quickly glanced back at the dog. The dog was still looking at her and waiting for conversation. But none came. She went back to sleep.

It was nearing four in the afternoon when she awoke. She first located the sun in the sky. She judged the colors of the clouds.

Then she looked at the dog. He was already awake and had been staring at her since she stirred. "Hey, dog. I think we slept well over eleven hours and I needed that, as that mountain we climbed last night was considerable. I think the plantain on my foot has helped and it feels better. Let us go to the stream, find what we can to eat, and then be under way." Caroline stood and rocked her foot back and forth, then smiled. "If my foot holds, I will attempt fourteen hours and that will bring me thirty-five miles closer. But if I speed my steps and there are no mountains, then forty miles is possible. I see no reason not to try."

Caroline dressed, rolled her blanket, and walked down to the stream. As she walked she prayed, "Lord help me find strength this day and provide me with sustenance for the trip. Protect my husband and protect my children." Taking off her shoes and leaving her bedroll on the bank, she waded out into the stream. Caroline saw five catfish about seven inches long swimming together. She moved slowly over to the fish and cupping her hands, she caught the larger one as it attempted to hide in the water cress. She took out her knife and cut it open and spilled out its innards. She closed her eyes and took a large bite. It was cold, so there was not much flavor, but she finished it in moments. She reached into the water and grasped a handful of watercress, swishing it back and forth in the water to dislodge any small snails living there. Satisfied, she quickly ate to cover the taste and texture of the fish. She found three other similar sized fish hiding in the watercress and again cupped her hands and caught another one, somewhat larger. After eating that one, along with the peppery hot watercress, she noticed the dog had given up searching for frogs or crawfish and returned to watch. Caroline returned to the stream and caught two more. She tossed them to the dog on the bank and he quickly ate both fish, still wiggling in the grass.

Clouds continued to gather that late afternoon as they started this night's walk. But it did not truly look like rain, only a cloudy evening. She listened for thunder but heard none. The terrain here was rolling and so the walking was easier. As the sun lowered itself one finger above the horizon, she passed two homesteads built close to one another. One was painted with whitewash and the second was not yet painted. Its front porch, likewise, was not yet finished and had five large irregular fieldstones gathered together for steps. The two homesteads stood about 900 feet apart, and both looked to have been deserted, as there was no sign of anyone near. Walking by the unfinished house, she looked beyond it to the white house and noticed it had a small garden in the rear of the house, and she could tell as she walked past it that most of the vegetables had been gathered. Plants had been pulled and scattered as if animals had gotten into the fenced garden and ravaged it. The fence itself had been knocked over, and the gate lay on the ground. There was nothing left standing. Caroline turned away and, spotting three apple trees near the barn, quietly walked toward the closest tree. While the tree had been stripped bare, there were several apples on the ground. Brushing off several ants, she found one and bit into it. It tasted sweet and juicy. She quickly found another and she put the second one into her haversack.

127

Caroline heard a rusted hinge of a door creak from the barn behind her as a large older woman walked out carrying a shotgun in both hands. This woman, who appeared to be over fifty years old, wore a tattered purple dress with a brown stained white apron over it. She wore no shoes. Her gray and black hair was straight and long, draped over her broad shoulders. The woman said nothing, but only stared at Caroline. At that moment, Caroline heard a door swing open to the right of her—she heard the familiar sound of a spring with its metallic twang, then the screen door quickly slapped shut. Caroline turned her head to see a younger woman, about nineteen, walk onto the porch with a large kitchen knife in her right hand and a hatchet in the left. This young woman, also barefoot and in a tattered blue-and-green homespun linen dress, stood on the porch yet did not advance. The older woman spoke first. "Well, young man, looks like you are traveling alone and that makes me think you could be a deserter. Are you?" The young woman stepped off the porch and walked slowly across the grass toward Caroline. "Answer my mother! Are you a deserter? You come here to steal and rape?" The older woman stood her ground and kept the shotgun aimed at Caroline. She noticed both hammers had been cocked and ready to fire. "I bet you are a deserter from the Johnny Rebs. Or maybe you are a spy. Well, the rebs been here, took our three cows, six pigs, and most all our garden. It took but twenty minutes and they wiped us clean." The younger woman took another step forward and raised the hatchet over her head, then stopped in a stance of defiance—her legs spread for action. "You know, there is a reward for deserters or spies. Both armies will pay to get you. Ten dollars! Speak up; what side you running from?"

Caroline did not want to answer for fear it would be the wrong answer, and so she thought of a young deaf man who attended her father's church fifteen years earlier. And so, she pointed to her mouth. "AAAHHH, AAAMMM, SOOORRRY." Then she pointed to her ears and shook her head back and forth rocking violently. "AAAHHH, AAAMMM. NOOO HEEEAAAR." The older woman lowered her shot gun slightly. "He's deaf. He is deaf. Are you deaf?" Caroline thought for a moment, and then pointed to her ears. "NOOO HEEEAAAR." Caroline raised her left hand to her mouth and pushing her hand outward repeatedly as if they would be words. NNNOOO SPEEEAAAK." The younger woman dropped her hatchet to her side. "Yes, he's deaf and almost dumb." Caroline moved her hands to her open mouth, motioning as if to say, "Do you have any food?" The older woman took a step back and shouted, "We ain't got no food. This winter comes and we might starve. There is no heartfelt one out here to help us. We all have been raped and robbed of all our sustenance. They took all my canned goods and all the chickens. Hell, they are starving too." She pointed the gun toward the road and waved her arm toward the road. "You move on. We ain't got enough food to feed ourselves. Why would we give you any? You move on, young man. Go fend for yourself, or you crawl into the woods and die." The older woman pointed again to the road. "You get out of here, you understand? Go ahead, and take that damn dog with you." The older woman took a step forward. "I said, get out of here! God damned you from birth, and there is no reason for you to live. You can starve to death like the rest of us." Caroline moved slowly between the two women and, looking over her shoulder, walked up the path and to the road. She looked back one more time and saw the two women standing there watching her as she left. Caroline walked quickly away from this ravaged homestead. She was taken aback that two women had rejected her, but then both thought she was a man and, like the raiding men before her, she represented only evil things. She thought of the many women who had helped her, but these two were different. They were desperate. Yes, she thought, she should be more careful in the future when she came to an isolated homestead. She had visualized many times how men could rape and kill her, but now she realized women could kill just as easily. It would be quick and unexpected. But in these times, it might be justified.

Walking briskly, with the dog leading the way, Caroline was 900 feet from the homestead, when she heard footsteps running from behind. She turned to see the younger woman running toward her, but without the hatchet or the knife in either hand. The dog turned and quickly rejoined Caroline ten feet behind her, in a guarding position. The black and brown dog started to growl a low warning. The young raven-haired woman glanced at the dog, and stopped twenty feet away. She spoke slowly and loudly. "Listen, mister, my mama don't mean no harm, but we are desperate. I know you are too. I brought you this. Beet roots. The rebs did not dig up our root vegetables. I have a few carrots too. You take 'em."

The woman leaned forward and made a gesture as if eating. Caroline stepped forward and took the three beets and two carrots and nodded a thank you. The young woman continued as if Caroline could understand. "You know most of the young men are being killed off, and when this war is over there will be few young men alive. If you come back this way, you stop in. I would make a good wife. We could work it out. You are slight, but together we would be strong. Together, we could run this farm. Mama could help too. I want to have a family and just because you are deaf and dumb does not mean you could not father a family. Please come back. I will make a good wife." The young woman turned and gestured back toward the homestead. "As you can see, this land here is very fertile. I bet I am too. Come back. I do not want to die alone. You hear? Come back." The woman gestured with her arms pointing to herself. She turned and started to walk away, and then she stopped for a moment and turned. She smiled and reached up with both hands and touched her heart. She then pointed toward Caroline. Caroline nodded "yes" to her as if she understood. The woman stood there and stared, as Caroline placed her hand over her heart, smiled, and, turning, walked on. As she did, something deep within her stirred and tears formed in her eyes. This young woman had seen her possible future. Few men would return from this war—whole and with arms and legs ready to start a family. Many would never return, but would rest in the soil hundreds of miles from home. This young nineteen-year-old woman's life was tied by a thin thread to her fluttering dreams. Within the next minute, tears started running from her eyes. She cried for the young woman

131

hoping and longing for a husband and a family. For in that young woman, she saw herself. She saw her own recent desperation and the fragile hope she held tightly within her soul. Maybe Caroline would find him alive. Maybe she would find something else.

Part Two

It did rain that morning. A light and sometimes uneven rain started at six but lasted only for moments. With the sun now three fingers up, Caroline came to a grove of sycamore trees, the type holding leaves larger than a man's hand with fingers spread wide. She found a spot 200 feet up the hill under a large sycamore tree that had diverted the rain. It was dry on the soft grass near the trunk. She laid out her bedroll and sat, taking off her shoes. Leaning back against the grey-and-green bark trunk, she reached into her bag and pulled out the beet roots and the carrots. Brushing off the largest of the three beets, she ate one and followed that with a single carrot, including the green leaves. Still she was hungry and reached back into her bag and found the last biscuit and ate it too. She knew there was a lone apple in the bag, but wanted to save that for when she was thirsty and could find no water.

The dog had followed her up the hill and, seeing the bedroll spread, he turned and ran back down the hill to the road and over to a grassy field and disappeared into the grasses which stood at his eye level. "He's probably after his dinner too. He never begs for food; maybe he is smarter than I imagined. He sees how hard it is for me to find food, and yet for him it comes easy.

From that night's long twenty-nine-mile walk—the valleys, the ravine, the difficult mountain, Caroline was exhausted. She soon fell asleep, as the sun rose higher in the morning mist. The rain stopped, and red-winged black birds started their morning ritual song fest, but Caroline heard none of it. In her thoughts, which came like waves, her husband appeared and disappeared. He was alive. He was dead. He was dying of wounds. He was not hers. He was waiting for her. She thought if she could make even thirty miles after she woke, she could be but forty miles from Elizabethtown. She realized Elizabethtown was located at the cross point of three roads, and thought how she might find news there about the war and the whereabouts of the Kentucky Volunteers. Further, she could write a letter to Missus Millar, telling her she was in Elizabethtown, and to let the children know she was in good spirits. Also, she would write a letter to her husband care of the Confederate Army, Kentucky Volunteers, saying she was only a few days away and her travels were going as planned. She thought the letter to her husband might not find him. So she would send one more. And that was to Ruth Abernathy, the Confederate Army nurse, care of the Shelbyville Baptist Church. She was the woman who had written to Caroline reporting the condition of her wounded husband. But the chance of a letter reaching her husband soon would be remote. Maybe her husband had fought off the gangrene and returned to battle. Then too, maybe the gangrene had overcome the medicine, and he had lost his arm. Maybe he was so weak that death overtook his life, and he was buried somewhere out in a broad field with a single crude white cross. She tossed and turned, and around noon as the sun peeked through the leaves, she found it hard to sleep. She woke many times, and the words "perseverance and plight" came into mind. She opened her eyes to see the dog had returned and was sleeping about twenty feet further up the hill. She got up and walked down to the road and turned to the west, walking back toward a small stream that ran down the hill. She stopped when she realized the dog had followed her. She bent over the stream, and drank for a while. Caroline tossed water in her face, realizing she had not washed her hair, which had gathered much dust from yesterday's roads. She cupped her hands and pulled up water and splashed it over her hair. She did this several times, then crouching low toward the clear waters, she splashed her face. She was looking down into the water when she spotted a tea cup with its handle missing and partially buried in sand pebbles in the middle of the stream. She stared at it suspiciously and slowly realized other people had stopped at this very stream for water, leaving this single cup by accident. But when? Was it this year or ten years ago, or maybe a hundred years ago when this was but an Indian trail, and only French trappers ventured this deep into the west. Who last drank with this cup? Where were they now? Maybe it belonged to that old woman and her daughter. Maybe it belonged to the Indians who had traded furs for plates and bowls and silverware— when trappers were the only white faces that traveled these hills. Caroline reached down and pushed the pebbles away, then gently pulled this evidence of civilization out of the water. She held the cup in her hand, examining the small yellow and green flower design along the rim. She rinsed the cup in the water and decided that she would be the next one

135

to drink from it. She dipped it in the water and brought it to her lips. Yes, she thought, this is how I used to drink water. She pictured herself standing in her kitchen with a large glass pitcher filled with water drawn moments earlier from their well. Cool and refreshing and in a bone china cup much like this one. After drinking a second cup of water, she placed the delicate china back down into the stream, thinking someone else may use this sometime in the future. It could be a year from now or a hundred years. Would it be someone like her, walking alone, discovering this stream and this cup? No one knew the future. She stood and walked back up the hill, and to her bedroll. Quickly, she fell asleep.

About three that afternoon, the rains returned and they awakened her. She stood, watching the black clouds travel from east to west, and decided she had slept for six hours and that would have to be enough for her. Caroline felt if she traveled now until six the next morning, or fifteen hours, she would easily make thirty-five miles. She pulled on her hat and rolled the blanket back into a bedroll. She was not going to let the rains slow her down. Back on the road, she took off her shoes, knowing that wet shoes would cause her blisters to only worsen. She tied the shoelaces and hung the shoes around her neck. This felt normal, as many times, like her children, she would walk around the homestead barefoot. The road turned muddy in places, and puddles of brown water formed in the road, and so she walked in the grass along the right side of the road. After two hours of walking in this manner, and after many conversations with the dog about the weather and terrain, she smiled for the first time this day. Her mind fixed on the apple she had eaten the previous day, and of the one still in her haversack. She thought of the apple pie she made for her children many times. She thought, "Maybe Priscilla is attempting to make an apple pie today and would not that be wonderful. Yes, it would be almost heaven to be there to watch my daughter standing by the stove in my apron watching it cool—smiling and proud of accomplishment." Caroline quickly ran from the thought, realizing thinking of her children and the homestead was causing sadness—pulling her back and slowing her down. She vowed to think only of the mission she was on. To only think of today, which would quicken her steps. She thought, "The children are fine. Missus Millar will keep an eye on them. They are probably having fun, laughing and ruling the roost, playing 'find me if you can.'" After that realization, she had no thoughts. None. It was just the road and the dog and her. Just the next step, the next minute, the next mile. Yes, she just thought of the miles to walk. Miles to be moved under her feet and behind her. After four hours of arduous walking, and at about seven in the evening, she came to a burned out homestead. The house had burned to the foundation, and the barn was reduced to its basic ribbed structure. The huge twelve-by-twelve oak beams had survived the fire, and stood like a skeleton, waiting for a new roof and new siding. Maybe it would happen this year, maybe years from now, or maybe never. But the barn stood there ready. Waiting to be barn again.

Caroline could see no one was there, and so she walked down to the stone foundation and looked for anything that could be useful to her. There was not much there. But in the fading sunlight, she did find some women's clothing that had been partially burned. They smelled of yesterday's smoke and were useless. But near the kitchen, she found an empty quart jar with a lid and red rubber ring. "This is good. I can use this to hold water." She spotted the well half way to the burned barn and walked to it. Standing there, she tossed the wooden bucket into the darkness, and felt the rope tighten as it filled. Caroline cranked up the overflowing bucket, and resting it on the wooden plank that ran over the top, she filled her quart jar with water. What was left in the bucket she brought up to her lips and drank the mineral water with its familiar taste. "Hey, dog, this tastes like the one we have. It's been filtered through miles of sandstone. I know, I dug out a lot of stones. God has put water down there, and ours is the best water far and wide." Caroline lifted the bucket off the plank and placed it on the ground. Dog looked up for approval and, seeing her smile, he walked over and drank. After the dog had finished, she lifted the bucket and tossed it back down into the well. "You don't want a bucket to dry out, because then it will leak. But you know that don't you, dog?" Actually the dog did not know that, but then dog knew a lot of things that Caroline did not know. Sadly, the dog had no way of communicating those things to Caroline. Only his actions spoke for him.

Nearing sundown, and after five hours of walking, Caroline heard horse hooves, not running but walking slowly. It was surprising to see someone that late, traveling so close to dusk aided only by failing sun and early moonlight. In the distance, she spied three wagons, all heading west and toward her. The first two wagons were pulled by oxen, and the third with two very tall black mules. All three wagons looked newly constructed and were the Conestoga design with hoops and white canvas over the top. She slowed her walk and thought whether she should hide, but upon seeing a woman sitting next to a man in the lead wagon, she walked on. In that valley with its wall of trees on both sides she could hear the sound of a woman singing a hymn and a baby crying. As the wagons approached, the woman who had been singing in the lead wagon leaned over and said something to the bearded man seated beside her. Then she turned and waved toward Caroline.

As the wagon came to a stop, the woman shouted down to Caroline. "I told my husband that man, meaning you, walks like a woman. So, who are you and why are you dressed that way? Cause I can tell a woman by the way she walks."

Caroline stopped and pulled off her cap, revealing all her hair as it came spilling down. "All my clothes got burned in a fire and these were my husband's, but now I find they are easier to walk in. I'm Caroline and I am on my way to Shelbyville to nurse my husband who has been wounded."

Three young children lifted the canvas on the side of the second wagon and gazed at Caroline, and then they started to whisper to each other, laughing at this woman dressed like a man. The driver of the wagon, speaking with a German accent, pointed to himself. "Mennonites do not support either side. We are heading to Missouri and away from this war. We have left Mount Horeb, where a great Union Army is now gathering for the final battle. We have seen thousands of blue-coated men—like an endless flock of birds. And horses I could not count. A line of cannons a mile long. Only God will stop them. Many of us, including Anabaptist, Shakers are going to Missouri, where there is little war, where our children will be safe." The woman, placing her hand on her husband's arm, interrupted. "But on this road today we saw a line of Confederate soldiers coming from the south. We counted over 700 men. Forty-two cannon. A hundred wagons." The woman, wearing a simple black dress with no buttons, only pins to hold it together, pointed to the second wagon. "As you can see, I am a mother. Many young soldier boys will be dead in the approaching days. I do not wish evil on anyone, but I believe you traveling east is not providential for you."

The man with the frayed straw hat spoke up again. "You should be cautious. Dressed as you are—like a man. Some will think you are a suspicious one. A spy or even a deserter. They say Kentucky is neutral, but it has become a prize to fight over. Both armies should leave, but their hearts are filled with hatred, seeking only dismemberment and death."

Caroline took her hat and pulled it back on. "Thank you for that advice and your offer of safety, but I must get to my husband, who lies wounded in Shelbyville. And I..."

The man leaned over the side of the wagon and interrupted loudly. "Since he wears the gray uniform, and since you are coming from the west, then both of you are danger. That is bad for him and you! He is probably dead, or carried off to a prisoner camp where many die of their wounds. You must understand you will never see him again. Yes, to you this is new, but we have witnessed these wars before, for there is endless wars in the old countries. It is a disease that has now traveled to this country. Sadly, there is no cure for this dire infection but the sacrifice of many."

Caroline looked down the road. "Thank you for your advice again. But I have come too far to turn back. I wish you happiness in Missouri. But I need to warn you, there is ahead of you the Willems Gang. A gang of murderers, robbers, and deserters. They are robbing and maybe killing those heading west. I have witnessed it. I hope you are armed."

"No, we are not armed. We are peacemakers. Like Jesus. We will not resist. It is not within our hearts to resist. May God walk beside you. Goodbye."

The man slapped the reins against the oxen and the wagon lurched forward. The woman smiled and raised her hands into a prayerful position in front of her face, then closed her eyes. The two wagons that followed started again but no one looked down at Caroline as they passed. They looked forward as if she was not there. For she was not one of them.

The night proved uneventful. The road was dry, and Caroline knew she was walking faster than earlier that afternoon. She ate the second beet and at midnight, she ate the remaining apple. Caroline wanted to walk to sunup, as that would be fifteen hours and her stamina was good. Her bruised ribs were still painful, but the comfrey was soothing both her side and the blisters on her right foot. Her new-found water bottle had been refilled several miles back at the only stream they had come to that night. Dog had been a good companion as he walked side by side with Caroline. All of this cheered her and caused her to occasionally quietly hum a song to lift her spirits. Dog would look up at her, thinking how much prettier a melody was than her talking words, which he never understood.

At about four in the morning, she heard a cracking sound and a thousand feet to her left, she heard a great tree start its fall to the ground. She judged the tree to be long dead, as the branches snapped loudly as it fell. The earth beneath her feet trembled and she ducked low, not knowing how close the tree was to her. The dog did not run, but only looked in the direction of the falling tree. Birds that had been living in the tree signaled their displeasure at losing their nests by calling to each other loudly. Moments later, a breeze stirred by the falling tree struck her face, and with that, silence returned. Caroline listened for the tree's echo for a minute and, hearing it, she walked on.

Nearing six in the morning, when the sky turned pink, she heard hoof beats from the west and she hurriedly moved into the trees on the left side of the road. She barely made it into the trees when ten men in blue uniforms came riding by with a quickness that suggested something important was about to happen. Barely five minutes later, rode fifty men also in blue uniforms racing by in full gallop. Caroline stayed deep in the woods while the dog lay beside her, sensing a fear in Caroline. This tension put the dog on edge, and he looked to her for some sign of reassurance—waiting to do something but not knowing what. Caroline did not look at the dog, but turned her head left and right, listening to indiscernible sounds. Several minutes passed, and the road was now quiet again. She started to stand. Listening for a moment and sensing some noise in the distance, she turned her head to the west, for that was the direction of the noise. It was a sound similar to popcorn popping on the stove. An echo arrived and in that echo she discerned the roar of gunfire. This continued for five minutes, and then slowly the shooting subsided and eventually stopped. She waited as one or two more shots rang out. Finally, silence returned. Caroline thought, "What was that about? Were the Mennonites in the middle of that? Did the blue-shirted soldiers run into an ambush? Was the Willems Gang involved?" This uncertainty only added to her fears, and so she decided she had traveled enough that night. With what she thought was thirty-one miles behind her, she called it day five. If her calculations were correct, she could be about ten miles from Leitchfield, and more than half way in her journey. She walked deeper into the woods and took out the last beet and ate it; she drank some water from her quart jar. Gathering leaves to sleep on, she undid her bedroll and went to sleep. The dog got up and ran off, back down to the road and disappeared into the tall grasses on the other side. Twenty minutes into her sleep, she heard in the distance three more gun shots, followed moments later with a large volley so big she could not count them. Then again silence. She felt safe here in the woods, yet with an understanding that war was within arm's length from her. No one would escape this unscathed. Men, women, children.

Somewhere during her restless sleep, she awakened to an unfamiliar sound. It was not a noise a man would make. It was like no other she had ever heard. She awoke and looked around. It was no longer morning, but early afternoon and the sun was high in the cloudy sky. She had done as she had always done, and pulled the hat over her eyes to shield it from any sun that leaked through the leaves above. The whooshing sound grew louder and was followed by a grunt. She quickly pulled her hat up then turned on her back. There before her, ten feet away, positioned on all fours was a large black bear. Its coal-black fur shone in the sun. Its glistening black nose sniffed the air. Its torn and ragged ears stood erect. Caroline made eye contact with the beast, and the 500-pound bear, staring eye to eye back at Caroline, sensed her challenge. With one loud roar, the bear exhibited its ownership of these woods. Her ears rang as she felt the hot air from its opened mouth strike her face. The bear stood on its hind legs, revealing its seven-foot size. He quickly started switching his weight from one leg to another, rocking back and forth, agitated and ready to fight. Caroline sat up, then froze and began speaking quietly. "Easy. Easy. I mean no harm to you. Easy there." Without taking her eyes off the bear, she moved to a crouched position, and slowly stood, all the while speaking in hushed tones to the bear. But the bear did not like her standing, and so let out another roar, this one even louder. Hearing that roar and now seeing its brown-stained teeth bared, Caroline froze and tried to look away, trying not to challenge the animal. The bear stopped moving from side to side and stood there observing. Caroline sensed from the bear's low grumble that it was not happy that Caroline had entered its woods. The bear smelled the air again and turned away for a moment, looking to its left and then right. The 500-pound beast went back on all fours and, not smelling food, turned and started walking deeper into the woods, looking over its shoulder as it walked away. Suddenly the bear started running. But the bear was running away from Caroline, deeper and deeper into the woods then quickly, as if it had done this many times, or by instinct, it turned left and started gathering speed running in an arc and racing toward this new intruder. Caroline sensed the bear was about to attack, but she felt helpless. In that instant, the creature came roaring back full of anger. With its huge four paws striking hard on the ground and with its head down, it impacted Caroline, knocking her backwards and to the ground. She gasped for air, as the strike knocked the air from her lungs. But the bear ran on. Running in another arc behind her, it turned and started its second attack. This time Caroline hugged the ground, shielding her head with her arms, but the bear lowered its head and flipped her sideways causing her to flip over several times landing ten feet away. The bear continued its run, circling for the third time, and started its approach when out of the tree line twenty feet away, the dog came running at full speed with no fear, and growling a noise Caroline had never heard from this dog before. The bear slowed and started circling again, but with its attention to the dog as the dog moved between the bear and Caroline. Then the bear stopped and looked at his new foe. There was silence for a moment as the two measured each other's sizes. The dog watched the bear, attempting to understand the beast's method of attack. The bear growled loudly and walked slowly toward the dog on all fours.

The dog spread his front legs wide and lowered his whole body to the ground then went into repeated barks mixed with threatening growls. He started jumping to the left and right quickly, daring the bear to attack. A standoff started with the bear growling at the dog and the dog growling back at the bear. It seemed like forever to Caroline, but in truth this lasted for no more than a single minute. Caroline got to her feet, and without taking her eyes off the bear, from her waist band she pulled out her knife. Suddenly, the bear decided it was larger than the dog and rushed with lightning speed to the dog. Grabbing the dog with its huge open mouth by the dog's neck, the bear shook the dog violently left and right repeatedly, and with a final growl tossed the dog thirty feet to the right. The dog let out a scream when bitten and rolled in the grass coming to rest against a tree. But the dog was not about to give up, and so, bleeding now from its wound, the dog decided to attack with abandon and ran full into the bear, who had turned his attention back toward Caroline. With its teeth exposed, the dog attacked, leaping midair into the bear and viciously bit deeply into the bear's nose. The bear twisted, and swatted the dog with his large paw and sent the dog flying into the grass, the bear's paw ripping a gash in the dog's side. The bear, with its nose bleeding profusely, attempted to stand but failed to do so then dropped to its four feet again and watched intently the dog, who was readying itself for the third attack. Quickly running at full speed with the knife firmly in hand, Caroline jumped on the back of the unsuspecting huge beast, and plunged the knife into its neck directly under its head then pulled back sharply. The bear recoiled, letting out a huge roar and rolled to its left, knocking Caroline off his back and onto the ground. The dog jumped forward and made a fourth run at the bear, but seeing the beast was bleeding, quickly pulled up ten feet away, raising its head to let out a noise that sounded much like a wolf. Both bear and dog knew they were injured and so they stood their ground roaring at each other, hoping the other would back down. But the dog, for some reason, felt an advantage. And that advantage was in this woman who had wounded the bear. The intensity of the bear's growls seemed to be building. Caroline sensed at any moment the battle would begin again and the 500-pound beast would prove victorious over the eighty-pound dog. She found herself twenty-five feet from this confrontation, but had lost the knife somewhere in the grass and started desperately searching for the only weapon she had. She kept her eyes on the battle and pushed weeds aside to her left and right. She glanced several times over at the two combatants. The bear's growling was increasing. In desperation, Caroline returned to the search. The knife was not to be found. She turned full circle and bent low toward the grass as if that might help find the knife. But it was of scant use. She glanced again as the snorting bear and the growling dog moved closer to each other. Caroline realized at any next moment the bear would attack and kill the dog. She moved to her bedroll and haversack, and there, resting beside those two things, was the glass quart Mason jar half filled with water. She stepped forward and grabbed the glass jar, raising it over her head and smashed it hard down on the only rock

147

within her sight. The jar exploded into three large jagged glass pieces. She pushed the broken glass apart and found the largest piece. This shard was only about seven inches long, but it did have an extended sharp and narrow point. She grabbed the glass in her hand. This thought raced through her head like a lightning strike. "I have only one shot at this. Eye! I must aim for the eye. I have no other chance." The dog started moving forward and bared his teeth to the bear again. The 500-pound black creature snarled and kept his eyes fixed on the eighty-pound dog. Caroline started her run, but like the bear who attacked from an arc she appeared to be running away and when she was fully behind the bear and running at full speed, she turned and charged from the rear. At the last moment, she raised her arm high with the broken glass shard firmly in her right hand and with her left hand, she grabbed the bear's left ear and pulled back hard, plunging down the glass shard into the bear's right eye. The bear twisted and turned to its right, swinging violently with its left paw ,striking Caroline and sending her flying sideways into a tree, knocking the air from her lungs. She gasped for air, but had flown twenty feet away and watched in horror as the bear stood on its hind feet and let out a scream of pain echoing off the valley around her. The bear came back down on all fours and focused not at the dog but turned its head toward Caroline. It raised its head back to the sky and roared out a second time in anger. Caroline thought the bear was about to attack her and so she got to her feet, but the bear shook its head and let out a high pitched whine of pain, which contained no roar of anger but now a cry of pure distress. Caroline could see the glass shard covered with blood still stuck in the bear's eye. The animal was bleeding profusely from three wounds. His neck, nose, and his eye all were covered with blood. Raising its paw to wipe away the biting obstacle, the creature's crude action only caused more pain as the glass shard plunged further into its eye. Now half blind, the bear realized he had two enemies. The dog and this human who possessed the power of sharp, blinding pain. The bear growled another roar then violently shook its head. The blood-soaked beast stood a last time, and Caroline could see the blood had blinded the bear now in both eyes. He turned and ambled away, shaking his head from side to side, as if this would restore his sight and cause the pain to subside. Caroline stood watching the bleeding bear and realized it could return at any moment. She, for the first time, felt pain on her side and understood that she was bleeding low across her stomach. Her hand that squeezed so tightly the glass shard was also bleeding. Taking her eyes off the disappearing bear, she looked and saw her shirt was covered with blood. She pulled up her shirt to inspect the wound and saw a four-inch gash an inch deep. She placed her hand across the wound and walked to the dog. The animal lay on its side and started to lick its wound. When Caroline approached, the dog laid its head down and panted. Caroline raised her hand, petting the dog's head. "There, there, boy, you did good. You did the best part. You did it. You kept him occupied. You did. You knew what to do. You saved my life. Let me get some nettle leaves for you. Let me get you fixed first. You took the worst of it. I'll be back. I need to find a patch of nettle." Caroline got to her feet and limped down to the side of the road. There on the other side of this wagon trail among the milk thistle, burdock, and yarrow she found the herb she was looking for. Caroline gathered several tall stalks, and slowly and painfully climbed back up the hill. The dog stirred as she approached. "Here's what I am going to do, I will chew this and make a poultice and place it on your wounds. It may sting a little, but it will stop the bleeding and that's what we have to do." Caroline found three long cuts on the side of the dog's ribs. She chewed the nettle until it was softened and she rolled three long lines of nettle and laid them gently on the claw wounds and held them in place for a moment. The dog lay quiet, as if he knew this was for the best, even though her pushing against the cuts caused serious pain. The dog tried to wag his tail, but did not have the energy to do so. He laid his head down and closed his eyes.

Caroline chewed the remaining nettle and lifted her bloody shirt and placed the poultice on her wounds. "There now, we will stop the bleeding. I will move my bedroll up here and we will take the next day off to heal. This will set us back a day, but I should think we will be better off in the long run. Don't stir, as I will return."

Caroline moved her bedroll up near the dog and decided both she and the dog deserved the rest after expending so much energy fighting the bear. She searched and found her knife fifteen feet away in the tall brush and was relieved to have it back. Ripping part of her shirt, she bandaged her cut hand. Both she and the dog, covered with blood and in pain, slept the afternoon, the evening, and all night.

Twenty hours later, Caroline woke at eleven in the morning. She cautiously stood for the first time since the bear fight, and felt the pain of the slashing cuts and the pain of bruised ribs. She had a conversation with the dog, explaining that she had to travel on and if the dog wanted to stay and heal that would be okay with her, as she knew the dog took the brunt of the bear attack. As Caroline rolled up her bedroll and slung it over her shoulder, the dog stood cautiously and took some steps. She looked one last time at the dog and started walking down the hill and out of the tree line. When she reached the road, she turned to see the dog slowly walking behind her. Glancing up into the sky, Caroline noticed the sky south of her, where buzzards lazily circled over a valley three miles away. What she did not know was three wolves and a pack of seven coyotes were waiting and watching a wounded and dying bear as it slowly bled out, wallowing in the muddy ground, unable to raise its head, unable to show its sovereignty any longer.

The dog and Caroline walked in pain and in silence during the morning and afternoon. There was only one wagon that passed them, and the man and woman just waved as they quickly passed by heading west. The wagon, being pulled by a team of black mules, disappeared in moments, and Caroline could hear the wheels and the sound of hoof beats for minutes as it disappeared. "Well, here we are walking in broad daylight; it certainly is a change for us, huh? Those people did not even want to stop and talk. Maybe they are running from something bad, or maybe they saw all this blood on my shirt and think I am a bad man who is out to steal and kill. I cannot blame them. You and I are both covered in dried blood. But I do believe the poultices have helped me. If I had a needle and thread, I would sew myself back closed, but so far the bleeding has slowed and maybe when we get to Leitchfield, then I may find someone to sew a few stitches." Caroline slowed for a moment and turned to the dog that was now walking step by step beside her. "Oh, yes. Dog, I have finally found a name for you. You may not like it, but I think it is perfect since you fought a bear. Therefore, I am going to call you 'Bear,' because you inherited his name, by beating him. What's more, he is most probably dead and can no longer use it. So, Bear, I do believe we make a good fighting team. Caroline and Bear, which is who we are."

No more was said that late afternoon, as she realized it was painful to talk as it required more breath, and her bruised ribs and cuts were painful. At three fingers from sundown, they came to a wide stream and Caroline removed her shoes and waded into the water, walking upstream a hundred yards. There in the pebbled bottom, she spotted several catfish hiding along the banks; one was wiggling and digging into the earth with his head pointed inward into the muddy bank. Bear quietly walked the bank behind her. Caroline slowly reached under the water and felt the tail of the twelve-inch catfish and she slowly placed her hand around the fish and pulled it out, tossing it on the bank in front of Bear. The dog put his foot on the wiggling fish and held it down. Caroline returned to her hunting, finding an even larger one and pulled it out, tossing it on the bank. "Go ahead, Bear, you can have that one, and this one is mine." Caroline stepped out of the water, then took her knife and cut open the flopping fish. She cut off his head and bit into the cold flesh. "I should like some watercress to go with this, but there is none in this stream. I have read the Japanese eat most all their fish raw. So, I will pretend I am Japanese. You, Bear, do not have to pretend, since you eat most of all your food raw. The texture is odd, but a little akin to a plum, and so that is what I will think of with each bite."

After finishing her catfish, she waded back into the steam and found a third smaller catfish. She tossed that one to the dog and he ate it quickly in six bites. While Caroline stood in the middle of the stream a hundred feet from the road, a lone rider in a torn blue uniform rode by. He carried no gun and wore no hat. His eyes only fixed on the road ahead. He was riding toward Leitchfield, and Caroline thought maybe he was a messenger or maybe he was just lost. Nonetheless, when he rode by, she ducked low while standing in the middle of the stream.

Back on the road, nothing more was said about catfish or the Japanese, or even Bear's new name. The pace was slowed quite a bit by the pain in her ribs and the gash from the bear. The dog at times trailed behind her by a hundred to two hundred feet. Occasionally, she stopped and rested herself, waiting for the dog to catch up. She noticed he limped at all times, favoring his right foot over the left. He held his head low and rarely looked up. At other times, he stopped altogether and lay down in the road, only offering a slight bark to alert Caroline he was stopping. Two hours of this slow going and she came to a split in the road. The more traveled road bore a five-foot-high post with an arrow and lettering that read, "Leitchfield 5." The lesser road had a sign that read

"Roundhill 21." She chose the more traveled road to Leitchfield.

It took two hours to reach Leitchfield. The sun was reluctant to leave that autumn afternoon and appeared to hold the sky hostage, but imposing gravity won, pulling it down surrendering quietly to a mountain range that lived in the west. She found a small town with twenty-five houses all in one long straight row. They appeared to have been built in one afternoon. The orange colored clouds had turned the houses the shade of sunflowers. A single unpainted new store bore a sign that read "Hyatt's General Dry Goods and Feed Store," and it sat on a double lot boasting a wide-planked porch. But Caroline, now favoring her right leg, stopped at the first house she came to and knocked on the door. An older man opened the door and looked first at her shoes then the rest. When she spoke, he realized it was a woman before him and invited her inside the house. The dog sat on the porch and soon fell asleep under a chair. The man introduced himself as Martin J. Doylesman and his wife, Emma. Caroline explained she had been attacked by a bear and had some wounds. She asked Missus Doylesman if she had needle and thread. Missus Doylesman went into the kitchen and returned with a thick button-hole thread and a large-eye needle. Missus Doylesman assured Caroline she had done this many times to her husband and proceeded to lift Caroline's shirt to examine the two wounds, both about four inches long. Missus Doylesman pointed to a kitchen table visible from where they were standing. "Let's go to the kitchen table, as there is better light." Caroline sat down nearest the window and told Missus Doylesman to proceed, then watched as Missus Doylesman dabbed iodine over the two wounds. Caroline tried not to flinch as ten stitches were completed in the first smaller wound. They took a short pause as Missus Doylesman came out with a small amount of whiskey poured in a coffee cup. "I should of thought of this before; this may help with the pain." Caroline drank the whiskey and made a face. "I don't like the taste, but if it helps the pain, so it will be." The second wound required thirteen stitches, as it was longer and deeper. Mister Doyleton stood by the kitchen door with his back to the proceedings as Caroline was partially unclothed, but he turned his head halfway in her direction. "I never heard of a woman fighting a bear. I have heard of early trappers, and some were killed, but to actually, with a kitchen knife and a piece of Mason jar, kill a bear, I should have thought that was near impossible. I will tell this story for years to come, and many men will not believe me, but I have seen your wounds and can tell they are from a bear, as no animal has claws wide like that." Mister Doyleton turned his head toward the front porch. "I will remember your story word for word. Your dog out there on the porch bears testament as to your bear story." Missus Doyleton interrupted, "Bears around here can get 600 to 800 pounds. When it stood, how tall did it stand? And after you lost your knife, what caused you to think of the glass Mason jar? And most of all, what made you think to stab it in the eye?" Caroline just smiled and shook her head. "I have no answers. I did what had to be done." Missus Doyleton stood and poured a little more whiskey into the coffee cup. "You know, Missus Duncan, you did not think of these things yourself. Someone gave you the answers, just like He did David. God was there and if not Him, then angels." Caroline took a deep breath, "The angel God sent was a dog, which I have named Bear, for he fought a bear and helped kill one. He has inherited the name Bear." Missus Doyleton moved to the larder. "I have four pork chops here, and your dog will get one of those tonight." Missus Doyleton stood and went to the kitchen and walked back with a tin pie plate and a single pork chop. She opened the door and placed it before the dog, then watched the dog attempt to stand. Leaning against the doorway, she observed the dog for a moment. "He don't look too good. He can barely stand, and he might not make it." She closed the screen door and walked back to the kitchen, then sat at the kitchen table with Caroline. "You might want to spend a couple of days here. You can sleep in the attic. We have a new feather tic mattress up there and some blankets. You need to rest and get well. I still have some older dresses. When I was younger and thinner, they fit me. You are welcomed to any one you want—your bloodied shirt I will take and burn." Missus Doyleton touched Caroline's hand. "Dear, you have been though a lot. Stay with us a while. Until you feel like moving on."

Caroline sensed the Doyletons had kind hearts, and explained the rest of her story about her husband being wounded and in a hospital tent in Shelbyville. Missus Doyleton said she understood. She said she took no sides in the war, but a wife possessed an instinctive need born deeply inside to protect her family at all cost. No more was said about the war. Caroline said she was very tired and wanted to sleep.

Missus Doyleton went to the kitchen, brought out a bowl with a large helping of berry cobbler and placed it in Caroline's hands. "You need to build up your strength." After finishing, Caroline went up the stairs into the attic and took off her shirt and pants and fell asleep in her underclothes, still stained with dried blood. Outside on the porch, the dog rested his head on his folded paws and took shallow breaths to keep his pain at bay.

Caroline had many dreams that night. None were about the bear, but all were about her children. In one, she was trying to get her daughter out of a tight place in a small black cave. Caroline pulled and pulled until her arms were exhausted, yet her daughter continued to cry out for help. In another dream, her eldest son, Isaac, was caught trapped in a barn which was on fire from an overturned lantern, and while she pulled unsuccessfully on the locked door, she could hear her son cry out in the flames. The most frightening dream was that she was alive in a pine coffin, paralyzed and could not speak. She tried to move her hand, but only three fingers would move, and no one saw it. Lying there in the coffin, she saw the lid placed on top and she heard the nails being driven in the coffin's lid. She heard her husband's voice praying, then dirt being shoveled onto the lid. She awoke screaming her husband's name as Missus Doyleton, in her night clothes, raced up the stairs and took her by her shoulders. "Missus Duncan, wake up! Wake up. You were having a dream. That, whatever it was, weren't nothing but a dream. You are safe here." Caroline slowly sat up in bed and hugged Missus

Doyleton for comfort. "I'm sorry. I have not slept well in days. I am so tired."

Caroline slept for the next twelve hours straight and awoke to the sound of children playing out in the street. She arose and found a selection of clothing on a chair near the door. She discarded her bloodied undergarments and found new ones. Selecting a green homespun dress, she came down the stairs, carrying her bloodied pants. "If I could borrow some soap, I wish to wash these."

Missus Doyleton pointed to the high-back chair. "I'll take care of that; you sit there and I will make a platter of eggs and pork chops for your breakfast. Well, the good news is your dog looks better than he did yesterday. He's been walking around this morning. He limps, but that does not stop him. I saw him down at the creek eating something. Probably a rabbit. We got hundreds of 'em. All colors, all sizes. I want you to rest this afternoon, dear. I just made beef vegetable soup and some sourdoughs. I collected some honey this morning, and it goes good on those biscuits. That will be dinner. I see you found the clothes I laid out. I think I will look at your stitches after breakfast. I want you to spend a few days with me resting up." Caroline smiled politely, knowing she would not waste any more time. She realized within minutes of getting out of bed that she had lost time and she needed to be on her way. But said nothing to Missus Doyleton about it.

After eating, Caroline thanked the woman repeatedly and said she must travel on to Elizabethtown. "You have been very kind, but this wound is not as bad as what my husband has experienced. Therefore, he, not me, is my priority." Missus Doyleton decided not to argue, saying the stitches looked good and applied Cloverine salve to the wound. Finally, she took a damp wash cloth and washed some blood out of Caroline's hair. Two hours later, Caroline walked out on the front porch and reached down and patted the dog's head. "You ready, Bear?" Caroline picked up her bedroll and haversack from the front porch. She reached out to shake Missus Doyleton's hand, but instead the woman kissed Caroline on the cheek. Walking down the stairs, Caroline saw Mister Doyleton waiting for her in front of the house. He stood with a walking stick in his hand. "I made this only this morning for you. It will help with the walking. And I honed your knife and made a leather scabbard for it. It is razor sharp now." Caroline thanked Mister Doyleton and placed the knife and its scabbard in her waistband. She turned and started off, with Bear slowly following her. Walking past several whitewashed homes, she heard someone call out to her. Caroline turned and saw Missus Doyleton was walking briskly toward her. At that point, the woman shouted, "Wait!" and hurriedly ran toward Caroline, stopping a foot away. "Yesterday, I didn't know you, and now today here we are new friends. I never had a daughter, wanted one but she never came. So now, I know what it feels like saying goodbye to a daughter, who I may never see again." Missus Doyleton raised one hand to her face and Caroline could see her eyes were filling in tears. She gently placed a folded peach colored handkerchief into Caroline's hand. "This was my mother's. She gave it to me for luck and I think it will bring you the same." Missus Doyleton kissed Caroline one last time on the cheek and stood there for a moment, and then turned and walked back toward her house.

Walking that morning was unusual, as it was daylight and the sun burned through the gathering of clouds, making it warmer than expected for Caroline. Within the first mile, she realized her loss of blood had weakened her stamina. As Bear walked behind her, she glanced over her shoulder. "Bear, you are doing good, considering you were about to killed by that bear. But so far, we're doing good. We're doing what has to be done. Aren't we?" Caroline felt dizzy and stopped for a moment; she moved her feet several times, trying to find balance and finding none, she fell to one knee. She took several deep breaths. Bear walked up from behind and licked her cheek. Caroline smiled and pushed on the new walking stick and stood. "If you can do this, Bear, then I can also." The two walked on, with the dog no longer following, but walking beside her.

As the day wore on, the pace slowed as each step produced a pain in her side. She noticed Bear was increasingly favoring his right leg and at times fell back a hundred feet, and so Caroline stopped to allow Bear to catch up. About seven that evening, Caroline realized her energy had waned markedly and so she stopped for a prolonged rest. She took off her right shoe and added some plantain to the back of the shoe near the heel where it rubbed against the blister. She sat near a stream with one shoe off, and dipped her right foot into the cooling water. Reaching into her bag, she pulled out a small bundle wrapped in a piece of paper. It contained a sourdough biscuit with a piece of honeycomb and a smoked piece of pork chop, all wrapped tightly with a piece of sting holding it together. It was a gift from the woman who stood on the road and cried when she left. She offered half the pork chop to Bear, but he walked away into the trees. As she ate, she listened but heard nothing except the evening birds. Bear was nowhere to be seen or heard. After she finished, she stood and inspected her stitches; once satisfied, she looked for the dog and spotted Bear about 200 feet upstream. He was searching and then plunged his head down into the tall weeds. In his mouth was a small mouse. Caroline reached into the haversack and pulled out the man's pants, still slightly damp, and pulled them on. She pushed the green dress inside the pants and put on her vest. Placing her hand back into the haversack, she found the handkerchief and smelled its perfumed lavender sachet. Caroline put the handkerchief in her dress shirt pocket close to her face. Now she stood and pulled her hat over her head. "There, I look more like my new identity. Gathering her bedroll and bag, she stood and whistled once. The dog jerked its head up and with great effort came running—his limp still quite apparent.

At about eleven that night, a light rain started to fall. There was no thunder. There was no lightning. She had only traveled seven miles in the last four hours. Even though it was raining, she decided she had to walk all night. "Bear, we must push on tonight as we are moving much slower. I know I hurt and I know you hurt. I hope I can make it to sunup. We can rest late tomorrow." At about midnight, the rain stopped, and she noticed the pace was even slower and it took more energy to walk the wet slippery hills. She was glad she had a walking stick to help push her forward. In the moonlight, she could discern several small mountains ahead and the walking stick would be very useful there. Nonetheless, she stopped at one point, finding the frequent little stops helped gather her strength. At about three in the morning, with fireflies flashing not around her but about a mile ahead, she had to stop, sit, and catch her breath for a while. Bear also sat beside her and searched the area with his canine hearing, moving his head right and left, listening to the night's sounds. Caroline noticed the pain in her side was still the same with no improvement. "I think when we get to the top of that mountain, we can call it a day. That should be about six in the morning. We'll find water and drink before we climb. I wish I had asked for a quart jar at Missus Doyleton's home. I am so thirsty. I am forgetting so much now. I think I may be getting delirious from all this pushing. Nonetheless, I must have perseverance, or I will fail at what I need to do."

At the base of the large mountain, Caroline found a signpost that read, "Duvall's Gap," with an arrow pointing ahead. There, Caroline discovered the water she had expected. Both she and the dog drank, and then started the trek up the dark mountain road that turned and twisted like the many streams she had crossed. Ten times the road changed its mind and headed in the opposite direction, but with each reverse course it climbed higher and higher. Caroline's legs were aching at each turn, but the walking stick helped to push her forward. She removed her hat to cool herself, and only slowed for that moment, then pushed on in the darkness. The blackness was so stark she could only tell she was on the dirt road by the manner her right foot struck the grass growing along the roadside, and so she redirected herself toward the center until her left foot struck grass on the other side. After two hours, when they made it to the top, she noticed three stones stacked on top of each other standing near a post that read, "Duvall 1723" She looked over the valley, and with the moon on this side of the mountain, she could see several buildings at the base of the hill. Bear followed her by one hundred yards, but did not make a sound. She could barely hear his steps behind her.

"Don't take another step, mister." The man stepped out from behind a tree and stepped onto the road behind her. The moonlight revealed to Caroline a man about forty-five years old. He had a pistol pointed at her. The man was about fifty feet away and slowly walked forward. He looked to be well above six feet tall with a torn hat, and he wore a pair of boots with no heels. His hat was pulled down over his ears with a red bandanna tied over the top and under his beard holding the hat in place. His black suspenders were tied under and around a raw leather belt holding his pants up. Caroline glanced at the man and could see Bear was slowly approaching the man with his tail tucked down between his legs, and the hair on his back was bushed in a straight line, ready for an attack. At a distance of thirty-five feet, and seeing a pistol pointed at Caroline, the dog lunged forward, growling as he did with the bear. With the speed of a ferret, the man turned and fired a single shot at the dog. The noise was extremely loud, and the explosion filled the air with intense white smoke. It happened so fast that Caroline did not have time to take her eyes off the man. She heard a cry of pain from the dog; what followed was a long continuous yelping as the dog disappeared into the woods. There were two painful cries, a whimper, and then a sudden silence. The noise of his gunshot continued to scream a high pitched ring in her ears. The man turned back to Caroline. "Caught ya! Don't move a horse hair. Not one. Yep, you are what I have been waiting for. Worth a pretty penny. Yep, there is a price on your head! I heard there was spies—women dressed as men and some say men dressed like women. All clever spies. Mostly Confederate spies. You just stand still." Caroline shifted her weight to the right foot. "I am no spy. I am on my way to Shelbyville..." The man moved to about six feet away, then raised his hand over his head, ready to strike. "Shut up! You are a lying damn CSA whore spy. Trading sex for secrets. And Yankees have a reward—a twenty-dollar gold piece. You start walking." Caroline did not move. "Sir, I cannot be a spy, nor even a messager. You can search my bag. I am on my way to help my wounded husband. I need to go to him. I am from Hopkinsville ninety miles back."

"Women are the best liars. So, you shut up and I'll do the talking. Start walking, I said. No more damn words or I'll knock you in your lying mouth." At that close range, Caroline could smell the man had been drinking. Still, he did not appear to be drunk, only angry. She glanced at him again and saw his pants had been patched repeatedly. His jacket was too short for his long arms, but he had tied a leather strap about the waist, holding the coat closed.

There was silence for the next thirty minutes as they walked down the switchbacks on the east side of the mountain. Now and again, Caroline would glance over her shoulder for the dog. But the dog was not there. As the sun was about to come up, the two of them approached a rundown crude log cabin set back from the road 2,000 feet. The cabin appeared to be sinking into the earth at one corner. Flagstones stacked four high held the cabin a foot off the ground at the other three corners. One planked door stood closed, and two windows were made blind with flour sacks covering the glass. Three small shacks stood further back from the cabin near the tree line. "This here is my place; keep walking—we are going to the first shed in the back. Caroline examined the single-room cabin as she walked to the shed in the back. The man's hand pushed hard on her shoulder. "Go on, get in there." Caroline walked through the half opened door, and observed a darkened small shed which could hold a single cow or single horse at the most. Its roof was flat and was barely six feet high. The man bent his head low to clear the rafters. There were empty crates on the dirt floor and two wooden spoke wheels from a wagon, but no wagon. In the corner was a small pile of men's shoes, dusty and dirty, tossed in no order. There was a single pair of women's lace-up shoes on top. Two twelve-inch oak posts, still with their bark, held the roof in place. Bolted to the wood posts, thick and rusted iron rings stood ready to hold tight an animal. Or a human being. The man kicked the wood crate against the wall then pointed at it. "You sit here." Caroline sat slowly down on the crate. "Sir, you are making a mistake. I am..." The man raised his hand over her head.

"Shut up, you lying whore. We will see you tell the truth in a day or so when the Union Army men come by."

The man pushed her down onto the crate, then pulled her arms behind her. Grabbing a long leather strap hanging on a nail, he tied her hands tightly behind her. Then he took a second strap of the same length and tied her elbows together. "I ain't giving you no food or water. That shall loosen your tongue. And what's your name anyway, I know it's gonna be a lie."

"I am Caroline from Hopkinsville; I've been walking five days now to get to my husband who has been wounded and is somewhere in Shelbyville. I am originally from Louisville and my father is the pastor of the Fairbrook Methodist Church there. I have three children who I left at home for this journey. I know nothing about the war or the plans or anything."

The man laughed then spit on the ground. "Good lies. Real good lies. But because you were dressed like a man makes me questionious. How I know? I heard over in Wickersville a week ago. It was a woman spy dressed like a man and that fits you like a suit. Hell, I set a trap at the top of that rocky top. I've been hiding out there like a nigger for three days now, waiting. I knew if there was a CSA woman spy in these parts she'd stay off the main roads and be sneaking up and over Duvall's Gap—walking by herself. Looky, spooky, looky, I was right. Twenty-dollar gold piece. That's a month's pay if you want to work for it. Anyhow, you ain't goin' no place. I'll see to that." The gruff man took down another leather strap and wrapped it three times around to her ankles and to the five-inch iron ring on the oak post nearest her. He grunted and groaned as he pulled it tight. "My daddy taught me that knot. The Garland knot." The man took another leather strap off a hook and tied it around Caroline's knees. "My daddy called this the four-way bind. No man ever escaped it." The man stood, brushing the roof of this shack with his head. Walking toward the door, he spit once, and then stepped outside. He paused and pushed his head back inside the shack. "Now, you rest there, my little spy. I am goin' in and get some sleep. I will send my daughter-wife to check on you. You be nice to her. Her name is Jezebel."

"Is she your daughter or your wife?"

"Hell, makes no difference to me. One is the same. One is the same." The man turned and walked out of the shed. Caroline sat there, her hands tied twice behind her, and her ankles and knees tied to the post. At first, she struggled to free her hands, but the man had tied them extremely tight. Caroline tried a second time, but slipping the leather straps off her wrist only proved to tighten them. Caroline was tired, truly exhausted from the night's walk and so attempted to lean against the wall and think. She had no plan. Yes, her knife was still hidden under her waist band, but it was no use. She closed her eyes to think of any escape, yet nothing came to mind. After a few moments, exhaustion and weakness from her bear wound took control and she could not fight sleep any longer. She woke several times and looked around the shed. Nothing had changed, and so she closed her eyes to think, but fell into a shallow restless sleep.

"You really a real spy?" A young woman stood in the doorway, yet not coming in. Caroline looked up and saw a seventeen-year-old girl standing before her in a homespun and well-worn linen dress with an assortment of mixed colored buttons holding the front closed. She wore no shoes. Her hair was bright red and tied in the back with two yellow ribbons. On her right hand, each finger was wrapped with a dandelion flower tied with its stem. Five bright yellow flowers in all. She held her left hand behind her. "My name is Joyellen. Not Joellen, no, but Joyellen. He said you were a good liar. Show me how you do that. I wish I could. Tell me a lie that doesn't sound like a lie. A real good one. Maybe a story that is hard to believe."

At that point, Caroline noticed the young woman had a knife in her left hand, which she held tightly by her side. Her arm stiff and her grip tight, pointing down. "I am not a Confederate spy. I admit I support the Confederacy because my husband is an officer in the army. The South."

"No! That is not a good lie! A good lie is like him, who tells everyone I am his daughter. I am not his daughter. He never had a daughter. Never had a son. Least while one that lived. His wife died trying to have one. So he went up to Elizabethtown, and kidnapped me while I was picking black berries. I was but thirteen and a half. He brought me here and made me cook and clean and mind him. Then he made me his wife."

"So, you are not his daughter?"

"But he tells passersby I am. I've been pregnant twice but the babies died. Now he tells the men he brings here I am his whore. Yeah, he is a good liar. I watch him lie, and he does not flinch. When I lie, I most always blink, and my hands sweat. I'm not good at it like he is."

"So, you were intimate with him from the start?"

"What do you mean into mint?"

"Sex. I am talking about having sex."

"You mean fornication? Then, yes. He made me take off my clothes and get in bed. It started the day after he brought me here. And I'm not allowed to say his name. His name is Ezekiel, but I can only call him 'sir' and that's all." There was a long pause and the girl looked to the ground. "Yes, he does that. Into mint. He fornicates me.

Caroline twisted against the straps. "Have you ever told anyone this?'

The young woman now stepped inside the shed and walked near Caroline, the knife still tight in her hand. She whispered, "No, I am not allowed to talk to anyone who passes by. If I see 'em coming, I have to run and hide in the cabin. He keeps me inside, so I haven't been off this homestead for four years—since I came here. I know I'm now seventeen years old; my birthday is in June. June twenty-one. My name is Joyellen Hollister. But he calls me Jezebel."

"Why don't you run away? Run away when he leaves."

"Oh, he'd track me down and whip me real bad. I did once the first year, but he tracked me down and whipped my backside with a leather strap. I bled. He said if I tried it again, he'd go to Elizabethtown and murder my mama and daddy and my little brother. That's exactly what he said, and I believe him. I saw him kill a man right here in this shed two months ago. He invited him in off the road for supper and robbed him. Tied him like you are and strangled him with his bare hands. He took his money and he carried him up in the woods and left him. It's his woods, so I walked up there two weeks later and there these bones scattered everywhere. I counted. There are bones of nine people up there. There is a small one. I think she was a woman. This belt I am wearing, I found up there. There's their shoes in that pile. He tells everyone we are hunters and farmers, but we only have chickens and two goats. This ain't no farm. This is a trap."

Caroline nodded her head toward the door. "Listen, if you untie me, we could get away."

"Oh, no! He'd track both of us down, and he is good at tracking. I was hoping someone stronger would kill him. Like when he is trying to rob a bigger man. Some man would cut him real bad. He never robs Negroes. He says they ain't got nothing to steal. Lucky them. Besides, they would fight him."

"We could do that."

"You mean we could cut him real bad? He's strong."

"But we could do it."

"That would be murder. I can't be no murderer."

"David killed Goliath. You know that?"

Joyellen thought for a moment. "Yes. I remember from Sunday school. David killed Goliath with a sling shot."

"Then David cut off his head with a sword."

"I forgot that part. The sword."

"Listen, Joyellen, you untie me and we will go into the house and while he sleeps, with a rock we will knock him out just like David."

"You would have to do it. I would be ascared."

"I think together you and I can do this. Will you help me?"

"But if we don't kill him dead, he would come after us."

"Leave that to me. So, untie me now." Caroline nodded over her shoulder to the leather straps around her wrist and elbows.

"What are you going to do, cut off his head?"

"You do not have to see. But are you sure he killed other men?"

"Yes, I saw one right here in this shed. Tied to that pole and choked to death. A young man with a carpet bag and real nice boots."

Caroline leaned forward and locked eyes with the seventeen-year-old girl. "Then untie me right now and let's do this now, let's not wait. He could kill me. You would not want that, would you, Joyellen?"

Joyellen took a step forward. "No! No! You are a nice person."

"Then untie me."

"I want to, but I am afraid. He is powerfully mean."

"Joyellen! When he finds out I am not a spy, he may kill me in a rage!"

There was a silence in the small shed, and Joyellen started breathing fast and pacing back and forth. "No. No. No. He's so strong it would be impossible. It would be a never be."

"I will do it."

"You're just a woman and he is a big man. He is frightfully strong."

"But when he sleeps, he is not a big man, is he?"

"Well, seems it's got to be a hard thing. And if you don't kill him, he'll go to Elizabethtown and kill my mama and my daddy and my little brother."

"He might do it anyway to teach you a lesson."

"No. He promised if I didn't run way he wouldn't."

"Yes, but you said he was a good liar."

"Oh, he is."

"So, how do you know he is telling the truth?"

"I don't, but...but wait, let me think."

"But if we take care of him, he can't."

"I don't want to take care of him. I wish him dead."

"That says it perfectly, Joyellen. He may kill ten or twenty more men and women too. You want that to happen? Do you want to see that?"

"No! But this is too much to understand. Why did you have to come here?"

"I came to help you."

"You did?"

"I came to free you."

"That's different then. I never thought of that. You came to free me?"

"To take you home."

"Home?"

"Yes."

"We could go home?"

"Yes, Joyellen, I can take you home."

"Promise?"

"Yes, I promise."

"Then, okay, I will untie you. But I don't want to do it. To kill him. So, I just untie you and that's all I have to do?"

"That's all I am asking."

Joyellen took three steps forward and to Caroline's back. "Okay, but it is your idea and not mine." The young girl reached down and started to untie Caroline. Then she stopped. "No, this ain't right. He will whip me real bad if he finds out I untied you."

"He'll never find out. Satan is on his side, but God is helping us."

"I forgot about God. Yes. God and Jesus and angels. Then I will do this."

The young girl, with scars on her arms from leather strap beatings, moved to the back of Caroline.

"He ties everything tight."

"Please, quickly. Be quick!" Caroline felt the young girl's hands on the leather straps.

"There, that's one done. And now these second others. He ties 'em really strong." The young girl fumbled for a moment and grunted but finished and then stepped in front of Caroline.

Caroline pulled her hands around her front and rubbed her wrists quickly, and then reached down to the leather straps around her knees and ankles. The knots were tight and so it took several tries before the straps fell lose. Once done, Caroline stood and felt dizzy for a moment. She steadied herself by holding on to Joyellen's shoulder. "See that hammer over there? That is what we use."

Joyellen turned and looked at it. "No, you said a rock or a stone like David. You got to use a stone."

"Okay, then, we will use a stone."

Joyellen walked to the door. "Out by the well, there is a whole big pile of stones."

"Okay. Good. Before we leave this shed, let me take off my shoes. We need to be quiet."

"Caroline, he sleeps light. He hears everything."

"He won't hear me."

Caroline took off her shoes and then stepped outside the shed and spotted the pile of large stones at the well site. She slowly walked there, glancing back at the open door of the cabin. Taking a stone in both hands, she bounced it back and forth, judging its weight. It was the size of a large man's big fist. She handed that one to Joyellen, and then bent over and took a larger one for herself. She whispered, "If I miss on the first strike, or if he turns on me, you will have to help me. Do not run away, but you run at him. When you do, I will hit him from the back." The young girl nodded as Caroline held her finger to her lips. "From now on, Joyellen, we do not say a single word. We cannot make a noise. Show me where he sleeps."

The young, red-haired girl with the yellow ribbons hanging down her back and dandelions on her fingers pointed to follow her. In twenty quiet steps through the morning's wet grass, the two of them, walking barefoot, approached the cabin. Caroline reached out and stopped Joyellen, then walked past her. She was the first to step on the porch. She heard a slight squeak, but the second step produced no sound. The door was partially opened, and so she pushed it just enough to slip inside the cabin. This caused another squeak. She stopped suddenly in the dimly lit room. Standing there silently just inside the cabin, she observed a shape of a man sleeping on the bed, covered only with the dark shadows of the darkened room. Caroline locked her eyes upon him. He was fully dressed and sleeping face up on his back. He had removed his shoes and they lay scattered at the foot of the bed. His jacket was tossed on a chair. Caroline lifted her heels off the floor then quietly walked on her toes to the bed. She paused and looked at where the man's head lay on the pillow. As her leg barely touched the edge of the bed, a mere two feet away from the sleeping man, without pause, in one quick motion she swung the rock high up over her head and quickly plunged it down with full force and onto the man's forehead. His eyes both sprung wide open and he looked up to Caroline. The man raised his head and started to sit up, reaching out with his hand toward Caroline, when she quickly swung the rock sideways hard against his right temple. The man fell backwards into the bed. Caroline raised the rock a third time and with both hands swung quickly against his right temple again. She was about to strike a fourth time, but the man lay motionless. Caroline could see the man was still breathing. It was shallow but quickening. Joyellen, who had been standing at the door rushed forward to the foot of the bed with a rock still in her hand held high over her head. "Is he dead? Is he dead?"

Caroline turned to Joyellen. "Joyellen, get out of the house. Now! Get out of the house." Joyellen looked at the motionless body, then dropped the rock and ran out. Caroline turned and pulled the knife from her waistband and, without pausing for a moment, she raised it high and plunged it quickly into the man's neck below the right ear and pulled forward. Instantaneously, blood pulsed out in rhythmic beats onto his collar. Caroline put her knee on the bed and reached over and grabbed the man's hair and turned his face toward her, and with a second quick movement, brought the knife across the left side of the neck. The man's heart was pumping blood at a rapid pace, and blood pulsed onto his left shoulder. For a moment, his right arm tried to feebly rise but fell back. Caroline stepped away from the bed and picked up the rock from her feet and stepped to the side of the bed. She raised the rock over her head with both hands, ready for whatever would come, but the man did not move. Silence descended upon the room. The only sounds she heard were her own breaths and a shallow, high-pitched moaning coming from the man lying before her. She did not move an inch, frozen there until his last breath escaped through his opened mouth. She noticed fingers on his right hand twitched for a long moment, then slowed, and finally locked tight as if holding onto something invisible. Maybe a gun, maybe a knife, maybe life itself.

Standing there, she watched a stream of crimson blood slowly flowing down from his neck and then behind his head and onto the pillow. His body, lifeless at the moment he was hit with the second stone strike, did not move. She took another step backward, keeping her eyes on his six-foot-four-inch body. "God, forgive me for what I have done. But he is a Goliath, and today I am David's daughter." Caroline turned and walked out onto the porch. She was surprised how quickly all of this killing had taken. A man alive one minute and in the third minute, dead. She stood there a moment and took a deep breath. The air felt fresh. Spotting Joyellen standing by the well with tears running down her cheeks and holding two rocks in her hands, Caroline raised her hand and waved to come forward. The young girl shouted out, "Is he dead? He is, ain't he? He is dead! Tell me he is dead. Tell me he is dead. He is dead, ain't he?"

Caroline nodded and shouted out, "Yes, he is dead."

"Damn you, Ezekiel, damn you! Damn every part of you. Damn your soul that tried to make me like you. I ain't that at all."

Caroline nodded and quietly spoke. "Yes, for the wrongs you have done, damn your soul, Ezekiel."

Joyellen continued to stand by the pile of rocks. "Well, I am me again. I ain't his wife. I ain't his daughter. I ain't his nothin'. This is right. This is real right. Oh, you don't know how long...he is dead, ain't he? Oh, God, is he dead? Tell me, Caroline! Tell me he is dead!

Caroline again nodded 'yes' and looked at the young girl for a moment standing there, shaking in fear, and holding the two rocks. She took her first step off the porch and walked to the girl. Reaching forward, she attempted to take the two rocks, but Joyellen held them tight. Caroline understood this fear and, instead, with her left hand touched the frightened girl's shoulder. Her right hand still held the bloodied knife gripped tight at her side. Joyellen was breathing fast and shaking, almost convulsing. Caroline looked the girl in the eyes. "Look at me, Joyellen. Yes, he is dead. You can go in now and see him. Let's both go in together and see him. I want you to look upon him dead. He lives no more. This whole God-forsaken thing is over. You have nothing to fear."

Caroline, realizing she had her bloodied knife in her hand, bent down and wiped it in the grass. The two of them walked cautiously across the grass and into the cabin, with the young girl still holding two rocks in her hands. Upon seeing the bloodied body, the girl stepped forward cautiously to the bed. She dropped the rocks on the bed and reaching down, she slowly lifted his arm, letting it fall back lifeless. She stood there staring at the man that had caused so much pain. Her face showed no emotion, but only amazement that this evil was dead. Joyellen looked to Caroline. "You said we could do it. You told me and it happened just like you said. I didn't think we could. I didn't think it was possible. But there he lies dead. I need to tell someone." Joyellen turned and walked back out onto the porch and, standing there, spoke quietly to the woods that surrounded the cabin. "I've seen him and he's dead. All you dead people up there on the hill. Ezekiel is dead. He ain't gonna kill no more. He ain't gonna kill my mama and my daddy 'cause he is dead. And I've seen it." Caroline walked out onto the porch and put her arm around the girl again. The captive girl turned with a surprised smile on her face. "At first, I thought this was a dream. But just like you said, Caroline. About David and Goliath. He is deader than I ever thought he could be. Lord, I hope he burns. I hope he burns in hell." The young woman stopped, turned, and quietly spoke. "You know, we could cut off his head."

Caroline took a step back. "I don't think that is what we should do. Why don't you gather your things? Anything you want and let us get out of this hellish place. Here, I will go back in with you."

The young girl went in and gathered a handful of clothes, and a small doll she made from thread-tied grass, sticks, and some yellow ribbon. She found a flour sack and filled it with hardtack, and salted pork. In the kitchen, Caroline spotted preserved food on a long shelf and took two quart jars of plums. "We will be walking for the next two days, so you find your shoes, if you have any, and if you know where he kept his money you get that too. It's all yours now."

The girl nodded and walked slowly to the death bed, where she knelt down; there, sitting under the bed and inches away from a pool of blood, was a tobacco tin. Joyellen slid out the small red box and then quickly opened it. The seventeen-year-old girl poured out its contents on the bed near the bare feet of the dead man. She gathered a handful of paper money, a silver pocket watch, and five single gold coins. She walked to a shelf and found a scarf. She put the money and the watch in the scarf and tied it tight, then put it into her sack. Caroline watched, and thought of a young, trapped bird being freed for the first time. "Joyellen, if you want we could burn this place down. With him in it. You want to do that?"

Joyellen turned. "No. Let's leave him for the animals. And I know they will come. There are wild pigs up there. They will come and drag him and eat at him till he is nothing but bones out into the yard. Maybe somebody else can see." Caroline nodded, turned, and walked out onto the porch, then to the shed where she found her bedroll and haversack. She took a single leather strap, once wrapped around her ankles, and wrapped it around her waist three times and then tied it. She sat on the dirt floor, not wanting to sit on that death crate again. She laced up her shoes and walked out of the shed but stopped to witness Joyellen standing out in the yard looking at the house intently. "I've changed my mind; let's burn it, let's burn every dirty thing he touched."

181

Caroline nodded silently and walked past the young girl and back into the cabin and looked one last time at the man still in bed, eyes opened and looking at the ceiling. His shirt now completely blood soaked. Crimson pooled around the man's body and soaked into the mattress. She found two coal oil lamps and poured their contents onto the mattress and the man himself. Seeing a shelf with books, she looked and located a Bible. Also on the same bookshelf inches away was the Colt 36 Navy revolver he had used to kill her dog. She took the revolver and placed it in her waist band. Caroline took the Bible and placed it on his blood-soaked chest. She called Joyellen to come in, and once inside the room, she nodded and handed the seventeen-year-old girl a kitchen sized box of matches. Joyellen walked over and spit on the man and then without a word, Joyellen lit a match and threw it on the bed. As the flames started to build, Joyellen stepped back. "Hey, Ezekiel, this is how hell is going to feel." She dumped the entire box of matches on the man, and then turned and walked out. Caroline stood there looking at what she had done. There was sadness in her face for the ugliness of it all. A killing. As she was about to walk out, she spied a box of cartridges and caps for the revolver and took the box. Smoke started to fill the room. Caroline took one last look at the man now burning. "Yes, Joyellen is right, you are destined for hell. Reap what you sow, Ezekiel. This is the whirlwind."

Ten minutes later, Caroline and the young girl were a quarter mile down the road heading east. Behind them, black smoke fueled with flames rose 900 feet into the sky, as fire engulfed the crude cabin and poured out through the two windows and open door. Caroline thought she heard a man scream from the cabin, but realized it was the sound of burning wood releasing its sap in the intense heat. In the hills, animals stood silent, listening to the roar of the flames and watching their sky turn black.

As they walked that midafternoon, the young girl talked excitedly without pause. "Excuse me if I am me too much, but I have not had anybody to talk to 'cause he said I had to be silent around him." She asked Caroline many questions she had quietly formed in her mind in the last four years. Caroline calmly and honestly answered each one, and the young girl nodded understanding. At other times, Joyellen smiled at the answer, as the answer was so obvious or so amusing. Thirty minutes later, after they had walked in silence, Caroline noticed Joyellen was crying, as tears dripped off her nose and ran to her chin. Mixed with the tears, Caroline sensed a fear that sent the young girl's body trembling. She stopped and took the young girl's right hand, still covered with yellow dandelion flowers. "Joyellen, listen to me. You are to forget about all of this. You were never married to him, even though he called you his wife. No. You were his prisoner and you do not have to tell anyone—anyone at all— what happened inside that cabin. You may want to tell your parents, but as you get older this will dim. Just think of this as a bad dream. Like a nightmare that ends when you wake up. And your new life starts today. The minute you walked away from that burning cabin. This will be your second birthday, and you have been freed. Do not think of yourself as soiled or dirty, for, dear, you are clean, fresh, and whole. It's a new you today."

The young girl nodded. "Should I ever tell my husband, should I get one? I mean should he know about me?"

"No, I would not. It is a secret. Not a bad secret. But a good and great secret. God sent me to help you, and God sent you into that shed to help me. Think of it that way. It's our secret—Caroline's and Joyellen's great secret. We should celebrate the secret. Yes. Hallelujah. God set us free. It is a good day and not a bad one. Caroline squeezed Joyellen's hand hard. Joyellen started crying again, but it was an emotion mixed with relief and joy, and yet the trauma was still there hiding. "I am so happy you came along, Caroline. I am so happy we did what we did. But I am not going to think about that anymore. No, not one minute's worth. I have been thinking about this now for the last hour. I never thought about it before, but I am gonna find me a young man and marry him proper and I am gonna name the firstborn after you. Caroline if it's a girl, and Carolina if it's a boy. That is how I will forget this."

Caroline nodded and smiled. "You do that and I would be honored." They walked on together side by side and silently for the next five miles. At one point, tears again started running down Joyellen's face, but she smiled through all of it. Another time, she stopped in the middle of the road and Caroline walked on but then she stopped and turned backward. Joyellen raised her arms over her head. "Thank you, God." Caroline turned back around and looked down the road and quietly said, "Yes, thank you, God. I thought you left me, but you were right there." A tear formed in her eye, but she wiped it away. As she was wiping the tears, she noticed dried blood on her right hand—the hand that held the knife. She tried to wipe it away but saw she could not. The hand that drove the knife was the same hand that drove the shard into the bear's eye. They were the same. "Please, God, no more."

As they walked, more homesteads appeared and were passed by. Many of the homesteads were located, not near the road but up in the hills and away from the streams and creeks which could flood in the spring and do damage to the home or the people who lived there. Many times Joyellen waved to a woman or man going about their daily chores. One woman who saw them ran into her home and then came running down the hill and carrying something in her hand waving it back and forth. The woman, who was out of breath when she reached the two on the road, explained she had written some letters that she wanted mailed but that the local post office, which was located in the town's only dry goods store five miles ahead, refused to send mail that was addressed to anyone in the Confederate Army. She asked the two if they were headed toward Elizabethtown, and if so, would they take these ten letters to the Seven Valleys Baptist Church and the Minister Reverend Herbert K. Manchester. She said it was known in these parts that the minister had no allegiance to any side and would see the letters reached the woman's two sons who wore CSA gray uniforms. The woman invited Caroline and Joyellen to stop and eat with her, but Caroline said she had to make up lost time and could not stop for dinner. The woman pointed to the side of the road. "Sit. Sit here, and rest for but a spell and I shall be back." The woman, who never said her name, ran back up to her house and in five minutes ran back down the hill and brought with her half an apple pie and a large slice of ham, all wrapped in a dish cloth. The woman said she would pray for Caroline and Joyellen. As the two walked away, Caroline could hear the woman singing a hymn. After a moment, when she turned around, the woman was still standing in the middle of the road and waving. Five minutes later, as the two of them rounded the crest of the hill, Caroline and Joyellen looked back once more and the woman was still there in the middle of the road swaying back and forth and waving. The connection this woman had just made with Caroline and Joyellen was the only connection this mother had to her sons. There was hope there.

At six in the afternoon, finding a small thicket, they stopped and ate some of the pie. Caroline, still feeling the effects of the bear attack, inspected the wound and noticed the swelling had increased. She examined the stitches, and saw that yellow pus was running out of the wounds. Her bruised ribs were painful, especially when she trudged up steep hills and was forced to inhale deeply. Searching one hundred feet up the road, Caroline found some milkweed and applied the white sap from the stem to the stitches, hoping that would have some effect on the pain. Caroline further told Joyellen they could sleep the evening and maybe, if she felt better, if the milkweed had a desired healing effect, that she could continue on after midnight. Joyellen said she would not travel on by herself and would stay with her new friend. As they unrolled their bedrolls in a thicket of young alder trees, Joyellen watched and then moved her bedroll within inches of Caroline's. At one point when they lay down, Joyellen reached over and took Caroline's hand; her eyes were filled with tears. Caroline spoke quietly. "You have something to say, and I fear I will get no sleep until you speak it."

Joyellen's cheeks rose as she smiled. "I will say it and then I will be silent. This is so, so wonderful. It is hard to understand I started out this morning a slave and prisoner, and now look at me. I am on my way home. Home! This is a wondrousness I have never felt before. Something I never thought I would ever feel again happened today. Caroline, the minute I saw you in that shed, I knew you were different. I have thought about angels since I was a little girl, but I did not think one would come in those muddy pants and stained shirt with worn out shoes. But that is how you arrived. My own angel. Thank you! Thank you! Here I go crying again. And tonight, I see you also came with a gift. I can't see what it is. But I feel light. What a wonderful gift. That's all I have to say."

The two women spent early evening sleeping side by side on leaves gathered from the alder trees, but Joyellen would wake frequently with a start, and in seconds she would glance quickly around the strange location, and to where she was sleeping on the ground, especially to Caroline sleeping beside her. When Joyellen closed her eyes, she revisited what had happened that morning. Every image, every detail, every word spoken was fresh again, culminating with the burning cabin. At that moment, the realization of her hours-old freedom caused a renewed smile to burst upon her face. She wanted to shout with pure joy, but stifled it, not wanting to wake her rescuer. From that point on, Joyellen barely slept, but at times laughed quietly to herself. It was joy she had not felt for four years.

After six hours, sometime after midnight, great horned owls calling to each other stirred Joyellen. She lay there looking into the pitch-black sky and started counting stars. When she got to 300, she smiled and rolled on her side, speaking softly saying this was the time to wake. In the end, Joyellen had to shake Caroline vigorously to awaken her. Caroline's eyes opened quickly as she hurriedly looked around, and then realizing Joyellen had awoken her, she laid back and forced a smile. Joyellen leaned close. "You said you wanted to travel after six hours of sleeping. Did I do wrong? Did I do wrong again? I'm sorry. I am so sorry." Caroline rolled over, turning on her back, looking up. "Joyellen, no. No, you did right. See, I have these dreams. All the time, every night. Now, just now, my middle boy and my girl were up in one of our apple trees. Hiding from me in a game. I could hear my little girl laughing, but I could not locate her, and so I said, 'Is that a snake I see climbing up that apple tree?' And she jumped down out of the closest tree, then ran to me and hid her face in my apron. It never happened, but the dream was so real that when you woke me, I was there." Joyellen stood, rubbing her eyes. "Well, I want no dreams when I sleep, only when I am awake; that way, I can see they are not real." The young girl untied her hair ribbons and waved them in a circle over her head. She laughed and looked to the west. "We, Caroline and

Joyellen, were there and that way is all yesterday." She quickly turned and pointed to the east. "And that way is where we are going. They look the same, don't they? But they ain't." Joyellen gathered her hair and took the yellow ribbons and then retied them. "I know I seem silly, but I have not been allowed to be silly in so long, it feels good to laugh again." As Joyellen adjusted her hair, Caroline ran her fingers through her own hair and pulled on her cap. "Well, the sooner we get walking, the sooner you will be able to be with your family again. So, time has already started, and we need to catch up to it. You gather your things and roll your bed, then we will have about three bites each of that apple pie and I think that will be our breakfast."

Joyellen watched as Caroline stood and she saw the pain Caroline bore. Reaching down, she rolled Caroline's bedroll and picked it up, slinging it over her shoulder. She did the same with her own bedroll. "I like carrying two because they balance each other. You just carry that haversack, that's all you have to carry. You need to walk light."

As they walked that night, Joyellen started singing to herself and occasionally skipped down the road. The moon produced a shadow on the road and Joyellen chased after it for a while then returned. "You know what I was thinking? What I was thinking right now? I was thinking today, tonight, I will be sleeping in my old bed. Yes, sundown this very night, I will be home, sleeping in my upstairs bed! Under my clean covers. My brother across the room. My mama and my daddy will be down the hall. And in the morning, or any time I want, I can climb out the window and sit on the porch roof watching people come and go. Horses and people. Women dressed for church. Men driving wagons carrying sacks of flour and corn, and girls on their way to school. All carrying books on leather straps over their shoulders and laughing." Joyellen paused for a moment and stopped in the middle of the road. "I miss school. I do. Caroline! Do you suppose I can go back to school? I missed so much. Wouldn't that be just wonderful? I was in the sixth grade with Missus Harkins. And if I go back to the sixth grade, I will be much older than the other girls. But that's okay with me. See, I want to get to the eighth grade. But I am scared!" Caroline looked to Joyellen. "Whatever are you frightened of?"

"My mama. She may be mad at me. I mean I have been with this man. He...well he did that to me. Sex! You know. He fornicated me. Am I bad? Am I bad now? Am I like him?"

Caroline took both Joyellen's hands. "Listen to me and listen well. As a mother, I would understand. Remember what I said. You are a new person. Today, start thinking about what you will be. What you can be. What you desire to be."

"If I am a new person, maybe I need to change my name. Maybe I don't want to be Joyellen, maybe I want a new name. Yes, maybe I need to be new. Caroline, what is your daughter's name?"

"Priscilla. Priscilla Leigh"

Joyellen smiled. "That sounds so pretty. I wish my name was Priscilla Leigh."

They started walking again. Joyellen laughed quietly, for she could not be contained. "It's just now I have a future. And I have so many thoughts. For so long with him, I had no thoughts. None. I just thought about what he would do. That's all. What he would do to me, and now when I get home, I could go back to school. I could go to dances and dance. I could go to church and sing in the choir. I could find my old girlfriends and we could go to Feller's Creek and picnic and swim. I could get a job at the dry goods store. I could sew a new dress or even ten dresses. I could take the train with my brother and go on up to Louisville to see the Ohio River. I could find a young man and we could court. I could do so many things, it is wondrous. You don't know how this feels. I feel so wondrous today and you were right, Caroline, I am a new person. You saved me! Yes, you did. I almost feel like running to get home as soon as I can. I will. When I see my home, I am gonna run all the way down the street and into the house. I am gonna shout. Mama! Daddy! I am home!" Joyellen stopped there in the middle of the road. Her happy demeanor turned serious. "Do you think they will recognize me? I have grown. My hair is so long now. I am almost fully a woman now. They won't be getting back their little girl. They will be getting back an almost grown woman. You think they will still love me? I am so different. He really changed me. He made me bad like him. I saw so much, and didn't do nothing about it, and how do I get it out of my mind? How do I do that, Caroline?"

Realizing this was a serious problem that would not go away, Caroline reached out and took Joyellen's arm and stopped in the middle of the road again. She put down her haversack, then reached over and pulled Joyellen's hair back out of her eyes. "Maybe you are right about changing your name. What would a new name do for you? Would you think of yourself differently? Would you forget about the last four years?"

"Yes, I would, if I were new."

"Okay, then. Choose that new name for yourself."

"Funny, I have been thinking about this since you told me. Caroline, your daughter's name is so pretty and it sounds clean. Priscilla.

"Priscilla Leigh. Do you know Priscilla is in the Bible?"

Joyellen shook her head that she did not know that, but thought for a moment and said the name silently. "Priscilla." Then she said it quietly, almost as a whisper. "Priscilla. Priscilla." She curled her lip and looked eye to eye to Caroline. "Then, if it is okay with you, my new name will be Priscilla. Priscilla Leigh. That's me. I am Priscilla now. Joyellen is the old me. She died back there in that hell for sure cabin. I am Priscilla now." She turned and started walking and shouting. "Yes, I am!" In five steps, she started running and jumping, and then turned and ran back, laughing at a new thought. "Priscilla, get up and make your bed. Priscilla, run to the store and get some eggs for breakfast. Priscilla, don't be late for school. Priscilla, dinner is on the table, put down your books and get down here. Priscilla, your boyfriend is walking down the street, and he is carrying flowers." Together, the two of them walked on, side by side, hand in hand. Joyellen lost in her thoughts. Caroline thinking about what lay ahead in Shelbyville.

Homesteads became increasingly more frequent, but it was night and the houses stood silently dark, collecting the moonlight on their slate roofs. Many of these whitewashed clapboard homesteads sat on 200 acres and most had vegetable gardens located on the morning sun side of the homes. Horses, mules, cows, goats took interest in this pair of travelers walking quietly in the moonlight. Soon they came to a fork in the road. One sign with a pointed arrow just read, "Elizabethtown17." The sign below it read, "Howe Valley 23." Nothing was said, but then nothing had to be spoken. Joyellen only turned and smiled.

After traveling for the next hour, they passed two homesteads, each with identical homes. There was a wide front porch, a side porch, a barn in the back, a chicken coop near the garden, and a hand-dug well that resided twenty feet from the back porch near the kitchen. The two did not say much to each other as they walked. Now and again, Joyellen, with a smile of perfect white teeth, would look at Caroline and Caroline would smile back. Joyellen turned at one point and said, "I hate to say this, but I have not worn shoes in three years. When I get home, I will have to go to the dry goods store and buy a pair. I will need them for school and church. Black ones with brown velvet buttons on the side. I might be able to wear some of my mama's dresses, but I will make all new ones, three, four, five new dresses. All brand new—yellow, green, blue cottons from the store and with white collars and pretty buttons. Funny, how I missed making pretty dresses."

After rounding a small hill and coming down to a stream on the other side, Caroline heard something behind her and stopped and listened for a moment. Hearing nothing, she walked on. A few moments later, she stopped again and heard something. Joyellen stopped too and cocked her head. "It's a dog. I hear a dog." Caroline squinted in the night but saw nothing. The dog barked once again. Caroline dropped her bag to the ground and started walking toward the sound. "Bear, is that you?" There was no more barking. "Bear, is that you? Bear, come on, boy." Quietly and in the distance, there was a bark. Now, two weak barks in a row were heard and finally three long barks. Caroline started running. At a hundred feet, Caroline could make out a dog hobbling toward her. Now Caroline ran as fast as she could. "Bear! Bear!" Bear stopped in the road. As Caroline approached, she saw the panting dog lie down on the road and whimper. His head and his sides were covered with caked blood. He tried to raise his head, but the exhausted dog could not. Caroline knelt by the dog and lifted his head and turned to Joyellen. "Joyellen, bring my bedroll. We are going to have to carry this dog. He's mine! He is the dog that saved my life."

It took about twenty minutes, but the two of them made a sling of Caroline's bedroll. Two corners were tied together, and then repeated with the other two corners. The leather strap Caroline had tied around her waist at the shed was affixed to one end of the sling, and a rope from her bedroll was tied to the other end. "He is too heavy for me to carry, but together I think we can share the burden." Caroline took one leather strap, tied it into a hoop and lifted it over her right shoulder. Joyellen did the same with her rope. With that done, the dog was suspended between the two of them. Caroline took the lead out front and, with Joyellen directly behind her, the two women took their first steps, and soon got into a rhythm. The dog pushed with his back paws and stuck his head out of one end of the sling and looked up at Caroline. Reaching in her bag, Joyellen pulled out a piece of salt pork and handed it to Caroline. Caroline smiled and gave it to the dog, which ate it quickly. A moment later, the black and brown dog closed his eyes, barked once, and fell asleep.

There was little talk for the next four hours as they walked nine miles. Both Caroline and Joyellen struggled with the extra weight of the dog. They stopped at one stream and placed the sling on the ground near the water. The dog stirred and wiggled out, then feebly walked into the water and drank. While standing by the stream, Caroline cupped her hands and washed the dog of the dried blood. She located the bullet hole in his shoulder and saw the bullet had come out the other side. When it came time to leave, the dog walked out of the stream, past the sling, and back to the road. Shaking the water from his coat, he looked to Caroline, and he gave a short quick bark. "So you think you can walk by yourself? Bear, you have been shot." Bear turned and started walking down the road. After gathering her bedroll and bag, Caroline attempted to catch up. Joyellen turned. "He may have been shot, but he is already a hundred feet ahead of us."

"I think Bear is close to home and he knows it. I found him with a wagon heading west. It may have come down this very road."

"Then they probably come, passing through Elizabethtown. We have lots of people who pass through. Or maybe he is from Elizabethtown. There's about a hundred homes around here, and way out in the hills there's a couple hundred more. That dog of yours may be walking home. So, Caroline, he may not be yours very long."

Two hours later, as the sun was one finger high, they came to a sharp rise, and they stood on the hill looking down into Elizabethtown. Joyellen quickened her pace. "I know this hill. I have been up here hundreds of times. Over there! Over there! That's where we live. Among those houses. I can't believe it! That's my home right there. The one with the little building out back." Joyellen started running. "I have to run, I just have to!" Joyellen started running down the hill, and when she reached the bottom, she turned and waved back at Caroline. "Follow me. Follow me!" Joyellen ran now in a full sprint. As she passed houses, she shouted out the family names. "Hendersons, Webolts, Meachams, Randolphs, Latimeers." Then she stopped and shouted back toward Caroline, "This one is mine!" She looked at the home, with tears running down her face, and then she shouted, "Mama, Mama, it's me, Joyellen! I am Joyellen!" The seventeen-year-old girl, still barefoot with two yellow ribbons in her red hair, ran up the steps of the house and threw open the door. "Mama, Mama, it's me! It's me!"

Walking quickly out of the kitchen, Joyellen's mother rushed forward, but stopped in the long hallway and looked at the young woman standing in the doorway. She started breathing quickly as tears formed and she rushed forward to take hold of her missing daughter. At the last moment and halfway down the hallway, she stumbled, and her legs gave out. She fell to the floor, but reached up toward her daughter at the same time. Joyellen rushed to her mother and fell to her knees, embracing her mother, who had burst full into tears. "Mama, I'm home. Mama, I'm home. I'm home. Mama, I did not think I would, I did not think I would. I am Joyellen. Do you recognize me? I am your daughter. I am home. Oh, Mama!"

Caroline reached the bottom of the stairs and stopped and listened to Joyellen. Climbing the stairs, Caroline found a chair then sat on the porch, not wanting to intrude. Bear followed closely behind. Caroline could make out much of what was said and soon she heard a woman's voice, quietly weeping, saying the name over and over. "Joyellen! Joyellen! Joyellen!" The mother did not say words that could be understood other than a mother's sobs and the name Joyellen.

All that morning, the house was filled with laughter, and as Joyellen's relatives and friends came running, screams of joy echoed loudly. And every time a new person arrived, Joyellen would lead the person to the front porch and introduce Caroline as the woman who saved her life. Her brother came running home from school, timidly looking at his older sister, who he barely recognized. Next-door neighbors arrived carrying food for the growing gathering. Soon, a line of people stood outside the home and Joyellen walked from person to person. Joyellen's father, after embracing his daughter and standing watching her, returned back to his shop and cried privately. At times, his joy overwhelmed him and he gasped for breath.

After her pastor and Sunday school teacher came and prayed together, things started to quiet down. Wherever Joyellen walked in the house that morning, her mother followed closely, reaching out and touching her daughter's arm, hand, hair, or just placing her hand on her back, as if this touching was a way of holding her daughter close. Later, as her mother prepared lunch, Joyellen wandered continuously from room to room, looking and touching everything that made this her home. "It's all the same, Mama, you did not change anything."

After lunch, Caroline asked if there was a place to sleep, as she was quite tired. Joyellen's mother took her upstairs and into her bedroom, saying she could sleep in her bed. Caroline asked Joyellen's mother if she would look to her wounds. Her mother returned with a bottle of iodine and some clean gauze. As they sat together alone on the bed, Joyellen's mother took Caroline's hand. "Joyellen told me you found her with this man. I want to know what happened to her. She won't tell me, as she is afraid to hurt my feelings, but you are a mother and so you understand why I would want to know these things. What did you discover when you found her?" Caroline took a deep breath, "No, I think your daughter should tell you everything, not me."

"No, I can tell she does not want to speak of it, and that is only right, but it will ache on me until I know everything. Please, you saw it, I know it was terrible, but if I don't know how bad it was, therefore, how can I think upon it? How can I be a help to her, and how can I be her mother again?"

Caroline shifted herself toward Joyellen's mother and told the story as she found it. She hesitated but shared everything Joyellen had told her. How she was kidnapped and turned into the man's slave—called a daughter and then a wife and how she became pregnant twice and lost both babies. Finally, she told of how the man was killed. The mother sat there in frozen silence, her mouth open in shock. She had no tears. But she looked only at her hands folded in her lap. "Do you think Joyellen will be scarred forever?"

Caroline took a deep breath. "We are all broken and damaged goods. Some more than others. If she were my daughter, I would get back to normal as soon as I could. You need to fill her life with new possibilities." Caroline adjusted herself on the bed. "While we were walking here, she said she wanted to be a new person, so you let her be that new person. She wants to be called Priscilla Leigh. Let her do that." Joyellen's mother nodded her head. "Embrace her. She will be fragile for a long while. Yes, you lost a little girl, but now you got back a grown, yet still a young, woman. And do this. In the kitchen on the wall, write her new name, Priscilla, and let her put a mark behind it for each new day since she came home. Start tomorrow morning. And every day, have her put up a new mark. She will see it on the wall, and she will know that she is new again. Celebrate today as her new birthday."

199

Joyellen's mother nodded at the idea, but a frown soon appeared. "One very last thing I need to know. Did Joyellen have any part in killing this horrible man? I want the truth."

"I killed the man with a stone she gave me, and with my knife I cut his throat. Joyellen was my helper. Without her, it would not have happened. She freed me and helped find the stones and when he was dead, she lit the matches and set him on fire. She burned down that cabin. Him on the bed."

"Good, very good. I am glad she did that. That is all I need to know. She had the strength. That man did not break her. She is not broken. She is hurt, but not broken. Caroline, thank you. You will never know what this means to have her back. I feel like her—reborn. So, then here's my bed, sleep as long as you wish. Joyellen said you wish to travel on tonight, so I will wake you about nine. I will have food ready for you."

Joyellen's mother stood and walked to the door. She stopped and turned. "You know, for four years, every night I prayed God would send an angel to protect my little girl. I didn't know if she were alive or dead. But He did. He did more. He sent a new brave angel to free her, and now I stand here and I see that brave angel."

Caroline slept a deep, quiet sleep. She had no dreams, she barely stirred. She woke once and heard laughter. When she looked down at the foot of the bed, she noticed that Bear had come up the stairs and was sleeping on the wood plank floor three feet away. She reached over and petted him once and then went back to sleep.

At nine that evening, Joyellen came into the room and said it was almost nine and she had some food gathered in the kitchen. She implored Caroline to stay another night, but Caroline said she had lost so many days traveling to her husband, and that each day was crucial for his survival.

Downstairs, Joyellen's father told Caroline that the best and quickest way to Shelbyville would have been the new railline, but the Confederate Army had burned all the trestles and tore up the track and so, the safest way was to head north along the Louisville Road to Shepardsville. But he added that because both armies were staying on the major roads, then take small farm roads that ran the valleys. He also said he noticed in Caroline's bag that she had a Colt 36 and asked whether she knew how to load it and fire it. Caroline explained the gun belonged to the man who had kidnapped his daughter, and she was familiar with this particular gun.

As she walked away from Joyellen's home, the whole family stood on the front porch and waved. Caroline stopped and waved once and turned and walked on. Bear followed closely behind, still limping. As she walked, she heard Joyellen shout out, "I love you, Caroline, and I always, always, always will."

The Louisville Road was called that because if you stayed on it long enough, you would get to Louisville, but there were many Louisville Roads from many parts of the state that linked little homestead gatherings attempting to become a town along the way. When there were a hundred homesteads, a small general goods store would spring up to supply the families with items they could not provide for themselves.

Coffee, sugar, flour, thread, shoes, matches, nails, coal oil, axes, and yards of bright cotton fabric were neatly stacked on shelves that reached twelve feet high. Additionally, it was the official post office for the community. It was where mothers and fathers came to mail letters to their sons fighting in the war and hopefully to get one back. Many times, it was the place where a mother read a letter saying a beloved son would not be returning.

Caroline, along with the dog, made slow but steady progress. Bear had a limp from his shoulder wound, but his face never showed any pain. Caroline herself felt a steady and pulsing pain in her side from the bear wound. She thought the wound was healing, as it itched somewhat, and to her that was sign of cells knitting themselves back together again. Caroline felt she was now about three days away from Shelbyville. At four in the morning, she heard a man's voice off in the distance and somewhere behind her. She started to walk into the grass and up the slight hill to her left. But the man was shouting at her. She reached into her bag and held the pistol in her hand. Realizing the man had seen her, she saw no reason to hide or to keep on walking. Finally, she could make out the man's words. "Hey there, sir, you mind if I walk along with you?" Caroline did not answer. But as she heard his footsteps behind her, she turned. Bear also turned and started a low growl. "Call off your dog. I mean no harm. I am Douglas Winterspoon and I am...oh! You are not a man, you are a woman, and you got a gun."

Caroline raised the Colt 36 Navy revolver, cocked the hammer, and placed her finger on the trigger. "You stop right there. The man heard the seriousness of her voice and saw the shine of a gun aimed at him. "Yes, I will. As I said, I am Douglas C. Winterspoon, and I mean you no harm." Bear continued to growl at the man, who had stopped twenty feet away. "Besides, I am walking faster than you, and it gets lonely out here. Anyway, I am on my way up to Ohio and Cincinnati."

Caroline noticed the man's voice was that of a very young man, almost a boy. "And how old are you and why are you walking at night," she asked.

"Oh, well, I am almost eighteen and I am in a rush before this war ends."

"And why rush so?"

"The Union army of the North is paying thirty-five dollars on the day you sign up and twelve dollars a month once you are wearing a blue uniform. And if I sign for the duration, they will deed me 235 acres once the war is over.

"So you mean to join the Union Army?"

"If I didn't, then my older brothers would force me to join them with the Confederacy, and they are having a pretty poor time of it. They joined up with General Bragg and he is pushing them hard, and they got no pay for two months, and no sign-up bonus. And, well, I got a girl, and we want to get married, but I need the money. Heck, I don't mean to shoot nobody, and I hope nobody shoots me, but Darlaney Louise is impatient, and she lives in Memphis, and so when this war is over, and I think it will be sooner than most think, then I can get back to Memphis and marry Darlaney Louise. We could homestead on all those 235 acres in Missouri."

Caroline turned and started walking again but kept her hand on the gun. "Walk ahead of me. And don't make a sudden movement." The two started to walk again. Caroline waited a while in the silence, then she slowly lowered the gun but kept it in her hand. "So, you don't care who wins the war?"

The man kept walking but turned his head toward Caroline. "No! My hope is the Confederates win, but they don't pay horse droppings and they are not giving free land away. It is a good sign, as I have been walking for thirteen days now, and not one Yankee or one Reb I have seen. I think that is a fortuitous sign. I believe I got four more days before I arrive at Cincinnati. They say you join right across the river. I could train for two weeks and in two weeks more, I would have forty-seven dollars! I will send most of that to Darlaney Louise."

"She's a lucky girl to have you."

"Oh, no. I am the most lucky one. She didn't want me to do this. She begged against it. She's afraid I will be killed. Anyhow, the sooner I get there, then the sooner I may send my sign-up money. I do think this war will be over in less than a year, and I will end up with good money and 235 acres plus Darlaney Louise. It is a sure thing for me. So it's been nice talking to you. I did not ask why you are out here at night, but that is your business—none of it is mine. I wish you the best and I hope you get where you want to go with desired safety. Goodbye."

The almost eighteen-year-old man tipped his hat and walked on. As he walked, Caroline could hear him singing the *Bonnie Blue Flag* song.

Caroline, realizing how his future was in doubt, could not get the young man's forethought out of her mind. Yet his love for this girl, Darlaney Louise, could cause his demise. She thought it would be wiser for them to head off to Missouri and wait out the war, safe and secure in each other's arms. She spoke it out loud to Bear, who was walking ten feet ahead of her. "I hope my two sons do not fall for some young girl so thoroughly that they risk their lives for a possible future. Not even a real and solid one but a maybe one, full of uncertainties." Caroline smiled at a new thought. "Bear, if we make it to Shelbyville and back home, you are going to love my boys. They will take you hunting and swimming and chasing rabbits. And my daughter is going to pamper you with food under the table. But there are difficulties hiding ahead of us. For it is certain, difficulties seem to inhabit this road. But, Bear, I am glad you found me, or I would be dead today. Killed by a bear and left rotting on that hill."

Caroline rounded the top of a hill and, stopping, she saw in the distance a mile ahead a sea of white tents in twenty long lines that filled a clearing as far as she could see. The morning mist had settled over the valley and many men were stirring. In the center, were ten larger tents, and four wagons sat near the road surrounded by a dozen men who were greasing axels and changing wheels. Five cook-wagons were alive with activity as fires were fed kindling wood and a dozen three-gallon black enamel coffee pots stood filled with coffee brewed minutes earlier. Even from this distance, she could smell biscuits being baked in wood-fired camp stoves. Ten-foot-tall tin chimneys poured out white smoke. She tried to count the tents and when she got to a hundred, she realized there were three times more tents. The cannons numbered well over thirty and were in a long straight line, all attached to caissons ready to travel. A rope corral held in a herd of horses so large she could not count them.

"Hey, over here." The voice whispered and then repeated, "Over here, it's me, Douglas Winterspoon." Caroline quickly walked into the tall grass where the young man she had met earlier that night was hiding. Caroline ducked down into the grass beside him. "They are Rebs. Must be 3,000 of 'em. Confederates! I can't let them see me or they will think I am a deserter—put me in a gray uniform and hand me a gun. That don't plank in my plans. I guess I am gonna have to go deep up into the woods and sneak around them."

Caroline poked her head up and looked up the hill and then to the valley. "They'll have lookouts deep in the woods, and I am surprised we have not been spotted by now. So, you will have to go into the woods a half mile or so, and it will be easy to get lost; therefore, you keep that big star, the north star, you keep that dead ahead for a half mile, and then turn and keep it on your left for another three miles through the woods. Then, put it over your shoulder and behind you, and don't let it get to your right or you will travel in a circle—walk until you don't smell campfires, then back out on the road. I wish you luck, Mister Winterspoon."

The young man tipped his hat and, crouching low, headed up into a grove of maple trees. Caroline waited for him to disappear and then went back to the road. Once there, she started singing as she walked toward the Confederates.

In a quarter of a mile, three sentries with muskets pointed at her jumped out of the tree line shouting for her to stop. Caroline stopped and raised her hands over her head, then waited for the sentries to walk down to where she was, surrounding her. Two of the soldiers kept their eyes trained in the direction from where she came, thinking this might be some sort of a distraction prior to a Yankee attack. Caroline kept her hands over her head as she explained to the gray-coated soldiers that she was on her way to Shelbyville to attend to her husband, a wounded first lieutenant in the Confederate Army. One of the men, with corporal stripes on his sleeves, told her to walk ahead of him. As they walked down the hill toward the sea of tents, the young soldier occasionally would glance backward at the hill behind him and shouted to his men to take up their ambush positions. Bear, noticing no one was pointing a gun at Caroline, followed at a distance, looking over the encampment and still limping from his wounds. As the three walked, the corporal said nothing, and Caroline spoke just once and that was to Bear. "Easy, boy, everything is going to be alright." The dog, sensing calmness in her voice, still intently watched the corporal as they walked to the encampment. The corporal pointed the way down an almost endless row of neat, white canvas tents all in straight lines toward the larger officer tents. The corporal walked close behind Caroline; at one point, she pulled off her cap, revealing her long, light brown hair, which had been stuffed up under it.

The soldier took her first to a sergeant, who was shaving, and was told to take her to the captain. Other soldiers, who were standing by their tents getting dressed, turned to face her as she walked by. Many of the young men tipped their heads and bid her good morning. One twenty-year-old said loud enough for all to hear, "I do not know who she is, but if she can cook, sign her up!" The other men laughed. One man knelt down and called to the dog, but Bear, looking left and right as they moved through the tents, ignored the man.

A bearded man was buttoning up his butternut tan uniform as the three of them arrived. Caroline recognized the bars on his shoulder as that of a captain. "Well, corporal, looks like you caught a little bird." The corporal spoke up, "She was walking by herself with this dog. She says she is on her way to Shelbyville. She looked suspicious to me, so I brought her here." The captain sat down on his camp chair and pulled on his boots—he said nothing for while, but looked at her suspiciously. "You know there is a war going on, and to find a woman walking by herself dressed as a man is indeed odd. We have been alerted for spies to give away our position, our numbers, and our capability. So what is your name and why are you traveling in a disguise?" Caroline spoke up, "Sir, my name is Caroline Emily Duncan. My husband is a Confederate officer, First Lieutenant Charles Duncan, and he was wounded and so I am traveling to him." The captain cut her off. "Made up stories tell me nothing. Could be you are a Union courier carrying military messages. Could be you were observing us. So you will be searched. And if we find communiqués on you, then you are a spy and spies are shot. No questions. I have the extended authority to execute spies. I hate to do it to a woman, but a spy or courier's information could kill hundreds of my men. Corporal, search that bag for written messages and be careful; I can see a revolver outline from here." The corporal took her bag and dumped it on the ground. The gun landed in the grass. The young, gray-coated corporal looked at the Colt's paper cartridges, hard tack, a handkerchief, and a small amount of coins. He shook his head. "There is nothing here, Captain."

The tall captain stood and pointed to Caroline from top to bottom and the corporal walked to her and started his search. He first reached into her pants pockets and pulled them inside out. All four were empty. The captain pointed to her breasts and the corporal lightly patted over and around her breasts and then, finding nothing, he felt her back and buttocks. The corporal stepped in front and knelt, then pulled up her trouser legs to her knees, revealing only legs. The captain pointed to her shoes. The corporal pulled off her shoes and inspected the inside of those. "Captain, there is nothing in here except leaves."

"Sorry for the intimate search. There are a lot of spies about and you appear suspicious. So, once more with a few more details, why are you walking by yourself dressed so?"

"No, sir, I understand. My name is Caroline Emily Duncan and I come from Hopkinsville; my husband is First Lieutenant Charles Matthew Duncan of the First Kentucky Volunteers, and he was wounded in two separate skirmishes and is in a Confederate hospital tent in Shelbyville. I am traveling there to attend to his wounds. He was shot in the shoulder and the leg. I have been traveling now eight days, all on foot. I wish only safe passage through your lines to get there."

The captain buttoned up the rest of his shirt, then reached down and picked up the revolver. He opened and inspected the large handgun. "It's been shot once and recently. What did you shoot?" Caroline took a deep breath. "The man who I took it from shot my dog." The captain took a long slow look at Caroline and then the dog. "How did you take it from him?" Caroline felt she was getting backed into a corner but decided to tell the truth. "He died and so I took it from him."

"And how did he die?"

"I killed him. He was asleep in his bed."

"So you were in bed with him and pulled a knife and cut his throat?"

"No. He held me captive. Tied me up. I got free and when he was sleeping, I struck him with a very large stone and then I cut his throat."

The captain smiled for a moment and then his demeanor turned serious. "This is interesting. I have never met a woman who admitted to killing a man in his sleep. You do not hesitate in telling that story, and yet you do not look the part of knife-wielding murderess."

"He had kidnapped a thirteen-year-old girl and raped her repeatedly for four years! I just happened to come upon them. And it appears he had murdered travelers for their money. The girl said she saw the bones of nine men and she thinks one woman."

"What did you cut his throat with?"

"It's a plain ordinary kitchen knife, which I keep in my waistband. Your corporal missed it."

"Show it to me."

Caroline pulled out the knife and held it in her hand presenting the handle end to the captain.

"So, you know how to handle a knife, and apparently you know the value of a gun. You ever shoot a gun like this?"

"Yes, sir, my husband taught me with his revolver before he left. I can load and shoot a musket rifle too."

"I would image you can, and so tell me what happened to the money? The money this man stole."

"I told the young girl to take it—her name is Joyellen and she lives in Elizabethtown. All I took from that house was the gun."

"And how do you know the man is dead, he could have survived. Maybe you only wounded him."

"No. I cut both arteries. Then we burned the cabin and him with it. He's dead."

"Alright, that settles that. I do have other questions." The captain pointed at a camp stool and motioned for her to sit down.

Caroline looked around, not knowing what was going to come next, but she sat on one of the two camp stools by the front of his tent. The captain turned to the corporal. "Get this woman something to eat and bring us both some coffee." There was silence for a while and then he pulled up a stool and sat facing her. "In all your walking, have you seen any Union military and if so, how many and where were they?"

Caroline took a deep breath, realizing maybe this officer was accepting her story. "I saw maybe 300 to 400 men with fifty or so horses and I would say about a dozen cannons two days ago west of Elizabethtown by about thirty miles. They were heading west. And moving fast. Before that, and further back, maybe sixty miles back, I saw a town that was burned to the ground and the boy there said about a hundred Yankees did that, but that would have been five or six days ago that he told me that. He said nine Yankees were killed and the town lost about twenty men. Well, actually, all the men were killed. The rest of the Yankees burned the town down, all of it. There is one other group of men I saw, about ten of them. I think they are the Willems Gang. There are a couple of deserters among them. Confederate deserters."

"Yes, very good. We know about the 500 men, and other homesteaders around here have verified that. It's Keelson's Raiders." The captain whispered to Caroline in a low tone, "I am going to do you a favor; I am going out on a limb, but what you have told me today seems truthful, so, from one officer to another officer's wife, I am going to help out. If my wife heard I was wounded, she too would travel to me." The captain leaned back in his chair. "Around one today, I am sending four supply wagons up toward Louisville but eventually to Frankfort. They will pass near Shelbyville. I am under orders not to give passage to civilians. But you get in back of one and keep low and you should be in Shelbyville by this time tomorrow."

Caroline took a deep breath, a surprised smile starting to form on her face. Inside, she felt a joyous tingle in her stomach. Finally, something good and unexpected was starting to happen. The days she lost had been given back to her.

The captain continued without noticing the smile. "I am going to give you one of our uniform jackets and hat. You wear those. Keep your gun, because this group of suppliers will be lightly armed. There will be but a small escort." The captain stopped for a second and sat back upright. "I pray your husband is still alive when you get there. It's well known the Yankees are taking our wounded soldiers from hospitals and transporting them up into Ohio to a prisoner camp near Lancaster. He may not be in Shelbyville when you get there.

As you may or may not know, Shelbyville has been in the middle of this conflict for the last month. You eat your breakfast and use my cot for some sleep. I will have my sergeant wake you when the wagons are ready to leave." The captain stood. "You may ask yourself why I am trusting you. It is because you are forthcoming in all my questions. Including a killing of a man. No spy would have admitted that. God speed to you, Missus Duncan. I hope your husband is alive and you find him."

The captain tipped his hat and walked away. Caroline sat there watching the soldiers form long gray lines at the mess tents. She was lacing up her shoes when the corporal arrived with a tin cup of coffee and a plate of biscuits and gravy. After eating much of her breakfast, she put the plate on the ground for Bear. As she walked into the tent with her bedroll, her bag, and her gun, she placed the knife back into her waistband. The dog followed her into the tent and, after inspecting it, he returned back outside and stood guard. Caroline lay on the cot and looked up at the shadow of leaves as they moved about on top of the tent. Her last thought was tomorrow she might be with her husband. She attempted to smile at the idea, but was overcome with fatigue.

"If you would do me the honor, I would like to take you out to the Fourth of July picnic, Caroline. Since I have joined your father's church, I have become aware of you, and I think you have become aware of me." Charles stood there, with his hat in his hand, looking down at Caroline collecting the hymn books after the service. Her father turned from the pulpit and smiled as he walked away. "You have caught me glancing in your direction several times. You have returned those glances with a smile, and so I assume you would be...you would be...you would be agreeable to my...to my...to my invitation." Caroline placed the hymn books down on the pew seat and pushed her hair out of her eyes. She said nothing. "There will be a dance and so we would start with a picnic, watch the bicycle race, and then end the day with a...end the day with a...dance by the river front park. I would then walk you home."

Caroline smiled but tried to hide it. "I barely know you, Charles Duncan. You have come into my father's church three months ago from who knows where and you pretend to be a perfect gentleman, but there are many secrets about you. I am only eighteen and you look like you are well into your twenties. Old."

"Caroline, I am twenty-two."

"See there, that is what I mean. You are handsome, yes, but there are others as handsome as you. What makes you think I have not already been asked?"

"Well, have you been asked?"

"Well, no, but it's still a whole week away."

"Good, because that will give you time to practice your dance steps because I am a very good dancer."

"You are?"

215

"You will find your local boys do not have the technique or style that I have; further, I will not pull you awkwardly close to me when we dance, as it will be like flying on a cloud."

"And when you walk me home, you would be a perfect gentleman? You would not..."

"One brief goodnight kiss is all that I ask."

"We have yet to pair, and you are already talking about kissing. No, that will not do. I realize some girls are easy to kiss, but I do not believe I am among those. I should have to explore my feelings, so I would possibly allow a brief kiss once, just the once. Caroline looked to see if no one was near. "The girls have noticed you gaze upon me at length, and so I do not want to let them down. I want to tell them a good story the next day."

"Then you shall give them a good story to hear. First, I plan a close embrace, then a romantic long kiss under the slender thread of the moonlight."

"I would never acquiesce to that! Courting is about getting to know one another, not about kissing. For you have yet to discover who I am, and let me tell you, Mister Charles Duncan, I am no shrinking violet. I am not merely an ordinary shy girl. I can ride a horse faster than any young man my age, and I am quite good with my father's rifle. I am an expert with archery. I have acted in three plays at school. I have strength of mind. You will find that out soon enough."

Caroline woke with a start. The corporal was standing beside her. "Hey, Missus Duncan, your wagon is gonna leave in about fifteen minutes. They won't wait. There's some more coffee outside. Here's your uniform jacket and hat as the captain requested. He said to put a handful of fresh cartridges for your revolver by your bag. I wish you luck. Oh, yes, my name is Jimmy Overmeyer and I am from Bowling Green, which is close to where you come from. You get that way, you stop in and tell my mom you saw me. West of town three miles on the Hopkinsville Road. Everybody knows us. The Overmeyers. That's us."

There were now five wagons all in a single line and positioned near the medical tents. Caroline soon realized that wounded Confederate soldiers were being loaded in the last two wagons. She counted four men who had been laid on straw mattresses, two to a wagon. In the next wagon, she watched as men loaded guns taken from surrendering northern soldiers. In the front two wagons were fifteen captured Union men, who had been bound together with ropes and their boots taken from them. Most had been wounded, as they were heavily bandaged. After looking into the front wagon, which held nine, one of the young Northern soldiers smiled at Caroline. "Good morning, ma'am. I see you are in uniform, and I had not realized the rebs were having women fight for them. I hope you are the one that shot me, 'cause it makes my wound a little less painful."

Caroline looked away and said nothing, as one of these men could have been the one who shot her husband. The corporal took her to the last wagon in the long line and helped her step up and into the back of the wagon. There was just enough space between the two Confederate soldiers for Caroline to sit on the hard oak boards that made the floor. Neither man spoke to her, and the one with a bandage on his thigh sat on his mattress staring at the floor of the wagon. He glanced at her but said nothing. The second had a bandage across his face and both eyes. He moved his legs several times as if he was attempting to move quickly away from something bad. He mumbled a jumble of words, but Caroline could not understand a word of it.

Looking through the front flap, she could see at the head of this wagon train, six Confederate soldiers on horseback aligned in a double line, side by side. Through the back canvas flap, she saw two men ride up and take a position behind it. No one said a word, as all communication was done with hand signals. Within minutes, the lead wagon was underway. The sudden lurch of Caroline's wagon caused one of the wounded men to groan. Caroline, sitting in the rear of the wagon with her back to the tail gate, leaned forward and patted the man's foot. "It's alright, just relax. I think you are headed toward a hospital and proper doctors. There is a water tin with us and so if you want some water just ask. My name is Caroline." The man with bandaged eyes said nothing and Caroline was not sure he had heard her. The man with the bandaged thigh looked at her, expressionless, but nodded. He leaned forward and took off his boots. Caroline saw he wore no socks. She saw dried blood covered his left foot.

An hour into the morning's ride, Caroline suddenly thought about Bear. She quickly glanced behind the wagon as if the dog would be following her, but, alas, there was no sign of the dog, only a cloud of dust stirred by the five wagons. She thought maybe it would be best for the dog to be back there with all those men. Surely, several would take a liking to the dog and take care of it. Still, she was quite sad to see him left behind and wondered whether the dog felt he had been deserted. She thought, "Bear probably went looking for breakfast in the woods this morning right before I left. How could have I forgotten Bear after all we have been through?"

As they traveled, they passed homesteads along the way and occasionally small children would run out of the houses and wave to the wagons as they passed. Young boys would shout out encouragement to the gray-suited soldiers. Mothers would stand by clotheslines or would lift up from their gardens and wave. Two young boys, both barefoot and carrying fishing poles, started to run after the last wagon. The older boy, who appeared to be fourteen years old, shouted out, "How many Yankees have you killed today?" The two gray-coated escorts who followed the wagons said nothing. A moment later, the youngest soldier turned and shouted back at the boys, "I killed five this morning before breakfast and I aim to kill five more before sundown tonight." The other soldier just laughed and the two boys stopped in the middle of the road, unable to keep up with the wagons. They took their fishing poles and pointed them like rifle muskets, singing, "Connor Meaney, mighty reb, shot ten Yankees in the head. Shot 'em dead. Shot 'em dead. Connor Meany shot 'em dead. Hoo-rha. Hoo-rah. Shoot all Yankees till they're dead."

Three hours into this convoy, the driver of the last wagon turned around and shouted to Caroline, "We are going to stop at the next creek and let the horses have some water and if you need to relieve yourself, I will have all the men on the right side of the wagons, and you can use the left side. Also, there is a sack up here with some hard tack and jerky. Those two men you are riding with are Private Jenkins and Private Murphy. Thanks for giving them water, both are too wounded to eat."

At the creek, the drivers brought canvas bags of water to the horses, then walked around the wagons and inspected the wheels. The driver of Caroline's wagon took a wrench from a box bolted to the side of the wagon and tightened a wheel nut then inspected the brake. Caroline got out of the wagon and took two water tins down to the stream and refilled them with cooler water. Most of the captured Union soldiers got out and went to the stream for water. As Caroline walked back to the last two wagons, she looked down the road from where they had come, speaking quietly. "I am so sorry, Bear. I was only thinking of me, wasn't I?" Forty minutes later, they were four miles down the road and making six miles an hour as the terrain flattened out. As they passed a man walking alongside the road, Caroline calculated the wagons could be saving her two days of walking.

Homesteads on both sides of the road appeared and disappeared like they were the ones traveling, not the wagons. Yet to Caroline it looked so normal. Women stood out by wash lines taking down dry sheets and pillowcases. Men, with their young sons helping, were digging holes for new fence posts. Young girls stood under apple trees picking up those apples that had fallen that day, bruised but destined to be made into apple butter that afternoon. Occasionally, Caroline smelled a familiar sweet cinnamon smell of apple pies baking, corn chowder simmering in kitchens, or bacon being fried for dinner. In front yards, side yards, and backyards, chickens moved in unpredictable patterns, picking at insects in the grass. It all seemed so peaceful, and yet here she was in the back of a wagon with wounded soldiers, captured enemy, and hundreds of rifled muskets. How could this be? How could sane men march off in hopes of killing each other? Could they not see as they rode by that they were passing a wonderful way of life? And what of the two boys with fishing poles who inquired about the war? Would they someday be in uniform shooting at their fellow man? Yet, Caroline understood she was now a participant in it. There she was with a gray coat on, a gray hat, and two gray-coated men traveling together. In her rucksack only inches away, was a revolver ready to fire at someone. This was the world of suddenness—where the unexpected event ruled the day and then decided who won the battle. Caroline thought of the man she herself, with sudden intensity, had to kill while he slept in his bed. The bear she blinded with a sudden plunge of a glass shard. Of a pair of pants she still wore from a town suddenly burned to the ground. Men killed and after they killed, they in turn were killed. She also thought of Joyellen, the young thirteen-year-old girl, who had been thrust into the unrelenting hell created by an evil man. Why had the world so descended into this morass of death? With these mixed thoughts, she felt divided and conflicted inside. Was it alright to confront evil with evil? She looked at the two soldiers who rode with her, and wondered had they ever contemplated those thoughts? Kill or be killed? And that was it. Kill or be killed. "I am on a journey. I am on a journey to find my husband and take him home with me to reunite our family. To take him away from the never-ending circle of bloodletting. The tears formed but held in her eyes. She wondered why her emotions surfaced so easily. Was she exhausted and feeling vulnerable? Did the bear wound sap her of her strength? Maybe resting and even sleep would help and so she found a place between the two wounded men and lay down. She pulled close the haversack she made years ago, now containing a fully loaded revolver. She pressed it up into her stomach, as this represented home to her. And so she slept.

A lone dog, barking its presence, stirred her awake and she raised herself up to see the five wagons and escorts were passing through a small village. She glanced out the back and realized the rear guard was no longer behind them. Several stores stood in a long single line in this little town. She saw the largest store sitting by the side of the road with a sign over the front porch. "Gambee's General Store." Three men sat on chairs near the front. Beside the store stood "Vila's Dry Goods." One woman was standing there with a small child in her arms; two small children stood beside her. The barking dog that woke her ran past her wagon and continued to bark. Then she faintly heard something new. It was familiar. Another dog was returning the bark. "It sounds...it sounds like Bear. How can that be?" She rose up and walked hunched over to the front of the wagon. She shouted to the driver. "Is there a dog up front? Is there a black and brown dog up front? In one of our wagons, is there a dog?"

The driver turned his head. "Yes, we got a new passenger. A dog. He appeared about two hour ago. He's been running hard after us. Private Billington, our escort in the rear, heard him and went back about a thousand feet and picked him up. Billington put him up in the front wagon. Now and then, he glances back at me. Billington said he looks injured." Caroline looked past the driver into the back of the front wagon. At first, she could not see much, as the dust obscured her vision. But eventually, the dust cleared, and Caroline could see a shadow in the front wagon. She squinted, and next to the driver was a shape lying on the seat. Caroline shouted out, "Bear, is that you?"

The dog obviously did not hear, and so she shouted out one more time, but this time much louder. "Bear!" The dog quickly turned his head and, catching sight of Caroline, he barked and stood and jumped into the bed of the wagon. He quickly moved past the captured Union soldiers and came to rest at the tail gate. The dog did not bark again, but sat there with his tongue hanging out. He raised one paw and rested it on the top of the gate. Caroline shouted out loudly, "Bear, I'm sorry I forgot about you. I am sorry, boy. I'm sorry." The driver of the wagon smiled and turned to Caroline. "Do you think that dog understands you? He's just a dog." Caroline did not take her eyes off of the dog, "I used to think so too. No, he is smarter than any dog I ever met. He saved my life from a bear. And he took a bullet for me."

They traveled this way for the next hour, with Caroline seated next to the driver and Bear sitting with his head resting on the tail gate, both looking at each other. At the water stop, as the horses were drinking in the creek, Caroline got down and walked forward to the back of the front wagon. She lowered the tail gate and lifted the dog to the ground. Together, they walked upstream and drank from the cool spring water. Sitting on the bank and watching small fish swim by, Caroline shared with Bear some hard tack and a piece of dried pork. When it came time to leave, with the help of the rear escort soldier Private Billington, Caroline lifted the dog into the fifth wagon. Underway and sitting on top of her bedroll, she leaned back against the wooden tail gate observing the two wounded men, neither of whom had moved. Bear jumped into the driver's seat and lay beside the driver, with his head looking back at Caroline. At other times, and despite the wagon's noise, Bear appeared to hear something and searched the surroundings for game as the wagons moved through the virgin woods.

The wagons picked up speed along the flat terrain. Isolated homesteads came and went. Smaller horse trails led off from the main road, but those homesteads, hidden by the hills, remained anonymous. Caroline realized hundreds of homesteads lay scattered along these unnamed roads that snaked back into the hills for twenty miles or more. These were innocent roads that imitated the trees around them. Branches that led to branches that led to branches, finally ending at a single isolated homestead. One little town they came to appeared normal, except two stores had been partially burned and there were no people visible. Smoke rose from a single home still smoldering. What she noticed was the lack of livestock. There were no cows, no sheep, no horses; occasionally, she spotted a few goats hidden away near the tree lines. Once, they came to a mule walking down the road looking for its way home.

Twenty minutes later, an escort rider galloped forward from the five wagons and approached a homestead near a small settlement. An older woman came out onto the front porch and pointed eastward down the road. The escort rode back to the stopped wagons and word was passed that a small contingent of thirty Union soldiers came through the area late yesterday and skirmished with five men—most likely Confederate deserters, all wearing gray uniforms. They had taken refuge in the settlement's school and during the confrontation, a fire broke out. The woman said the deserters rode away with the Union Army in pursuit. Sergeant Wilcox selected three men to ride a mile ahead and to fire signal shots if they encountered the Yankees. The three escorts rode off, leaving only two escorts and the sergeant up front for protection.

Nearing four in the afternoon, they approached two signposts. The main road continued north, and a smaller road split away. The larger sign read Louisville and the smaller read Frankfort. The escorts were waiting at the fork, and they rejoined the wagons. The three took their place at the head, and Private Billington returned and spoke to Caroline. "Tracks on the road show the Yankees went north to Louisville and so we should be free of them all the way to

Frankfort. We plan to stop and spend the night at about sunset. We should pass near Shelbyville about ten, eleven tomorrow morning."

As she had been doing since the start of this travel, Caroline attended to the two wounded soldiers with water and kind words—only one man wanted anything to eat. The soldier with bandages over his eyes groaned when the wagon hit a deep rut in the road. The other soldier, with the bandaged thigh, spoke rarely to Caroline, but spoke occasionally to his wounded fellow soldier. "Sooty, I heard once we get to Frankfort, they are going to put us on a train back to Atlanta and let us go home. I think this is it for us. We are no longer useful." Then to take his mind off his pain, he hummed a tune, but he only knew part of it. At one point, Caroline changed the bandage over the man's leg, as it had started to bleed. When she looked at the wound, she could see a shattered bone through the blood. She also saw infection, maybe gangrene. She found a chest of medicine under the driver's seat and applied a dusting from a glass jar marked sulfur, then bandaged his thigh. She realized his leg might have to be amputated. Now and then, she heard him say, "Sooty, they ain't gonna' cut me. I will shoot at any damn doctor comes at me with a saw."

At sundown, the wagons came to a small settlement composed of thirty-five houses, a general store, a school, and a livery stable. With a signal from Sergeant Wilcox, the wagons pulled up to the rear of a blacksmith shop. The sixteen horses were unleashed and tied to the side of their wagons. Five drivers set about watering and feeding the horses. An older man came forward to inquire if help was needed, and then left and returned forty minutes later with three ladies of his age who brought three cast iron pots of green beans, sausage, ham, and fried grit cakes. Without talking, the three women put the pots on the ground, looked into the eyes of the soldiers, and quickly left. One woman returned moments later and passed out tin pie plates. The four Confederate wounded men preferred to stay in the wagons, and food was passed to them on the pie plates. Sergeant Wilcox ordered the captured Union soldiers out of the wagon and gathered them in a circle and told them to sit. Hard tack, water, and salted pork were passed around and were quickly eaten, as it was the only food the blue-coated soldiers saw that day.

Standing guard over them with two revolvers stuck in his belt, a gray-coated escort, Corporal Leadon Kellermans, sat on an empty water barrel, eating his plate heaped high with green beans, sausage, and fried grit cakes. The other escorts and five drivers rolled out blankets on the ground and under the wagons. Caroline took her bedroll and, with Bear at her side, went inside the blacksmith barn and found a pile of hay to make herself a bed. A minute later, she returned to the rear of the wagon and picked up a tin plate of food. Since there were no utensils, she used her fingers to eat. The single slice of ham she gave to Bear. After eating, she returned to her bedroll inside the barn and, without removing any clothing or shoes, Caroline fell asleep. Bear walked around the inside of the barn several times, smelling and sniffing the place, and in the end he walked to the large barn door and found a place in the opening half outside and half inside. It was as if he was guarding something on the inside of the barn.

Caroline's mother stood in front of Caroline, who sat in a chair in the dining room—her mother held a note in her hand. "Caroline, you are thirteen now and no longer a child. I think we need to have this talk. It is long overdue, because people are talking. Your teacher is concerned. What I want to know is why do you make up these incredible stories?" Caroline adjusted herself in her seat. "Mother, sometimes I am bored in class and so I close my eyes and I see stories come to life. And if I keep my eyes closed long enough, I see me in the stories. I talk and they talk. These are conversations that make me think. And so I am writing a play about it all."

"You told your teacher that you swam the Ohio River? You have not done that. Why this falsehood?" Caroline sat in her seat quietly for a moment and adjusted her dress. "Mother, I saw it like it was real. Then I placed it in my mind as I saw it. And once that happened, I knew I can do it because it will be the second time I have done it. All I have to do is walk down to the river and do it again."

Caroline's mother looked her over and exhaled. "And who is this new friend, Amanda? Did you also make her up?" Caroline wrung her hands for a moment. "I will have a new friend some day and until I learn her real name, I will call her Amanda. And on the day she arrives, I will already know everything about her." Caroline's mother sat down in a chair next to her. "Alright, you can make up stories, but do not tell other people, just make them up quietly and keep them to yourself." Caroline stood up from her chair and looked her mother directly in the eye. "Mother, when I turn fourteen on my next birthday, I will swim across the mighty Ohio River to Indiana. And Amanda, my new friend, will swim it with me. You watch and you will see. Amanda was not born with fear. Neither was I."

At five a.m., as the sun was about to rise into the pink sky, Sergeant Wilcox, who was not happy that a woman was traveling with them, came into the barn and said they would leave in thirty minutes. He further stated those same local ladies had returned with corn bread, coffee, and a platter of fried eggs with bacon. Caroline pushed her hair up under the gray hat and walked outside. One of the ladies walked toward Caroline to offer a plate of food, but seeing how feminine she was and hearing her voice, she was surprised and stood there in amazement.

The other three ladies quickly came over and started asking questions, saying they were unaware there was a woman traveling with the wagons. One woman, about the same age as Caroline, said if she had known Caroline was sleeping among men, she could have stayed with them in a proper bed. Another woman, a much younger one, asked how it came to be she was traveling dressed in that manner, and traveling with the wagons of wounded men? Further, she asked was Caroline a nurse? Caroline responded that she was not officially a nurse but had been acting as one. She gave no further details, as she felt any information she provided could fall into the wrong hands. The youngest woman turned and ran back to her home, and within minutes, came running back with a plain yellow print cotton dress. "This should fit you. It's my favorite dress but you need it more. Yankees could shoot you. I do not know why you are wearing that uniform, but they shoot anything that's gray. I mean, here you are, and you are a nurse of sorts. Please put this on when you can, as there are Yankees everywhere." The woman thrust the dress wrapped with a string around it, into Caroline's hands. Then along with the other ladies, she excused herself, saying it was Sunday and they had to prepare for church. As she walked away, she slowed for a moment and, looking over her shoulder, she smiled and then raised her hands together as if to say, "I will pray for you." Caroline smiled and returned the gesture; taking the dress, she placed it into her haversack next to the gun and two boxes of ammunition. As she walked to her wagon, Sergeant Wilcox came away from his men and three civilians. He motioned and stopped her at the back of the fifth wagon. He informed her that the next part of the trip was going to be fast, as he had been informed minutes ago that the Union Army was very active in this area. "If you hear shots, stay low in the wagon, as we will attempt to outrun them. I have been doing this a long time and I assure you, Missus Duncan, this is not a game. Those are real bullets. And we will fire back at them with real bullets. I hope you understand the danger you are taking. You can stay here if you want or travel with us."

The next part of the road was hillier than before, with large oak groves mixed with pine woods both to the right and left. Caroline sat in the back of the wagon, watching the two wounded men who seemed to be in less pain. One asked for water repeatedly but would only take a small sip. The one with the bandaged thigh tried to have a conversation with the blinded man, but the answers he got back were one word answers and nothing more. At one point, he again attempted to sing a song, but failed to remember the words and only hummed the part he knew. Bear was invited to sit next to the driver, and Caroline noticed the dog preferred the view, being able to see hills and creeks they passed. Taking out the package containing the dress, Caroline inspected it, and was surprised at the fine hand stitching and the jade green buttons with orange thread. She held part of it up, facing herself, and thought in Shelbyville she could change into the dress while searching for her husband. She thought the dress would look more like her old self than the gray woolen jacket she wore over men's dark gray pants. She leaned back and looked at her brown shoes, now worn badly, their stitching torn, and covered with dried red mud. She thought she might also find a general store and purchase a new pair of button shoes to go with the yellow dress. She refolded the dress, tied it with the string, and held it close. Lifting it to her face, she could smell the familiar potpourri of lilac, rosemary, and honeysuckle.

The first sound Caroline heard was like that of a single tree branch being snapped sharply by an explosive burst of wind. That first shot sent thousands of birds flapping into the air and struck the corporal riding escort to the right of Sergeant Wilcox. It tore through his chest and knocked him sideways to the ground. A strange silence lasted only the time it took for a quick brief inhale of air. Suddenly, there was the sound of hundreds of branches being ripped from the trees by high

231

winds. This was a fusillade of shots that exploded from the pine woods to the left of the wagon-train and struck down a second lead escort rider. This rapid gunfire continued, exploding into the wooden sides of the first wagon and striking four of the captured Union soldiers not visible beneath its canvas. In the second wagon, gunfire struck the driver with three bullets, instantly killing him. In that wagon, two of the Northern soldiers were struck; one died immediately, crimson splattered on the white canvas above his head. In the third wagon, carrying only the captured rifles, the driver was struck in the calf, thigh, and arm with three bullets. In the fourth wagon, a Confederate wounded soldier who had been sleeping was hit in the arm and cried out in pain while the driver was hit in the foot. Three shots tore through the canvas of the fifth wagon and one shot sent splinters flying into the air covering the blind soldier with bits of wood. Bear jumped out of his seat and ran back towards Caroline, as if to protect her.

Sergeant Wilcox, the lead rider with the first wagon, grabbed his revolver and fired three shots over his left shoulder into the woods, shouting to the first driver, "Go! Go!" He turned his horse to the left and fired two more shots, then turning to the right, he whipped his horse into a gallop as the drivers slapped the reins hard against the horses. More shots rang out from the left side of the road. One shot slammed into the floor of Caroline's wagon inches away from her foot and sent splinters flying into the side of her face.

Whipping his horses even harder, the driver of the first wagon leaned forward and fired his revolver in the direction of the ambush, but immediately was struck in the calf and once in his wrist. Caroline ducked low into the wagon, her face flat against the floor, and reached back for her bag. Twenty more shots rang out, as the five wagons sped away from the ambush. One of the escorts in the rear was struck in the arm but held onto his horse. The second rear escort, Private Billington, had his revolver knocked from his hand. The driver of the third wagon pulled out his revolver and was firing to the left and behind as the wagons sped over the crest of the hill and down the other side into safety.

Sergeant Wilcox slowed his horse and allowed the first wagon to speed by. He came along the side of the second wagon and was whipping the air with his revolver, screaming, "Go! Go! Go! Moments later, the second part of this ambush exploded from the right side of the road. Forty Union soldiers, hidden above the tree line, fired on command and seven bullets struck Caroline's wagon on the right side, sending wood splinters into her arm and leg. Four of the bullets tore into the canvas and out the left side harmlessly. One shot whistled inches from Caroline's face. As it sailed by her ear, red hot and whistling, Caroline sensed its finality. Private Billington, one of the two escorts in the rear, now without a gun, tried to ride past the fifth wagon, shouting to the driver, "I need a gun! I need a gun! He then rode on to the fourth wagon, only to find the wounded driver had collapsed onto the seat. Private Billington was attempting to jump onto the wagon when a second series of shots rang out and he was knocked from his horse and onto the side of the road. The second part of this ambush lasted only the time it took for the wagons to speed by and yet in that short time everything seemed to challenge Caroline's senses. Noise, heat, smell, and impact all overwhelmed her. No sense was left unaffected.

In all that cacophony, Caroline heard gunshots from the rear of the wagon and lifted her head from the floor and, looking over the tail gate, she saw five blue-coated men whipping their horses in a fury and approaching, while quickly firing their revolvers at her wagon. Two shots tore into the tail gate and continued into the driver's seat. Without thinking, and only reacting, Caroline grabbed her haversack, pulling out the Colt 36 Navy revolver. She lay low with her eyes peeking over the wood gate. She drew the gun sight over the lead rider, now bouncing left and right, and pulled the trigger. Her shot went wide right, and so she sat upright and tried it a second time, holding the revolver with both hands. She closed her left eye and slowly pulled the trigger and watched as the lead rider was torn from his horse. She took a quick look at the second rider and aimed this time for his leg; she pulled the trigger and this shot found its mark and the man grabbed his leg and soon pulled up on his horse.

The third rider, wearing an officer's gold-braided uniform of a captain, forged ahead and fired three fast shots toward the fifth speeding wagon. The movement of the horse, and the officer's long outstretched arm, caused two of the three shots to strike the wagon's tail gate, but one went high into the back of the driver's head, killing him. Caroline took aim with the weapon and fired at the man. A bump in the road caused her shot to crease the man's left arm. Caroline squinted her eyes and said to herself. "Sir, please do not come closer." Without thinking, she shouted out one word, "Don't."

The Union officer whipped his horse, hoping to get closer for a better shot. As he drew within twenty feet, attempting to aim his gun at Caroline, she looked into the man's blue eyes and blond hair, his teeth gritted tight, and she shouted, "No!" The officer lowered his gun over Caroline's chest and fired another round. His shot went left of her by mere inches. A gray arm pushed her down and the wounded Confederate soldier, now with a revolver retrieved from the driver's belt, instinctively fired with a well-aimed shot. The officer's shoulder exploded, splattering blood onto his face and sending him backwards off his horse. His weapon went flying out of his hand and into the weeds beside the road.

The fourth rider, with corporal stripes on his sleeve, pulled up and stopped to attend to his fallen captain. The fifth rider whipped his horse hard toward the wagon and fired three shots in a row, all wide, missing their mark. The wounded Confederate soldier fired a single shot that tore into the man's arm and sent the revolver flying out of his hand. Now without a weapon, he pulled on his horse hard and turned his horse left, retreating quickly back toward his fallen fellow soldiers. Caroline raised her head above the tail gate. The wounded Confederate soldier collapsed back onto his straw bed and closed his eyes, gun still in his hand. Caroline looked forward to see her wagon was without a driver. Crouched low and walking quickly, she made her way to the driver's seat and, standing over the man, she took the reins and whipped them hard.

The five wagons, several without drivers, sped ahead, led by Sergeant Wilcox, who was riding next to the two lead horses. This continued unabated for ten minutes, with only the sound of hoof beats and wagon wheels striking bare ground replacing the crescendo of the gun fire left behind. No one said anything except for the sergeant who kept shouting, "Go! Go!" Coming to a large, flat bottom land, Sergeant Wilcox slowed his horse and motioned to the wounded driver of the first wagon to do likewise. "Square 'em up. Square 'em up!"

Entering the large open field, the wagons veered right and in one hundred feet they formed a haphazard defensive circle. The remaining escorts and drivers jumped out of the wagons and off horses, gathering captured rifles from boxes in the third wagon. Several of the wounded riders hobbled off their horses and crawled underneath. Sergeant Wilcox shouted to the captured Yankee prisoners, "All of you get out and stand alongside our wagons. Show yourselves to your Yankee brothers." All his gray-coated men took positions under the wagons, pointing their weapons westward to the road. The sergeant shouted out instructions to the three remaining drivers to lock their brakes for fear the horses would pull away and separate the wagons. Moments later, he dispensed powder and ball to the three. One soldier took six captured Enfield muskets from the third wagon and loaded six and laid them on the ground next to him ready to fire all of them. Caroline stepped over the seat and to the rear of the wagon with the two wounded men. Bear jumped from the wagon and stood facing the threat. Coming to the last wagon, Sergeant Wilcox yelled to the two men and lone woman to get out of the wagon and into the grass under it. Caroline helped one of the wounded men out of the wagon, but found the second one, the blind soldier, had bled out from the shot in his neck. Caroline grabbed her haversack and took a place near the large rear wheel. Opening her bag, she pulled out ten cartridges for her Colt revolver and in two minutes reloaded her weapon. Realizing the dead driver's Colt revolver was left up in the rear of the wagon, she climbed up and back into the wagon and retrieved the weapon that rested on a straw mattress. She quickly ducked back under the wagon. She handed one to the soldier who had shot the union captain. He took it, reloaded, and lay facing down toward the rear of the wagon. "You know about Colts, don't you?" Caroline turned and lay down beside him but did not answer that question. "The bag has twenty more cartridges; I'll take ten, and you take ten. There may be more up by the driver. You stay here I will go check." Caroline, keeping her revolver in hand, crawled the length of the wagon and up and over the front wheel. She pushed the dead driver over onto the side and pulled away his opened leather bag which hung near his seat. She climbed back down and ducked between the two wheels. Crawling back to the rear of the wagon, she took her position. "Got it. Let's see. It's got only one box of six. But to answer your question, yes, I have shot before but never at people."

Sergeant Wilcox, crouching low with bent knees, appeared, his left hand covered in blood. He never looked at Caroline or the wounded man but kept his eyes on the road in front of him. "If they come, if they come on horses, we have the advantage, but if they come with rifles on foot, there will be many, and it will be a shootout. I see no advantage for us. There are but thirteen of us. Three cannot hold or fire a weapon. If the Yankees don't come in the next five minutes, then they are attending to their wounded. One of you two killed their officer and so they will think twice. I am going to wait five minutes, and then we are gettin' the hell out of here. Missus Duncan, I will need you again to be the driver of this wagon. When I give the signal, you get up then help this man get in, and when you are in place, you shout it out. We are going to travel fast, and I mean fast. Do not hang back. Do not straggle. I will leave you. I swear to God I will. You whip those horses hard."

Five minutes passed and the Sergeant whistled loud and shouted, "Mount 'em up!" Gray-coated men scrambled out from under the wagons and climbed aboard. Three Union soldiers climbed back into the wagons; nine others went running barefoot across the meadow toward the tree line. Caroline helped the wounded man to board the wagon and he took a position in the rear. Climbing the front wagon wheel, she took a seat and grabbed hold of the reins. She pushed the dead driver to the side and slid into his place on the bloodied seat. Bear looked up from the ground and Caroline motioned for the dog to come up and join her. Bear climbed the front wheel spokes and into the wagon, standing behind Caroline. She grabbed the brake release and held it in her hand, shouting out, "Five is ready." Seconds later, she heard wagon two and wagon three shout out. Wagon number one, driven by Sergeant Wilcox, jerked as he whistled loudly and whipped his reins over the rear of the horses. All five wagons lurched forward and started to build speed. The six horses which the escorts had been riding on, still saddled, ran off in six different directions, but three turned and followed the wagons. Sergeant Wilcox could be heard over the sound of the hoof beats, "Go! Go! Go!"

This quick escape continued for the next fifteen minutes at gallop speed and without relenting, and once past a fork in the road the lead wagon slowed. As they traveled, Caroline continuously looked over her shoulder to see if the wounded soldier was still upright and watching. At one point, she shouted back, "Is everything alright? What do you see? You see anything?" The answer came back, "Nothing. I see nothing back there; they're not coming."

A moment later, the lead wagon came to a creek, and stopped at the edge. Sergeant Wilcox jumped out of the wagon. He held a revolver in one hand and had a second stuck under his belt. He shouted loud enough for all to hear. "I do not think they are coming. "Water 'em." The three remaining drivers pulled their wagons up to the stream, and the horses started drinking. Sergeant Wilcox came walking back to Caroline's wagon. "That road we passed about a quarter mile back, Missus Duncan, that is the road to Shelbyville. We are heading to Frankfort, and that is this road. You stay with us. It is another forty miles to Frankfort. Shelbyville has changed hands several times now and I think Frankfort may be safer."

Caroline looked down from her seat. "But my husband is in Shelbyville, and that's where I have to go."

239

"Was in Shelbyville weeks ago. Was! Today, he could be in Frankfort—could be anywhere. We tend to move our wounded as we travel. You come to Frankfort, and I'll find out more when we get there."

"No. I am going to go to the last place, the place where he was last. And that is Shelbyville."

"You don't seem to understand. We are always moving. I've been to Shelbyville and there would be no strategic reason to hold that place. I bet they moved him weeks ago to Frankfort or even to Lexington, or he is..."

"When I get to Shelbyville, I will find out, won't I? Beside Shelbyville is merely fifteen miles, wouldn't you say?"

"I would say more like twenty, but you do what you have to do, lady; you seem to have gotten this far and I do not know how you did it. Where did you start from?"

"Hopkinsville."

"That is 180 miles from here. You walk the whole way?"

"There was no other way to do it."

"Okay then, you do as you wish, but you get out of those grays as soon as you can and good luck. We will be here for no more than another ten minutes and then we are going again. It will be your last chance."

Caroline stood, stepped over the seat, and went to the back of her wagon to get her bedroll and bag. She placed her revolver back in the bag and gathered some hard tack and salt pork from the food box in the wagon. She said goodbye to the soldier who was still guarding the back of the wagon. "I think you are the new driver. I wish you luck."

The wounded soldier stood up and walked cautiously to the front of the wagon. As he did, he turned. "If you find your husband dead, you come on down to Mayfield, Kentucky. I would marry you in a whisker's width of time. You got a backbone, lady. You got backbone." Caroline smiled but said nothing and walked away.

The sergeant was true to his word, and within moments of her and Bear walking away, she heard the wagons start to pull away quickly. The driver of the fourth wagon, a young man with blond hair, shouted out, "Ma'am, either you're nuts, or God is on your side. So, put in a good word for me. Private Marshall K. Washburn, Sassafras Ridge, Kentucky."

It took Caroline five minutes to walk back to the road that led to Shelbyville. Looking at the sign, she read the words chiseled in the wood, "Shelbyville." It was blunt on one end and on the other it came to a point angled toward the north. There was a second sign that pointed west which read "Elizabethtown." The third sign pointed east and read "Lexington." This northbound road climbed up for the next three miles to what, at first, appeared to be a rocky summit. On a large rock formation, someone had written with a rust-colored rock, "Franklin and Geraldine. 1857." There were others but most were unreadable, as rains and weather had washed away the red stone markings. One chiseled stone

241

lettering which she could make out, read "Tomas Elihu Sloan, 1807." Since the big rock was ten feet from the road, she walked over and, finding a red stone at its base, she wrote, "Caroline Emily Duncan and Bear. 1862." Looking down at Bear, who stood by the road, she said, "No one will know who we are, but this proves we were here."

Bear, limping from his wound from the bear attack, took the lead and was only five feet ahead of Caroline. It was a slow pace but Caroline, in pain also from her bear wound, could not have walked any faster. After a mile and a half, she realized this was more than a hill, this was a small mountain. Six switchbacks later, they rounded the top and felt a breeze of cool air while observing an expansive open valley below. From that position, she could see what appeared to be twenty miles in all directions. Behind her and miles away, she thought she observed a dust cloud from five CSA wagons moving toward Frankfort. Ahead of her and to the north, the road ran straight through a small settlement of fifty houses, all in a line, hugging the road as if the road provided safety. Scattered to the left and right as far as the eye could see was a checker board of homesteads. Fences and fence posts divided the green pastures in geometric shapes of all sizes and configurations. Herds of black, brown, and auburn-colored cows grazed in groups of ten to twenty on hilly pastures. White kitchen smoke rose from chimneys to the right and left. The closer she walked, she could discern clotheslines fluttering with different colored shirts, dresses, and white sheets. This was not Shelbyville, but the peacefulness of its appearance was comforting. She squinted her eyes and saw what appeared to be a larger town; a single white steeple rose above all else about fifteen miles in the distance. "Bear, I think I see Shelbyville. It's a flat road to there. We could be there soon."

By three in the afternoon, rolling black clouds swept across the sky and thunder signaled the approaching storm. A breeze that had earlier felt good in her face soon became stronger and trees began fluttering their leaves high up on the very tops. One, two, then three cool droplets of water danced on her forehead. Miles ahead, jagged coils of terrifying lightning, searching to ground itself on the tallest trees, found their marks and shot their bolts of brilliant light and intense scorching heat down grey tree trunks and stabbed themselves deep into the black earth. The air turned chilly and demanded surrender with its overpowering forces. By its cold and biting wind, Caroline knew it was moving in her direction. She quickened her pace and, at times, almost ran. In five minutes, the downpour started, and she spotted a single homestead that stood by itself near a tree line. As the rain intensified, she broke into a painful run and raced to the small barn that stood to the side of the house. Bear was quick behind her and found a place to rest under a hay wagon. Caroline wiped the rain from her face with her gray coat sleeve. A lone mule stood in the corner, watching the intruders. Three minutes later, as the wind increased, the back door opened and a man ran out and across the yard to the windmill, which was turning at a high speed, making a cracking sound. The man pulled hard on a metal lever which ran up to the brake on the wheel and slowed the blades, causing it to finally come to a high-pitched stop. Like a cat playing with a mouse, the tail whipped and see-sawed around, as the gusting wind twisted and turned the tin tail as it saw fit. The man continued into the barn, holding his hat tight. "Boy, this looks like a humdinger." Caroline looked the man over, seeing a thin man of middle age with a kind face. He held a rag in one hand and a wrench in the other. "I saw a funnel cloud about ten minutes ago down that away, over near the Huntmere's homestead, but it never touched down. We had one of these two years ago and they said it was from a hurricane coming up from Georgia. I do not know where this came from—probably a northerner. You from around here?"

"No, I am from Shelbyville, and I am on my way there. My name is Amanda."

"You got a gray uniform on, Miss Amanda, and there are a lot of Yankees around. I'd be careful. What you wearing that uniform for?"

"I lost my jacket in a river crossing and found this one in a pile of clothes someone left behind, and it was the only one that fit. I take no sides in this war."

"Me neither. I just lost my brother's boy. He was shot a month ago in a skirmish near Shelbyville. He wore a gray uniform like that. He's buried up there someplace I don't know where. My son, Hilbert, packed up two months ago and high tailed it to Colorado. We are peace-loving folks, Calvinist, and we want no part of this. Bueller is my name. Peter Bueller. My wife is inside and why don't you come in and dry off. Your dog can stay on the porch."

"Thank you, sir. I can stay the storm out here."

"No, you won't, you will come inside, as my wife has not had any women visitors and she is housebound and at times she gets a little delirious and so you might be able to help."

"But, sir, I need to get to Shelbyville as soon as I can and from that hill south of here, I could see it."

"That's Shelbyville alright, but you don't want to go there. Yankees are everywhere and they have been ambushed by the Grays only three days ago, and they lost a lot of men, so they are seeking revenge."

"I have no other choice."

"Go ahead and go inside. Just see her and talk to her; she needs company real bad. I don't know what to do. I was about to make some soup and you can have a bowl. Please come in, if for just a moment. I need help."

Caroline looked to the darkening sky. "Alright, until the rain clears. But I need to get to Shelbyville."

"You know, I question whether you are from Shelbyville; most people would have said I need to get home. You didn't."

"I wrongly spoke. It's been a while. I need to get home."

The man pointed to the house. "Give us an hour of your time and I will provide a good warm meal, and if you spend the night I will leave you have my son's room."

Caroline looked at the black sky and looked to the house. "I certainly can give you an hour. This storm may be over by then, but I am urgent in need. It is life or death for my husband that I travel."

Once inside and standing in the warm kitchen, Caroline took off her wet coat and the man returned with a dry towel and a jacket. Handing her the coat, he said it belonged to his son, and he was keeping it, hoping his son would one day return. The man pointed to the darkened bedroom and led the way. Caroline followed with caution. Inside the room with the tall pine head-board flat against the wall, Caroline made out the form of a body in bed with several blankets piled on top of the form. A tin bucket on the floor held several bloody towels. On the table sat the Bible and a single lit candle. Caroline saw the tired grey face of a sick woman as she pulled a chair next to the bed.

"Hello, my name is Amanda, and your husband invited me in to see what I can do. How are you feeling?"

The woman stirred out of her sleep. "What? Peter, who is this woman? What is happening?"

The man leaned over her. "This is Amanda, and she has come to help you."

The woman opened her eyes and Caroline could see intense fright in her face as her eyes frantically searched the room. "I see things. Snakes. Snakes everywhere. I cannot sleep. My son is gone. I am weak. I have been bleeding down there for a week now and I think I have lost a lot of blood. I feel so tired. But kill the snakes, please. I beg you."

Peter turned to Caroline. "I change the towel beneath her three times a day. The doctor is miles away and he himself is too sick to travel this far. My neighbors have nothing to do with us since we will not take their sides in the war. They think my son should join the blue army. I am alone. I thought the bleeding would stop by now. Help me, please."

"Mister Bueller, if your wife has been bleeding for a week, then she may eventually bleed to death, unless we stop it."

"Yes, but how do you know what to do? You have not seen what I have seen."

"This is abnormal uterine bleeding. We need to go gather healing herbs, now."

"But how do you know?"

"I have read about this before. I suspect she has torn a blood vessel in her womb. It can happen to women who have weakened blood vessels from giving birth or exertion. Doctors call it menorrhagia."

"Alright. I will go with you; there are many, but which ones do you need?"

"I need nettle and lots of it. We need to make teas and most of all, I need to make poultices."

"You mean stinging nettle? I think I know where there is a whole drift of it."

"Good, let's get a knife and a basket."

At that moment, a huge thunderclap jolted the ground, and the little white house shook on its flagstone foundation. The woman in bed screamed out. Caroline stood and went into the kitchen. She opened a drawer and pulled out two knives. "These should do; I will take this basket, and you take that one." Caroline turned and went for the door. "Which way? Which way? Mister Bueller, where is the nettle?"

The man pointed to his right as he walked out the door. "It is up there in those woods. I will lead the way." The man ran out into the rain and toward a tree line 900 feet away. Caroline followed closely. A second thunderclap struck and the two froze for a moment then ran under a group of trees. "Over here. I usually stay away from it. Is this it? I call this nettle. It itches my skin when I touch it."

Caroline bent down and pulled up a handful and to her nose, breaking the stems and leaves. "Yes, this is it. I will need both baskets full, and I need the roots—especially the roots." Caroline started cutting and lifted the nettle in the basket. The man pulled up the plant roots still clinging to the black soil. A third lightning strike struck a tree a hundred feet away, its sound deafening. As the man stood to look at the strike, a fourth one hit a pine tree 300 feet up the hill and the top burst into flames for a moment. Continuing to gather the nettle, Caroline glanced over her shoulder as the rains nearly hid the small house 900 feet away. Then everything went white hot for a brief moment, and Caroline found herself on the ground, her ears ringing and the rain striking her face. She sat up and saw Mister Bueller had been knocked down too. He was face down, and so Caroline shouted over to him, "Are you okay. Are you alright?" The man did not move. Getting up, she walked over and turned him on his back. She could see he was still unconscious but breathing. His eyes fixed straight ahead. Then he muttered something. "My wife, attend my wife. Leave me be. Attend my wife."

"I don't want to leave you here."

"My wife. Attend my wife. I will be there. Give me a minute. Let me be."

"Caroline reached for her basket of nettle and the man's basket. She added some more herbs and looked once again to the man. He was rubbing his face. "Rub mud on your face if you itch. I will be back shortly." Bear, who had followed them up the hill, watched Caroline turn and run down the hill. Bear circled the man for a moment, then sat down next to the man, who moved his arms about, but his legs remained dead. Caroline ran back though the rain to the house. Once inside, she rushed to the kitchen, and finding kindling wood she added some to the stove. She walked back into the bedroom. "We're back and everything is okay."

"Where is Peter? Who are you?"

Peter is gathering more herbs; he will be back soon—you just rest."

"Where is Peter?"

"Up in the woods. He will be back. I need the water to boil first and I am sure by that time, he will be back."

It took twenty minutes for the water to come to a boil. As she waited, she dumped the nettle onto the table and started chopping it into small pieces. Then she washed the roots, returned to the table, and, taking a saucer in hand, she beat them with the edge until they became pulp. Occasionally, she tasted it to determine its strength. She was not entirely satisfied but it was all she had. Once the water had come to a boil, she dumped five handfuls of nettle leaves and roots into the pot. Then she removed it from the fire and started stirring it briskly, letting it steep. As it swirled, she looked for a cloth and, finding nothing, she walked into the bedroom and to the chest of drawers. She found a dress folded there. It was a summer white dress, worn and thin. Caroline took it and returned to the kitchen. With her knife she started ripping long six-inch strips then she cut them into six-inch squares. Looking around the kitchen, she spotted a sewing kit. She pulled out the white buttonhole thread and returned to the table. She stirred the nettle again and saw the water had turned a bright yellow. She took a spoon and tasted the tea. "Good."

Bear wandered in from the front porch and sat near the table watching the activity. Searching the drawers, she found a large spoon. She dipped out a spoonful of the simmered herbs and placed them in the middle of a cloth, then pinched the sides up and tied it with the white thread, creating a small poultice the size of a grape. This continued for a few minutes until she had six of these tied and resting in a bowl. Pouring a big glass of tea, she drank half herself then walked quickly into the bedroom with the bowl.

"I am back now, Missus Bueller. I have poultices and I need to place these in inside your vagina, your womb. I need for you to relax. I have seen this done before. I have six of them. These will stop the bleeding. But it will take several hours. I will be replacing them with fresh ones every two hours. I have tied them with a long string. That's how we will remove them."

Caroline pulled the blanket back and saw the woman's night gown was stained with blood from her waist down to the top of her knees. She pulled up her nightgown and saw a towel under her, stained scarlet with blood. "This will hurt a little, but after the first one the rest will be easy. Caroline took the half glass of tea then poured it over the poultices. "I can insert these, or you can, which would you prefer?" The woman said nothing, and so Caroline reached in with her fingers, opening the way for the first poultice. The woman stiffened for a moment but then relaxed. Caroline smiled slightly. "Good, very good. Here goes the second one."

251

The lady stirred slightly. "They are awfully warm, aren't they?" Caroline did not answer, but started with the rest of the poultices. After all six were inserted, Caroline stood and went to the bathroom and came back with a fresh white towel and placed it under the woman as best she could. She reached into her waist band and pulled out her knife. "Your nightgown has to be removed. But I dare not move you, so I think it best if I cut it off." Caroline cut along the seam and cut up the front, then the sleeves. She pulled it out from under the woman. "We will cover you with a folded sheet. We can change those when necessary. I want you to drink some tea also. I will bring that next."

Over the next four hours and into the early evening, Caroline repeated the procedure three times. But in all that time, Mister Bueller never returned. The rains continued to fall through the grey darkness, and after sunset the blackness descended out of the hills, surrounding the little white house. Caroline looked for a lantern and, finding one hanging from a hook on the front porch, she went back into the house to light it. She looked in on Missus Muller who was asleep and quiet. Caroline went back out onto the porch. "Come on, Bear, and let us go find Mister Bueller."

It was hard retracing her steps, but she knew there would be a path that they had left through the tall grass. She held the lantern high over her head and called out to him. "Hello. Where are you, Mister Bueller? Hello, are you out here? Mister Bueller?" Bear sprang in front of Caroline, barked once, and then disappeared into the darkness. He barked several times in a row, and Caroline turned to follow the barking until she came to Mister Bueller on his stomach. "I'm okay. I just can't move. My legs feel asleep and I cannot get up. I even tried crawling, but I have not the strength. This is how far I have crawled. Maybe fifty feet. I have a wheelbarrow down by the barn. You get it and bring it here. It's just inside the barn. You bring it here. Please. I need to be near my wife. How is Missus Bueller? I cannot hear you. My ears are still deaf. How is she? Shake your head."

Caroline smiled and shook her head "yes" then raised the lantern, as she walked down the path to the barn. The rains continued unabated. Once inside the barn, she spotted the wheelbarrow leaning against the wall. She walked by the house pushing the wheelbarrow, but stopped and went inside and into the woman's bedroom. She was still breathing and still asleep. Caroline lit a candle and then a coal oil lamp in the kitchen. She went back outside and took the wheelbarrow and started up the hill. Bear followed closely behind her. "Go find the man again, Bear." In the darkness, even with the lantern, it was hard to see the path, but she could hear the dog bark now and then. She followed the sound until she came upon Mister Bueller. "I'm back. Let me turn this downhill and get you in it. I will pull you in backwards with your feet dangling by the handles. First, I need to turn you over." Caroline turned the man and pulled the wheelbarrow close. Using his hands, Mister Bueller pushed his body up and backwards into the wooden carry-it-all. It was difficult, but together the man squirmed until he was in. Caroline lifted the handles and balanced the man. "Mister Bueller, do not move, as it will cause me to lose balance and you will end up

253

on the ground again. Please hold the lantern high so I can see."

In moments, they were underway through the tall grass. Near the garden, Caroline stopped to rest. Her bruised rib and bear wound caused a shooting pain in her side, but she continued, and within five minutes arrived at the back porch. The man asked Caroline to place the front of the wheelbarrow to the porch and he pushed himself backwards onto the porch. "Good, I can move this way." The man pushed and crossed the doorway on his rear and into the kitchen. "Put two chairs together and I can push up and onto a chair." Grabbing two chairs, she slid them as close as she could to the man. He pushed against the seats and then raised himself onto one of the chairs. "Well, thank you! Thank you! I don't know what I would have done without you. And what of Missus Bueller? What have you done with the nettle?"

Caroline explained the procedure, and how she had seen it done to several women after childbirth to cease the bleeding. She said it would take hours to work, but that it always worked clotting blood. She said she would continue to replace the poultices throughout the night. Caroline went to the stove and added more wood, then went onto the porch and out into the yard. The rain continued and in the pitch black darkness, she felt the rope and bucket and drew more water from the well. Returning, she poured it into a large soup kettle. "I see you have canned sausage and tomatoes and corn and okra. I am going to make a soup, and I think your wife might be able to take some, at least the broth. I also saw her canned beets on the shelf and I want her to eat some with every meal, as they will build blood over the next week. As for you, I don't know what to do. But I will put a hot compress on your spine. This could be a temporary thing or it could be permanent. We will see hints in the next twenty-four hours."

All went according to her plan. The woman did eat some soup and consumed a whole beet. The man likewise ate a large bowl of soup, and, for good measure, he ate three beets. Caroline had two bowls of soup with some pone bread she had prepared. She opened a jar of cracked pickled pig's feet and gave that to Bear, who was getting used to eating what people were eating. Caroline watched as Bear crunched the bones and then swallowed.

At about midnight, Caroline tilted the man's chair backwards and pulled it on two legs into the son's bedroom. She helped the man into bed, and he reported some feeling was coming back in his toes. He moved one foot slightly to show Caroline. Returning to the kitchen, Caroline stoked the fire and added a few pieces and then started the process of making poultices again. At one o'clock, she entered with fresh warm poultices and changed them for the old. Caroline noticed there was less blood on the towel and took that as a good sign. Removing a single feather pillow from the bed, she laid it at the foot of the bed for her own place to sleep and lay on the pillow. Covering herself with her bedroll, she reached down and removed her shoes. Bear came into the room and lay briefly on the braided rug next to Caroline. But after a few minutes, Bear got up and went back out onto the porch as the rains continued. Caroline was unaware of Bear's movements, and still wearing her damp clothes, she soon fell fast asleep.

At five in the morning, chickens started crowing and Caroline got up and looked to Missus Bueller. She relit the coal oil lamp and pulled the quilts back and saw only a smatter of fresh blood on the towel. She walked on her bare feet into the kitchen and restarted the fire in the stove. Bear heard the movement and came in and lay near the cast iron stove. A coffee pot was located and some coffee beans were discovered nearby in a box marked "Caffé" in gold letters. A coffee grinder was put to use. Caroline reached for the coffee pot and poured in some water. Adding a handful of coffee, she placed it on the rear and hottest part of the stove. Caroline went in and woke Missus Bueller. "You are looking better, as your color is returning. How do you feel?"

Missus Bueller rolled to one side, facing Caroline. "Better than I felt yesterday. I do not remember your name. Where did you come from? Where is Mister Bueller? Has he gone to fetch help? I feel better. I don't think I have a fever. Were you the one who did the poultices?" Caroline started to answer, but Missus Bueller had more to say. "I can't remember much, but I do remember I saw snakes everywhere. Not today though. Where did you say Mister Bueller is? What is your name? Yes. Now I remember. You are a nurse. Am I right? You came in here with the poultices. Many times. I feel better. I might take a breakfast if you would be fixing one. And I will have more beets, please. Oh, and I must to pee."

Caroline told her that was a good sign then pulled out the commode pan, placing it near the woman. She helped the woman arch her back and slid the pan close. She carefully removed the poultices. "Do the best you can and what spills will go into the towel." When the woman finished, she rolled back onto her back. "I suppose that was the nettle tea you had me drink. I remember that. But please. Please send Mister Bueller in to see me. I want to see his face."

Caroline walked into the next room and looked in on the man, still sleeping. "Storms over. I'm making some coffee, and your wife—well, some of her color is coming back. She seems better. How's your legs?"

Mister Bueller slapped his leg. "I feel nothing here. I can move my foot a little. We can do some more hot compresses after you fix the poultices with my wife. Oh, yes, there will be eggs out in the henhouse this morning. If you desire to have a chicken for dinner, grab a red one. The hatchet is hanging in the barn. I cannot thank you enough. You are an angel that God has sent. Yes, you are. You may not know it, but you are. Ruth would be—Ruth would be dead. I know it. Yes, you saved..." The man started to tear up. "You saved two lives last night."

That day, Caroline applied nettle poultices at six, nine, and noon. At one in the afternoon, it looked like the bleeding had stopped altogether. Missus Bueller got up, then cautiously, with Caroline's help, walked out to the kitchen and sat by the warm stove for a while. Caroline had her drink another full glass of hot nettle tea and chew on some goldenseal root. Caroline explained Mister Bueller was in the second bedroom but had been knocked down by lightning and could not move his legs. Missus Bueller slowly got to her feet and went in to see her husband. Sitting on his bed, she reached out and touched him—Caroline could hear them talking. Going out into the garden, Caroline found some carrots, onions, and butter beans and returned to the kitchen to prepare another soup with the fresh vegetables. Exhausted, Caroline sat near the stove and dried her shoes by the fire. After the soup had simmered long enough, Missus Bueller had a small bowl with another helping of pickled sliced beets. Mister Bueller ate a large bowl of soup in his room and asked if he could have a single finger of whiskey. Caroline said no and left it at that.

That afternoon, Caroline sat out on the porch and watched the white clouds dipping so low she knew they would hide the mountain ridges behind her. She wandered down to the garden and picked a small pail of red raspberries. Near a small stream, Bear searched along the bank for something alive to eat. Then he turned and raced after three rabbits caught unaware of his presence. Two escaped. Walking back to the porch, Caroline observed a flock of well over one hundred cardinals land in a beech tree near the barn and pick at the beech nuts. This sight was something she had seen at home only weeks earlier. Caroline thought how the world seemed to be the same no matter where one traveled. A lone black cat with white paws and white chest wandered out of the barn and positioned himself under the single beech tree watching the birds. Bear readjusted himself on the porch to watch the cat watching the birds. He knew the protocol and sat quietly.

Occasionally on the road, 300 feet away, a wagon would come up from the valley heading south and she thought wouldn't it be a miracle if one of those wagons carried her husband? During that afternoon, there was no sign of either army, just a few homesteaders going to Shelbyville, now so close. She waved as they came by, and Caroline felt good to see women with their husbands traveling this road. She glanced at the dog. "If Missus Bueller continues to get better today, we can travel on early tomorrow. I will stop and talk to the doctor, and let him know the circumstances here at the Buellers. My bear wound is healing, but there is a soreness underneath that worries me. Bear, you are behaving almost normal, although I feel you hide your true condition to protect my feelings. Nonetheless, we should be in Shelbyville tomorrow, maybe before noon. It's only fifteen miles because I saw it from atop that hill. You feel up to it, boy? Huh? Do you?" The dog looked up and wondered what the question was. Bear thought when people's voices went up at the end of sentences they were asking questions, but it was never clear what was being asked and so he always barked once to say, "yes," because "yes" was always a good answer.

That afternoon, Mister Bueller tried to leave his bed, as he had regained feeling all the way up to his knees, but his left ankle was still too weak, and so he sat back down. Missus Bueller came into his room and sat beside him. They chatted quietly and then prayed together. Eventually, she lay with him and said she would spend the night there beside him. Later, Caroline went into her bedroom and removed the sheets. She found the bloodied towels and took them outside and placed them in a large copper tub and filled it with lye water to soak.

Sleeping in the main bedroom on clean fresh sheets, Caroline tossed and turned, thinking about the day which had finally arrived. The anticipation was overwhelming. The uncertainty of what she would find raced through her mind. Would she find him? Would she find a man barely alive? Would she find a grave? Would she find any answers? Her sleep was shallow and she woke several times and fought to get back to sleep. Fatigued, and with her muscles aching, Caroline turned repeatedly looking for relief. Outside the cabin, Bear slept on the porch, and once wandered off in the direction of three rabbits heading toward the garden. He snatched and then carried the slowest rabbit off into the tall grass. All of this happened in near total silence, with the rustle of grass and quick silent steps blending with crickets to barely puncture the darkened stillness. A lone barn owl watched the movements of Bear and the rabbits, then flew silently out into the darkness in the opposite direction. Caroline heard none of this, as her mind was twelve miles away in the next town. Shelbyville.

At five a.m., the rooster started crowing and Caroline sat straight up, but immediately started thinking this was the day she had been looking forward to for the last eleven days. No longer would she count the days, but now she could count the hours. The rejoining of her husband and her could occur this day. She closed her eyes and prayed that everything would be as she hoped it would be, and that she would find her husband, nurse him back to health, and then take him home. After she finished, she said the 23rd Psalm, then without delay, she put on her clothes. She wanted to save the yellow dress for when she arrived in Shelbyville, and so she put on the gray jacket with the dark grey pants and her shoes. Caroline walked out into the kitchen. She stood there thinking she should say goodbye to the couple, but realized she had informed them of her plans yesterday and so she walked out onto the porch to observe the orange sun attempting to light the sky. She breathed in the air of this day. It was different than yesterday's air because this was the day she had been waiting for. Maybe this was the air she and her husband would be breathing together only hours from now. A smile formed on her face. Bear was already standing out by the road, glancing back at the house as if he knew what Caroline was about to do. He commenced wagging his tail at her presence on the porch. She knew what that meant to the dog. It meant to travel. To the dog, it was where adventure lay.

The road was muddy from the storm and so she walked to the side on the grass that grew near the road. And while the storm had passed, to Caroline the sky looked as if it might repeat itself this day. Bear ran his usual fifty feet ahead and only stopped occasionally to wait for Caroline to catch up. A sudden brisk burst of winds caused Caroline to realize a second storm could happen, but she watched the now darkening sky for the speed of the clouds as they moved overhead. "Bear, I am afraid we are in for more rain, and I hope it is light and quick, then moves away, or that it rains to the west of us and not here. I see there are more homesteads ahead, but stopping anywhere would delay me and I will walk on even in a downpour. I hope you understand and stay with me through whatever comes our way."

Moments later, a light rain started to fall, and she could see there might not be any sun today. The rain formed droplets on her grey jacket, and the wind caused her to feel a chill both on her legs and her face. A flash of lightning lit up the sky, and the thunder, ten seconds later, rolled across the valley. "I am not stopping, Bear! If I have to, I will walk the rest of the way to Shelbyville in a downpour. I am this close." A second, then third lightning strike struck miles ahead and far to the east as she walked north. Bear fell back and started walking directly in front of Caroline only a few steps ahead.

The downpour she feared swept in from the right, and the noise of it striking the leaves of the trees alongside the road was similar to standing on the banks of a raging river. She stopped and pulled the hat down, so that the flap of the cap would shield her eyes from the rain. Water started running down the middle of the road, and at times she had to jump over the water that was running six inches deep. "You know what this is, Bear? Ole Satan does not want us to get to Shelbyville. This is like Job. Well, pour it on, because this will not stop me." Suddenly a lightning strike hit a thousand feet ahead of her and struck a tall pine tree. The loud crash caused her to take a step back and she ducked low and raised her arm to shield her face. Bear jerked quickly to his right and went low in a defensive position. "Is that the best you can do? Well, it will have to strike me dead right here in the middle of this road to stop me. Let me make this clear, I will not be stopped." The top of the pine tree that was struck smoked for a while, and then burst into flames. Even the rain was no match for the fire.

The next two miles proved the same. At one point, she faced a five-foot-wide stream of muddy brown water running across the road. Caroline removed her shoes and tied the laces and held them in one hand, then leapt, but her bare feet slipped on the muddy landing, and she fell backwards into the stream. She stood, and picking up her rucksack and her shoes, she walked on barefoot. From that point, when she came to a stream crossing the road, she walked through it, much like Bear, who appeared to have no thought of attempting to keep dry.

At the bottom of a hill where a stream would usually cross, she encountered something she had not planned for. The stream had overrun its banks and was twenty feet wide, running quite fast. Without hesitation, Caroline started across the stream and felt the pull of the water, but it was not strong enough to pull her downstream. Her adjustment was to make very small steps. She leaned to the left from where the water came. This seemed to work, as the valley was wide, so the stream was likewise wide, not deep. In the middle, the water came up to her knees, but she kept her right leg extended out to the side, and that stance kept her stable. Once to the other side, she looked back to see that Bear had stopped and was watching with interest. "Come on, Bear, it's not that deep." Bear stood and took his first steps into the water. A moment later, he was over his head and swimming, but the current was taking him downstream. "You can do it, Bear. Come on!" Water splashed over Bear's head, and at times it covered his head entirely, but that did not deter him. As the brown water churned and pushed him downstream, he kept his eyes trained on Caroline. "Good boy. Good boy. Come on. You are almost finished." Caroline started running on the bank downstream to position herself as a target for the black and brown dog. A minute later, Bear was on the other side but downstream sixty feet. Once back on the grassy bank, Bear shook his whole body from top to bottom and then, without looking at Caroline for her approval, he trotted back to the road, turning to signal Caroline with a glance that again he was ready to complete the last day's walk.

Once back on the road, the two of them walked side by side. The rain lessened slightly as the sun attempted to peek through the storm clouds. The terrain in this central part of Kentucky had proven to be a disadvantage for homesteaders since the first Europeans walked these rugged hills. For Caroline and her dog, it was still the same hindrance as they struggled to climb hill after hill. And while the descending was always easier than climbing, the downside of the mountain road proved to be a slippery challenge. By the eighth hill that morning, Caroline was tiring and stopped to have some hard tack and salt pork. Sitting there, and sharing some food with Bear, she looked down and spotted chimney smoke from a lone homestead at the bottom of the hill. The house was of unpainted oak plank, and the roof was of wood shingles cut from cedar plank. Caroline stood and started the downhill walk, slipping and sliding until there was enough grass on the side of the road to walk on. Once at the bottom, Caroline came to the lone homestead 300 feet from the side of the road, and, like many homesteads she had encountered, it was tucked close near the tree line. A woman sat out on the porch and waved to Caroline to come over and get out of the rain. As she approached the woman, Caroline saw a gun resting in the woman's lap. Caroline stopped when she saw the woman take hold of the gun. The woman, who appeared to be in her fifties, stood with the gun at her side. "You stop right there. I could not see you were wearing a gray jacket when you first approached. There will no rest here for you." The woman took two steps forward and stood on the flagstone step in front of the porch. "Sir, you better move on. We don't take well to no rebels here." Caroline took a step backward. "I am not in the Confederacy. I was given this jacket to merely to keep warm."

"Lies! I hear there are spies everywhere and I am believing you are one. Get the hell out of here. You will find no sympathizers in our home. You would do well to rid yourself of that ugly garment 'fore I put a new hole in it."

"I take it you have lost a son in this war."

"Damn it, that I have, and not one but two. Sadly, one more has joined the fight to save the Union and I am in mourning for his life, for I do not know his whereabouts or his condition." The woman ever so slowly raised the gun and pointed it at Caroline. "If you are wise, and my belief is you are, then you can see God has smiled on you this rainy day, for my anger will be held for a time while you retreat from my land."

Caroline turned and, without saying a word, walked back to the road. Her hand was still in her haversack on the revolver in case the woman came running after her, firing her rifled musket.

The rain looked like it would drizzle the whole day, and to Caroline that was better than the downpour she had experienced hours earlier. Bear walked beside her as she came down a hill and past a grove of hickory trees to a place where the road went in three different directions. Nearby, sitting in the middle of a dozen large rocks, there were three road signs. The smallest road was labeled "Burnsville," while the second road was marked as "Treat's Crossing." The last road sign, and the largest of all three, was labeled "Shelbyville." There were no mile markings and so she paused for a moment. Then she heard something behind her.

Three men quickly emerged from out of the hickory grove. Two appeared to be in their twenties. The third looked to be ten years older and in command. Two were armed with rifles, and the youngest one wore a belt over his coat that held two sheaved knives. All were dressed in worn and patched civilian clothing. Two of the men wore shoes; the youngest was barefoot. Caroline turned and watched as the men, walking briskly, came upon her. Bear, seeing the speed of the men and their guns, started a low growl.

"Hold up. Hold up. Hold up!" The oldest man led the way with his gun pointed at Caroline. "You stop right there or I will shoot your gray ass right there where you stand. No. You are not fooling me. I can tell you are a woman. I can tell you there are spies among us. Spies dressed to deceive, and those spies take information back to the rebs. But looky here. You are dressed in a Confederate jacket and hat, and you are not a man but a woman. What am I to think?"

"Sir, I am a neither a soldier nor a spy. I was cold, so I found this jacket and hat. Do I look like a spy to you? Do spies travel with their dogs? Do spies walk in broad daylight?"

"Spies be spies. I have heard spies are trained how to spin a story. Went to school for that. Trained to cleverly hide what they really are."

"No, sir, I have not been trained to deceive."

"Boys, see how good she is? She already is practicing on us. Well, miss gray coat spy, there is a bounty on your head and all I have to do is take you ten miles the other side of Shelbyville to the Grand Army of the Union, and if I show evidence, I will collect a reward. I will say no more. You just start walking. Go ahead and start walking or you will feel this rifle butt on your head." The man with the torn hat turned to his two young men. "Boys, you stay here, and we might catch another one." The two men turned and started back to the hickory grove. The older man pointed down the road with his rifle. "I said git!"

Caroline started walking down the road labeled Shelbyville. The sun had come out as the two of them walked on the side of the road in the grassy part. The man took out a piece of tobacco and started chewing it. He did not point his musket at Caroline, who walked thirty feet ahead, but carried it slung over his shoulder upside down and pointing ahead. Observing the two of them, and walking a hundred feet behind them, Bear watched this new man-made threat, waiting for a signal from Caroline. He noticed Caroline did not appear frightened, and so much of his gaze was upon the man with the torn hat. In the next fifteen minutes, not much was said as they passed homestead after homestead. At one point when no houses were to be seen, and as they approached a large wooded area, the man walked closer to Caroline. "You know, I am somewhat older than you, but I have been with women your age, though less attractive. Paid-for women. And women of wholesomeness. I have a feeling I could pull you into these woods and have my way with you. Have some relations. The Yankees would not care. I mean, you are a spy. You are trained to lie, so I can lie too."

Caroline stopped in the middle of the road. "Take me into the woods if you dare, but God will punish you all your days."

"God is happy I caught a spy. God is on the Union side not yourn."

"You would be cast into hell the instant you die."

"I will take that chance. Now go ahead and walk into the woods, right where I point." The man gripped his musket and pointed it at Caroline, then pointed to a small grove of pine trees. "Go ahead, lady. Get up into those woods."

"Sir, your life is at risk. Do not do this for I..."

The man thrust his rifle and struck her left shoulder hard with the butt. "Git up there, you whore, and give me that sack." Caroline handed the man the haversack. While walking thirty feet up the side of a hill and into a group of young trees the man struck her shoulder a second time with the rifle butt.

"This is far enough. Take off your clothes!" Caroline hesitated and looked around for a plan of escape. She did not see Bear hiding in the tall grass, but she slowly took off her gray jacket. The man, watching Caroline closely, smiled and hurriedly took off his own jacket. "Faster, I ain't got all day." Caroline unbuttoned her pants and watched the man intently, looking for any sign of weakness in him, thinking of what Missus Millar had told her about surrendering and acting passive yet waiting for the right moment. The man unhooked his belt and pulled his shirt from his pants. He took an aggressive step forward pushing her backwards and hard to the ground. Caroline fell on her back but quickly rose on her elbows and cocked her knees into a half sitting position. The man took a step toward her and pushed his foot against her shoulder, kicking her back down. "On your back. Get down." Caroline, resting on her back, felt for the knife she had carried for the last eleven days. She felt its handle through her waist band. "Let me get a good look at you. Yes, you are the prettiest one I have ever caught." The man, fumbling with the last buttons on his pants, dropped them to around his knees. He wore nothing underneath. "Take off those damn pants or I will hit you again."

Caroline unbuttoned the pants but slid the knife behind her. The man with the torn hat stood there gazing at her. "Show me your breasts." Caroline did not move. "I said, show me your breasts." Caroline hesitated and the man reached down and struck her hard across her face with the back of his hand. "You bitch, I said show me your tits." The man lifted his rifle over his head as if he was about to strike her with it in the face. Caroline, bleeding from her lip, unbuttoned her shirt and revealed her underclothing. "More. I want to see your tits!" Caroline lifted her garment up under her chin showing her breasts. "That's what I wanted to see. Naked tits. Yes, those are beauties. Now, lay back, whore!"

Caroline looked to the right of her and saw her haversack three feet away. She looked back at the man, who was smiling as he gazed at her. Caroline looked for Bear and spotted the dog a hundred feet away, slowly creeping low in the grass toward the man. Bear started to growl. The man looked over his shoulder at the dog and raised his musket, pointing toward the dog. Caroline, seeing this, shouted out to Bear, "No." Bear stopped and quickly moved to his left, lowering himself and disappearing again in the grass. The man turned and pulled off his hat and tossed it sideways, then took a step forward toward Caroline, who lay in the grass. The man, in his haste to move to her, took a large step and, forgetting his pants were gathered around his boots, tripped and stumbled. He fell to the ground on his face three feet away. Caroline instantly rolled to her left and shouted, "Bear!" She sprung to her feet with the knife in hand and took three fast steps forward. Turning her body, she leapt on the man's back as he struggled to stand. Bear came running from out of the weeds and bit hard into the man's right wrist as he tried to turn himself over. Bear pulled hard and would not let go. Caroline grabbed the top of the man's head and pulled back on his hair. He reached around with his left hand and tried to grab at her leg. She swung and sliced the knife across his left hand and he pulled away in pain. The man, collapsing his face back into the grass, paused but for a second and then tried to turn the other direction, screaming, "Get off me, you damn bitch!" Caroline took the knife and pulled it across the man's left ear, his left cheek, his nose, and halfway across the right cheek, drawing instantaneous blood. Bear continued his biting grip of the man's right hand. The man pushed up with his left hand and attempted to roll over to face Caroline but, with Bear pulling hard, the man faltered and collapsed face down. He attempted to turn his face to confront this thirty-three-year-old woman. Caroline, still holding tight his hair with her left hand, pushed the knife against the right side of his neck and shouted loudly to the man, "Do you feel that? I have it within my power to kill you right now, but I will do only what you make me do. Do you want to live?" The man did not answer but gathered strength and attempted to roll over, but that proved difficult, as Bear pulled even harder at each attempt. The man's right arm proved useless. The man turned his face to Caroline and attempted to grab at her with his bloodied left hand. Caroline sliced across the palm a second time, and then pressed the knife tight against his neck. He faltered at this second attempt and collapsed again. Seeing her advantage, he stopped moving. "Hey, lady, you and your damn dog have the best of me, but seriously, God's honest truth, I was foolin'. God as my witness. This here is a joke."

"I am not fooling. Do you want to live?"

"Yes. Yes, ma'am! Now call your damn dog off!"

271

"This dog is a trained killer. You stay in that position or he will kill you. He will go for your neck, as he has been trained to do so."

Caroline got off the man and quickly stepped to where her haversack was lying in the grass and pulled out the revolver, instantly cocking the trigger. She looked back to the man lying in the tall grass and attempting to wipe blood from his ear-to-ear face wound. She pulled down her garment and buttoned one button on her pants. Releasing his bite and moving inches away from the man's face, Bear emitted a low intimidating growl. The man felt the heated breath of this eighty-pound dog.

Caroline, standing there with the revolver in one hand and the knife in the other, spit blood from her bleeding lip. "Roll over. I said roll over." The man reluctantly rolled over onto his back, still wiping blood from his face gash. Caroline took six steps back. "Okay, now slowly stand up. Sir, this gun is loaded with six rounds. One move from you and you will be shot. I do not want to do this to you, but you have narrowed my choices. I will let you live, but I require honesty. I need to know about your kind. Do you work or are you fully criminal? From your calmness and demeanor, I would say have you raped other women before. Have you? Before me? Have you?"

"Lady, I do not have to answer your questions. But truth is...truth is fickle. Hell, I was not born with land or money to entertain women. Who do they think they are? So I took 'em to teach them. They are no better than me.

Caroline interrupted. "These women ran from you? Resisted?"

"Lady, I have been drunk, and things happen. And by that, I mean most of these women were where they should not have been. Like you. What are doing out here walking by yourself? Aren't you asking for it? I would say so."

"So, you have you raped other women. Women like me?"

"Well, you call it what you want. I push 'em down and they start crying. I do not knock them out. I rarely strike them. It takes me no more than five minutes. Then they can be on their way. Me on my way."

Caroline, realizing what the man had just admitted, did not become angry, but she realized she had become judge and jury. Her demeanor was calm and thoughtful. "Today, I only wanted to pass. I have reluctantly killed a man, maybe three men in the last eleven days. I did not set out to kill, but God has put this in my hands. I do not want this cup. But it lies before me. What am I to do? If I walk away, are there more women you will rape, maybe kill? There is no answer but one. So, you will do as I say or I will, with those women standing beside me, shoot you right here on this piece of grass. I am not a killer, but I will kill to protect. I have one last question, are you, sir, ready to do what I am asking you to do?"

The man, with his hand across his cheek and blood pouring through his fingers, nodded his head. "Yes, ma'am! I will let you go. I will not harm you. I will send you on your way, untouched."

"No. That is not the answer. Then understand you are about to die here! For it is here, on this hill, your life will end."

"No! No! You have the gun and so I will do as you say. I will."

"Listen to me and listen well. I have here a knife. Razor sharp and you now realize that by the slash on your face. That sack that hangs beneath your sexual member. Doctors call it by its Latin name, scrotum. Scrotum! It holds two glands called gonads. There is not any muscle in that sack, so it will not be painful. You are to cut that sack off. You cut all of it off. Not your other thing, for you have to urinate, but the sack. I offer you now this knife."

"Wait! Wait! Are you asking me to cut off my manhood? My balls? Lady, you are crazy."

Caroline tossed the knife to the man's foot, and he reached down and picked up the knife. His right hand was bleeding from the dog's bite. His left from two deep cuts across the palm. Caroline centered the gun on the man's chest. "One step forward and I, without hesitation, will pull this trigger. You know what a Colt 36 will do?"

"Dammit, do you know what you are asking?"

"I am asking you to castrate yourself. You can keep your penis, for that is necessary. But I am demanding, in exchange for your life, that you castrate yourself right here and right now.

After today, you will no longer desire sex. You will no longer be a rapist." The man, who wore no undergarments, standing in his pants gathered around his legs, made another plea. "For God sake, lady! What the hell, do you think I am crazy? You will not force me to do this. I would be a weak man to do as you say. No woman has ever forced a man to castrate himself. No. I will not do this."

"I will count to ten; if it is not done by ten, then I will shoot you there in your manhood with a single shot."

"Lady, this is crazy. I will not do this. Please. As God is my witness, this was just foolin' around. I was joking."

"One, two, three, four, five, six, seven."

"This means I will never have children."

"Or rape again. Seven, eight, nine."

In one slow move, the man pulled up his blood-stained shirt, then hesitated for a moment. "I can't do this." Suddenly, he lunged forward toward Caroline, reaching for her neck with his bloodied left hand and, in his right hand, the knife raised high.

"Bang!" Caroline fired a shot into the man's shoulder. He jerked backwards and cried out in pain, "Ahhhhhh!" The man took a second step backward and, grabbing his shoulder, he looked into Caroline's eyes. He saw determination as he had never seen in a woman. "Please, one more time, I'm begging. Do not make me do this." Caroline said nothing but kept the Colt 36 revolver pointed to the place below his stomach. He reached down with the sharpened knife and hesitated for a moment then looked down and pulled the knife across his scrotum. He let out a scream of pain. "Ahhhhhh!"

Caroline took a step backward. "Show me! Show me them."

The man held up his severed scrotum in his left hand as blood started dripping down his legs.

"Okay, lay back down. Put your shirt on it and it may stop bleeding in an hour or so." Caroline reached forward and snatched the knife from the man's bloodied hand. "I am not a spy. I am a woman looking for my husband. I am taking your musket. If I see you following me, I will take it you seek retribution. I will end your life. You may not believe it, but you are a lucky man today. God let you live. Maybe only to repent of your sins."

Caroline called to Bear, who was standing a foot away from the man in an aggressive stance. Caroline picked up the man's musket and her rucksack and backed away slowly. Glancing backwards, she walked out into the tall grass and back onto the road. As she walked away, she heard the man cry out again in pain, cursing her and then cursing God.

Nothing more was said for the next twenty minutes, as she was lost in thought of what she had just done. She looked at Bear several times. "Good dog. You are a very good dog." Her right hand, the hand that fired the Colt 36 revolver, the hand that smelled of gunpowder, started shaking and would not stop. "God, why are you testing me? Haven't I done enough? I have! I have! Why then are you allowing this evil to come against me? Please, Lord, I am not that woman you desire to carry your banner. I have no strength left. I desire just to find my husband." Caroline realized she was carrying the man's weapon and so she tossed it into the high weeds along the road.

In the second hour, she cried briefly and decided she needed to have a conversation with Bear. "Well, Bear, do you see what I have become? I have lost sympathy for my fellow man. I have killed. I have wounded. I am no better than they. If God came today, could He forgive me? Those were His created creatures. I have taken His law into my hands. Have I dispensed punishment? Should I not have sacrificed myself? Should I not have turned the other cheek? Jesus! Did He not give his life? What was it like for Him? He could have saved himself. But that is what I did. I chose me over them. Was that anger inside me all the time and was I never aware? I resolutely do know this. My husband and my children is what I care about most. Those men I have killed and wounded could not weigh equal against my family, for my family stands innocent. Yes! Oh, dear Lord. I pray this damnable war to end, so that peace descends from the heavens once again. What I have done, as evil as it is, will remain a secret, as I do not want my family to love me less. I cannot and will not speak of this again." Caroline wiped the tears from her eyes and walked on for the next six hours. In all that time, she never said a word to her dog. She never hummed a song. She felt totally defeated and in despair. Much of the time, she only wept, but she kept walking.

At one point, a flock of twelve bright red and brown cardinals flew over her head and landed in a holly tree covered with red berries, which stood by itself, not near other trees, but as if it had been planted years ago just for this time, for this day, for this moment. They fluttered about, eating and chirping loudly. Caroline stopped and observed the cardinals. "Bear, look there. They are unaware the food they eat possesses seeds they carry to start other holly trees. Twenty years from now, their offspring will eat the berries from the trees they will start today. But at this moment, they are unaware of what they are doing. I would tell them, if I could, of their future, but they only know of today, much like me."

Three miles down the road, Caroline came to a rocky part of the road and slowed as she stepped over the rocks, which had been deposited there after hundreds of years of rain cascading down from the hills. At one point, her left shoe caught between two rocks and as she pulled hard, the heel dislodged from the rest of the shoe. Caroline immediately noticed it and, when she looked down, she saw the heel and the nails that held it in place. She picked up the heel and walked to the side of the road to sit, attempting to pound it back into place. But the nails were so bent they would not be driven back. The heel was now useless. Caroline stood and walked on unevenly. After 500 feet, she realized this was much like a limping man and was slowing her steps. She sat down in the in the grass and took her knife and, after much effort, pried off the right shoe's heel. She started walking again. This was even footed, and it felt similar to when she walked barefoot around the homestead. Her speed returned and she was satisfied. Twenty minutes later, and walking quickly side by side with Bear, she came to a small wooden bridge made of recently cut logs over a stream. She crossed over and found a homestead in the next quarter mile.

As Caroline approached, a homestead woman walked out of the garden carrying a basket filled with greens, calling out, "Hello there, stranger. Stop and rest yourself." Walking beside her was a young teenage girl holding on to her mother by the way of a thin rope tied around her mother's waist. "Over here. I am out in the garden. My name is Alma. What's yours?" The forty-year-old woman stopped at the edge of the garden and rested the basket on her hip, held there with her right hand. The young girl spoke, "Mama, don't forget me." Alma turned to her daughter. "Yes, this here is my daughter, Coriander." Caroline walked across the grass and to the garden and stood before the lady and her daughter. Caroline could not take her eyes off the beautiful young girl who was so perfect in face and smile, yet with eyes closed tight. "Yes, she is blind. Born that way into this world fifteen years ago next month." Caroline dropped her haversack to the ground. "It's nice to meet you both, but before we talk, could I have some water to drink?" The woman took a step forward and pointed to the back of the home. "There is a well in the back and you drink all you want. And I have a plate of yesterday's cornpone and some fried chicken on the table in back." Caroline smiled. "Yes, that would be very nice, for I have not eaten today. My name is Caroline. I can do chores to pay you back." The woman walked forward, and Caroline could see the woman was barefoot and her feet were covered with mud. Likewise, Coriander was barefoot, but what stood out was that Coriander had honeysuckle flowers woven in her hair. Coriander took a step toward Caroline. "Ma'am, you have such a sweet voice. May I see how pretty you are?" Coriander reached out with her hand toward Caroline and Caroline took a step forward and placed the girl's hand on her face. "Oh, you are very pretty. You have a graceful nose and high cheeks. I cannot tell if I am. Mama says I am, but what do you think?" Caroline kissed the girl's hand. "You are most beautiful. If I had a daughter as pretty you, I would be proud." A tear formed in the young girl's eyes. "Is my mama pretty? I think she is." The woman took the basket of beans off her hip and handed it to her daughter, then picked up another bushel basket of beans standing at the edge of the garden. "This rain is making a whole mess with my garden, and I got at least five bushel of green beans I need to sell. But first let's get you some water to quench your throat, for I hear it in your voice that you have had a tiring time today."

Caroline took off her bedroll and placed it on the ground. "I am on my way to Shelbyville to find my husband."

"Well, you got an eight-mile walk ahead of you. Come on in and get some ice-cold water. Our well is fifty-six feet deep, and it is the sweetest of any one around. Oh, by the way, my name is Alma Washburn; what's your whole name?"

Once inside the house, Missus Washburn offered a seat at the kitchen table and poured a glass of water out of a tall blue ceramic jug. The young girl took a seat and reached her hand over to Caroline, her face earnestly looking toward this new visitor with the pretty voice. The woman went to the pie safe and cut a piece of cherry pie and returned with that. "Here's some pie. And let me get you a piece of chicken; they go together. My mother did, and now I do. We always have pie with chicken. Well, that is whenever I have a chicken. Yankees came through two weeks ago and took our last cow and all our chickens. Except I have a hidden wire pen up in the woods with nineteen chickens and a goat tied to a tree. Anyhow, I will have eggs and milk. Lord, I hope I am not talking too much, but a chance to talk to another adult woman comes nearly never. So, it is odd to see a woman walking alone on my road. I bet you have relatives, a husband, in Shelbyville?"

Caroline explained the situation with her husband. The woman leaned back in her chair. "This war is the stupidest thing I ever saw. My brother's son, Tad, is fighting with the Unionists, and my sister-in-law's two sons, Frederick and Homer, are fighting with the Kentucky Regulars, the Confederals! They could be shooting each other today. Cousins! For what? Let us just sign a peace treaty and keep out of each other's business. We're Kentuckians; we may or may not break away from the Union, but our state and ten others have not moved anywhere. We are still bumped up against Illinois, Indiana, Ohio—northern states. We still speak the same language. George Washington is still our founder, along with Jefferson and Franklin. So, why come down here and start shooting? It's greed. Lincoln wants to be president

281

of a big country. He doesn't want to be president of a country half the size it was. But I got a solution if they would listen to an old woman who only owns one pair of shoes. Ain't nobody's fight except Lincoln and Davis. Let 'em go and fight it out bare knuckles in a town square." Missus Washburn stopped talking a moment. "I am sorry if I am talking too much. You know, we don't even have a church around here so I could get to know some women. We got a circuit rider comes riding into town twice a month and he speaks down at the school." Missus Washburn leaned back in her chair and clicked her fingers. "Come to think of it, would you like a ride into Shelbyville? My husband, Mister Washburn, is going in about an hour to get some more nails and some hinges and lumber for the barn. Last night's storm blew the door open and broke it off real bad. And he broke the handle on the hammer, so he could not pound nails even if he had them."

"Missus Washburn, you said he leaves in about an hour?"

"He'll take the wagon, 'cause he will take some of my green beans in for the city folk that have no gardens, and with the money I make, we can get a new handle for the hammer, ten pounds of nails, some lumber. Then I need a sack of flour, some coffee, sugar, and what else, c-a-n-d-y?" The young girl spoke up, "Yes, Mama, yes, ribbon candy for me." Missus Washburn nodded 'yes' and turned back to Caroline. "So, there is room for you and your dog. Eat your pie; if there is one thing we have, it is pie." After eating the pie and a small piece of chicken, Caroline stepped into the bedroom and put on the yellow dress. She looked to her brown, worn-out shoes and grimaced at the sight. When Caroline came out of the room, Missus Washburn remarked how pretty she looked in yellow. Her daughter, Coriander, wanted to feel the dress and said it felt like the color of apples. Missus Washburn explained that she had taught her daughter colors by the smell and taste of fruit. The color yellow was apples. The color red was cherries. Blue was huckleberries. Green was grapes. Orange was oranges. Black was plum. White was pears. The young girl exclaimed, "I adore the color yellow. You must be beautiful today."

Missus Washburn's husband loaded the five bushels of green beans. A single horse stood waiting, already hitched to the wagon. Mister Washburn did not say much. He wore a torn brown canvas jacket and blue bib pants with a pair of shoes that had been cut away on the sides for a wide foot. Missus Washburn and Coriander stood on the porch and waved goodbye. As they traveled, Mister Washburn hummed a song, but it was not familiar to Caroline. Chewing on piece of sassafras root, he spit occasionally to his left and then wiped his right sleeve across his face. Caroline looked over the back of the wagon with its five bushels of green beans, eight pecks of cucumbers, and six crates of sheep-nosed apples. Bear sat way in the back and enjoyed not having to walk.

Part Three

The ride to Shelbyville took two hours. Upon seeing the outskirts of the town, Carline's anticipation started her heart beating faster. Homesteads appeared and were located closer together. A sign by the side of the road read, "Welcome to Shelbyville." Finally, there was a line of houses—no longer homesteads, but city houses side by side with white picket fences. Stores started appearing between houses. A blacksmith barn and a small corral sat on the left side of the road, and across the way was a lumber yard with wood stacked twenty feet high. One house had a sign that looked like a tooth, and the name of a dentist, Abner Pomeroy, painted in red. Caroline glanced in the window of a ladies' clothing store and saw a yellow dress much like the color of hers. Finally, after a long line of homes, she spotted a church on a hill off to the left and up from the street. She glanced at the church and turned to Mister Washburn. "Is that the Shelbyville Baptist Church? The one up the hill?" Mister Washburn looked and then grunted, "Yep, that's it. But there is a Methodist church at the far end of town. It's the new one. And the Quakers have a small one that looks like a plain house to me. It's two blocks over to the right by the farmers market. We'll go right by it."

"You can drop me anywhere here."

"I was told by Missus Washburn to drop you off at the market, same as me."

"Okay, yes. And I appreciate the ride. You saved me a long walk."

"I don't think the horse knew you were back here, so he did not slow down a bit. You know he is fourteen years old and I think I might get another six years from him."

The farmers market was located on the grounds of the school and, thus, central to town. It was a piece of land large enough for the school to expand in the future. Caroline saw a long line of thirty wagons, all gathered in two columns, fifteen wagons to a side. The horses had been unhitched and tied to a long rope that ran between two posts about 150 feet away. Farmers who had brought in baskets of corn, beet roots, tomatoes, and beans were likewise unloading their produce on the ground in long straight lines. Several women stood by tables with peck baskets of eggs and butter, and glass gallon jugs of milk, fresh from cows or goats that morning. Townspeople walked the lines, buying the produce. The market was held on Mondays, Wednesdays, and Fridays, rain or shine. Children ran freely about the school grounds, while their parents shopped. Caroline got off the wagon and helped unload the green beans, the apples, and the cucumbers onto the ground. She thanked Mister Washburn once more, shouldered her bedroll and took her haversack, then started walking uphill toward the church. Bear followed closely behind, watching all the activity of the townspeople. Twenty houses away from the market and drawing closer to the church, Caroline saw two ladies walking toward her. The women, both dressed alike with large white bonnets, smiled as they walked by. Caroline turned toward them. "If you have a moment, ladies, I am looking for my husband. My name is Caroline, and I am from Hopkinsville, and he was wounded near here. Do you recall a Confederate field hospital that was in the area only four weeks ago?"

The older lady of the two, who was carrying a basket of tomatoes and yellow beans, turned and pointed over her shoulder toward a clearing about a half mile. The younger lady said nothing but looked sad and stared straight ahead. "The hospital tents were over there on Mister Ramsey's pasture. You can see from here, the grass is still brown from all that went on. Well, actually, there were three hospital tents. All white and all facing south. They used a big tent where they operated on the men. There was a wagon parked next to it with all the instruments, bandages, and medicine. But about one week ago, they brought in ten wagons and packed everything and left."

Caroline smiled briefly. "Thank you for that, but what happened to the men? The wounded men?" The older lady frowned. "Most of the town's ladies never went over there. The big tent. The surgery tent. I could not bear all that moaning when they operated on the men; it caused me to cry." The woman put down her basket on the ground and reached forward to shake Caroline's hand. "I am Missus Ollinger. I still feel bad for those boys weeks afterward. There were some dead and most were carried up near the woods and they buried them by that tree line. You can barely make it out from here. They put up no individual markers. Somebody put up a single white cross, but that is all that is up there. No names or anything. They said there were twenty-three men buried up there."

Caroline shielded her eyes and looked at the hillside a half mile away. "Is there anything else you know that could help me locate my husband? He was one of the wounded."

"Well, they were here only a fortnight—two weeks—and then they put some of the lesser wounded on wagons and moved them, they told us, down to Chattanooga. At least that's what they told my husband."

"To Chattanooga? Not Frankfort?"

"Yes, Chattanooga, that's what he said. It was a terrible sight, there were men who had arms and legs amputated and they were the first to be moved. Of course, some of the boys were so badly wounded or had advanced gangrene with terrible fever, so they chose not to take them. The army left one large tent, a surgeon, and one nurse. Both were overworked and three days later, they got orders to leave, which is why the nurse asked for lady volunteers. They said they would send a nurse, but they never did. So we ladies did the best we could. The shame of it all, there was scant medicine."

Caroline turned her attention again to the hill with the lone white cross. Missus Ollinger turned and looked at the hill herself. "Some of the last soldiers under our care grew weak and died, and we buried several of them, not up there, but up behind our church. Those poor boys told us if they died, they wanted a proper burial with a marker and, especially, by a church. Missus Henninger was sort of in charge of that." Missus Ollinger turned around facing Caroline. "That surprised us that the Confederate Army would just leave those men. They said the Union Army was coming this way and so they had to leave. That was so sad when they left those men. It was the most sorrowful thing most of us had ever seen." The woman reached down and picked up her basket. "I have to go; Mister Ollinger is ill at home."

Caroline reached out and touched the woman's arm as she took a step forward. "My husband may have been one of those men. Do you recall a Charles Duncan? First Lieutenant."

"No, I tried not to learn their names."

"I understand. But this woman in charge, Missus Henninger, where would I find her?"

"Oh, well, that could be a problem; she is over at her sister's house in Nicholasville. She herself took sick caring for those boys. She stayed with the sickest fourteen hours a day."

"Who else would know about the men?"

"Well, we all took turns. I helped. But, as I said, the army, the Confederates, did not leave us much medicine to help, so we made do with what little we had. Usually, about one man died every three days. There was a lot of fever and pain. We cried a lot for the boys—especially the youngest ones. Our own doctor, Doctor Baumridge, helped all he could, but after a while he just ran out of medicine. He collapsed to his own bed with the fever. So, it was just six of us women. Emily, Nettie, Harriet, Ermal, Ruth, and me. No one told us much."

"How would I find out what soldiers left and who stayed and who died? Are there records of some sort? Any records at all would help."

"Go up to the church. They tried to, but there was so much confusion everywhere, and the Confederates never told us much." Missus Ollinger shifted the basket to her other hand. "We just felt it was the Christian thing to help our fellow man. But you go up to the church. There may be somebody up there to help. The pastor might have recorded something. But God bless you, young lady, I hope you find your husband and that he is alright. We never thought we would see something like that in Shelbyville, did we, Alice?" Alice did not say anything, but just looked down at the ground with tears in her eyes. "By the way, this is my daughter-in-law, Alice Dean." Alice Dean looked up and forced a smile then looked back to the ground. "My son, her husband, is somewhere with General Jackson, that's all we know. Well, that's all any of us know about our boys." Missus Ollinger reached out and touched Caroline's hand. "God bless." Missus Ollinger smiled, then turned and walked away. Alice Dean followed, but several steps behind, she looked over her shoulder at Caroline and forced a smile, but the smile ended, and her face returned to sadness.

The little Baptist church sat on a hillside. It had been painted white when it was first built in 1839, but some of the paint could not withstand the ravages of rain and snow. Bare wood peeked through where water splashed against it. The front door, painted red only two years ago, still had a gloss that reflected the blue colors of the sky, turning the door purple in the late afternoon. Caroline climbed the steps but found the door was locked, and so Caroline made her way past the church and up a small well-trod path on the right side of the church. Bear followed her but lay down in the shade, keeping his eye on Caroline.

Before her, in neat rows, lay the small cemetery. Five rows of slate and marble headstones started twenty feet behind the church and ran in a curved line hugging the hill. Twelve gravestones stood in each line. Most were simple white marble with names and dates but not much else. The site ran uphill and hugged a line of chinaberry trees at the top. Standing there at the bottom, Caroline could see two rows uphill near the trees that appeared to be recently dug. Fresh dirt, the size of a body, was mounded on top of the graves, and small, crudely made white wood crosses stood attention facing downhill. Caroline observed an older man pushing a wheelbarrow toward a pile of earth, thirty feet away. The wheelbarrow was filled with earth from a newly dug grave. She looked to the right and saw a six-foot-long trench with a shovel standing at its head. The opened earth standing ready to receive and hold tight a new someone.

Walking cautiously up the hill, her feet slipped occasionally on the grass, but she caught herself from falling and walked to the first row of freshly dug and recently covered graves, which ran to the left of her. Slowly walking down the line, she started reading the names that had been painted with black paint on the crosses. "Henderson, Clarence. Tuleberry, David. Menke, Lawrence. Babbit, Jonathan. Clarkson, Henry. Lemoore, Hamilton. The last one read Morgan, Isaac. She stepped uphill past the last grave and started walking to the right and down the last row. She slowly mouthed the names as she walked. Millhoff, Derek. Baines, Alexander. Foshee, Garland. Barksdale, Enoch. Duncan, Charles.

There was a silence in that moment the likes of which she had not encountered on this long journey. A stillness that weakened every muscle in her body. For there it was. And it was all there was left. Duncan, Charles. It said no more. Nothing. Caroline stood there staring at the name and hoping she had misread it. The air in her lungs lost its strength and her lips allowed the air to leave. Quietly, almost in a whisper, she spoke, "No." Silence stilled the air around her. "No. No." Blood drained from her face as her skin turned white. She felt a numbness sweep through her arms. The earth started to slow beneath her feet. She noticed tears forming and gathered in her eyes. Things on that hillside got blurry. "Charles, is that you?" Caroline's legs trembled. She stumbled and took a step backwards. For the next minute, she stared only at his name on the white cross and the mounded dirt before it. Duncan, Charles. "God. No." Caroline's legs weakened, and she fell to her knees. Tears were slow to fall, but rolled gently down. "No, God. No!" Her next words were never formed on her lips. Only fragments hung on her lips and were said sadly in a little girl's voice. "Please, God, take this away." The earth around her—the trees, the sky, the clouds—seemed to move, yet his grave stood centered and solid before her. Unmovable. Something driven into the Earth with a force greater than man could resist.

The next ten minutes were of a new realization she fought against. In that moment, she suddenly and without wanting it, became a new person. She was no longer a wife looking for her husband. She had found him. Minutes passed. Quiet tears streamed down her cheeks and neck. Caroline could only stare at the white cross. Finally, she gathered herself and stood; her tears slowed, and quiet questioning entered into her mind. What? When? How? Exhausted from her eleven-day walk, weakened from a bear attack, fearful every day of her trek, it had culminated in this place behind a small church in Shelbyville, Kentucky. Two pieces of white-painted wood forming a cross was the evidence of a life ended. But it did not tell the story of this man and his wife. "So, this is all? Duncan, Charles? This is so small a cross, so nothing. He was much more than that." Caroline turned to the other graves and raised her hands, pointing in both directions. "These other men, who are they? I should be buried next to you, Charles, not them. That is not how it is suppose to be. I am...I am your wife. Wife! But why are you here?" Caroline continued to speak quietly, as if speaking to her husband in hushed tones. "This is not how it is supposed...not how... it is supposed to end! You promised when you left, Charles!" Caroline started to cry again but weakness overcame her, and she fell forward on her knees, then fell over and embraced the earth. The shock was over and now something new came forth. Her words were barely audible. "Charles. I love you. Do you hear that? I love you. I do desperately so love you." After a moment, she pushed hard the earth and raised herself off the grave and into a kneeling position. She sat back on her heels. She raised her arms to the side as if pleading. Anger started to reveal itself. "Lord! Why? Why have you deserted me? Why have you...have you turned your face...your face against me? Did you take your hand off him? I prayed. Yes, you know I did. I prayed every day. Many times a day. Throughout the day. But this? Have I...have I done something wrong? Oh, Lord? Have you forgotten us? We were your children. The two of us. Charles and Caroline. Why, God? Why have you forgotten us? Why did you remove your hand from him?" There was a long silence and finally Caroline screamed out, "Oh, God, how could you?"

Caroline pushed herself up and stood erect, looking still down at the grave. She did not hear the birds or the wind in the trees. She felt death's shroud had surrounded her and could not be thrown off, but slipping tighter around her. Maybe permanently. "Lord, I cannot go on. I am tired. I am so tired. Please, Lord, let me rest. But no, you will not. I know that. I am a mother. I have children. If this is a test, then I have failed it. Have I not? Lord, why? Answer me, Lord, please. Let me hear you. Did I do something wrong? Is it because I killed a man? But I had to. I saved someone, didn't I?" Caroline sat there waiting, but only silence returned to her as she realized it was no use to argue with God. Gathering strength, she got back on her knees and read the cross one last time. "Duncan, Charles." The silence from God filled the hillside and she realized nothing in front of her would change. Caroline slowly got to her feet as the anger started to drain. She wiped the tears from her face. Red dirt from the grave mixed with her tears covered her cheeks where she wiped. Her new yellow dress, stained from the fresh dirt on the grave, showed where her knees first fell. "He died alone and now I too am alone. Lord, have you left me too?"

The old grave digger pushed his now empty wheelbarrow past Caroline. He stopped and the old black man took off his hat, revealing white curly hair.

"Pardon me, ma'am, but God don't leave his children. He takes us through it. He carries us."

Caroline turned to the man standing on the other side of the cross, her eyes still filled with tears. "But I do not want to go through it."

"But pardon me, ma'am, you will have to."

"How can I? I have no strength left."

"How far have you traveled, Ma'am?"

"I have walked here for eleven days now."

"That is a long time to walk. But pardon me, ma'am, I have been walking this earth for sixty-seven years now. I think that is longer than eleven days. Wouldn't you say that?

"Yes, it is."

"So, you weep a spell and then you thank God that He gave you this young man for as long as He did. He didn't have to do that, but He did."

"But we had plans."

"Pardon me, ma'am, but they might not have been God's plans."

"What do you know? You're just a grave digger."

"Yes, ma'am. I dig the holes and then I bury the holes."

"Did you dig this hole?"

"Yes, ma'am, I dig that hole. Maybe nine days ago."

"This is my husband's grave."

"Oh, let me see the name."

The old man took several steps forward and looked at the name. "Oh, yes. That one. I even helped put that box down there."

"What kind of box was it?"

"Just a plain pine box. They make 'em up the road a bit. John Washington Henderson makes all of 'em. He does nice work too. It's a handsome box."

"Who paid for it?"

"Army won't pay much. Relatives pay for most. Some are paid for by the church here. But some of 'em are empty."

"Empty?"

"Well, the army bury a lot of the boys out in the field where they fall at the battle."

"But these here?"

"Most of these men were wounded but died later. After the army left, the women of the church, they was in charge. They had 'em buried here."

Caroline stared into the old man's brown eyes. "I do not understand. Make it clear. You said some of the boxes are empty."

"Oh, yes. Some of 'em was empty."

"Well, this one, this one right here, was it empty?"

"I remember that clear like. I always put a few rocks in it to give it some weight. A soul should weigh something. So, yes, I put rocks in the Charles Duncan one."

"So, maybe he is not here?"

"Oh, no, ma'am, his body is not there. That is an empty grave. You should go and talk to Missus Simms. She is the pastor's wife. "

"Missus Simms knows something about it?

"Yes, she knows more than most folks around here."

"And where does Missus Simms live?"

"Ma'am, she is in the yellow house on Church Street. Yellow house with a porch swing. A blue one. I painted it myself."

Caroline thanked the man and gathered her bedroll and bag and walked down out of the cemetery and past the church. Bear followed closely behind. She stopped and looked up at the new white crosses at the top of the hill. There were thirteen of them. Back out on the street in front of the church, she asked a woman walking with two small children where Church Street was, and the lady pointed in a direction south of the main street.

The yellow house stood out from the others on the street, as most were painted white. In the front yard, a flagpole stood with a red, white, and gold Christian flag flying in the breeze. Caroline told Bear to stay in the front yard, and she climbed the steps and knocked at the screen door. A woman in her mid-fifties, dressed in a cream-colored dress, came to the door.

"Hello, can I help you?"

"Yes, ma'am. My name is Caroline Duncan, and I have traveled a long distance to be with my husband, who was wounded, and I received a letter about some ladies in your church, signed by Nurse Ruth Abernethy, stating my husband was being cared for by them, here in Shelbyville. This morning, I have discovered a grave with his name behind your church."

"I am sorry to hear that."

"But an old Negro man told me that the box is empty; it doesn't have his body."

"Please, come in. Let's us talk privately."

The lady opened the screen door and Caroline took off her bedroll and placed it on the porch. She kept her bag with her, placing it on a table as they walked into the living room. The woman sat in a chair, but Caroline took a seat on a long settee nearest the woman. Caroline sat there with cheeks still stained with dirt from the grave, and her dress bore the same red dirt. She was unaware of herself and her appearance. "I take it you are the pastor's wife, Missus Simms?"

"That I am, and, Missus Duncan, where do you come from?"

"My husband and I have a homestead near Hopkinsville."

"That is a long way from here."

"The thing is, I need to know why there are empty boxes being buried, and do you have some records of the men, who they are, and when they died, things like that? For certain, I want to know where his true grave is. Where his body is buried, for I want to go there. Place a cross. Be near him for while."

"Let's do things first. Many men on both sides are killed on the battlefield and are buried in mass graves. But their relatives want to grieve and have a proper burial in a proper church cemetery. They come to us and request a Christian service. They want a coffin and a headstone. John Henderson makes the coffins and the crosses and we provide a burial space."

"Who pays for this?"

"If they live close, the relatives who travel for the service. Or the army may pay a very small amount. Mister Henderson gets a dollar a casket and the church sells the plot for two dollars. We pay Amos fifty cents to dig a proper hole. Pastor Simms officiates at the service."

"So, the army paid for my husband's coffin and the burial plot?"

"I would think not. It may have been someone else."

Caroline leaned forward with hands together in a pleading manner. "The ladies from your church who helped care for my husband. I wish to talk to them. I need to know what his last days were like."

Missus Simms leaned back in her chair. "Toward the end, that would have been Miss Ermal Fiske and, unfortunately, Miss

Fiske left with the wounded men and traveled with them down to Chattanooga. They had but one nurse; these men were left alone."

"But the records, who has the records? Like when he died? Where he is actually buried? Where he is now?"

"Well, I have some here. Miss Fiske did most of the record keeping and she gave them to me when she left. Let me get the ledger."

Missus Simms stood and went to the cabinet in the corner. She pulled out two books and stood there. She appeared to want to say something but changed her mind, and so she returned and sat down with the ledger then started quietly and reverently turning pages. She came to a page and ran her finger to a single paragraph.

"Well, on the twenty-third, Miss Fiske wrote she and Missus McCumbers and four other ladies, she lists their names here, were helping to care for twenty-eight wounded men. There were but two army nurses and a single surgeon. She writes several men died, and recently wounded soldiers arrived that week. She lists a Lieutenant Charles Matthew Duncan arriving on the twenty-third with several wounds. A wound to the leg and a bad wound to his shoulder Then, let's see, his care continued until the first of October. She writes on that last week of September, nine men died of their wounds and seven were healed enough to return to limited duty. There is a notation that both Sergeant Lionel Moriston and your husband, First Lieutenant Charles Duncan, died on the second of October. She notes the cause of death was serious infection, a burning fever, and blood poisoning for both men on the same day. Missus Partridge volunteered to write to the relatives of the deceased."

"So, Charles died on the second of October?"

"According to this, yes."

"Who else did these notes go to?"

"There were official forms they filled out every day. Missus Partridge sent those to the surgeon who was in charge, but by that particular time, the Confederate Army and their surgeons had to leave, and so the forms were signed by two witnesses and mailed to Frankfort."

"Then, that's it, then? That's all there is?"

"No, we have church records of sorts."

"What do you mean?"

"The relatives of those we buried and the date and how much they paid, and where the deceased are located behind the church. Whether they paid for a marble, stone, slate, or a simple wood cross."

"Could I see those records?"

Missus Simms stood and moved back to the secretary cabinet and pulled out a red leather ledger and moved her hand through the pages. "Here. Let's see now. Okay, alright. Well, here it is. Mister Hopkins...Mister Louis Hopkins paid for your husband's coffin and a plot. He ordered and paid for the coffin and the marker. This is dated the third of the month."

"Do you know Mister Hopkins?"

"No. I do not think he is from around here."

"Did he sign for it?"

"Yes, everyone has to pay and has to sign."

"Could I see it?"

"Certainly, it's on line 31. Charles Matthew Duncan deceased, signed by Mister Louis Hopkins. Here."

Caroline took the book and looked. She stared intently at Mister Louis Hopkins's signature. There was a silence in this little room that caused her to shake. She started breathing quickly. A sense of disbelief mixed with hope came across her face. She raised her hand to her mouth.

"No. No, that's my husband's signature. Yes! It is. That is my husband's signature. Yes! The way he makes the 'L' and the 'O.' That is the way he makes an 'I' with the circle dot, I am sure of it. And this is his 'S.' The 'S' on the end with the sweeping swirl. Louis."

"Oh? Well maybe he knew he was going to pass away and signed for his own funeral in advance."

"Has anyone ever done that before?"

Missus Simms took the book from Caroline's hand and then folded it closed. "Missus Duncan, I am going to put this book away now. I do not remember you coming here and, as far as I am concerned, that grave is your husband's up there or somewhere else. I advise you to speak to no one about this matter and return to your home."

"You mean he might be alive?"

"I am originally a Shaker, and I and Reverend Simms are for peace and the sooner the soldiers return home...return home...the sooner this hellish war will be over. And that is all I am going to say. Would you like to stay for supper?"

"No, I have much of the day left and I must make my way home. Back to my children."

"Some trains are running again. You can catch one here at about six this afternoon—it will run to Louisville, and then you change for the Nashville-Louisville line. But there may be a problem with the track being torn up. North of Bowling Green is, I understand, the problem. Several trestles over rivers have been set afire. My sister lives there. Ella Bruckheimer. Look her up and spend the night there, if you get there. She will have more information about traveling."

"Thank you. I have one more question. Did you ever meet Mister Hopkins? He would be about thirty-six, tall, with a beard, curly long hair, and he might be walking with a limp."

"That does seem familiar. But my eyesight. My memory. And oh, yes. I want to refund the two dollars he paid for the plot,

303

and I think he left a donation of another three dollars, and you will need it for the train." Missus Simms stood and walked to the secretary again and pulled out a small leather purse. "The train to Bowling Green will cost about two dollars. Missus Duncan, I would hurry home if I were you. As I said, I cannot be seen as siding with one side or the other. We are a valuable resource here. If it were a Unionist boy, we would do the same thing."

Caroline took the money and stared into Missus Simms's eyes and saw her tears but a slight smile. "Hurry, dear, or you will miss the train." Caroline grabbed her bag, then her bedroll. The dog jumped up and ran to the gate. Caroline walked quickly down the stairs and followed the dog out onto the street. Twenty minutes later, she was standing near the Shelbyville railway siding. Her face was still stained with red dirt, her yellow dress stained at the knees.

That day, the train was thirty minutes late and slowed to a crawl a hundred feet from the station. Passengers crowded the platform and inched toward the edge, holding their bags. A lone mother held tight the hands of her two children. A dozen Union soldiers moved away from their wagons; each blue-coated soldier was armed with a bedroll, a haversack, and a musket. The train started to move again cautiously, only to stop under the huge wooden raised water tank. The engineer jumped out and walked quickly to the water funnel and pulled on the cord, swinging the funnel spout over the engine's tank. The second engineer climbed on top of the black engine and took off the water tank's steel cover. The first engineer pulled a second rope near the tank and water gushed into the tank. The conductor shouted to all on the platform, "All aboard for Louisville." Caroline and the dog walked to the last car and boarded from the rear of the car. Finding the first seat on the right, she placed her bedroll in the rack above her head and took a seat near the window. She looked down to her well-worn and heelless shoes and thought how funny they looked next to this bright yellow dress still stained from the dirt from the grave. She brushed the dirt from the dress, but it helped only a little. Exhausted, she closed her eyes and leaned back. "Father, forgive me for doubting you. I am sorry. I am weak. But that is no excuse. For my body is weak but my mind is not. You have brought me through this. Forgive me. Amen." Caroline opened her eyes and caught her reflection in the window. "I must look a fright, Bear." She pulled her hand through her hair and looked out again. There, she saw Missus Simms standing by herself. She had a serious look on her face but was discreetly nodding her head "yes," then, seeing Caroline's face in the window, she smiled and mouthed the words, "Go home," then walked away.

Caroline had not noticed the three military men standing on the left side of the train platform, all wearing blue uniforms. One was smoking a cigarette, one smoked a pipe, and the last one only looked to the ground unsmiling as the others talked and joked. When the second engineer finished taking on water, he signaled to the first engineer, who gave a short blast of the steam whistle. The three men boarded the train in the car just ahead of Caroline. The conductor walked forward from the last car toward the first car taking the fare.

"Simpsonville is the next stop, then Middletown, and finally Louisville. Ladies, use the restroom in the first car, as it is the only one with a lock." He stopped at the couple who were seated at the front of the car and repeated his message.

The train was slow in taking off, but within ten minutes, it was building a full head of steam. It seemed to Caroline, who walked at two miles, sometimes three miles, an hour, that this train was racing away in breath-taking speeds. She watched almost shocked at how fast the trees raced by. Bear had moved to another seat ahead of her and stuck his nose out the window. Then after a moment, the dog jumped off the seat and moved across the aisle to the left side, as if this was somewhere else he had never seen. A moment later, and not wanting to miss what was on the right side, he crossed the aisle and secured his place by the window. "It's the same, Bear. Both sides are the same." Bear, not understanding Caroline's comments, jumped up and went to the left side again, not wanting to miss that view. As the train rocked from side to side, Caroline, still exhausted from the last eleven days, fought off sleep. And like Bear, her eyes gazed out the window at the homesteads flying by. Each home was alive with people doing everyday normal things. But most of all, Caroline looked for children. In them was hope for the future. She saw in these young boys and girls, her own children 190 miles away. Closing her eyes, she battled sleep, but soon dozed off.

"Mama, it's coming! It's coming!" Priscilla ran to the kitchen but stood at the door, waving for Caroline to come and see. Priscilla, not wanting to miss anything, ran back to the barn. Caroline wiped her soapy hands, removed the stew from the stove, and undid her kitchen apron. She caught up to Priscilla as they both entered the barn. There on the floor kneeling, was her husband, Charles, positioned at the back end of the horse. Her two sons, Isaac and Noah, sat on top of a hay stack looking down with interest.

"Caroline, I'd say in the next five minutes Methuselah is going to be a proud papa donkey and Evie here gets to be the mom."

Isaac waved his hand in the air. "Hey, Pa, I got a great name for our mule. Aristotle, 'cause that will make him smart." The younger boy, Noah, who had moved higher onto the beam and was sitting cross legged, shouted down, "No. Excelsior." Priscilla spoke up, "Mama, please, I want to name it! I want Emma."

Caroline clapped her hands over her head several times as if to draw attention and quiet. "You three can call it anything you want, but I will name him Coffee because if she or he is the color of their mom, then she will be coffee colored. Coffee!"

Charles moved over by the horse. "Noah, you come down here and you too, Isaac. All of us will have to pull to get 'em out. Caroline and Priscilla, you comfort Evie as we pull. I imagine she is in a lot of pain right now."

"Ma'am, you care if I get and sit across from you?" The young, blue-coated man who had been standing with the two other military men back at the station quietly waited for an answer and then, seeing none, he slowly sat down. She woke from her sleep and looked at the man, and for the first time saw that he was in handcuffs and wore leg chains. She glanced at the end of the car and saw a man standing there. He wore what looked like a revolver on his hip. He pulled back his coat to reveal a small silver badge resting on his vest. The man was staring at Caroline.

"No, please sit down, no one is sitting here."

"Look, ma'am, I ain't bad. I gave up. That's all. I just gave up."

"You have been arrested?"

"Oh, yes, ma'am. I have been apprehended. Not captured, mind you, but apprehended. When I got on the train, I saw you looking at me with sad eyes and I don't want a woman such as you to think poorly of me. Many people have looked away from me, as if I should not be looked upon because of these chains."

Caroline looked again at the man standing with the revolver and noticed he had pulled his coat further back and rested his hand on his revolver.

"No, I ain't bad. Like robbery or nothing. I just seen what it is." The young soldier reached over to shake her hand but realized the handcuffs were restricting him. "My name is Josephus Lumford. And I am proud to say I am from Nelsonville, Ohio. I got shot once in the foot at the Swallowfield skirmish and I got healed enough, and so they put me back in line and I got shot in my left foot and right arm at Drexalville. I said twice is enough and I am going home. Nelsonville. That's a small town west of Marietta. I joined when my older brother joined, and I believed in it at first, but they lied to us. They want us to stand there in a long line and shoot at each other. This whole thing is a slaughtering field. And here is what I think, if you don't mind hearing me."

"No, go on and tell me about it."

"So, we shoot one of theirs and they shoot one of ours. All day long this goes on. One of theirs, one of ours. Pretty soon there will be no one left but the generals way in the back. I got a girl back in Nelsonville. Annelle McKinsey. She is waiting for me to come home so we can get married. But stupid me, see, I got carried away and I joined. I do not know what I was thinking at the time. But that blue uniform looked so pretty. They had a brass band and said we would all be heroes to save the Union. They said it would take three months. But now I understand if a few states left, we would still have a union, only it would be smaller, so that was a lie. Anyhow, it was this damn blue uniform that made me do it. And so, five days ago I threw my gun down and started walking back to Ohio. They said I could not do that. I said I joined voluntarily and so I should be able to unjoin voluntarily too."

Caroline looked at the two soldiers who had brought the young man onto the train standing in the front of the car as one took out his pipe and lit it. He shook his head left then right, as if to say don't believe the young man.

"They said I was a deserter. I said, no, it was not in the middle of the fight that I ran. I stood there and fought, but afterward, and after the fight was over, then did I walk away. At Cynthiana, I counted thirty-six of my fellows dead and fifty-three with shots in arms and legs and faces. I should not want to be dead, and I did not want them to cut off my leg. So, I said enough is enough. They caught me at Briars Fork. I was wading across the creek, and they rode up and put me in chains."

Caroline looked the young nineteen-year-old soldier in the eyes. "Where are they taking you to? Will there be a trial?"

The young man shifted in his seat and looked at the armed guards watching him, and to the third man in a suit with a badge. He leaned forward then whispered. "They don't tell you nothin' but I suppose I will go to prison. I honestly believe that is the smart way. These people here say five years in prison. I think Annelle will wait for me. I don't know that for sure, as she is sure desirable. Five years for not robbin' or killin' or rapin', just for walking away, that don't seem fair. No, ma'am, that ain't fair. Thank you for listening to me. I just don't want people like yourself thinking the worst of me. I ain't no criminal. I just walked away."

The young man stood and scuffled with his leg chains back up the aisle, stopped for a moment and tipped his hat in Caroline's direction, and then turned and walked back to the front of the car.

The train made its first stop in the small town of Simpsonville, where twenty new recruits in their new bright blue uniforms got on. Most of the young men looked to be in their early twenties, and two of them appeared to be seventeen or eighteen and had not yet started shaving. All the men joked and laughed as they boarded the train, carrying their haversacks and their muskets. They all sat up front in the car and whispered to one another. One pointed to the soldier in chains and laughed. The captured young man from Nelsonville, Ohio, smiled at the insult and spoke quietly. "There's twenty of you now; in three months there will be ten. One year from now there will be only two of you left. Laugh if you want; I will still be alive." Caroline heard none of this but noticed the laughter had quickly changed to a solemn quiet with the twenty young recruits.

Traveling on this flat rolling terrain, the train sped ahead at well over forty miles an hour and rocked left then quickly right. Occasionally, the engineer would sound the whistle as it passed a town or came to a road crossing. Caroline remembered being told by her father that a normal steam train on flat tracks could attain a speed of sixty miles an hour, and the record was set at seventy-three miles an hour, across flat Iowa. The train slowed as it climbed a hill and cautiously turned to the north. Caroline could see a town ahead and she could see a water tower and brick buildings forming the small town. A three-story, red brick courthouse marked this town as a prosperous location. As the train slowed to five miles an hour, she read the name "Middletown" in big block letters on the water tank written in white paint, with an American flag

311

flying from atop the tower. One young boy, about eleven, had climbed the ladder to the top of the wood structure and sat with his bare feet hanging over the side; his young sister stood at the base of the tower looking up, envious of her dare-devil brother.

After the stop, the twenty new recruits got off and stretched their legs and joked around. One recruit grabbed another's blue cap and tossed it to another, who, in turn, tossed it to a third recruit. The young recruit grabbed the cap of the recruit that stole his and jumped back onto the train. After the train took on eleven new passengers, the conductor walked through the car and shouted that the next stop would be Louisville, and that would be in thirty-five minutes.

At the first sight of Louisville, which was from atop a hill ten miles away, Caroline craned her neck for a better look and smiled. This was her hometown. The town she was born and grew up in. This was the town in which she met her husband. She noticed Bear had moved to the window and was fixed on the sight. Caroline thought, "I wonder if this dog has seen something so large as this? I will never know the story this dog has to tell." She herself soon became transfixed on the number of homes and buildings that dotted the landscape. It had been three years since she was last here and she was amazed at all the new roads being made and homes being built. She strained her neck to see the mighty Ohio River. At one point, she made out six paddlewheel steamboats travelling in a long straight line and moving west. All the boats seemed to be heading toward the Mississippi River 370 miles to the west.

Soon, Caroline caught sight of coal black smoke from another train on a set of tracks a half mile north of hers and heading in the same direction. She thought, "This could be the one. This could be the Cincinnati to Nashville line with a stop in Louisville. This could be the train she would catch to get home. Yes, it would let her off in Bowling Green, and that was merely a two and a half day's walk to Hopkinsville. And maybe her husband, if he was alive, took this exact train only days earlier. "I pray that is what he did. I'm not sure, but maybe, yes, maybe that is what happened. No, he was not buried under that white cross. He signed the registry! He paid for his own burial! Did not Missus Simms say, 'Go home?' 'Go home.' Is that what she meant? Was there a message in that? She couldn't say the truth. She could only hint. But she said it with somewhat of a slight smile. I remember the smile. Or was it just a consoling smile?"

That was the first time Caroline thought of home this day and especially her children. Was this eleven-day trip merely for naught? Had she put her children in jeopardy for nothing at all? Was her husband buried back there in an unmarked battlefield grave? Was there a mistake? Was that really his hand writing? Maybe someone else had a similar hand, and who was Mister Hopkins who signed? Missus Simms said there was haste and confusion. Overworked ladies attending the men and boys dying in fever and pain. If the record was true, then Charles died on the second of October. Gangrene had festered in his shoulder and blood poisoning pulled him down into a deathly fever he could not overcome. A tremble started in her stomach and shook her core. She noticed her

313

hands and legs were shaking. She took deep breaths and pulled her haversack close to her and reached around the revolver and found a piece of hard tack. She thought this might quiet her nerves. After eating half of the dried cracker, she offered the second half to Bear, who took it and ate it. Bear returned to the window, which offered endless interesting new things to see; occasionally, he would turn his head to Caroline, hoping she was still there, as she was to him the only connection to the overturned wagon and those people who fled the trauma.

Rounding a second curve, three young boys, aged five, seven, and nine, looking like brothers and all riding a single large black mule, waved furiously at the train. No one noticed the boys except for Caroline, who gathered energy to wave back. Caroline thought of her three children, often riding a mule like this one. At that moment, a thought came to her and she realized it seemed like several months had passed since she last saw them. The many events that happened to her in the last eleven days were occurrences that required years or a complete lifetime to encompass ordinary people. She closed her eyes to picture her children hiding deep in the woods, disappearing into the shadows, hiding in tree tops or maybe deep in a cave while Union soldiers searched the area for food.

Five miles outside of Louisville, Caroline noticed the second train had moved closer. Yes, it was the Cincinnati-Nashville line and was turning south, approaching merely a thousand feet from her train. To people on the train, it appeared the two trains would soon collide in a flaming explosion, but without warning, the Cincinnati-Nashville train went down into a deep man-made ravine and her train climbed up and over a trestle as the other train passed directly underneath. Soon, both trains were traveling side by side but had changed their positions. The two trains whistled at each other in some sort of fraternal acknowledgement. Eventually, both trains decreased their steam to thirty percent, as inertia carried them into Louisville.

Caroline strained her neck to see the eastern part of town where she spent her childhood. She spotted the white-painted steeple of the Methodist Church where her father was pastor and where she married. There was something emotional and pulling hard in her that wanted to rush off the train and quickly walk the ten blocks to her old home. The home where her mother and father now lived. To the church where her husband once stood at the altar, waiting for her to walk down the aisle. But that was not to be. Those were yesterday's emotions. That girl in white was the young Caroline. No, she could not waste time. Eleven grueling days had got her here. But this was not her destination. She had one ache and one desire that pulled at her insides, which was to catch the Cincinnati-Nashville Line. The train running to her left would take her to Bowling Green and from there, a walk to home. Yes, that is where she desperately wanted to go. She longed for her family, but more than that, maybe to find her husband. If only this hope had substance. A flame flickered inside her and only her mind and his image kept it burning.

The Louisville train station was a mass of confusion. Soldiers in blue uniforms shuffled across the platform from one train toward another. Jute bags of unknown items sat next to wooden crates. Kegs of gunpowder stood off by themselves stacked three high. Travelers with leather cases and carpet satchels stood watching with anticipation. These men in suits and woman in long dresses huddled, talking to each other with a seriousness that comes from not knowing what lay hidden in the next hour, the next day. The two soldiers in charge of the young deserter joined with other men and other prisoners in leg irons. The detective in a suit with a badge followed closely behind. Wounded soldiers sat in wheelchairs, some without legs and some without arms. Many had bandages over their heads and over their eyes. Over to one side, a group of women with red, white, and green badges on their capes stood over three extended wooden tables with bowls and spoons and a twenty-gallon cast iron pot containing soup. Three baskets nearby were mounded high with biscuits and pone bread. Two serving bowls overflowing with bright yellow butter stood at the ends of the tables. Blue-coated soldiers stood in line getting the last hot meal they would have before the next battle. Maybe forever. The two trains, which had earlier raced each other, sat perfectly still on the opposite sides of the platform. Overhead, a wood structure topped with a metal roof designed to shield passengers from the sun and rain was filled with hundreds of sparrows that occasionally flew down to the wooden platform to retrieve pieces of bread tossed by sympathetic soldiers. A sign hung near the train that carried Caroline here. It read in green and gold letters, "Louisville-Frankfort-Chattanooga." She walked to the other side of the platform, and she approached a sign lettered in red and yellow. It read simply, "Louisville-

Elizabethtown-Bowling Green-Nashville." As she stood under the sign, she felt Bear rub up against her and with each step she took, the dog followed closely behind. Occasionally, Bear glanced up with a questioning look on his face. "It's okay, Bear, there is a lot of confusion here, but you stay with me, and we will soon be on our train and out of this depot of confusion. Yes, I know, boy, there are too many people for you to watch."

Caroline walked to the cashier's window and bought a ticket to Bowling Green. The man selling the ticket said the train would leave on time, but that three trestles were being repaired and if those repairs were done, then the train would be in Bowling Green in five hours or about midnight. But if just any one trestle was still damaged, then the trains would stop north and would wait until the army was finished with the repairs. The man volunteered that the trestles in question had been partially burned by the Confederates trying to stop the resupply of the Union Army marching to Nashville. The man wore a black shiny hat with a black vest and nickel-plated badge. Ink smears covered both hands, but especially his right hand. He had smudged his chin and pulled on his ear and so they were black, but he was unaware. He said both trains were full and so the dog could not sit on a seat, but had to sit in the aisle. He stamped her ticket and told her, "There are no refunds on this ticket. Even if the train does not get to Bowling Green, there are no refunds. It is war-time rules, and we make no promises." She moved away from the cashier, as the line for tickets was growing. As she walked away, he repeated his message to the next traveler.

The cashier was correct, as the train was full. Like her earlier train ride, she selected the last car and was the first onto the car. Bear rushed past Caroline and ran toward a seat on the right side—a similar seat to that she had taken earlier. Bear jumped into the aisle seat as he had done before. Caroline smiled. "Bear, you learn fast. This is the seat I would have taken. But the train is full, so you will have to sit in the aisle." Caroline positioned herself at the window and placed her haversack and bedroll in the brass rack above her head. Thinking further about it, she stood and took down her haversack and placed it at her feet. The car started to fill with passengers, and most were weary and silent from the wait. Many were men, dressed in dark drab clothing, but there were women dressed in bright reds, blues, and greens. One young woman carried a small baby wrapped in a pink blanket. Caroline looked at her yellow dress, the dress she thought she would wear to see her husband in. But it now seemed out of place and ordinary. She brushed at the stains on the front, but they resisted.

Once the train car filled, four more men crowded their way in and stood near the front of the car. They appeared to be in their twenties and wore Union Army uniforms. Two of the men appeared to have been wounded and wore bandages over the heads just above their eyes. A third one had a bandage that covered his right hand. The fourth man bore no bandages but appeared to be stunned and had to be told where to stand. He stared straight ahead without focusing on anything in the car. He moved his lips but said nothing loud enough to be heard.

The train pulled out on time and Caroline had no idea who was in the other cars. She noticed the four men and motioned for one to come and sit in the seat next to her. Bear promptly moved to the aisle and watched the man with a bandage over his head come and sit down.

"Thank you, ma'am. That's a nice-looking dog you got there. I used to have a dog, but he is still at home with my younger brother. My name is Eschol Tilliams. Funny name, huh? In school, the boys used to call me Echo. Like the sound you hear in a well. It's not biblical or nothing. It was my grandfather's name. What's your name?"

"I'm Caroline and the dog's name is Bear."

"Funny, he sort of looks like a bear, but I bet there is a good reason you named him that."

"Yes, he and I together met up with a black bear, and the bear lost."

"What did you shoot it with?"

"We killed it with courage. This dog attacked from the front and I came at it from the back."

"Is that the God's honest truth? I bet you used a big knife."

"Yes, it is. And sort of. How did you get your wounds?"

"Poolesville. We had a skirmish with about a hundred rebs. They say we got nine of theirs and they got nine of ours. The four of us are going back today. They said we would be fit to fight in a week's time. Hell! Excuse me. I mean heck. I can barely see out of my right eye, and Luke sees everything in a blur. Nevin lost two fingers and a thumb. Jonathan is so scared he just stands there. He'll be killed in our next fight. He just stands there. He won't even talk no more."

"That's sad. Eschol, I will pray for you."

"That won't help. My mama prays for me every day. That's what she writes. But look, I still got shot anyhow. I would rather have a good tree to stand behind than have God's help."

"I'll still pray for you, and I will pray for your three friends. Eschol, you hold to what you have been taught all your life, not what this war has taught you."

Nothing more was said about the war, wounds, or even God. The train picked up speed and small villages and scattered homesteads, both surrounded by large areas of virgin woodlands, raced by. Occasionally, the engineer would blow his steam whistle at young children who gathered at road crossings waving and jumping up and down in excitement to see the train running again. After ten minutes, Eschol, got up and walked to the front of the car and whispered to the young man who appeared to be in shock. He took the young man's hand and led him to the seat and had him sit. Eschol took off his hat and then reached down and took off the young man's hat and placed it in his lap.

"Ma'am, this here is Jonathan. No use talking to him. He won't talk back. He's been that way for a whole week now. But then he hasn't talked to a woman, so he might. Just talk to him. He's from Indiana."

Eschol left and returned to the front of the train car then stared down its length to the rear door window. Caroline turned and looked at the young man seated next to her. His eyes seemed fixed on something a hundred yards away. She took notice that the hat sitting in his laps was torn and bore a dark brown stain that appeared to be blood. She noticed his boots had blood stains.

"Jonathan? Would you like a biscuit and ham? I just bought it at the station. I would be more than happy to share it with you. A woman named Benita made it."

There was no reaction from Jonathan.

"It has a fried egg, bacon, and tomato on it. It looks to be made this morning. It's big enough to share."

Slowly, Jonathan turned his head. "Do you know my mama?"

Caroline appeared surprised the young man was speaking. "No, I don't. Wait! Wait! I think I do. Yes. Jonathan's mom. What is her name?"

"Emmalee."

"Yes, I know Emmalee."

"Could you...when you see her, could you tell her you saw me? Don't tell her about this." Jonathan pointed to a fresh red scar held together with stitches that ran from his mouth across the left cheek and to a part of an ear lobe.

"No, I won't. What else do you want me to tell her?"

"Tell her, I love...I love her. No to worry about me."

"I will do that."

"See, I don't want to fight no more."

"No, I am sure you have done enough."

"Just ask for Emmalee Pinter. East Mount Carmel on the Wabash River. Indiana."

"Yes, Emmalee Pinter. Your mother. Jonathan's mother. In Indiana."

"Tell her not to let Gideon join up. He's my friend. Cause it's no use. No damn use at all."

"No, it is of no use."

The young man raised his right hand over his eyes. He fought for air and gulped it like it would give him strength. Caroline could see tears running down his face. He wiped his eyes and sat there silently, then he whispered into his lap, "It's all lies. And it's been that way since the first day." Jonathan turned to Caroline. "My older brother, Clavell, said to me, 'Hey, let's go kill some Johnny Rebs,' and I followed like a stupid puppy dog. Well, the rebs probably said the same thing, "Let's go shoot some Yankees. Well, they shoot back and sometimes they were better shots than we was. Clavell, he was out front, brave like, and he was shot three times within twenty minutes of our first firefight. They cut off his left leg and he went home. I wanted to go with him, but they wouldn't let me. Three weeks later, at Rainstree, I got shot in the foot and five minutes later, in the face. I thought I could go home, but no, and now they are sending me back. I would cut off my right foot if I could go home, but they got that figured out too. If I do that, they will send me to prison. I don't think there is a way out except death. So I guess I am going back and get killed. That is the only thing that will satisfy them. I got no other choice. No damn choice at all." Jonathan took his hat from his lap and placed it on his head then stood. "Thanks for talking to me, ma'am. You see my mama, you tell her I always loved her. Emmalee Pinter, East Mount Carmel. Everybody knows her." He nodded to Caroline and walked forward to his three friends. He hugged Eschol when he got there and sat down on the floor facing the rear of the car. After a while, he took off his two boots. He sat there with his shoes off, looking at his single brown sock filled with holes. His right foot revealed only a dried crimson bloodied bandage wrapped twice and tied below the ankle in a knot.

The train made excellent time through this northern part of the state. Caroline noted how, occasionally, a homestead had been burned. In one location, four homesteads in a row were only ashes now, and along the road that ran beside the track there were the carcasses of two dead horses, bloated and rotting in the evening sun. Later, she saw where the telegraph lines had been cut and the poles burned. The travelers all looked out onto the carnage and whispered to one another. The train slowed for a time as it approached a damaged track. The Confederate Army had earlier pulled up the track, and starting large fires, they heated the steel rails red hot and carried the hot rails to nearby trees bending them into a 'U' shape. The Union army had reheated the track and attempted to bend it back straight but they were not entirely successful. At those times, the train slowed to five percent steam and carefully rolled over the uneven tracks.

Ten miles later, the train approached a river, where sections of the trestle were burned but partially restored with new timber that afternoon. The train slowed as the charred timbers beneath it groaned under its one-hundred-ton weight. Union soldiers were still adding fresh cut green oak logs for bracing as the train's engineer leaned out his window and looked to the river ninety feet below. When the train approached, the workers, who were stripped to the waist and covered with perspiration, quickly climbed down the beams and waded waist high in the slow-going stream. Most moved away from the trestle, not knowing whether it would collapse, plunging the train to its demise. Two Union soldiers stood on the tracks waving yellow flags. Caroline could see both jump out of the way. As the train passed one soldier, he shouted out, "Slow down. Slow down. For God's sake, slow down!" Several passengers stood and looked down to the muddy brown river below. One passenger got out of his seat and ran to the back of the car. He opened the back door and jumped off the slow-moving train. Moments later, two more men ran to the back and did the same. The train moved very slowly across the trestle, and the groaning of the wood could be heard above the sound of the steel wheels and engine, now running on five percent steam. Halfway across, a half-burned cross timber gave way and the train shifted suddenly to the left, dropping two feet, but other timbers held fast. This caused an audible gasp from the passengers, and one lady let out a scream, pulling her baby close to her while closing her eyes. Several men stood and looked out the left side of the train, watching the soldiers below scatter and run for the river's banks.

Caroline took a deep breath and held tight to the seat in front of her. The thought instantaneously crossed her mind, "If the train falls, it will fall to the left and the window to my right will be my escape." Caroline instinctively reached up and opened the window as the train proceeded. The conductor, who had been seated in the rear seat, stood and shouted out, "Everyone sit down. Sit down and don't move." One man refused to sit and stood in the middle of the car, caught in inaction not knowing what to do but wanting to do something. The train inched itself forward to the middle of the trestle and Caroline could hear the cheers of the men who had been repairing the trestle. The engineer started to apply more steam and it started to pick up speed. In moments, the engine moved from the trestle and back onto the land side, and the men below gave out another loud shout. Caroline could hear one fellow below shout out, "Hip, hip, hooray. Hip, hip, hooray. Ole Abe Lincoln smiles on you today."

Several young passengers joined in the celebration and started applauding each other. One man stood and walked down the aisle, slapping men on their backs for their courage. "We did it. We did it!"

As the train regained its speed, Caroline stood and closed the window. Sitting down, she looked to Bear lying on the floor near her feet. "Come on, Bear, you sit up here next to me so you can see where we are going." Caroline tapped the seat and the dog understood. Soon, they sat side by side, equal survivors. "Bear, after that, I am hungry, and I bet you are too. Let's share this last biscuit to celebrate that trestle passing." What surprised Caroline was that when she placed half the biscuit, egg, bacon, and tomato sandwich in front of Bear, he licked his mouth, but took no bites. He only looked at Caroline. She nodded "yes" to Bear, but still the black and brown dog only looked at her. Finally, she cupped her hand and raised the sandwich within an inch of his mouth. Bear curled his ears to ask but still only looked at Caroline. Finally, she moved her mouth as if she were eating something. And that is when Bear understood and took his first bite. The sandwich disappeared in moments. "Good Bear. Good dog. I think you have a reluctance to eat human food. It is not as good as rabbit or crawfish or catfish. But you will have plenty time to do that when I get you home."

Forty minutes later, the train slowed as it approached a town she had been to only days earlier. The conductor walked down the aisle. "Elizabethtown is next. This is Elizabethtown. We will take on water and coal. This is a thirty-minute stop. Get up and stretch your legs. This is Elizabethtown."

The little town with a population of 800 looked different to her as she sat ten feet up in the air looking out her window. The sun was almost down. This was the town that her new friend, Joyellen, lived. She thought, "It seems like ages ago I was here, and I thought a lot had happened at that point. How little did I expect what has happened since then. To see Joyellen and her family again would be wonderful, but that is not prudent for me. Maybe sometime in the future when this war is over, I will stop for a joyful visit but not today. My mission is not over. I have sadly accomplished nothing at all."

Once the train had come to a stop at the station, fully half the passengers got off and she could see what appeared to be fifty people standing on the rail siding with luggage and tickets in hand. At this point, she heard a huge clunk in the rear of the train as another car was added from a siding rail. The conductor walked down the aisle. "Munfordville is the next stop. That's a two-hour, fifteen-minute run. If you want to get off the train, for any reason, fold your coat and leave it on your seat or there may not be a seat when you get back. Hold on to your tickets; I will be checking those once we are underway. Munfordville is next. Munfordville in the great state of Kentucky is next. Thank you for your patience." The conductor went to the back of the car and observed the new car being added. Then he descended the stairs and went inside the depot. Twenty minutes later, he walked back and stood on the platform. He shouted out to all who stood there, "There has been a delay. There has been a delay. There is a burned trestle south of Upton and we will not proceed until it is reinforced. The army is working on it. It can be in an hour or more. Stay close, because when we get permission, we will move out."

The one hour turned into three then five. People on the train tried to sleep. Those on the platform lay down on the wood planks. Some opened suitcases and took out coats to sleep on. Others covered themselves with whatever they could find. Men cleared out the depot so women could find warm shelter there. Still seated on the train with Bear at her feet, Caroline reached up and took down her bedroll and covered the lady with the baby who was attempting to sleep to her left. At four that morning, the conductor shouted out a new announcement. "There is hot coffee and soon biscuits in the depot. We are re-stoking the fire in the locomotive. It will take an hour to get up a head of steam, and we are scheduled to leave at five. Once again, we are leaving at five. The trestle has been repaired."

Caroline glanced out the window to the platform, lit only by five coal oil lamps hanging from the side of the building on great iron hooks. She searched the faces of the people standing up and gathering their things. What she saw was fear—frightened faces of mothers holding tight their children's hands. Many of the men stood close to their wives, wondering what was lying in wait. But on a grassy knoll to the side of the depot, blue-clad soldiers were starting to rise from the ground. Bedrolls were rolled up. Haversacks were slung over shoulders. In the middle of this gathering of young men, stood twenty muskets forming a single pyramid of wood and shining iron—locked together and perfectly balanced. The young men milled around waiting to pick up their weapons.

No one wanted to add weight to their already tired shoulders. No one was smiling, nor was there any laughter from these battle-weary veterans, for they knew what was waiting for them—yet another killing battle. Civilians too were not smiling but were happy for the morning coffee and biscuits. No one had expected this long delay. But there was very little complaining going on. This was war and this was the new way of life. Looking to the front of the car, where Jonathan and the two soldiers had earlier stood, she saw they were no longer there. In the next thirty minutes, men and women started boarding the train from the front and back. There was no pushing, as most were overly tired and silent. Some of the women carried baskets and their husbands carried their repacked leather luggage, which they pushed into over-their-head, brass-railed bins. Men stood by seats and allowed the women to take the window seats. After the women were aboard, the men filled in the remaining seats. But many men found no seats and stood in the middle of the aisle. Caroline motioned Bear to sit on the floor near her feet and so the seat next to her was empty. A young woman took the seat and nodded hello to Caroline. No words were spoken, only looks exchanged.

Thirty minutes later, exactly at five in the morning as the sun was breaking the morning sky, the train pulled out of Elizabethtown and several men inside the car applauded. One bearded man, wearing a long black coat and gray pants, stepped into Caroline's car looking for a seat; seeing none, he stood at the front next to an older man. Glancing around the car, he came to Caroline's face and then quickly turned away, facing forward. The older man noticed this new man was trembling, and so he put his arm around the man's shoulder. "It's okay. It's okay, young man. No matter what you went through, God is on your side." The trembling man gripped the handle, opened the door, and went back into the forward from which he came. He said not a word.

The young woman seated next to Caroline shuffled her feet and reached down and scratched her leg. "Pardon my movements, but poison ivy has found a place on my legs. We walked two days to get to Elizabethtown and we traveled through the woods for one whole day. I was smart and covered my legs with mud—that's what the Indians do. But it still found a place." The woman leaned back up into a sitting position. "I'm Alma Huddleston. We are from Nag's Branch. Where are you from?"

Caroline smiled politely. "I'm from west of Bowling Green. Hopkinsville. We are west of that. We're homesteaders there. I am Caroline."

The woman with scratches on her face from walking through briars brushed her hair back from her face. "My husband and I are dairy people. We had a herd of thirty-two cows. Guernsey and Brown Swiss. But the Union Army come through and took all our cows. Every one. Left us a piece of paper. A receipt. Conscripting cows, they said. So we are heading to his brother's place in Russellville until this thing is over and we get our cows back." The woman forced a smile. "He worked hard to make the best cheese in the county, but now no more. So, I guess we start again when this is over. Carl's in the third car with our son. We are lucky though, as they say this is the first train out of Louisville in six days." The woman reached down and scratched her leg again. "That's why there are so many of us on it. The Confederates burned all the trestles and so trains have not run. And bridges too, so there are no coaches. We walked for two days to get away because there's something big about to happen near us. Nag's Branch.

Caroline looked at her seriously. "What do you hear about that?"

"I have heard over sixty thousand men are gathered with the Confederates. And the Union has even more. How do you feed all those men? I shall tell you how. You steal. You plunder. You conscript anything that can be eaten.

"Where do people say is this going to take place?"

"Some say near us, that is why we rushed to get away. My husband would walk to Russellville and his brother's place, but my boy is sick and exhausted. I am too."

The door opened in the front of the car and the strange man with the long black coat entered. He had pulled his hat over his eyes, ducked his head forward, and walked down the aisle to the back door. He slowed once and looked at where Caroline was seated, but continued to the rear door and entered the fifth car.

Most of the next leg of the trip was uneventful. Alma, the young woman with the poison ivy, said no more about the war, and fell asleep. Her husband came into the car with their

331

son and stood toward the front. The boy occasionally reached down, scratching his bare legs covered with red poison ivy welts.

At one point, Bear rose and shook his body and then walked out into the aisle, did two turns, and returned. Caroline watched outside as the trees raced by at forty miles an hour. She had not gotten much sleep back at Elizabethtown, so time seemed to pass slowly even as the hills raced by. At other times, her head nodded forward, and she briefly fell asleep, but fought back against it.

Five miles outside of Munfordville, the conductor walked into the car and made his presence known by clapping his hands over his head. He shouted out in a loud voice, "Munfordville is next. Munfordville! All those wishing to depart at Munfordville, we will be exiting on the right. Please take your things with you. All those heading to Bowling Green, please stay on board, as this stop is only a twenty-minute stop."

At Munfordville, the station's platform was much smaller than Elizabethtown, and the depot office was little more than a one-room building, but like Elizabethtown, the platform was full of people waiting for the train. Travelers, including the young woman with the new-born, got up and left the train, and many new passengers crowded onto the car. The conductor tried to stop people from crowding onto the train, shouting, "There will be another train through here in three hours. Please, we cannot take everyone. There will be a second train in three hours. Please be kind to one another." Nonetheless, people packed onto the train. As the train lurched forward, those standing lost their balance and several men bumped into each other. As they pulled away from Munfordville, Caroline looked out her window and saw all of the Union Army men had gotten off the train and a long line of military wagons, pulled by mules, stood waiting for the men. She counted the number and saw there were sixty such wagons, all painted olive drab green and each one covered with white canvas tarps. Behind those wagons, stood thirty cannons and caissons, each pulled by six large dark brown horses. She noticed army crates stacked six high were being loaded into the wagons. Kegs of gunpowder were being rolled to the caissons. "Bullets, gun powder, and men," she thought, "soon to be used to kill other men." Once underway, the woman with poison ivy stood and then leaned back to Caroline. "I'm going to sit with my husband; a seat is available now. Good luck."

As the woman stood, the gruff man in a long, black coat standing near quickly moved and sat down next to Caroline. He placed a small, black, well-worn carpet bag at his feet. Tilting his head forward and shielding his face, he sat there trembling, then inhaled rapidly. The smell of perspiration was about him and his hand was shaking, even resting on his knee. Caroline noticed it and thought the man was ill. He turned and whispered in a low, raspy voice, "Whatever you do, ma'am, do not look at me nor become frightened." Caroline started to turn to look at the man. The bearded man quickly pushed his leg sideways into her knee. "No! Do not look at me." Caroline turned her eyes forward and remembered the knife in her waist band. "I am a wanted man to be killed or shot in the next moment." The man pulled his leg back. "At the next bend of the train, pretend you are looking out the left windows at the scenery. You can glance at me then. But do not react. Just a quick glance. For I fear the sight of me might shock you.

Caroline quickly glanced at the ragged, gaunt, heavily bearded stranger, then, with her face forward, spoke quietly. "Sir, why would your appearance shock me?"

"Ma'am, I used to know you before this happened to me. I am aware of who you are."

Unsure now of this man's identity, Caroline bowed her head low and spoke in a whisper. Her eyes fell upon his pant legs covered to his knees with mud. "You did? Where would that be?"

"In Louisville, Kentucky, many years ago."

Caroline paused and thought, but nothing came to mind. "I cannot recall, but I do not remember you. Maybe you are mistaken."

"I am not, but it is good that you do not recognize me."

"And, sir, why would that be good?"

"They say I am a dangerous man."

"Dangerous in what way? For you appear weakened."

"I was dead, but now I find myself immersed in a miracle I cannot comprehend. For moments ago, the earth did shudder and I stood amazed on its plane, unable to move.

"Sir, you speak in riddles to me, but you choose words like my husband. Did you know him? In Louisville? Maybe at college? Charles Matthew Duncan?

"Yes, I knew Charles well and I hope to again with God's everlasting, gracious, and merciful help."

At those words, Caroline suddenly gasped. There was an overwhelming and familiar accent in this man's weakened voice. A sudden possibility struck with an insight unimaginable. Like unexpectedly falling into a pond of cool water, her body quivered. "My husband...my husband, Charles, used those same words, many times—everlasting, gracious, and merciful—but rarely have I heard them from another's lips. Could it be...?" Caroline sat there with her mouth open. Her hand started to tremble, and her breathing quickened. Tears started to form in her eyes, but she made no eye contact with this man sitting so close. Calming herself for a moment, her lips formed to speak words that were hard to say and so she said them slowly and with fearful and measured caution.

"And, sir, if your name was ever Charles Matthew Duncan, please tell me so."

"Ma'am, hold steady and do not arouse attention."

"I have come many days to find him. And now, I believe I have."

"And now you have."

"But your voice is unlike my husband's. It is strange to my ear. I need more proof. My husband had a scar on his left wrist from a saw blade. An accident. May I see your left wrist?"

"There is no need to, Caroline. I am Charles Matthew Duncan."

"Then you will show me your scar. Please."

The man pulled back his coat sleeve, then the shirt sleeve, and there on his wrist was the evidence she wanted to see. The saw blade scar.

Charles turned and quietly folded his hands in his lap. Caroline gasped for air. There was a stunned silence between the two of them. The only sound was that of the wind racing by the open window. Caroline's face flushed. A chill started in her fingertips and ran throughout her body. This was not the reunion moment she had envisioned. Stunned and silent, side by side, they rode in this train car as one. Caroline noticed tears were falling from his face and landing on his hands. She reached over and took his hand. She could say no words, for none were worthy of the moment. Finally, Charles stirred. "For us, the past is written, the ink is dry, and the future is what we—you and I—will now write. All I hold onto is a fragile plan and maybe not much of one at all. I had a new identity. I was not your husband. I was someone else's husband. I cannot express anything emotional to you at this time. But there is no greater love than what I have for you. I have been waiting to say that for eleven months. I said it to you on my death bed. Over and over. And now I live. However, all my efforts may have been in vain.

Caroline, still looking straight ahead, lowered her eyes toward her lap and whispered," Charles, what do you mean in vain? For you are safe and you are with me. We are on this train, and we are going home."

"Caroline, if I am caught today, I would be considered a Confederate spy and imprisoned or shot. My wife would be equally charged if she were aiding me. If my own people caught me, I would be tried as a deserter with the same outcome. I do not fear death for myself. I only fear the death that would separate us." The man looked over his left shoulder then back ahead. Caroline squeezed his hand tightly. "Charles, I so love you, and now I am frightened. But this is far better. Yesterday in Shelbyville, I found you dead. I stood at your grave and bitterly wept. I cried out to God. And today I find you here next to me. Not dead but alive. I am filled with relief and a joy unimaginable." Fresh tears started running down Caroline's cheeks. Her voice barely understandable. "But you are right, for there is a new challenge we face. And we will do it together for now I am confident in my ways."

Charles took several deep breaths to calm himself. Caroline realized his hand continued to tremble. She had never seen her husband this broken and frightened. He was terrified of a single man with a badge and a gun when he had faced hundreds of guns in battle. Her thought was something had happened to him emotionally. She glanced at his face and noticed a gray pallor. He was a man once close to death, but today still running from it. "Are you still sick? Do you have a fever?"

"I've gotten use to the fever, but I feel dizzy at times. I have little strength. I've walked from Shelbyville to Louisville and then to Elizabethtown—at times in the woods, just off the roads. But I am glad I did all that now that I see you sitting right here. I will get stronger; I just need to get home.

Charles took a deep breath and quickly glanced at Caroline then back to the floor. She heard a smile in his voice. "When I saw you, I wanted with every muscle in my body to rush forward and embrace you, but, no, that cannot be. That will come later, but for now we need a new plan. I've been thinking for the last hour how we can do this. There are private people on this train who work for the Union, and they look with suspicion at all single men traveling alone. They have cast their eyes on me several times. They carry guns and have badges on their vests."

Caroline glanced up at Charles again, but her eye contact was brief. "How have you escaped them?"

Charles stared down at his carpet bag and kept his eyes there as he pulled his hat forward covering his eyes. "At first, I traveled as a Quaker pastor who had lost his wife and traveling to her funeral. I have a passage letter that states that. It appears to be signed by Confederate Colonial Willtrout, but I have forged it myself. It got me past Confederate lines, but that matters little to the Union. You have seen the blue coats and if they suspect me, they will search me and see my wounds and I will be branded a deserter from the North or a deserter from the South. Either way, I will be taken away as a prisoner. Or shot. So, I have thought of a new plan, and I will tell you more later." Caroline started to speak, but Charles continued. "Caroline, I cannot put you at risk. I will not sit here much longer, so listen carefully. In Bowling Green, you get off the right side and I will get off the left. Walk to the center of town. The big brick courthouse. West side. I will meet you there."

"Charles, I love you."

"I know, but please show no affection. Now, I am going to stand and go to the car behind this one. The last car. Caroline, in Bowling Green, get off on the right side and meet one hour later at the courthouse. Remember, the west side."

"Charles? I want to..."

"No. No more. In an hour." Charles stood, then reached down and secured his carpet bag. Tipping his hat, he turned toward the rear of the car then walked to the door and out of the car into the trailing car.

It was only in that moment, after this revelatory and sudden appearance of a dead man—a dead husband now brought back to life—did she sense a quickening pulse and a flushness that descended upon her face. Yet in this happiness in finding her husband, there was a fear she could soon lose him. She wanted to reach out and hold him, but to hold him, she had to let go. After he got up and walked away, she started to tear up. She tried to quell it but that proved impossible. Tears ran down her cheeks. She turned her eyes toward the window and pretended to shield them from the sun, but it was of no use. At one point, her body started to quiver. Through her tears, she looked at her hands as they trembled. She quickly dropped them to her side. A man who had been standing nearby took the seat next to her and smelled of darkened earth. His beard and hair looked unkempt. His brown-checked jacket was worn and covered with soil at the cuffs as if he had been digging with bare hands for root vegetables. His pants were stained with mud at his knees. For that reason, Caroline thought this man was a wonderful sight. Not a Union or Confederate soldier, but a plan ordinary struggling man attempting to move away from the turmoil that could erupt without a moment's warning everywhere it crept. Here was a man who may have slept in the woods and dug in the soil for something to eat. Or fell to his knees in front of grave. All that was now an everyday occasion and every day it happened with more people.

The next hour and a half appeared like hundreds of hours to Caroline. Knowing her husband, who she had not seen for eleven months, was fifty feet from her—alive and not dead. Not in a wood box buried under six feet of dirt behind a small white church in Shelbyville, Kentucky. No. He was not there. He was safe with both arms and both legs. He had lost weight, but she knew his kind voice. She knew all would be well once they were together again. She rode on for a while, as the train rocked side to side. At times, she would take a deep breath to quiet herself, only to feel the pain from the bear wound in her side. Only short shallow breaths kept the pain at bay, and this caused her to feel light headed. At one point, she leaned against the window and fell asleep. It seemed like minutes but it could have been hours. Over a section of damaged rail, the train lurched hard to the right, and she jerked herself awake. Looking around the train car, everything looked strange and ghostlike. People seemed living in another time. They seemed without emotion. While her emotion was raw and unbridled. Quickly, a dark moment happened. Caroline thought, "Was that a dream? Did I fall asleep and have a dream? Did that really happen? Was that Charles? Was there any evidence? Maybe it was a dream. Maybe I fell asleep and woke up. This has happened many times before. What is wrong with me?" She thought, "I am tired. I have not slept in a long while." Her joy turned to uncertainty. Caroline looked over her shoulder toward the rear of the train. She wanted to stand and walk to the last car to see for herself, but what if he wasn't there? Hope was better than uncertainty. And would the Pinkerton man sitting up front in the black bowler hat think that it was suspicious? What if he was there and the Pinkerton man followed her. She sat there and her joy was turning into confusion, then weakness. She turned to the man seated next to her. "Who was seated here before you took this seat? Did you see a man with a beard, a long black coat, a carpetbag? He was seated next to me."

The man looked around. "I didn't see nobody. Are you saving this seat? I'll get up if you want."

"No. You sit there. I think I had a dream."

"We all do. I dreamed once that I found a pot of gold out in the field. I woke up and searched the whole house. I knew I found it, but I never found it again. Is that what you mean?"

"Yes, that's it exactly. Thank you."

"You getting off at Bowling Green?"

"Yes, I am. Or I think I will."

"Pot of gold. This big. I went out the next day with my wife and we dug everywhere. The mind will play tricks on you."

The scenery was getting to be more familiar to Caroline, as the train was now thirty minutes away from Bowling Green. As Caroline sat there, her muscles started to move. Her legs would not rest quietly, and she noticed every minute she had to move. Bear looked up and noticed it too. She glanced down at her hands and saw they were moving much like the exercises she did when she took piano lessons as a teenager. The thirty minutes passed slowly, and she kept looking over her shoulder toward the fifth car. She looked for any sight of a tall man in a black coat. She saw none. She said quietly to herself, "Please. Please." Five minutes before they arrived, she noticed people on the left side of the train were pointing at the new brick buildings that were coming into view. Caroline could not wait any longer and stood. She grabbed hold of her bedroll and haversack and squeezed past the dirt-stained man and slowly made her way to the rear of the car standing by the door. The conductor entered the car from the front, clapping his hands over his head. "Bowling Green. Next stop Bowling Green. Do not forget your luggage. Bowling Green, next stop. Fifteen minutes stop."

This little town had been a bright economic force for the state of Kentucky. Tobacco was king, and the rich dark leaf cultivated in its "black patch" region was highly sought after. Exporters paid three times higher for Kentucky black tobacco, already a favorite of the European well-to-do and valued by royalty. But the war had stopped all that. Now, only a few wagons rambled down the town's brick streets. The train cars, which once upon a time carried this highly prized crop to New Orleans or Mobile for shipping, all sat empty, rusting as they waited on the side tracks. The train had barely stopped when Caroline jumped from the last step but, losing her footing, she fell to the ground. A male passenger helped her up and she was immediately engulfed by the crowd of departing passengers. She tried to glance back at the fifth car, hoping to catch site of her husband, but he was not in the men and women departing the car. She stood near the tracks and watched intently. Finally, the last man departed the car, and she searched again the men who had gotten off. But in that moment, his words came back to her. "Courthouse, west side." It was all she had and so she embraced the words, repeating them quietly to herself. Caroline quickly walked the five blocks, and as she hurried, she glanced ahead of her and behind her. Still there was no sign of Charles. She stopped at one point and adjusted her bedroll and haversack over her shoulder. She watched as Bear looked confused at all the brick buildings side by side with no grass between them, no grass in front. Brick and cement ruled this growing town. There were no woods to hide in and no tall whip grass to look for rabbits. No streams to catch frogs sleeping or catfish hiding in the watercress. Caroline walked on cautiously, surveying the streets, stores, and alleyways that made up this county seat town. Coming toward her, she observed a passing Union Army wagon loaded with barrels of black powder and two blue-coated soldiers driving four large mules dripping with sweat. Four soldiers followed closely behind, riding stiffly on dark brown horses. One of the men, an officer with gold braid on his shoulders, turned his head and eyed Caroline. There was no acknowledgement of her nor was anyone smiling. They were about their business and the business was in killing.

As she rounded a corner, she spotted it. A red brick courthouse. High above that building, pointing into the sky, were a trio of three flag poles. They held no Confederate flag, no Union flag, but only a single flag of the county. At this point, she started to run but then remembering what she had heard in the dream, she slowed and looked around. No one was following her. She approached the courthouse square, observing two older men standing by the front door, talking. Looking up into the sky, she realized she was on the east side of the courthouse and so she quickly walked past the two men on the sidewalk and around to the corner. On the south side, a mother and two children were waiting while her husband loaded suitcases into a carriage. Rounding the next corner, her heart started pounding with excitement. At this point, she was on the west side. The brick was covered in morning shadow—dark, as the new day's sun had yet to strike its face. This was the side where she was supposed to meet Charles. But there was no one here. She looked over her shoulder at Bear, who was following ten paces behind. A sense of gloom started inside her mind and her smile of anticipation was quickly waning. "This is it, Bear. This is the west side of the courthouse, and this is Bowling Green, and we are where we are supposed to be. This is what Charles said. Courthouse. West side in one hour. But has it been one hour? No, it has not. So I am early. But why an hour? Why did he say an hour? Why should we wait? Bear, I do not understand this. Have I been fooled? Is there something I don't know? No, God. Don't let this happen. Please, God." Caroline dropped her bedroll and haversack to the cobblestone walkway. Her stomach tightened and her hands suddenly trembled. The gift she thought was hers was being taken back. She turned in a full circle looking. There was nobody in sight. "Jesus, please do something. Do it now. Please, do it right now." She stood there in silence. The earth beneath her feet seemed to be moving. She felt unsteady. Spots appeared in her eyes as she steadied herself. Ten long minutes passed.

A voice came out of the doorway behind her. "Caroline, pick up your bedroll and your sack and walk over to the door behind you. Do it slowly." Hearing her husband's voice, Caroline's body started to tremble. Tears of many emotions rolled down her cheeks. It was the voice on the train. Her breathing increased rapidly as she picked up her bedroll and haversack. She wiped her eyes and looked around for anyone suspicious. She noticed there were only those two older men, now walking away, and so she walked backwards slowly to the door and found it partially opened. Caroline stepped backward and into the darkened room.

The man, standing on the other side of the door, quietly closed the door behind her and whispered, "Caroline. Caroline. Caroline. Caroline. Sweet Caroline. How I love you." Before Caroline could say a word, her husband, turned her around and pulled her tight to himself. "I love you, Caroline, yet I have no words. I am so taken with you. I have wanted to hold you for so long. It's you. It's you." Tears gathered in his eyes. Caroline, still in shock, said nothing but looked at her husband. Finally, she spoke. "Is it you? Can it really be you? Tell me. I want to hear your voice. Tell me anything, Charles." Charles brushed her cheek with his hand. "Yes. I am alive. I am very much alive. I have survived. But why, I ask myself? And the only answer is I am alive to be with you."

"Kiss me, Charles. Please, kiss me now." Charles looked down to his wife and, looking into her face, he paused to take in her very being, then he kissed her as he had kissed her when he left for the war. It was a kiss full of love and full of emotion. Happiness. It was of oneness, peace and resolve, tenderness and caring, desperation coupled with remorse. Her tears continued and soon gave way to joyous laughter of euphoria. His tears ran down his cheeks and disappeared into his beard. He laughed and then, realizing the magnitude of the first kiss, he gave a second kiss. But this time, he kissed her lips, her cheeks, her eye lids, her neck, and then he pushed her from him and just beheld her.

"You are the most beautiful thing in the world. I cannot believe. I cannot believe this at all. Why were you on that train? How did you get there? What did you know? Did you think I was dead? I could not write. Caroline, is this really you? Are you really here? I think I must be dreaming. First, why were you on that train? Go ahead. No, don't. Can I tell you how beautiful you are? God had to do this. I could not arrange it any better. So, I want to hear your voice. Tell me you are my wife, Caroline."

Caroline wiped away a tear. "Yes, I am your wife. The one you married in Louisville. The one you moved to a homestead at Hopkinsville. The one you had three children with, I am her, and I am yours. It is as simple and wonderful as that."

"But why were you on that train?"

"I was going home. I had traveled, mostly walked, to Shelbyville, the last place you wrote from, and when I got there, they said you were dead. I died there at your grave. At that little church, I lost all hope. I cried for what was lost. But two people gave me hope. They said you might not be in that box. I saw your signature for the burial site and then I thought, no, you are alive and maybe on the way home. So, I caught a train to come home.

"And I thought, if I could make it, I would come home to you."

Charles stepped back to look at his wife. "And you walked all the way to Shelbyville? By yourself? All the way?"

"I did get a small ride with Confederate troops going for ammunition, but, yes, I walked eleven days. I will tell you about it when I get home and you can tell me yours when once we return."

"What of the children? What of Priscilla, Noah, Isaac?"

"They're safe; the Millars are checking on them daily. They are probably living up in that old cave. There's lots of food. I would not have left them in danger."

"Did I tell you how beautiful you are? When I saw you on the train, I almost shouted out your name. I had to go to another car to collect myself. To quiet down. I had to put on a mask."

"And I thought you were a dream. I thought, 'no, this cannot be right.' I thought I was making it up in my mind. I cried all the way after you left me, until right now. I was so unsure of everything. Hold me tight. Hold me real tight. Tell me this is no dream. Please."

"This is no dream, Caroline, but we need to be consistently watchful. One false step on my part, and I would be revealed. Some would consider me a Confederate spy. Sadly, there is no fair trial. It can be and is certain death."

"Yes, Charles, I know of this as I have talked to one. Both Union and South are searching for those men who walk away. But let's get underway now. Let us get far away from here as soon as we can, for it may only get worse. We will walk home if we have to."

"If the stages are still running, we can be home midday tomorrow. The stages used to run every six hours. And if they have stopped running, I will buy a mule. I have money. I will buy a carriage, or a wagon. But we need to move out of this area fast. The Union Army is here and gathering strength north of here—troops are pouring in from Ohio, Pennsylvania, and New York. They want to take Nashville before Christmas. Once we are home, we will be safe. I see you have a dog and that is good too. So here is our story. We are Quakers and we don't believe in war, and we are going home to Hopkinsville, where I am a pastor."

"Yes and no. It is the Shakers and Mennonites that are all going to Missouri. I have talked to them, and we are from a little town called Hartville, Kentucky. It is a Shaker settlement. I know that for a fact. Bethlehem, Missouri, that's where they are going. And that is where we are going. Bethlehem, Missouri. Remember that. Charles? Now, kiss me again."

A minute later, Charles picked up Caroline's bedroll and she picked up her haversack. Back on the sidewalk, they walked out of the building and traveled down the street. Charles took her hand and squeezed tight. "The dangerous thing is there are Pinkerton men everywhere. They are looking for spies,

Confederates, their own deserters. The Union is paying a bounty, and the Pinkerton men collect half the reward. Three of them were on the train. Today."

As they entered the second block, Caroline looked up at Charles. "How could you tell? What should I be looking for?"

"Their eyes. They are always searching. Darting back and forth. They travel in pairs. They come from New York and Philadelphia, and you see that in their dress. If you see two men, both in black derbies, they are Pinkertons. They would consider me a spy or an escaped prisoner."

On the street that day, everything looked normal and safe. There were only husbands and their wives walking the sidewalks, carrying packages. Occasionally, a horse-drawn buggy would trot by. A wagon loaded with cotton bales stacked eight feet high passed by with two Negroes holding the reins and pulled by four mules. As they walked, Charles glanced over his shoulder but saw no one following him.

"If I remember correctly, the Overland Road Company is in two more blocks." Caroline agreed and they quickly walked down the brick sidewalk. As they continued, they passed a hardware store, a men's boot store, and a small restaurant with a sign in the window that read, "Farley and Farley Restaurant." Next to it was a small, white-front store with a green and yellow sign over the door that read, "Miss Hanna's Dress Goods and Millenary." She glanced in the window and caught her reflection, then slowed and pulled on Charles hand.

"This yellow dress is not right for Shakers. Let me run in and get a dark one. It will take ten minutes and no more. Charles, come in with me and get off the street."

Caroline led Charles into the dress store and walked to the readymade rack on the side. Miss Hanna pushed back her chair and stood from her sewing machine, walking over. A second woman stood over a large table in the corner, cutting from a pattern. Caroline held up a black dress and a dark blue, then disappeared behind a curtain and moments later walked out to stand before the mirror. "I will take the black. We are Shakers. Our women wear white caps. Have you any white caps?" Miss Hanna led her to a table and pointed out a collection of fancy bonnets and simple caps. After quickly braiding her hair, Caroline placed the white cap on and adjusted the fit. True to her word, she was back out on the street in ten minutes. "An unadorned black dress looks more Shaker to me. And the white cap is the tell-tale sign. I think we look fully religious now. I wish you had a Bible to carry."

A church bell off in the distance rang seven bells as they approached the Overland Road Company. Two stagecoaches sat in a straight line. Both were painted bright red with green and yellow pin stripes. The name "Overland" was written in gold. Men in leather pants were leading horses out of a barn on the other side of the street and starting to hitch them to the first coach. On the sidewalk in front of the Overland Road Company, two ladies stood with three pieces of luggage and two hat cases. An elderly man stood leaning on his cane, trying to light his pipe, a red-green-and-orange carpetbag resting beside him. As they approached the stage office,

Charles adjusted the bedroll on his shoulder and, with that action, Caroline was suddenly aware they were without luggage—something that would look suspicious to any Pinkerton man. She pulled her haversack off her shoulder and carried it in her hand. Trotting along behind them, Bear glanced around nervously at the spectacle before him and decided to walk between Caroline and this new man.

"Excuse me, sir, could I have a word with you?" A short, heavyset man in a bowler hat stepped out of a darkened space between two buildings. "My name is Gerstein, and I am with the Pinkerton Agency." The short man with a thin mustache pulled back his coat jacket to reveal a Pinkerton badge on his vest. Several inches below the badge, a small, 31-caliber pistol rested in a black leather holster. "Can I ask who you are?"

Caroline stepped forward. "He's deaf. He can't hear you, but he speaks a little. He reads lips. I can answer for him; I am his wife. His name is Sims. Abraham Sims. I am his wife, Elizabeth. We are Shakers and we are heading to Bethlehem, Missouri."

The Pinkerton man stepped back and looked them over. "And where are you from?"

"We are from a brotherhood of Shakers in a small gathering town east. Hartville. It is in the eastern part of the state, it is right..."

"I know where Hartville is," the Pinkerton man interrupted abruptly. "You Shakers are a devout sort, aren't you? I mean, you study the Bible a lot. Do you know the one hundred Psalms?"

"Yes, I do."

"Let's hear it."

"Yes, it says, 'Make a joyful noise unto the Lord. In all ye lands, serve the Lord with gladness; come before his presence with singing.'"

The Pinkerton man turned to Charles and shouted, "Go ahead and you finish it, Abraham Sims."

"I said he is deaf; he knows it but he has a hard time speaking.

Charles held up his hand to Caroline. "Knnnn-oooooow...yeee...thaaattt...ttthhhaaaa...Loooorrd...Heeeee...i sssssssss...Gaaaahhhd."

Caroline interrupted. "Yes, Abraham. Know ye that the Lord, He is God. It is He that hath made us and not we ourselves. We are the sheep..."

The Pinkerton man took two steps back. "Good. That's enough. But I got a question for you, ma'am. You got a new dress on, but your shoes look pretty worn and covered with dry mud. You been walking to avoid people? Hiding?"

"We walk and lead people to the lord as we walk. Could I pray with you today? And would you like to know the Lord? Let me take your hand and pray."

The Pinkerton man waved her away. "No! No! No! Alright, go on. You're free to go." The man in the bowler hat turned and started to walk away, then he stopped and turned. "But you know what really convinced me? That dog." The Pinkerton man pointed to Bear. "That's a family dog. He ain't no one-person dog. He's a true family dog. Anyhow, good luck in Bethlehem; they say it is pretty country. And by the way, I know the one hundredth psalm. My mother taught me. I ain't religious, though." The Pinkerton man tipped his hat, turned, and walked across the street. Locating a chair outside a tavern, he sat down, while a second Pinkerton man came out of a tavern nearby, placed his gun back into his holster, and also took a seat. Neither man smiled. Both wore bowler hats.

Two stages were set to leave that day—one at 10:30 and the other at 1:30—and both would be packed with nine passengers in each coach. Caroline and Charles boarded and took seats facing forward on the 10:30 stage. The driver said the dog could ride on the floor or he could ride up on top sitting next to the driver. Caroline stated she wanted the dog with her and so Bear sat on the floor.

The two ladies with a large amount of luggage, including several round hat boxes, rode backward facing Caroline and Charles. The older gentleman with a white beard got on and sat next to the ladies. A young man and his pregnant wife climbed in and looked to the seat next to Caroline. Charles got up and gave his seat to them, then sat in the middle row jump-seats facing Caroline. Two young brothers, dressed in matching shorts and jackets with bow ties and travelling by themselves, sat next to Charles and asked permission to pet

Bear. Caroline nodded yes, and then smiled to Charles. "You can pet him too. He saved my life. He's our dog, now."

The dry dirt roads were straight for the first ten miles, then starting into the hills, they twisted and turned as the terrain dictated. Many of these roads followed well known Indian trails established hundreds of years earlier. This trace, barely wide enough for a wagon, ran up and down the wooded hills, and many times through streams, following the paths deer, elk, and antelope had forged out before two-legged creatures came hunting game. The driver never slowed the horses, calling out to them to pull harder as they climbed the steeper red clay hills. The downhill ride was much faster as the driver rode the brake to slow the two-thousand-pound stage as it rounded perilous curves. At the base of these hills, Caroline found comfort in seeing the small settlements, many without names, which dotted alongside the road, gathered together for mutual safety and companionship. Coming into these settlements, young boys and girls ran from homesteads and out to the road. They would scream and shout to each other that the stage was coming. Several would run from the work they had been assigned, and raced toward the road, waving their hats. This was a sign of normalcy. It was a good thing. The driver would take off his hat and wave back at the boys. Young girls would come to the front porch, still wearing aprons and shielding their eyes from the sun, politely waving. At one such small settlement, twenty-three miles into the day's journey, the stage stopped at the outskirts near a small shed crudely marked "Overland Stage Company." A split-rail corral held four fresh horses. As the driver climbed down, he announced a twenty-minute stop for exchanging the horses and "stretching your stage legs." Two privies were situated at opposite sides of a small shed, marked "Hissin's and Gerl's." The pregnant woman was helped off the stage and walked quickly ahead of the other ladies to the privy. Her husband stood near the door and wound his watch, lifting it twice to hear its ticking. Two young barefoot boys ran to the stage and ran their hands over the painted letters on the door, shouting out each letter to each other in some sort of spelling contest.

Caroline and Charles walked to where there was a siphon pump over a water well and drew cool water to drink. An array of chipped enamel cups hung on nails next to the pump. Charles splashed water in his face and then walked over to the driver, who was giving water to the horses. "What's the name of this place?"

The driver turned and looked at Charles. "Don't have no name. Well, Calvin Bishop owns the corral we use, so we just call it Bishop's Rest."

The two young girls who waved from the front porch came briskly walking over the road, still wearing their aprons and each holding a cane basket. The older one, with a red bow in her hair, held her basket filled with biscuits forward toward the travelers. "Tomato-bacon biscuits with honey. Five cents. I also have biscuit egg, watercress, and cracklings." The younger girl, who wore her hair in pig tails, stopped in front of Caroline and held forward a basket with a wrapped item. "Baked this morning. No yesterday's here. Best turnovers in

Kentucky. The ones with the 'C' is cherry. The ones with the 'P' is peach. No more food for the next thirty miles."

Charles reached into his pocket and found a dime. "One biscuit and one turnover." The younger girl handed him a turnover wrapped in brown waxed paper, and the older one was quick with the biscuit wrapped in a similar way.

The older girl looked at Charles. "Beg pardon, sir, any war news? You hear something? My brother is out there somewhere, sir. The last letter from him was three weeks ago. Private Daniel Edward Fellerman."

Charles scratched his beard. "I hope it is over soon and your brother gets to come home and eat some of you girls' biscuits."

"Sir, you're the second stage that's been through here in the last two days. That one came through yesterday morning and that is what they said. "No news. But no news is good news. That's what my mama says."

Caroline walked over and stood beside Charles. "That turnover looks very good. Did you bake it or did your mother?"

"Yes, Fellie and me do all the cooking now. Mama's in charge of the garden and the chickens and the goats and canning. Fellie and me, we cook and do the laundry. Daddy is up at Timber Load, he's a logger. We only see him once a week and then he goes back loggin'." The younger girl smiled. "But all the money Almandine and me make, well, we get to keep half. That's why we were so happy to see the stage running again."

The driver called out to his passengers, "Get on board, we are leaving in five minutes. The other stage will not take you, as it is filled up."

Caroline bent down to Fellie, the littlest girl. "Tell your mother we think you are the two prettiest girls we have seen all day. And I will take another biscuit please." Caroline stood up and searched her pocket and found a nickel.

Almandine took the coin and smiled. "God bless you, ma'am. Thank you for being a customer." The man with the pregnant wife waved to Almandine and she ran over and handed the man a biscuit. Fellie followed and handed a turnover to the older gentleman. Then, the two ladies with the two hat boxes bought an egg, watercress, crackling biscuit, but paid for it with a dime and wanted no change.

The driver shouted down to the girls as he took his place on top of the coach. "There will be another through here this afternoon—but two hours. You girls be ready for them. And I'll take the two biscuits you got left." The young girls nodded and ran to the coach. Quickly, Almandine climbed the front spoke wheel with her bare feet, handing up her last two biscuits. The driver tossed two nickels into the air and Fellie dropped her basket and caught both in midair. She smiled and walked backwards, waving goodbye. The two girls joined hands and ran back across the road to their front porch. They stood there waving. After a minute, Fellie started counting the money.

Once underway, the road became straight and easy. Caroline leaned to the side and soon fell asleep. She woke once and pulled her haversack close to her and suddenly remembered there was a fully loaded revolver wrapped in a dishcloth inside, and so she moved it around to where she could not feel it any longer. She stirred and turned to Charles. "I should have told you sooner, but I have a Colt 36 in my haversack."

Charles looked around to see if anyone was listening. "I'm glad you told me. Caroline, slip your haversack toward my foot. Is it loaded?"

"Yes, it's got a fresh load of six and there are twelve more cartridges and caps wrapped in a rag."

"Have you fired it?"

"Several times. I am pretty good at it."

"Good. You had a steady hand with mine, so it only makes sense. Where did you get it?"

"From a dead man. I don't want to fire it again though."

"I understand. Caroline?"

"Yes, Charles?"

"We should be home in about five hours."

Every twenty miles, the stage was scheduled for a stop. The first one came in a small town named Wilford's Creek, and a second in a town that had just changed its name. The stage driver said they found the new name in the Good Book and so they called it Jericho. Its old name was Gilson's Gulch. The early evening sun was still a welcoming warm ball in the sky, now one finger high, but the driver shouted down he would not travel after sundown, as it was too risky. "My eyesight is not too good, and it gets damn dark out here."

The driver did not say much after that, but drove the horses hard, hoping to make Jericho with some daylight left. At half past seven in the evening, the stage pulled into Jericho, and he stopped beside the Overland Stage Corral just outside of town. "That's it folks, that's as far as we come today. The road ahead is treacherous in the dark."

The driver announced the stage would leave promptly at seven the next morning, then he recommended the new ten-room Whippoorwill Hotel or one of the two guest houses in town, which sat quietly off the main street one block away. Caróline said she preferred the quiet guest house, as the Whippoorwill Hotel was directly across from the town's only restaurant and tavern.

As the two of them, with Bear close behind, walked down the street, they saw two guest houses sitting next to each other. Both houses, identical in size and design, displayed hand-painted signs that hung over the porches and swayed in the breeze. One read the Sparrow Guest House and the second read Red Bird Guest House. The woman at the first one was about fifty years in age and wore a large apron that came down to the tip of her shoes. She spoke softly with a strong hint of Irish, and introduced herself as "Hanny." Her braided hair was hidden by a handkerchief that she wore when cleaning. She held a broom in one hand and said she had three rooms available. The room, she said, was fifty cents a night and a hot bath would cost an additional ten cents. Charles gave her a dollar bill and Hanny reached into her apron to make change. Hanny climbed the stairs and said room number three was toward the rear and the one closest to the bathing room. Hanny handed them the key and left only to return a moment later with a fresh bar of soap and two towels. She said she had started heating the bath water an hour earlier, and so it would be ready in another ten minutes. She pointed to the only white-painted door on the floor, and then walked the few steps and opened the door. Hanny said she was proud of the first copper and brass tub in Jericho. On the wall were pictures of Irish castles and Irish countrysides. A large potted palm rested in the corner. Hanny took out matches and lit the lamp. "When we had these two houses built, I said to my sister I wanted no windows in the bathing rooms. I wanted decorum. I wanted privacy." Hanny pointed to the tub. "See that? Our town, Jericho, has central water, so you yourself fill it halfway and then I'll come with ten gallons of hot water in ten minutes. If you leave those boots with me, I'll clean 'em and put polish on them for ten cents. Same for your husband's shoes. Oh yes, breakfast is at six prompt and that is fifteen cents. Now if you excuse me, I have to go gather eggs and tend my goats for tomorrow. I will be back in ten minutes with the hot water."

When Caroline returned to their room, she found that Charles had taken off his boots and coat and had fallen asleep on the bed. She walked to the window and pulled the curtains closed. She took off her shoes and dress and returned to the bed and, for the first time in six months, laid down beside her husband, placing her arms around him. Ten minutes passed and she heard a knock on the door; she sat up in bed not realizing she had fallen asleep. A voice on the other side of the door whispered, "Bath's ready. I just poured in the hot water. It's all yours now. Leave your shoes in the hall if you want 'em cleaned and polished. If you have underclothes you need washed, please leave them by your door. That's another ten cents."

Thirty minutes later, Caroline returned from her bath and said she felt different than she had for the last eleven days. Her light brown hair was wet but that felt wonderful. She patted her hair dry and realized she had nothing clean to wear for sleep. She stood there undressed but looking at the healing stitches on her side. "I guess I will have to sleep without bed clothes. I have no other choice." Caroline turned the blanket down on her side of the bed. "Charles, wake up and get undressed, as I am going to bed now. I have left the bath water in the bathing room. It is still quite clean; you should use it while it's warm. I am going to sleep. I have not slept properly in five days, and oh, yes, I love you more than ever before. But I am so tired, I think I will be asleep when you return. I want to hold you more than ever, but I so need sleep. Dear, dear husband, now we have tomorrows."

The first sound she heard that morning was that of a rooster crowing. She rolled over in bed and discovered Charles had bathed and returned without waking her. She got out of bed and put on her black dress and white bonnet, then walked down the stairs to the kitchen barefoot. She found Hanny standing by the stove, pulling out of the oven two cast iron skillets of corn pone. Caroline stood there barefoot. "Hanny, that was a wonderful bath and I have had a good night's sleep on a wonderful feather-tic bed, but I have a problem. I cannot find my undergarments. My shoes were there, but not my undergarments."

Hanny placed the corn pone on the table next to a bowl of butter and stood there barefoot. "Still drying. Could not get the blood stains out of the one. Have a cup of coffee and I'll get the iron out and iron them dry. Go ahead and sit down. You're the first down and the stage will leave in about an hour. As for your dog, he is on the back porch along with fur of a rabbit. Or maybe it's a squirrel." Hanny left the room and quickly returned holding Caroline's shoes. "You know, these shoes of yours are worn out. I restitched part of the left one and it'll hold and the right one was full of comfrey leaves. Odd thing is there's no heels. So you must have been in a hurry or you would have gotten them fixed."

Caroline did not answer, but poured herself a cup of coffee and added some goat milk. Sitting down, she looked down at her feet thinking of what story was best to tell. Hanny started ironing dry her under garments. "So, I take it you are running from something. I mean your feet—I can see the torn blisters from here, and there's two toenails missing on your right foot.

Both ankles looks cut up like you been running through the briars. Those stains on your top garment looks like s serious wound. You look to me like a nice person. So, I guess you have come through a lot."

"Hanny, you know the twenty-third Psalm? Though I walk through the valley of the shadow of death? That is where I have been. My words are pale to what I have witnessed and what I have done in the last eleven days."

Hanny stopped her ironing and moved over and sat down next to Caroline. She took her hand. "But you're here now. You have got your husband. Ain't none of my business, but don't look back, as the devil is always chasing us."

Caroline reached her hand on top of Hanny's hand. "I've not told my husband this. But I am in need of advice of a woman older than me. I have killed a man with a knife—a rapist and murderer. I have shot three men, two are dead for sure. I did not want to, but I had to. They would have killed many more had I not..."

"Have you asked God for forgiveness?"

"Yes."

"Then that is it. It's settled."

"How do I tell my husband?"

"So, what would you tell him? For what will it gain you?"

"No. I do not want to tell him."

"You don't have to. You tell him everything but that. You told God and now you told me. That is enough. Do not...I will say it again, do not mention that to him." Hanny lifted her hand from the table and pushed Caroline's hair back from her face. "Listen well, young lass. If you tell him, it will make him angry at those men. He will be angry that he was not there to defend you and he will carry that inside. It will churn on him—it will simmer all the time. Anger simmers until it forces its way out. Our men are going through enough hell now. That is all I am going to say. But remember this. Silence, once tis broken, cannot be put back. People have tried but people have failed." Hanny stood up from the table. "Now, Caroline, how do you enjoy your eggs? And maybe that is it. You broke some eggs, you scrambled them, you ate them, and now that is over. Done. Now go get your husband up. Here, take your underclothes. By the way, while I charge for everything I can here, this advice is free. You look to today and not yesterday. Now get up there and get that lucky man down here for breakfast."

One hour later, the stage was underway. Everyone had returned and they took the same seats they had yesterday. Caroline felt wonderful in her clean clothes and she felt good about the talk she had with Hanny. That burden was now lifted. She would remain silent about much of her journey. About the men. About her killing them.

The fair weather of yesterday had started to turn cold. A light, misty rain had started to fall and sent a chill through everyone on the stage. It looked like the sun would not come up this day, but dark clouds would be the rule. At one stop, the driver got down and went to the back and retrieved an oiled rain slicker for himself. The passengers pulled down the curtains to keep the rain out, although some rain came in and pooled on the floor. The young pregnant woman started shaking and so Caroline took her bedroll blanket and draped it over the woman. Later, Caroline herself became chilled and so Charles took off his coat and placed it around Caroline. As they drove on, the rain intensified. The skies drew darker. Flashes of lighting occasionally struck high in the hills around them, but the driver did not stop. There would be no reason to.

As the road became increasingly more muddy, the stage slowed as the horses worked harder to pull the stage up the hills that surrounded the valley below. At one spot where water crossed the road, the men and the driver, including the boys, got off the stage and grabbed hold of the spokes of the wheel and turned them to help the horses pull the one-ton wagon through the mud and up the hill. Once to the top, everyone got back in the wagon and the downhill ride proved even more frightening, as the back of the wagon slid one way then another and, at times, looked as if it were going to go over the side and tumble down the hill upside down. The driver rode the brake all the way down the hill, but still the wheels locked and slid until he reached the bottom. Caroline looked out the window and saw another hill in front of them much like the one they had just crossed. The driver shouted down to them, "I am stopping here to give the horses a break, and, who knows, it may stop raining. I am going to walk up the hill a little bit to the first turn to see what the road is like. You all just stay put."

Charles raised the curtain and watched the driver walk up the hill. Caroline could see three tight switchbacks from her vantage point. Lightning clashed into a faraway ridge line followed by a thunder that vibrated the air. Charles leaned toward Caroline. "We may have to stay here a while, until this clears. There are two more big hills like the last one before we get to Hopkinsville. The driver has driven these mountains for the last twelve years, so he knows what he has to do and whether the horses are up to it."

An hour passed and the rain slackened slightly. The driver returned after a second look and opened the stage door and climbed inside. "Folks, I will not attempt that hill 'cause the other side is a humdinger, with two tight switchbacks and we could slide sideways and overtake the horses coming down sideways, brakes or no brakes. I walked up there, and it is a river of water coming down that road at one evil looking switchback, and that is a very dangerous sharp turn. The road is decomposed granite, so it should dry quick like. Rest assured, I have done it before. All it takes is for the rain to stop. So let us sit tight. I've got some army hard tack if anyone gets hungry. Anyone here got a gun?"

Charles looked at Caroline and, with his eyes and a quick shake of his head, he signaled, "don't tell." The old man with a cane, reached under his jacket and pulled out a thirty-one caliber Colt pistol. He handed it to Charles. "Here, you take it. I'm not good with it. It's fully loaded with six."

The driver looked at the small caliber gun and smiled. "Well, it is a good start, and I got a revolver and a musket rifle up on top with me. There are wolves in these hills and we need to be prepared. They may attack the horses, but you are safe in the coach. We will just sit this rainstorm through."

Thirty-five minutes later, the rain slacked and then stopped altogether. Through the clouds, the sun started to break. The driver got out of the coach and climbed up on top. He sat there looking at the road for a moment. Then he bent over the side and shouted, "I think in another fifteen minutes we may attempt that hill. You should know that mountain has no name. But all us drivers call it cemetery hill, and the top last switchback we all call coffin corner. I guess you know why. So just sit tight. We have only lost an hour, so we might make it to Hopkinsville before one. Ladies, do not be frightened, as I know this road like I know the back of my hand, and I would not put us in danger."

Caroline raised her window curtain and watched as the sun started to strike the hill in front of them. She could see some birds had come off their branches and were starting to fly in circles over the valley. She glanced at her husband, then said words silently, "I love you."

Charles smiled and leaned forward, whispering, "You are the most beautiful woman in all the world. North. South. East. Or West. How lucky I am, you chose me."

At first, the sound was not recognizable, as it was so far behind them. But soon it was clear. They were horses. It sounded to Caroline like eight or nine horses and coming from the east. A second later, a gun shot was fired into the air. Charles glanced out the window and watched for a moment, then pulled the curtain down. He turned to Caroline. "It looks to be seven of them. They could be robbers, deserters, or worse. One or two rapists could be in the bunch. I will take the Colt 36 and, here, you take the 31. It fires just like my Colt. Cock and pull the trigger. Because I am the main threat, they will be watching me. So, you take the first shot, and you shoot the man who appears to be the leader. He will do all the talking to me. I will take the one on his left and you take the one on his right. Then whoever is closest. Don't watch a man fall. You aim, shoot. Aim, shoot. Aim, shoot. One. Two. Three. Fast is best. After the first shots, their horses will be jumping around so their accuracy goes bad. Do not fire until I sneeze. Then as fast as you can. Put the gun up your sleeve so they won't see it. I will put the revolver in my belt behind me. I know it's a lot to understand, but I have seen you shoot. We have surprise. Are you up to this?" There were no complicated thoughts in Caroline's mind, but only a single thought—now she had a partner. She quickly kissed him. "That is not our last kiss, but one for luck. I am ready."

Caroline looked out the window to the east and watched as the men rode closer. As they did, she noticed a young woman about twenty years old was with them. Her rose colored dress was soaked, wet from the morning rain, as was her hair. It appeared her hands were tied to the saddle horn. Seeing this, Caroline clinched her teeth then slipped her white bonnet on her head and slipped the pistol into her left sleeve. "God, steady my hand."

The lead rider raised his gun and fired a second shot into the air as the seven approached. He rode to the front of the coach and faced the driver. The other six came alongside the coach on the left side. The leader pointed his revolver at the driver. "You old son-a-bitch, I know you got a revolver up there and so you throw it down right now or I will blow your ass out of that seat. Do it!" Caroline glanced at the lead rider. He looked familiar, as did two of the men with him. He wore a pair of brown leather pants with a black jacket and black hat. But most important of all, she spotted the young man who had tried to shoot Bear a week ago. A yellowed, brown-stained bandage was still on his right hand. She glanced back at her husband. "This is the Willems Gang. I know these men."

The leader of the gang, Sercint Willems himself, shouted to the driver. "Stay right there where I can see you. Anybody inside, you come on out. We mean no harm, we just want your money." The rider next to Willems shouted, "He means it, cracks and dicks, all of you! Get the hell out here."

Caroline ducked down and opened the opposite side door. "Bear, go!" Bear looked once at Caroline and jumped out the door. In seconds, he went into the weeds and disappeared.

Willems shouted out again. "What did I say? Damnit, get out of that coach." Caroline looked again at the men. There were seven of them, each one with hollowed eyes and a sense of desperation about them. The young woman, who was tied to her saddle, was somewhat behind them, and the reins to her horse were held by one of the younger riders, who was twenty feet behind the leader. Only two other men held their revolvers in their hands, while the other four rested their hands on their revolvers, which were tucked under their belts or in holsters. Caroline looked at the man with the bandaged hand who shot twice at Bear and noticed he also carried a military sword tucked under his saddle. He wore a Confederate cap pulled tight over his head. Charles was the first to climb out of the stage and was followed by Caroline a moment later. She caught up to Charles and rested her hand on his back for a moment. "Trust me, Charles."

Caroline stepped forward. "So, excuse me, sir, are you the famous Willems Gang?"

Willems, who had his eyes on Charles, turned his attention to the woman wearing the white bonnet. "You heard of us?"

"With all great respect, sir. Everyone knows of you. It's in all the Louisville papers. You are quite famous. You are the Willems Gang. But no one knows much about you."

"Yeah, that so, lady?" Willems returned his eyes to Charles and the driver, who had raised his hands but stayed up in his seat. The driver's musket was hidden from sight and near his feet.

Caroline smiled and stepped closer to the leader and away from Charles. "I understand there was a wagon overturned near Elizabethtown nearly two weeks ago. They were just poor evacuating Mennonites. There was some blood on the seat. Do you know about that?"

"Yeah, I know something of it."

"What happened? The papers did not say."

"Hell! German Mennonites are damn stubborn people! I shouted for him to stop, but he whipped his damn horses. He refused to stop, so I shot for him and missed." Caroline could feel the weight of the revolver tucked into her sleeve. "But someone was shot."

Sercint Willems kept his eyes on Charles and the driver. "There was a young girl about thirteen riding beside him. The stupid ass girl aimed a musket at me, so I shot her. Hell, I don't like killing children, but better her than me. Was that in the papers?" Willems learned forward to hear and rested his gun on the saddle horn.

"I read it. Yes, it was in the papers. You shot her?"

"They had nothing but six dollars and two old horses. Nothing good to take at all."

"And why are you way over here west of Bowling Green?"

"Ain't no blue army here, ain't no gray army. Just easy pickins for us. Like stages. But, lady, you seem knowledgeable and educated."

Caroline's eyes went to the young girl and she noticed she was shivering in a thin dress, wet from the cold rain and stained with blood and soil as if she had cradled something wounded or dying. The girl looked at Caroline and silently mouthed the words, "Help me. Help me."

"We're Shakers. My brother is deaf and dumb, so it's of no use talking to him. I talk for him. Excuse me, Mister Willems, I am about to sneeze. All this rain." At that moment, Caroline started inhaling like she was about to sneeze. She glanced to her husband. All eyes went to her. "Ahh. Ahh." Then she let go. "Choooo."

Caroline raised her hand to catch the sneeze, but in that speck of a moment, like a snap of a twig, she pulled the small Colt 31 pistol from her left sleeve, cocked the hammer, and fired her first shot—*bang*—striking Willems centered in the sternum and into his spine. Charles, at the sound of Caroline's sneeze, pulled his revolver from behind his back but as he was about fire his first shot, he heard a second shot—*bang*—as Caroline pulled the trigger, targeting the man on her left who was attempting to aim his revolver on Charles. Caroline's quick shot penetrated an inch above his eyebrows and into his forehead. With his eyes still wide open in surprise, he went limp and fell out of the saddle. Charles's first shot was a half second later, and this shot from the Colt 36 ripped into the third man's chest, sending the man backwards from his horse. The four men who were scattered behind the first three men were reaching for their weapons after the initial gunshots. The fourth man, wearing a torn and dirty Confederate hat, pulled his weapon from his belt. Spooked from the gunfire, his horse quickly jerked left. The man, looking over his right shoulder, was attempting a shot, which went wide and missed Charles by twelve inches. The errant shot went through the stage door, striking the older gentleman in the calf. Charles fired his second shot into that fourth man, and he flew backwards out of his saddle, his revolver flying out of his hand. Caroline did not see any of that, as her eyes were on the nearest man to her, the fifth man. His horse was attempting to flee and had turned sideways to the right. It was Ryland Creech, the same young man who had shot at her dog a week earlier. She aimed the Colt 31 pistol as the man, his right hand still bandaged, was fumbling with his gun attempting to aim at her. But as his horse was jumping around, his ill-timed shot at Caroline sliced the air three inches over her right shoulder. Caroline's shot—*bang*—went slightly left and struck him in the left side of his neck, slicing an artery. This man reactively aimed his weapon toward Caroline's chest for his second shot when Bear came running out of the weeds from the back of the coach and leapt high into the air and grabbed the man's left hand. Caroline, squinting through the bluish smoke in the air, fired a second shot—*bang*—into the man's stomach. He fell from his horse backwards, snapping his neck upon landing. Instantly, she heard a round fired from beside her as Charles fired his third shot into the sixth man, holding the reins of the young, kidnapped girl. He fell to the road with the reins still tied around his left wrist, jerking her horse sideways. The seventh, and last rider still on a horse, kept shouting, "Damn, damn, damn," and was attempting a shot, but his revolver jammed. He instantly threw it to the road, grabbing a second revolver from his belt, and fired a single quick and random undisciplined shot toward Charles. Caroline returned two shots—*bang bang*—at the man. Her first shot struck the man in the right shoulder and a second tore into his right arm. His gun fell to the ground. In all this mayhem, the driver pulled out his musket from under his seat and laid it across the baggage and fired one shot into the man's chest, causing his arms to fly into the air and his head to jerk backward as he fell from his horse. In those sixteen seconds of exchanging gunfire, no one spoke. Not Caroline. Not Charles. Not anyone inside the stage. The only words heard mixed in the gunfire were curse words from the members of the Willems Gang. And while the gunfire was extremely loud, what followed proved more surprising.

The echoes of the shooting, all thirteen shots, had a life of their own as they bounced off the trees and repeated endlessly down the valley. Bluish smoke rose above the scene. Inside the coach, the air was filled with the smell of black powder and the new screams of a baby crying uncontrollably. Charles moved quickly from man to man, checking their condition. Willems was the only one still alive for certain. Lying on his back, he appeared to be reaching for a second revolver in his belt and attempting to move, but his legs were useless, as Caroline's Colt 31 caliber bullet had struck dead his spine. Further, he was bleeding from his chest and mouth. Charles bent over and grabbed the man's revolver and stuck it in his belt. He walked quickly to the other six men scattered and took their weapons, all scattered on the ground. Some men were bent in gruesome manners, legs and arms twisted as if they had fallen out of the sky and crashed into the earth while attempting to escape some unseen force. All were dead or were bleeding out and death would come in the next three minutes. One man, who held the reins of the young girl's horse, lay on his face, his body twisted and his hands still holding the reins. The young, twenty-year-old woman was attempting to scream, but no sound came from her mouth. Caroline reached up and rested her hand on the girl's arm while quieting the horse. "It's alright. It's alright. They're dead. They're all dead. It's alright, it's over." Caroline looked over the shooting scene and watched her husband move from man to man. She turned her attention back to the girl. "You're safe. You're alright." The air was filled with the smell of gunfire, as she untied the reins from the dead shooter's hand and slowly led the horse over to the coach. The girl took a deep breath then screamed loudly, "Wahhhhhh." Caroline touched the young girl's arm again. "Calm down, it's all over." She reached up and untied the girl's wrists. Charles walked over and helped the young girl down. The driver was already out of his seat and inspecting the six dead before him. Sercint Willems, the seventh man, was still struggling and trying to say something, but the blood coming from his mouth obscured his words. The driver kicked Willems hard in the stomach and the black-suited rider, choking on his own blood, fought for words. "What happened? What happened? Please. What happened?" Thirty seconds later, his gurgling stopped.

Caroline took the young girl in her arms and held her. "It's over. It's all over. They're dead. My name is Caroline, I am Caroline. What's yours? Tell me now, what is your name?"

The young girl was calming down but was still sobbing. "I'm Eleanorah. I am Eleanorah." The young girl could not continue speaking and so buried her head into Caroline's shoulder. Then she pulled away, angry. "Thank you! Thank you! Thank you! These men, these damn men shot my brother, Lucien, and took me. In Lewisburg, yesterday. Did I say I am Eleanorah Falkner? Yes? They said they were going to rape me and kill me if they did not get the money from my mama and daddy. The man with three fingers, Ryland, his name is Ryland Creech, and he was going back to get the money tomorrow."

Charles rested his hand on Caroline's shoulder. "Well, that is not going to happen. Ryland Creech is dead. They all are. This is my wife, Caroline, and we will take care of you." Charles turned and went to the coach to check on the passengers.

Caroline spoke softly to her, almost in a whisper. "We can take you with us to Hopkinsville and we can send word to your father and mother and they can come and get you there. You can stay with us, but I want to know this. Did they touch you? Eleanorah, did they touch you in any way?"

"No, Willems said my parents would pay more if they knew I was untouched. But they all talked about wives they had kidnapped, and they...did that."

"Well, you are not one of those, are you? God looked after you today. That's why we were here."

"But you shot all those men. Seven of them! You shot all of them. How did you do that? All of them? It was so fast. I was sure I was going to be shot. But you shot all seven. And you're a woman."

377

"Little David killed mighty Goliath with a single stone. Did he not?"

"Seven of them, there were seven. And you shot four of them. I watched you shoot. And you're in a dress. You're a Mennonite. I mean, I never thought, never thought that a Mennonite, a woman...four of them! And he shot three, and that dog. He took hold of that three-fingered man, Creech. I want to tell the world about this. I mean it was so fast! I tried to scream, but nothing came out. Please, can I go now and sit in the coach? I need that or I am going to faint. Yes, I feel it." Caroline helped the woman into the coach and the two elderly women helped her sit between them. Eleanorah continued to talk inside the coach. "I can't believe I am alive. I can't believe it. I thought they would kill me."

Charles walked over to Caroline and took her by the shoulders. "Caroline! I could not imagine. Your aim, your speed without fail. You did that. You shot four of them, one, two, three, four. Fast. I am spellbound. We, no you, shot my revolver maybe twenty shots at the homestead, but this was extraordinary. You never hesitated for a moment. Many hesitate. But you did not!"

Caroline, still holding the small revolver in her hand, pushed her hair out of her eyes. "Charles, I did not do this. Someone else was pulling the trigger. But I despised Willems. I suppose that's why. When Willems said he shot that girl on the wagon, I thought he would go on doing it until someone stopped him. That's when I knew why I was here. This cup was passed to me. And I gladly drank of it."

"I am still amazed how fast you fired that gun."

"I will tell you more when we get home. And you will tell me about your wounds and about Shelbyville."

"Yes. Let's search these men, get all their plunder and let's get their horses. Leave them where they fell and let's get the stage moving again. Is the young girl alright?"

"Yes, the two ladies have her between them and they are a comfort. The boys haven't said a word and the old man said I could keep his gun. He has been shot in the leg. But it is a clean wound. The young man is wrapping it."

The ride up cemetery hill was slow going. The fast ride down was a little scary but after the shootout, nobody seemed frightened—except for the driver himself, who rode the brake with his right foot all the way down. Charles rode up top with nine revolvers at his feet. Caroline rode in the coach and explained things to the pregnant woman and her husband, who said they had closed their eyes and did not look until the shooting was over. He kept asking how the seven men were shot and Caroline said her husband and the driver did all the shooting. The older gentleman with the white beard and the two boys shook their heads and said that was not the truth at all. They pointed to her and said, "She shot four of 'em herself." One of the young boys interrupted his brother and said, "She shot the leader, and she shot one man square in the forehead." The boy pointed to his forehead and then closed his eyes as if he was dead.

Caroline smiled. "Boys have the best imaginations." At that point, Caroline realized she still had the Colt 31 pistol in her hand. She opened it and looked into the chamber. "I had none left." She handed the gun back to the older man with the wound in his leg. He turned it down. "You keep it. It's never been fired and now it has. I watched and you hit four. It's yours now."

It took two hours to get to Hopkinsville. The rain had slackened west of cemetery hill and so they made good time, as the roads of crumbled granite were mostly dry. As the stage pulled into town, the driver stood and started shouting out to all who could hear, "We got the Willems Gang!" "We got the Willems Gang. All of 'em." Three men loading a wagon hurriedly walked over to hear the news. A man walking with his son came out of a hardware store. "They're all dead. Sercint Willems and all of 'em. Everyone is dead. We did it. We got the Willems Gang." More people rushed down the street and stopped to listen. "She did it. That woman right there in the black dress and white bonnet, she shot four of 'em. The Shaker woman. Herself! Come and see." A barber cutting hair rushed out to hear the shouting, still carrying his shears and comb. "We got their guns, we got their horses, we got a pile of money. I got his hat. I got Sercint Willems's hat. It is an amazing story, and I will tell you all about it. Buy me drink, and I will tell all." The driver jumped down off the top of the stage, holding Sercint Willems's hat high in the air. A crowd started gathering around the driver. "The Willems Gang shoot-out. We were there and we did it. I shot the last one myself with this gun." The driver held up the rifle musket and then held the black hat down low for a small boy to touch it. "This is Sercint Willems hat. I watched them die, all seven of 'em. Folks, the best part is, that woman down there shot four of 'em herself. One, two, three, four. Who would have thought from a Shaker woman?" The people on the street started cheering. Caroline took off her white bonnet. "I'm not a Shaker, I am but a homesteader like many of you. We had to do it. We had to save this young woman's life. My husband and this driver. They're the ones. But we saved her life. That's what's important. There is a wounded man in the stage, and he needs a doctor." The white-bearded gentleman with the cane got off the stage limping, his trouser leg crudely bandaged but covered with blood. "I don't need a doctor. I need a drink!" Cheers went up as the crowd moved toward the only tavern in town. The two young boys, the two older ladies, still holding their hat boxes, and the pregnant woman and her husband all climbed off the stage. Each passenger wanting to tell their part of the story.

Caroline and Charles took the young woman to the sheriff's office and explained the incident. The sheriff sent a deputy to the telegraph office to send a telegram to the sheriff in her town of Lewisburg. Caroline told the young girl she could stay at the only boarding house in Hopkinsville or come out another thirty minutes to their homestead. The girl started shaking and said she did not want to go to a boarding house by herself alone, but wanted to go to Caroline's home.

Charles took two of the Willems Gang's horses and borrowed a buggy. The valuables collected from the bodies and saddlebags of the Willems Gang were given to the sheriff.

Caroline went to the general store and bought new shoes for herself and a dress and coat for the kidnapped girl. The three of them were in Hopkinsville for only two hours before they left for the ten-mile trip to their homestead.

At times as they traveled, the young girl, realizing how close she came to an unimaginable ugliness only a day earlier, cried. Not only for her, but for her brother. As the buggy traversed down the curving trail through scattered homesteads, Caroline's thoughts were complicated. "I truly felt I would never see this blessed countryside again. This road. These homesteads. I thought at dark times this day would never happen. Was I so weak to have thought this?" She reached over and touched her husband's shoulder. Charles smiled back, not realizing what Caroline was thinking.

At one point, as familiar homesteads came into view, Caroline quietly said the names of the people who lived there, just as Joyellen had done days earlier. "The Carmichaels, the Bennetts, the Quigleys, the McCumbers." For Caroline, everything looked different from the day she left thirteen days earlier. Things looked greener. Homesteads looked whiter. And gardens looked neater. Animals that gathered near the fence lines looked whole and fresh. As they passed the Millars' homestead, the last one before theirs, Caroline stood in the buggy and waved, tears running down her cheek. "We're back! We're home!" Missus Millar ran out onto the porch and shouted out, "Caroline! Caroline! The children are fine. We saw them yesterday." I knew you could do it, Caroline! I knew you could do it." Caroline sat back down in the buggy and said quietly to herself, "I almost didn't. I almost failed."

As they approached the homestead, Caroline heard a scream and Priscilla came running barefoot from the house. She kept repeating the same words over and over. "Mama! Mama! Mama!" Caroline jumped from the buggy and ran to her daughter. Falling on her knees, there on the grass, the two of them hugged. "I told you I would be back. And I am. I'm home. I'm home."

Priscilla lost her breath and gagged for air; with tears streaming down her cheeks, she barely could be understood. "I missed you so. I missed you so, Mama! Mama, I love you. I love you!"

Caroline pointed at the bearded man. "Did you miss your daddy too? 'Cause I brought him back." Charles got down off the buggy and stood there. Caroline pointed at the tall man with a beard. "Yes, that is your father. He doesn't look it, but he is." Priscilla turned and looked at the strange man standing before her.

Charles took off his hat. "Priscilla, it's true, it's me. I am your father." Priscilla wiped her eyes to get a better look and, upon hearing his voice, she ran to him. She burst into tears, but no words were spoken.

Moments later, the two boys came walking out of the woods. One was carrying a freshly killed rabbit and the other was carrying three black squirrels. But upon seeing their parents, they both stopped and looked. They stood there frozen. Finally the youngest, Noah, dropped his rabbit and ran to his mother. Isaac, the older boy, picked up the rabbit and walked to his father, who was still hugging his daughter. "Pa, we have been usin' snares like you taught us, and we catch rabbits every day, and we built a lookout in that big beech tree you showed me, and we can see for ten miles. Priscilla's been sleepin' in the house, and I been sleepin' in the lookout. Noah sleeps in the barn with the goats and Priscilla learned to ride the mule all by herself now. There are three owls in the barn, and we've been cutting firewood for the winter. The mule pulls all of it down here." Isaac started to tear up. "Dad. Dad." He dropped his three squirrels and the rabbit to the ground. "I really missed you. I did. But I was strong like you taught me. And I knew you would come back. I told them you would not leave us."

Charles hugged his son. "You did a good job and I am extremely proud of you. I really am, but for now—for now go to your mom. She needs you."

In the waning moments of the day, the five of them gathered together and hugged. And after a bit, Caroline looked at Eleanorah, the kidnapped girl, who was standing a distance away watching. Caroline took a step toward her and waved her over. The girl walked slowly toward the family. She stopped a few feet away. "Caroline? I have heard from the time when I was a little girl that there are angels. My mother said that they come to help. They come to protect. And here I am. Looking at you. I am looking at an angel. Do you know that? Do you know you are an angel?"

Caroline turned to the girl. "Eleanorah, I am no angel. I am just a plain wife with ordinary skills. I had hard decisions to make. And so, I just did what was right to be done. That's how I saw it. And it is truly that simple."

Dinner that night was an unrivaled celebration. The Millars arrived with a beet, turnip, and carrot salad. The main attraction was a rabbit and squirrel stew overflowing with okra and potatoes, onions, and green beans. Priscilla made two skillets of cornbread and she and Caroline milked the goats to make goat milk butter. Peaches from a double quart jar were the dessert, served over two gingerbread cakes made by Eleanorah. Isaac, Noah, and Priscilla kept interrupting each other, telling stories of adventure. Of trips to the river to swim, of a thunderstorm that filled the pond to overflowing. Priscilla was most proud that she had learned to mount and ride the mule named Coffee without any help from the boys, and once rode all the way to the Jacobson farm five miles away. No one wanted to go to bed that night, and they stayed awake until after midnight when Priscilla fell asleep in Caroline's arms. The boys had a hundred questions to Eleanorah about the big shoot-out at the stage holdup. They kept saying over and over, "Our mother did that?" Charles and Caroline sat on the porch holding hands until sunup, talking about what it was like being apart. Neither wanting to go to bed, but waiting for the red-winged black birds to start the day.

The following days, Eleanorah's parents arrived from Lewisburg, and her mother and father had a tearful reunion down by the stream that fed into the fishpond. They spent hours talking to her there. The next two days, they walked the woods together, hand in hand, and talked about the brother who had been killed by the Willems Gang. The mother several times took Caroline's hand and said, "I only wish that I could have been there next to you with my own revolver. Thank God, they never touched Eleanorah. For I would not bear it."

A week later, an official letter arrived from a Confederate Army agency in Richmond, Virginia, explaining to Caroline that her husband, First Lieutenant Charles Duncan, had died from wounds suffered in battle and was buried with full military honors in Shelbyville, Kentucky. The letter included a death benefit check for half his salary, forty-five dollars.

The Union Army never got closer to their homestead than fourteen miles east of Hopkinsville. But later, two large armies numbering nearly one hundred thousand clashed at Perrysville, Kentucky with high casualties on both sides. Charles's unit, the Kentucky Volunteers, took heavy causalities.

Charles shaved his beard but kept his moustache. He never traveled far from his homestead for fear of being recognized. He said everything he needed was right there and only the boys went to town for supplies and things like coffee, flour, sugar, thread, and colored buttons for Priscilla.

Caroline did not talk much about her eleven-day journey. The only story she would tell was about the bear attack, and she did so only because she had the two scars on her left side that revealed the ferocity of the bear. However, over the next several months, she did write in exacting detail the whole day-by-day experience. When she finished the one hundred and thirty pages in her new leather-bound diary, she tied it closed with a yellow ribbon and gave it to Priscilla. Caroline told her not to read it until she turned eighteen. Priscilla obeyed and put it away in a new cedar chest made by her father. Caroline never told Charles of the Union men she shot, of the rapist who castrated himself, the Shivers River crossing, of the girl she rescued and the man they burned in his bed. She did mention the bear attack and how it is possible to kill a bear, if you attack like a bear. None of the traumatic things were mentioned because Caroline did not want to be that woman to her family. No. That was a woman she had to become to do what was necessary. Caroline simply desired one thing. She wanted only to be the wife of one man and the mother of their three children.

The Duncan family lived quietly and stayed away from other homesteads for the rest of the war. In June of 1866, they sold the homestead and moved away. They took four mules, two horses, a donkey, three wagons, and a dog named Bear. Some said they went to Bethlehem, Missouri; others said they moved to Oregon. No one knows for certain where they moved to, but one Christmas in 1867, the Millars, who lived in the next homestead, got a Christmas card from Colorado that read, "Every Christmas, I cannot help but remember your advice. I traveled at night. I gathered leaves to hide under. You saved my life. You truly did. Merry Christmas, my dearest friends. Caroline."

Ron Meszaros

How does a flower know it's a flower? It cannot see its colors. It cannot smell its fragrance. Could it be that it hears from the Almighty? I believe so. I do think we, like the flower, can hear when we embrace the stillness. For in that silence, we are joined with the invisible. I hear first. Then I see. I am a flower to Him who speaks softly to me. And I listen.

--- Caroline Emily Duncan 1829-1926

Made in United States
Orlando, FL
20 September 2024

51701265R20233